Oh, What a Tangled Web We Weave

When First We Practice to Deceive!

W.D. Jeffrey

This is a work of fiction. Names, characters, businesses, events and incidents are the products of the author's imagination. Any resemblance to actual persons, living or dead, or actual events is purely coincidental. The views, opinions and derogatory language expressed by those characters are not shared by the author. References to actual historical events are as accurate as the author can determine. The author apologises if there are anomalies.

Table of Contents

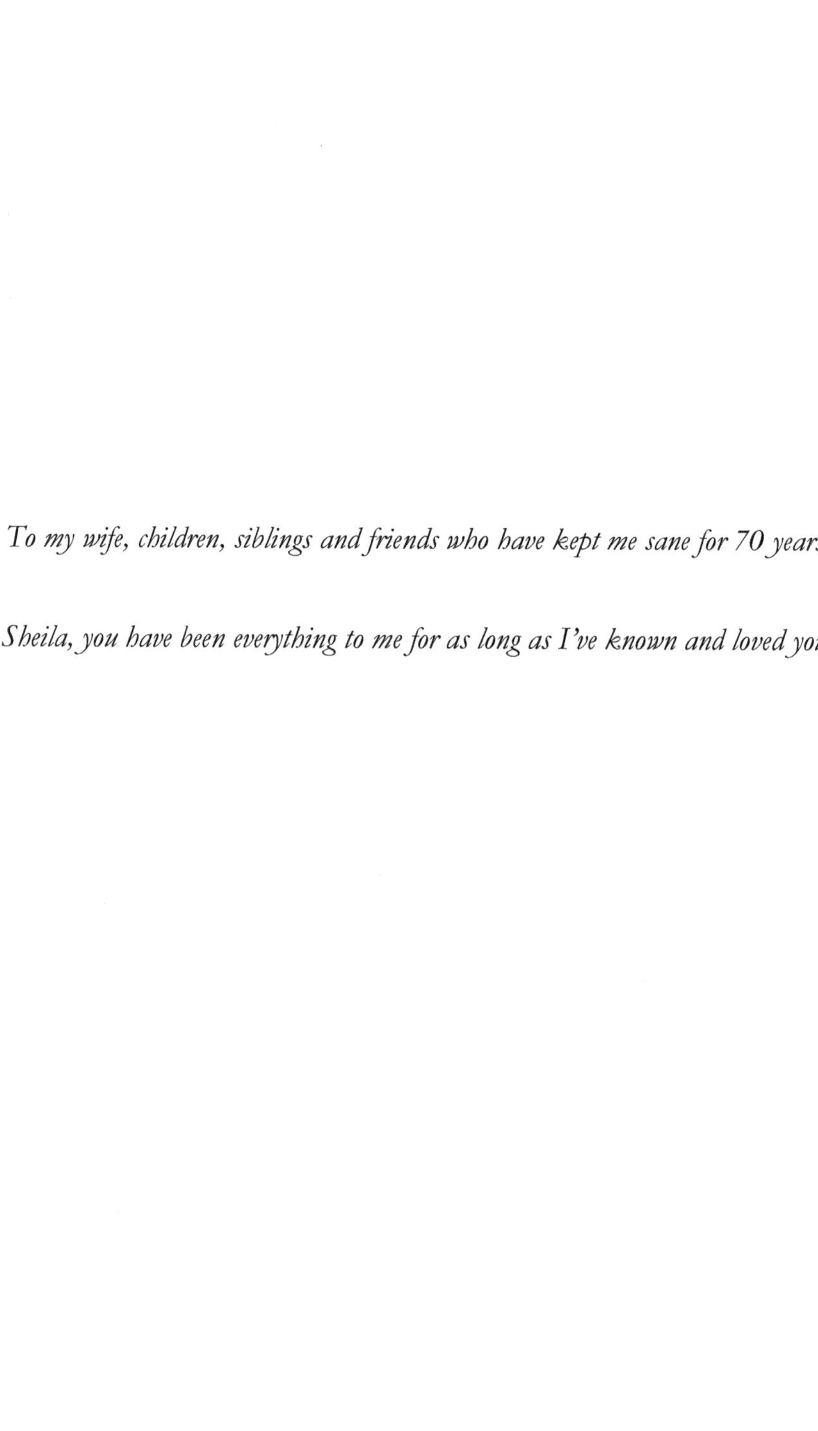

To my wife, children, siblings and friends who have kept me sane for 70 years.

Sheila, you have been everything to me for as long as I've known and loved you.

About the Author

ii

Born in England to Irish parents, lived and worked in West London initially in local government before moving to the private sector as an I.T.Manager for an engineering company. Married with three children he retired in 2018 and moved to Aberdeen, Scotland.

PART 1

Changes

1
Time to Stay Goodbye

January 2015

"What's with the beard, Jonah?"

"I couldn't be arsed to shave. Anyway, in these temperatures, at least it keeps me face warm."

"Hmm, not sure it goes well with the shorter hair. You look as though you just missed being a skinhead," Big Cliff said sarcastically.

"I just had a number three all over. It keeps it all tidy," Jonah replied.

"Looks more like a number two!" Cliff said to a few sniggers, "In fact, it's so bad it looks like you did it yourself…in the dark!"

Jonah just sneered at him.

"Christ, it's freezing out here. I hope it's a fuck sight warmer inside!"

A group of young men turned to the shivering individual. One of them answered, "It should be. After all, it's a bloody crematorium, ain't it?"

"Phil, did you not think to wear a coat, being winter and all?" questioned Lofty.

"The only coat I have is my donkey jacket and I didn't think it was very appropriate," Phil replied.

"At least it's black," said another.

"It certainly is, well-spotted Mush. There's not much that gets past you, Jonah. However, you may also have observed that it has a fucking great luminous orange panel on the back saying Hampshire County Council. Anybody would think I worked here!" Phil shivered.

"For fuck's sake, borrow a jacket then if you don't want to freeze your knackers off," was another comment.

"Mate, I wouldn't need to except for occasions like this, would I? And how many funerals are we likely to go to at our age, especially in sub-zero temperatures?" The group silently concurred for a minute.

"So, what happens with a cremation then? I know they burn the body, but what's the process?" Gump asked rather indelicately near some more mature mourners. The group moved away, and the rest of the guys spoke quietly, realising their friend's lack of tact.

Ollie provided the details.

"The only one I've been to was here, and they have the coffin on a sort of big marble plinth in front of a set of curtains. To start, they might play some music that the relatives have requested. Then, one or two people come up to the front and say a few nice things about the bod in the box. At some point, the relevant religious dude says something about everlasting life – you know, something to comfort the relatives. But everyone knows it's complete bollocks because once you're dead, that's it. Then, as they're finishing their little speech, they press a button, and the coffin goes slowly through the curtains on a conveyor belt."

"The final curtain, as the song goes," Paul put in. Ollie acknowledged that and then continued, "Out of sight of the mourners, they take the coffin off to the incinerator, burn it all, and stick the ashes in a vase or Tupperware container for collection later."

Billy contributed his tuppence worth. "The question is, do they really burn the coffin? I mean, they're not cheap, and it's such a waste to have it all literally go up in smoke, don't you think?"

Ollie replied, "The cynics among you might suggest that the crematorium guv'nor–"

Cliff interrupted with, "Also known as the Chief Stoker–"

Ollie nodded and continued, "The crematorium guv'nor, A.K.A., the Chief Stoker, takes the body out of the coffin to burn it but sells the coffin back to the undertaker at a reduced rate so that the man in black can sell it again…allegedly."

"And this is true. Years ago, they actually sold the corpse to interested people for the purposes of medical science. So, for all we know, they still do that!"

"It started in Scotland, didn't it, look it up – Burke and Hare body snatchers?" Billy queried. "And probably still goes on there as well…"

"That's outrageous!" GG said indignantly and then thought about it. "But if they sell the body, where do they get the ashes to give to the relatives after the ceremony?"

Ollie sighed with a certain amount of disdain, "Oh, GG, don't be as dim as Gump; they keep a stockpile from their wood burners, so for all anyone knows is that the urn sitting on the mantelpiece does not contain dear Uncle Bert's ashes but the leftovers of a few logs of dried spruce. Whilst Uncle Bert is cut up into a thousand pieces and pickled in some type of alcohol!"

"Oh, so it's not all bad news then!" GG stated, eliciting a few chuckles in response.

"If it's true about the casket, then it's a real con, but I've also heard that they just remove the brass fittings and sell them back because they're not going to burn anyway. Perhaps they should introduce coffin rentals, so the relatives only pay for the number of days the body is in it," Billy suggested. There were a few nods.

"Or give the coffin back to the family to use another time."

He let the lads think about it, then resumed with, "Anyway, I'm going to have a white cardboard coffin so the funeral mourners can write something on the side in felt-tip pen."

Billy was convinced he had hit upon a novel idea for farewell messages. Paul was the first to comment. "How about – *'come back and tell me the winning lottery numbers for next week'?"* he suggested.

"Or – *'You were right when you said you felt a bit Tom and Dick'*!" GG threw in.

"*'Can I have your golf clubs?'*"Lofty added with a grin.

"I know a good one for you, Billy – *'Fuck off and burn you twat!'*" Jonah spoke up, laughing.

"Bloody hell, Jonah, say what you think, why don't you?" Cliff glared at him. "Did your better brother dribble down your mother's leg?"

Jonah looked rather sheepish, given Cliff's rebuke. Cliff continued the assault with, "I'm going to call you The Thrush!"

"The Thrush? What does that mean?" Jonah looked confused.

"'Cos, you're an irritating cunt!"

It went quiet for a few seconds, apart from a few sniggers.

"Okay, maybe *'Good Riddance, I never liked you anyway'*!" Jonah suggested with a false laugh. He laughed alone. The others looked at him and, to a man, thought *'The Thrush'* was very apt.

"For fuck's sake, Jonah, just 'cos you got hair round your mouth doesn't mean you have to talk like a cunt." Cliff said before adding, "You can't help it, can you? It's like watching a two-year-old who's determined to stick a fork into an electric socket!"

A couple of guys laughed out loud before Cliff changed the subject.

"Sod the golf clubs. I think I'd write *'Can I have your missus?'*" he said before adding, "Burnt to buggery in a cardboard box with terms of endearment written on the side, yeah, I like it, Billy. Cheap, cheerful and no fucking class. Perfect for you mate!" and he ruffled Billy's hair. The group chuckled at Cliff's well-meaning putdown of his footballing teammate.

Billy puffed out his cheeks and responded with, "Well, that's a slight variation to the sort of stuff you normally get with flowers, but I can see there's a theme developing." He wasn't overly impressed with their lack of sensitivity but expected very little anyway.

"Is there a piss-up after this?" Steve asked, changing the subject.

"Yeah, they've hired the church hall just down the road, sandwiches and tea or coffee, but I'm not sure if there's alcohol though," Lofty answered.

"There'd better be – you can't have a decent funeral without alcohol. It's compulsory in Ireland, you know!" Billy seemed rather aghast at even the suggestion of a 'dry' after-ceremony event.

"Oh yeah, you've got shamrock roots, haven't you? You little leprechaun, you," said Cliff.

"I have, mate. Do you know, at an Irish funeral or wake, as they call it, everyone gets half cut in the kitchen with the body in an open coffin on the kitchen table or propped up in the corner."

"Really? That's bizarre!" Steve seemed quite shocked.

"Yep, and when they're ready, they go and bury the poor unfortunate soul and then come back to the house to get totally shit-faced… which usually ends up in a fight. In fact, any ceremony I've ever been to where Paddies were involved has always ended up in an altercation. They reckon it's not much of a do if there isn't a punch-up."

"Fuck off!" Phil said cynically.

"No, it's true. I went to a christening in Kilburn last year for two Irish families. Fucking hell, it was like a bar fight in a John Wayne movie. The best bit was that the mother of the baby started it when she poured her father-in-law's beer over her mother-in-law's head and called her a scheming, bullying witch. It was great entertainment as little by little more people got involved, supposedly as peacemakers, with the ulterior motive of thumping seven kinds of shit out of one another. It seemed to me that there was some unfinished family business, which isn't unusual for the children of a fighting race!" Billy added, without bothering to explain, that the phrase allegedly came from the Irish Republic's National Anthem.

"Ach, a great craic!" said Cliff, sounding more Asian than Irish.

"Yep, but it did get a little out of hand. Especially when the Old Bill turned up, and they became the piggies in the middle, no pun intended. They were getting grief from both warring factions. They had the last laugh, though, when they arrested at least six people," Billy said.

"Including the baby's mother?" asked Steve.

"Especially the baby's mother… and the baby who was done for assaulting a police officer when he had a technicolour yawn over one of the constables!" Billy added. They all laughed loudly, which caused a few neighbouring solemn heads to turn and look with a fair amount of contempt at their perceived disrespect towards the event.

"Don't worry about the alcohol – there's a pub just around the corner from the church hall," Ollie said to much relief from the assembled crew.

They were quiet again for several seconds before Phil, still shivering, said, "Jesus, it *is* fucking freezing out here, though…"

It was undoubtedly a bitterly cold January morning, plagued with a raw easterly wind that perfectly defined the term *'wind chill factor'*. The weak sunshine highlighted the stark plain lines of the crematorium building, but the manicured lawns and the Garden of Remembrance just beyond failed to soften the whole panorama. Nobody could escape the fact that it was a soulless, miserable place, which did nothing to relieve the despair and desolation of anyone in attendance. Some of the lads were unwittingly irreverent towards the occasion, but as a group, they were seriously trying to keep their grief well hidden under the camouflage of humour.

The funeral was well attended, and the car park was virtually full, with just enough spaces left for the stragglers of the 'last-minute.com' brigade. Groups of family, friends, and acquaintances grew rapidly to stand inside the entrance hall of the crematorium, waiting to be allowed into the chapel. There were many handshakes, hugs, and kisses for people who hadn't seen each other in years and had now met up for the worst of the three-line whip of hatches, matches, and dispatches. Sympathy and condolence for each other were the order of the hour, all trying to gain some strength and support to cope with the tragedy that had brought them to this dreadful day.

Arriving at the entrance steps was one very frail, old lady from Shoreditch in the East End of London, who determinedly refused a wheelchair and hobbled with her Zimmer frame to join the main party. Born in 1932, she had witnessed the Blitz first-hand long before she was evacuated to a family of *'sheep shaggers'* in Wales, as she called them. Everyone knew Harriet as a 'down-to-earth' lady who had endured and overcome the extreme hardships of civilian life during such a destructive war. Despite her years and obvious infirmity, she was as sharp as a tack and didn't stand on ceremony. She still ran her own stall in Columbia Road Flower Market every Sunday and had done so since 1950.

She was often described as a 'character', which covered her irascible and curmudgeonly ways as if advanced age allowed for some entitlement to such behaviour. One of her claims to fame was that she 'boxed' the ears of the Kray twins on a number of occasions during their formative years in Shoreditch and environs and maintained that had *she* been their mother, they would have turned out all right. Despite their infamous reputation for criminal violence in later years, they had a grudging respect for her.

"What a fucking waste…" She paused and drew a deep breath, which rattled through her. This was not the sort of language you would hear on the East Enders soap opera. "The older I get, the more I know that there is no Almighty God because…" she paused again to breathe deeply, "if he allows the heart-breaking catastrophes and tragedies that go on all over this world every fucking minute of every fucking day then he ain't no God of mine."

"Shush, Gran, please don't," implored her great-granddaughter, taking the elderly lady by the arm.

"Don't shush me, child… why did this need to happen? Why couldn't God have taken someone more deserving of such a fate? Like a child molester, or rapist, or murderer, or some scumbag drug dealer, or criminal that just don't care who they hurt with their selfish crimes?"

She didn't want an answer. She gasped deeply yet again, each breath a major effort for such a fragile old dear.

"It won't be long before I pass on. In fact, now I'm here, I'm not sure I should bother to go home, but I tell you, '*He*' is really going to get a piece of my mind."

"But Harriet, you've just said that you don't believe in God," said a nearby relative.

"No, I don't, and… I will tell Him as much when I get there!" She scowled and shuffled forward, nearer to the door. There were many understanding nods and a number of wry smiles.

"Did the bobbies get the bastard that did this?" she asked of no one in particular. The response was that someone had indeed been arrested by the police.

"Give me a hammer, and let me spend five minutes with them," the old girl said.

"Could you lift one?" asked a cheeky youngster.

"A knife then, I don't want to kill them, cos that's too good for them. They just really need to suffer for their awful crime," she coughed a type of smoker's cough that went through her like an echo chamber. Anyone could see that she was absolutely incensed.

On the dot at 11.00 am, the chapel doors were opened, and the throng silently filed in to take available seats. 'Time to Say Goodbye' by Andrea Bocelli filled the room. It is so poignant, so emotional, and *so* clichéd. Five times a day, twenty-five times a week, the crematorium staff had it on repeat and were sick of it.

"I'm going to have *Return to Sender,*" whispered Cliff.

"Shouldn't that be *Road to Hell* for you?" chuckled Paul.

"*Another One Bites the Dust*' was Phil's offering.

"*Show Me Heaven!*" mumbled GG.

"Ooh, Gorgeous Gary, you old romantic!" said Billy as he gave GG a friendly nudge.

"I want Elaine Paige dressed up in a very sexy catsuit, showing plenty of cleavage, standing in the corner singing *Memory*!" whispered Steve.

"Mmm, Elaine Paige, a definite MILF," Ollie added.

"Top dog!" said Gump.

"I think top cat would be more appropriate," Billy interjected.

"Give me *Highway to the Danger Zone*," Gump said in a macho kind of way, and they all sniggered again. Their camouflage was bearing up well.

The Civil Celebrant moved slowly from the back of the large room to the front. She was a mature, curvy, well-dressed lady, even if the blouse was deliberately a size too small and the skirt was a smidge too short. She had blond, tousled hair, and the walk down the aisle in her high heels drew a lot of attention as the heels clicked against the tiled floor. The male half of the audience was especially interested. When she turned to face the gathering, she had a kindly smile and a sexy pout that you could stick a sheet of glass to. She introduced herself as Louise and explained what Civil Celebrants were about before beginning the service.

"I don't know about you guys, but she can convert me anytime she wants!" GG whispered to his peers.

"I'll bet she could raise the dead!" Paul added. "With a pout like that, she could remove the contents of a mince pie through a small hole in the top with one suck."

"She's certainly raised my spirits," Billy said. "Christ, look at her boobs. You could have one in your mouth, one in your ear and talk to yourself all night. With a body like that, she'd certainly keep you warm on a cold winter's evening. I might have a chat with her afterwards about performing a service for me."

"She was only the undertaker's daughter but anyone cadaver, and she always knew how to deal with a stiff!" said Cliff quietly, which drew a few stifled sniggers.

"She was only the undertaker's daughter, but she laid on the slab and said fillet...," said Gump. They all looked at him quizzically before he thought about it and said, "Ooh, sorry. That should have been the fishmonger's daughter!" The others just shook their heads — it was classic Gump.

Ollie mentioned that she was about to start.

"Good, she can start on me," offered GG.

The Celebrant spoke with love and reverence, even if most of the congregation were really too numb to take any of it in. The lads were patently moved by her words, and there wasn't a dry eye in the house.

There was no alcohol at the gathering in the church hall, but the pub around the corner was full.

2

School's Out

July 1988

"Go on, JJ, at least put it in your mouth. I'd love it if you put my knob in your gob. I won't cum, honest!" Mike almost pleaded with her. "It really wouldn't be that much of a stretch to go upstairs and…make love, you know. I mean, we're both virtually starkers now, and we are really good friends!" He gave her puppy dog eyes, then blurted out, "god, I'd love to shag you!"

"No, and don't be uncouth, just be grateful I'm even giving you a hand shandy, now roll that Johnny on, and I'll take care of that fine stiffy of yours," Julia said, stroking his balls. Mike persisted.

"Well, get your lipstick on my dipstick…get your gums on me plums…get your smackers on my knackers," he knew he was wasting his time as she just stopped what she was doing and glared at him as he had one more go…

"Lips on me, pips…ok let's cut out the middlemen altogether – how about munch on me mutton…no?" he smiled meekly then asked, "We do this every time with a condom just for a wank…why?"

"'Cos, I don't want your baby paste over the sofa. Now, do you want it or not?"

It was better than nothing or doing it himself, so he let her continue and, minutes later, filled the bubble to almost bursting point. He was ordered to flush it down the toilet and make sure it was gone, which he did moments before her parents came home.

Julia Jane Fulton was born on the fourth of July 1970. Her dad always made the joke that she was so special that hundreds of millions of Americans celebrated her birthday on that date. Julia was the only child of David and Rita Fulton, a comfortably-off middle-class couple in their mid-twenties living in a small, central Hampshire village in the South of England. Both of her parents worked, and up to her sixteenth birthday, her maternal grandmother took on parental duties as and when required and also babysat on the weekend once a month or so. It was a small but financially secure family environment, and she was privately educated from the age of eleven.

Julia was beautiful and intelligent. Everything in life came so easily to her. Her parents were keen to give her every opportunity that they could but were also very careful to instil a sense of value for money and that she should be aware of how privileged she was. *'Money doesn't grow on trees, my girl'* was a statement she was beaten to boredom with. Julia understood it well after the first five hundred times and was sure they did not need to keep banging on about it.

During her early teens, she indulged in her passion for ponies and horses, and because her parents refused to buy her one of her own, she got a volunteering job at a local stable, which gave her ample opportunity to learn how to ride properly and also how to take care of such fine animals. When she wasn't studying, every spare moment was spent at the stables, and as she reached puberty, she found that her horse riding took on a whole new avenue of physical pleasure.

In her final year at school in 1987/88, she was appointed Head Girl, much to her parents' pride and delight. As a straight-A student in every subject, it bode well for entry into a university of her choice and a degree that would lead to something of merit, like law, corporate banking, or business management, should she so choose.

She was a popular girl, especially now that she had developed into a very attractive young lady. She stood a slender 5'7, had shoulder-length, strawberry blond hair, mesmerising blue-green eyes, firm, rounded breasts and the proverbial hourglass figure. Many people commented on her uncanny resemblance to her beautiful mother. She had a great sense of humour; she was confident without being conceited, arrogant, or vain, and she treated everyone in the same friendly manner. It was a skill her mother taught her, specifically when she was old enough to understand that her beauty was a major asset - *'sex sells and can open doors'.* With mature and intelligent parental guidance, she could cope with difficult situations, particularly involving the opposite sex, although very little could have prepared her to deal with someone with criminal intent.

The last few weeks of her final term arrived, and her best friend Melanie was allowed to host a pre-graduation party at her parents' swanky bungalow for around thirty or forty people. Unfortunately, this included one unsavoury and unpopular guy named Mark Timmins, who was besotted with Julia. He was a big lad, *'strong as an ox and almost as smart,'* was an off-the-cuff quip from a teacher in an unguarded moment, and if the cap fit, Timmins wore it with some misguided pride. He was also an overbearing oaf who bragged about his family's wealth at every given opportunity. He was to be avoided at all costs. The only friends he seemed to have were some of the other misfits that he hung about with. In any other school, he would have been classed as the school bully, but a private education also buys a certain amount of protection for all students. Therefore, he was always on the radar of the teaching staff and school administration.

Timmins wanted Julia, and this night would probably be his one and only chance. As Head Girl, she was always very approachable and friendly, which he and one of his followers took advantage of. Initially, he and Neville "The Nonce" Padfield cornered her to ask advice on applying to universities. Realistically, he had no intention of going to one as he was already lined up to work in the family 'firm'. Plan A was to get her drunk, but her dad had warned her about going to parties where there was a lot of available alcohol.

'People do very stupid things when they're pie-eyed. By all means, have a drink, but pace yourself so that you know when it's starting to take effect. Trust me; it's funnier to watch someone being a complete clown while you're barely under the

influence than to join them and be the star of a shit show.' She smiled at his repetitive lecture but knew he meant well, and she never forgot the words.

Trying to get her drunk wasn't working – time for the drastic backup plan.

His older brother Graham, who was even more odious than he was, had given him a small vial of a drug called Rohypnol that had recently come over from the US. It was infamous as the date rape drug because of its effectiveness in rendering the victim helpless for a short period of time. The elder Timmins had used it to good effect on two girls and encouraged his brother to *'have a good time.'*

Timmins Junior took his opportunity to spike her next drink and watched intently as he continued to bore her to distraction. With no apparent warning, she suddenly felt dizzy and said as much. He feigned surprise and concern but told her that she had better lie down. She could only walk in a stumbling fashion and, held up by Timmins and Padfield, was steered towards and into one of the bedrooms of the bungalow.

Alan McCann, one of Julia's many admirers, was a quiet, studious young man. He was quite popular but preferred to keep a very close circle of friends. He had noticed how Timmins and Padfield had cornered Julia but presumed that she could walk away at any time if she wanted to. Alan was perturbed but decided not to get involved. It was not his choice as to whom she made friends with, even if Timmins was as welcome as the Taliban at a Gay Pride march.

Alan went off to the kitchen to get another drink for himself and his mate Neil, asking him to keep an eye on Timmins. But when he got back, Julia, Timmins and the henchman had gone.

"Neil, where's Timmins and the others?"

Neil turned and looked at the empty space. "Oh, they've gone! Sorry, I got distracted."

Alan looked at Neil, who then pointed to Tina Sainz, who was wearing the tightest T-shirt and jeans that left nothing to the imagination.

"God Almighty, that's so tight she'll have to have that lot surgically removed!" Alan was aghast but turned to the job in hand. He was worried and told his buddy as much. They decided to look for Julia but not get involved if everything appeared normal.

They first went outside, thinking that they might have decided to leave the party and go elsewhere. They checked the front drive and road, which was quiet. Alan and Neil ventured into the back garden. There were a couple of girls smoking, one lad urinating into a drain, and another being sick near the fence - no sign of the missing group, though. However, further down the garden, there were noises coming from a dilapidated old shed. The pair snuck up to it. It was in such a state of disrepair that the frame was creaking.

"You're taller than me. Have a peek through the window." Alan asked Neil. Neil wasn't amused but did as he was asked.

"Oh fuck…things you wish you hadn't seen – that spectacle will be etched on my mind forever." Neil looked traumatised.

"What…what did you see?"

"Cassie Rogers bent over a mower with Andy Crumplin giving her one from behind!"

"Eugh! Cassie Rogers, Andy Crumplin…"

"More like the other way around, but that's basically what I saw…" Neil was still shocked.

Alan looked suitably disgusted before adding, "Well, they are engaged."

"If they weren't, they're fully engaged now. That said, she's been engaged more times than a public toilet in Southsea on an August Bank Holiday!"

As they hurried back to the house, Neil told Alan that Andy Crumplin's dad had set up Cassie and Andy with a new arm of his portable homes and garden building business as a wedding present.

"Believe it or not, it specialises in sheds!"

"Sounds like they have a fetish for it. Anyway, let's try to find Timmins and see what that skank is up to." Alan surmised that in such a short period of time, they couldn't have got very far.

In the spare bedroom, Timmins and Padfield had already undone her skirt and pulled it down before Timmins told his lackey to sit her on the bed but keep her upright.

"Right, you snobby, conceited bitch you're going to get it now," Timmins said to Julia, who could hardly keep her eyes open and was mumbling incoherently.

"Hold her still while I get her undressed," Timmins said. Then unbuttoned her blouse and pulled it off her. He then undid her bra and slipped that off as well.

"Mmm, you might be a cow, but what a fine pair of udders…!" And he laughed as he squeezed one of them before he took his shirt off. Padfield suddenly had second thoughts.

"Mark…this is wrong…"

"What? …what did you think was going to happen when we drugged her?" Timmins snarled at his friend.

"We? You drugged her, but anyway, I don't want any part of this…it's just not right!" He let Julia flop back on the bed and got up.

"I thought you wanted sloppy seconds?" Timmins sneered as he started to undo his jeans.

"Nah, this is so wrong, you have her…I'm outta here."

"Fuck off then, go and watch the door!"

Alan and Neil did another complete sweep of the main areas before heading towards the bedrooms. As they listened for sounds from the first one, Padfield exited from a bedroom further down the hall. He was accosted by Alan and Neil.

"Where's Timmins?"

Padfield was initially shocked to see them but then replied.

"He's in there – I don't want anything to do with it, got it? It's nothing to do with me!" and he quickly walked away. Neil went after him.

Alan was seriously worried now. He opened the door and put the bedroom light on to find Julia lying on the bed naked except for her knickers. He was immediately struck by how beautiful her breasts were, with her nipples hardened in the cool air.

Timmins was standing by the side of the bed, just wearing a grubby pair of Y-fronts. "Timmins, what the fuck are you doing?" Alan shouted angrily. Timmins was surprised to be disturbed, especially since he thought he had a guard outside the door.

"What have you done to her?" Alan shouted, moving closer to them. He stared at Julia again before looking at Timmins, who had now turned to face him. What Alan saw turned his stomach.

Timmins was speechless as he looked down at himself to find that he had climaxed and soaked the front of his pants.

"She…she wanted me to fuck her!" Timmins tried to brazen it out as he made a grab for his jeans.

"She's unconscious, you lying scumbag…" and looked down at Julia again, then reached for a quilt to cover her up, by which time Timmins was almost dressed.

"You disgusting, sleazy cunt," Alan had never been so angry and as big as Timmins was, Alan floored him one punch to the jaw. Neil came into the room, "Bloody hell, what's happened to him?"

"Don't ask, get Melanie as quick as you can. Don't make a fuss, but we need some medical help here. I think Timmins has drugged her in some way." Neil shut the door and was back a few minutes later with the party host.

Melanie was shocked to see a very groggy Mark Timmins lying on the floor and Julia lying on the bed.

"Wow, what's been going on here?"

"Don't worry about that prick. See if you can help Julia, please."

Alan then asked Neil to help him throw Timmins out of the window.

"But he might break his neck!" Neil half-heartedly protested.

"We're on the ground floor! But frankly, it would be no loss. Now grab an arm and don't touch his nether regions…he's made a mess of himself."

Neil recoiled at the detail, but between them, they managed to roll the bulky Timmins out of the window and onto the grass outside. Alan asked his mate to see if Padfield was still around, and when he left,

Melanie set about checking Julia's pulse and vital signs. Alan explained what he saw, although he omitted to tell her about Timmins' premature ejaculation; it was just too gross to relay. Mel was appalled at his revelation.

"She seems ok, but just out of it for the moment. We should send for an ambulance to be on the safe side, though," Mel said as she checked Julia's pulse again.

"Yeah, but the issue is how do we save her reputation with that crowd out there? You know what they're going to think…" Alan said pointedly.

"Hopefully, it would be no more than she was pissed…anything else would be a disaster."

"Being pissed would be bad enough!" Alan said, almost pleading with her to find some excuse for not calling 999.

Just as she was about to answer, Julia ever so slowly started to stir. Keeping her covered with the quilt, they sat her up slightly and got her some water, which she half drank, half dribbled but still had very little control over her limbs.

She came around gradually over a thirty-minute period, and although still very weak physically, her brain became more in tune.

"What…what happened? Mel, what's happened?" She asked drowsily.

"You were talking to Timmins and his brown-nosed friend Padfield," Melanie said, trying to look deeper into Julia's heavily dilated eyes, which she could barely keep open.

"I… I couldn't get away. He was… droning on and on…about nothing." She took a deep breath and, screwing her eyes up tight, opened them again, attempting to focus.

"Then I…got really dizzy and…so tired." Julia took another deep breath.

"Yes, I know, but you're okay now," Mel said, giving her a big hug.

"Did I… faint?" Julia said slowly. She was still a way off from being back to normal.

"I'll get out of the way, Mel, thanks for helping. I'm going to look for that cunt Timmins," Alan said. His relief was obvious, and he knew she was in safe hands.

"Okay, Alan, thank you," Mel said, giving him the thumbs up.

"Who was that?" Julia said slowly, still trying to focus.

"Alan, he found you, and just in the nick of time, I think," Melanie said, trying not to sound too dramatic and failing.

"Why? Did I faint? I can't remember?"

"He thought Timmins and that lizard sidekick of his were up to no good, and he also thinks Timmins spiked your drink," her friend said. Julia shook her head and, sipping at some more water, tried to make sense of what she was being told.

"Jules, I wouldn't put it past him. He's a slimy toad at the best of times, and no girl in their right mind is going to go near him." Melanie was quite emphatic in her judgment of Timmins.

"Can I just lie down . have a little sleep? I am just so tired."

"No, I don't think that's a good idea yet. Drink some more water, and we'll chat some more. When you're feeling better, I'll get someone to take you home." Mel was very concerned for her friend.

"Mel, I can't go home like this. They'll think I'm drunk. I don't get drunk. Where are my clothes? I don't have any clothes on," Julia slurred as panic started to set in. Melanie could see she was quite distressed.

"Don't worry, everything's fine. I'll sort it so that you can stay here tonight. It'll all be ok," Mel said reassuringly. She made the call an hour later when Julia could speak more normally, although she was still quite weak physically and would never have managed a flight of stairs unaided. Mrs Fulton trusted her daughter's excuse that they were having a good time, and she wanted to stay over. Julia often had sleepovers at Melanie's, so it wasn't uncommon.

Julia slept soundly in a made-up bed on the floor in Mel's bedroom so that her friend could keep an eye on her. In the morning, Mel made breakfast, although Julia ate very little, and they sat in the garden while Mel, at Julia's behest, went over the chain of events that Alan had relayed to her. She still couldn't believe Timmins would attempt such a thing, even if her friend wasn't so keen to give him the benefit of the doubt.

On the following Monday, which was the very last week for the sixth formers, everything was winding down. There was a lot of chat about how good the party was, with stories of 'naughty behaviour,' drunkenness, and the explosive aftermath of people who had significantly misjudged their limits of alcohol consumption. Timmins was putting about a story of how he and the Head Girl disappeared into a bedroom and, without saying as much, suggested to the minimal audience that he and Julia Fulton had 'enjoyed themselves.' When questioned by the gossip vultures of '*Did ya?*', the reply was, "We chatted for a good while, as most of you probably saw, so let's just say one thing led to another," and he left it for them to draw their own inevitable incorrect conclusion. He was enjoying the incredulous attention when normally people wouldn't give him the time of day.

Most people didn't believe it - nonetheless, the rumour spread like wildfire, especially as Julia had gone missing for an inordinate amount of time. When Julia was tackled about it by a few of her friends, inwardly, she was incensed. However, in a very dismissive response, she just asked, "Who is saying that, Timmins? Really? I remember talking to him, or rather, listening to him bang on about nothing for what seemed like a lifetime, but that was it. He had nothing to say and was saying it too loud."

The Chinese whisper was in overdrive. Melanie kept her up to date, although she was under strict instructions to bite her tongue, smile sweetly, and offer a little incredulity if questioned, just add that she had seen nothing.

Timmins had started a snowball that he thought might gain him some sort of kudos among a small number of peers, peers that really understood him for the unlikeable sociopath that he was. His whole family was known to be a herd of sociopaths and were essentially unwelcome outsiders.

By Wednesday evening, with only two days left of school, Julia decided the time was right to seek advice. Since the weekend, she had agonised about Saturday's events and she struggled to understand how, in all human decency, it was possible that someone could do such a thing? The issue was far too personal and emotional - her mum was the only person she could confide in.

Julia caught her alone in the front room, watching some mindless TV. There wouldn't be a better opportunity. She snuggled up on the settee with her maternal parent, laying her head in her mum's lap as she did occasionally, more so when she was little. Her mother knew, as only a mother could, that something was troubling her daughter. She said nothing apart from commenting on the TV program selling the dream of a life in the sun for the ordinary man in the street.

"How about a holiday home?" She asked her daughter, who was just staring at the garden through the open patio doors. There was no response. Her mum paused for a few minutes.

"Did you have any more thoughts about an eighteenth birthday party?" She said, changing the subject. Julia said she didn't, and that was the only prompt her mum needed.

"Sweetheart, we could batter a silly conversation around all night, but the sooner we know what we need to chat about, the sooner the issue could be resolved. What do you think?"

A few seconds of silence passed, and then Julia reached for her mum's hand to hold it. She swallowed hard a few times, and tears welled up in her eyes. She was grateful that her mum couldn't see her face, but the tears soaking into her mum's thin skirt would be evident soon enough.

"The party on Saturday—" Julia started, and those few words made her mother freeze. She tried to act calm, not least to try to keep her daughter in the same state, and she stroked her hair in assurance.

"Yes, and?"

Julia desperately tried to stem the tears. She hesitated again but then asked her mum to understand as she blurted out that nothing had happened; she was fine. It was just something that she hadn't anticipated, and while she knew nothing at the time, if it hadn't been for a couple of friends, things might have got…well, rather nasty. Between deep breaths and occasional dabs of her eyes, she conveyed a tepid version of what she had been told by Melanie. She didn't want to sensationalise or exacerbate a delicate situation.

"I'm sorry, Mum, really sorry," she sobbed. She didn't know why she said it, because she knew it wasn't her fault. Her mother made her sit up and gave her a big hug.

"Did you encourage the boy without realising, maybe, how you were dressed or something? I know it shouldn't make any difference, but some guys are just so unprepared for a lovely girl to talk to them that they think sex is being handed to them on a plate."

"No, I was just wearing my black skirt and pink blouse that you bought me last year."

"And do I know this lad?" her mother asked.

"I'd rather not say his name, but yes, you do know him or, rather, *of* him," Julia replied.

"Not Mike?" her mother questioned, desperately hoping it wasn't him.

"No, don't be silly. He wouldn't hurt anyone."

"Okay, well, look, you have nothing to feel guilty about, and your real friends have done you proud. That's the positive to take out of this. Don't concern yourself with what might have been – it didn't happen." She gave her daughter another big hug.

"But it's all over school, and the rumours are that I'm some sort of drunken slut – I'm the Head Girl, you can see how it looks," and she started to weep again.

"Do you want me to do something, maybe speak to the school?" Her mother asked, and they chatted about a possible course of action, but ultimately, Julia said she would deal with it herself as she wiped the last of her tears away.

"I just wanted you to know in case you heard it from somewhere else." Then, with a determined look in her eye, Julia nodded to herself and repeated that she would sort it. She kissed and hugged her mum before saying good night. Her mother asked her not to say anything to her father because it was best that he didn't get involved.

"The thing is, he'd want to kill the guy concerned, then I'd have to calm him down, and we'd agree to wait and—"

"And?"

"After he'd calmed down, he would go and kill the guy, probably quite painfully." Her mother then gave her a weak smile and raised her eyebrows as if to say *you know what your dad is like*. Julia smiled with an understanding nod and went to bed, thinking that if he knew the truth, he probably *would* go and kill Timmins.

Thursday morning, Timmins was occupying his corner of the Students' Common Room with his pals Padfield and another non-entity called Paul Green. It had been dubbed 'Rotten Row' by other members of the year. Julia was focused and fairly calm. She knew not to get angry – *'If you lose your temper, you lose the argument'* was another pearl of wisdom from her father.

There were several smiles and hellos from her pals, and she responded in kind, but people could see that she was on a mission as she headed directly for her target. Timmins didn't notice her until she stood over him.

"Hey, lookie here, guys, it's the Head Girl. They don't call her the Head Girl for nothing!" he said and sniggered along with Padfield and Green. She just stared at him.

"What do you want, another go?" and he laughed again.

She crossed her arms and said loudly, "Another go? Surely, another go would assume that there was a first go, wouldn't it? Although it appears that you've already been muck-spreading some utter bullshit about me."

"Hey, it's only what other people have been saying. I'm too discreet for that."

"Mark, you're about as discreet as a block of flats with much less charm!"

"Oh, come on, you know you enjoyed yourself. Or were you too pissed to remember?" Timmins sneered.

"I'll tell you what I remember, Mark," she still spoke quite loudly. There was a distinct hush in the room, so no one was in any doubt about what was being said.

"I remember being bored to the point of almost losing the will to live about your inane, pompous self-worth," she paused, "I remember how you liked to malign and insult people, teachers and students alike," she paused again and, like a politician, repeated the opening phrase for dramatic effect.

"I remember you telling me how rich your dad is and how you're going to join the family business, which I assume still indulges in illegal activities, allegedly." She continued to hold his gaze.

"I remember that your despicable brother spent some time in Wandsworth Prison for drug dealing, which was covered up in a lie about him going abroad for a gap year. Do you really think people in this county are so gullible? I guess you do - you pedal crap – he pedals drugs, and it won't be long before you're doing the same."

There was some sniggering, but you could have heard a pin drop, and people could see that he was getting very uncomfortable. She gave his sidekicks a withering look before continuing.

"I remember you giving me a drink which tasted a bit odd and then–" she took a deep breath, "And then... I don't remember anything more until a couple of hours later."

"Yeah, well, you were drunk, the Head Girl, drunk as a skunk and behaving like the slapper you are," Timmins sneered again.

"Do you know, Mark, I would rather pour boiling water in my eyes than have a vile, repellent wretch like you crawling all over me," she was measured in her delivery but was only just managing to restrain herself from punching his smug, ugly face.

"You didn't seem to mind me crawling all over you on Saturday!"

"So, to be clear, you're saying that we stripped off and had sex?" She said, watching him closely. He did not return her gaze.

"Yeah, and you loved it!" he said awkwardly, grinning at his mates but now trying to avoid looking at the interested spectators.

"What position did we do it in, then?"

Timmins hesitated. "The one you insisted on – doggy, probably because you're such a bitch," Timmins was getting cocky. Green laughed, but Padfield was looking decidedly ill at ease.

"You must have been like the SAS," Julia said, knowing he would be confused.

"Huh?"

She repeated herself and then added, "You were in and out without anyone knowing. Least of all me!" There were more giggles from the engrossed audience.

"Perhaps it was pitch black, and you couldn't see what you were doing. Did you have your weenie worm stuck in something else?" she suggested to more sniggering, especially from the girls.

Just then, Mel turned to Alan and said, "I forgot to tell you something," and whispered to him. There was silence, Julia could see he was on the ropes. He glared at her and then turned to his accomplices.

"Listen to this bitch trying to save her reputation," he then turned back to her. "You're just a two-bob slag, so don't try to be clever," Timmins scoffed.

"I should worry about what a lying degenerate like you thinks, then again, not. But if you are so convinced that your story is true, just stand up and swear on your mother's life that you had sex with me on

Saturday night." Julia paused momentarily before saying, "Before you do, there is something I want to share with you."

Timmins looked confused as she bent down to put a small item into his hand and then whispered in his ear.

"I'm going to spare you the embarrassment of giving you the used one from that night. Had you done what you've been crowing about for the last few days, that bed would have looked like a scene from the Texas Chainsaw Massacre. So, it's your call, you arsehole – brazen it out and get thrown to the wolves and the police, or get up and fuck off, you lying, worthless piece of shit!"

Timmins, breathing heavily, went red both with rage and embarrassment as she stepped away, staring at him. He stuffed the tampon into his pocket, and he knew he was being utterly humiliated. As he got up to leave, he indulged in one last act of bravado.

"Fuck you, Fulton, I'll make you pay for this."

Alan McCann was within touching distance of the pair of them and had kept his silence up to this point. He was not prone to violence but surprised everyone, especially Timmins, when he stepped into his path and grabbed him by the throat.

"Just remember what I saw of you and your little accident. Don't make threats, you bully. If anything happens to her, I will come looking for you!" and he pushed him aside. Alan then turned to Padfield and Green. "You tossers can fuck off as well."

Timmins was clearly shocked and barged past Alan to get out, as did his two sidekicks. The three of them ran the gauntlet of abuse and demeaning laughter from the onlookers. Julia's heart was pounding, but her relief at holding it together was all too obvious as she sat down. Mel sat beside her, and a few others came up to her, offering their support.

A month later, Mark and Graham Timmins were both attacked and bundled into a van. They were taken to a disused warehouse and stripped down to their underpants. They were then tied to railings with their legs wide apart, where the perpetrators catastrophically damaged their testicles with a baseball bat. There was a scrawled sign around the younger sibling's neck– *'Live long and think on what you did, you are scum'.*

An anonymous phone call to the emergency services saw them urgently taken to A&E, where nothing could be done to save their future prospects as biological parents. Over a period of three or four months, several incidents of vandalism occurred to the Timmins' family house, cars, and especially business premises. It was enough to see them sell up and move away.

A thorough police investigation into the attacks drew a complete blank. Subsequently, there were no arrests or prosecutions, and given the family's reputation, it was suggested that it was some form of criminal turf war. Nobody shed tears over the Timmins family's demise.

3
The Things We Do For Love

July 1988

With school finished, Julia contemplated her future. She had received unconditional offers from three universities but wanted to step away from education for a short while. The fact was, she was just so excited to be absolutely *free*.

She already had part-time employment as a waitress for a catering company that frequently serviced big corporate events at exhibition centres, sporting venues and large hotels. She was now able to work as often as she liked, and she enjoyed the more adult buzz of the working environment, especially from the larger events.

On one such occasion, a fund-raising dinner at the old county cricket ground near Southampton, Julia was assigned to a table of eight guys, all in their late twenties and mid to late thirties. They were a rowdy bunch but even though she was just out of school, she was well-versed in how to deal with boozy, boisterous men. *"Be humorous, be flirty, smile a lot, but don't take any nonsense"* was the sound advice that her mother had given her. She was also armed with one real gem from her father: *"If all else fails, kick 'em in the gonads!"* And so, with a deep breath, a tight blouse, a push-up bra, a short skirt and a welcoming smile, she went into battle.

Julia was informed that the host of the table was one of the cricket club committee members, Gerry Irvine. He was pointed out to her by her catering manager as the tall, dark-haired guy who was herding his guests towards their seats at the start of the evening. She was quite taken with his casual but smart dress sense and the fact that he appeared to have a fair amount of sway with them, even though most were significantly overdoing the cheaper prices of a members-only bar. Of course, as a committee member, he did have his reputation to uphold, and for the most part, he kept things under control. It was almost inevitable that, given the consumption of alcohol, the line of acceptable behaviour was under threat.

Julia was summoned and stood next to one of the more mature guys as she took yet another drinks order. From his seated position, he put his arm around the top of her legs and pulled her onto his lap, to a big cheer from some of the younger guests as her bottom landed side-on onto his crotch.

Gerry shouted over to him.

"Bob, stop behaving like the dirty old git that you are and let the young lady up, please! You wouldn't like it if a lounge lizard like you did that to your daughter!"

In the motion of sitting down, her skirt rode up, revealing the tops of her stockings, a juicy little titbit that Bob was not slow to share with the gang.

"Ooh, lookee here!" Bob exclaimed and, resting his hand on her upper thigh, proceeded to undo the clasp of one of her suspenders to more cheers from the captivated audience.

His hand gently stroked her smooth skin, and she could now feel that he was getting aroused as his erection pressed into her backside.

"BOB!" Gerry was more insistent now. "Let the young lady get up!"

"Oh, she doesn't mind Gerry, let her take the order, and then I'll let her go," Bob said as he held her with his right arm around her middle and his hand dangerously close to her left breast, all the while continuing to caress her outer thigh with the other. Julia appeared to be unfazed, but inside, she was a mixture of complete resentment and no little humiliation…nonetheless, her nipples responded to the physicality.

"Sir," she said, "I won't be taking any more orders for drinks until I'm allowed to stand, so please let me go." Her heart was pounding. The whole incident was getting out of hand, even more so when the guy fingered her name badge pinned to her breast pocket.

"One little kiss, then, Julia?" Bob said, still stroking her thigh. She looked at him, then leant in towards his ear and just as he was about to kiss her cheek, she said quietly, "If you don't let me go, I'm going to jab this pen so far into your eye that you will need surgery to either remove it or replace the refill. Failing that, I'm going to reach down and squeeze your nuts so hard that your resultant high-pitched squeal will probably shatter every glass on this fucking table."

He complied immediately, and as she pulled away and stood up, she loudly said, "I'd suggest sir should buy a different mouthwash as the one he's using doesn't appear to be working." Julia then pulled her rumpled skirt over her stocking tops and addressed the group.

"Now, gentlemen, if you're all going to behave, I will gladly take your order for drinks. What can I get for you?"

The rest of the table's occupants burst out laughing, and she received thunderous applause and a wink from Gerry.

"Well, that's us told, especially you, Bob. Now, guys, can you conduct yourselves with some decorum, please? It is a charity event after all - not some fucking chimps' tea party." Turning to Julia, he then apologised for the expletive. She just nodded in acknowledgement.

The rest of the evening went off without a hitch, and she received a very generous tip, not only to her delight but also to all the other waiting staff when it went into the shared gratuity pot. Bob even came to the back room to have a word and to profusely apologise for his behaviour. Julia was very magnanimous and brushed it off with, "Boys will be boys." He shook her hand and pressed a ten-pound note into it, whispering that he understood tips had to be shared but that he wanted her to have this for herself. She smiled, thanked him, and he turned and left with his metaphorical tail between his legs.

After clearing up, Julia went to the public phone to call her mum for her arranged pick-up. To her surprise, she was met by Gerry, who had waited for her.

"Can I give you a lift home? I'm going in your direction," he said confidently.

"But you don't know where I live, so how do you know you'll be going my way?" She was quite puzzled.

"If you tell me where you live, I *will* be going in that direction," he laughed.

"Ah, yes, very good. Mum warned me about men like you." She tried not to sound too enthusiastic, but she was warming to him.

"Men like me?" He asked innocently.

"Yes, what was it you called that guy at the table…lounge lizard!"

"Miss, I am no lounge lizard. A smooth operator, maybe, but no lounge lizard. I am mortally offended at such a slur," he said in mock indignation.

"I'm sure you'll get over it," she replied.

"So, can I give you a lift home and maybe tempt you to a swift drink first?"

"Haven't you had enough already?"

"Now, you know that you only brought me water tonight," he said.

"Ah, but for all I know, there might have been some surreptitious Sauvignon sampling," she replied, although she could tell that he was sober.

"Frankly, I prefer to be a Champagne Charlie rather than a Sauvignon Sid," Gerry responded emphatically.

"So, if I go for a drink – *one* drink, you'll give me a lift home afterwards and no funny business?" Julia said sternly.

"Scout's honour, one drink and no funny business, but you're not German, are you?" He asked.

"No, my grandparents owned a Dachshund called Fritzie, but apart from him, whatever gave you that idea?" She wondered where this was going. He quickly replied.

"Well, they're not renowned for their humour. I mean, German comedy is no laughing matter, so consequently, there is definitely no funny business."

She responded with a wry smile.

"But to be fair, the last time they had any real fun, it took six years and half the world to stop them. I guess once they get on a roll... You know, it's all about momentum," he said with a straight face. She laughed; she was undoubtedly warming to him.

"Okay, let me phone my mum."

"For permission?" He asked cheekily.

"No. Just to let her know that I don't need a lift," she sneered.

"Hi Mum, everything alright? Good, good. Look, some of us are going for a quick drink. I'll be home after that. Yes, some of them are coming our way, so thanks for the offer earlier... What? Oh yes, I've got my key. I promise not to wake anyone…yes, yes… Okay, g'night. Yes. Love you. Mwah!"

He led her out of the clubhouse and over to his Range Rover. He then opened the passenger door for her, anticipating a glimpse of her stocking tops, to which she responded,

"Hoping to get a quick flash, were you?" And made no attempt to cover up when the inevitable 'show' occurred.

"You never know your luck!" He smiled as he closed the door and went around to the driver's side of the car. She had managed to pull the skirt over her stocking tops by the time he was in the vehicle.

"So, just where do you live? We'll stop for a quickie on the way," he asked, fully aware of the double entendre.

"Quickie?" Julia was also on the same wavelength.

"Yes, a quick drink. It must be way past your bedtime!"

"I'm eighteen, so I'll please myself," she said bluntly.

"Gosh, eighteen and never been kissed!" Gerry exclaimed, trying to provoke a response. She laughed but gave nothing away.

"To be candid, I thought you were at least in your twenties, the way you kept all the lads at our table under control."

"Except one!" she said, contradicting him.

"No, I disagree. That could have turned rather ugly, but you dealt with it and didn't cause a scene." She thanked him and repeated her earlier line of "boys will be boys."

Julia told him where she lived. He knew of a little country pub nearby that would be ideal. Over the time span of a pint of lager and a glass of wine, she found out that he was thirty-two, divorced, with no kids, and worked as an independent financial advisor who also did a bit of estate agency work for a pal when required. She delved deeper into his marriage. He had been with his former wife for four years, married for three of those, and got divorced because he came home early one afternoon to find, "My darling wife in a threesome with two guys – riding one cock and sucking the other!"

"Oh, I'm so sorry. I didn't mean to pry." She was genuinely shocked at the graphic description.

"It's okay," Gerry assured her, looking rather melancholy. "She always was very gregarious."

Julia burst out laughing. "Wow, there are gregarious girls, and then there are just plain old sluts," she continued to laugh. He smiled, but she could see he was very hurt.

"I should have paid her more attention, but you know what it's like when you're trying to build a business. I guess I didn't see the warning signs."

Julia said she understood, but she had no idea of the amount of work required to get a business off the ground and make it profitable as soon as possible. She finished her drink and hoped he would offer another one, but he didn't.

Instead, he said, "Right, one drink, a promise is a promise," and getting up, finished the last inch of his pint. Outside, he opened the car door for her again and smiled. They both knew it was in the hope of another quick flash, she willingly obliged.

As he got in the car, she said, "What is it about stockings and suspenders?"

"I have no idea," he responded as they drove out of the pub car park, "but it may be something to do with the giggle band."

"Giggle band?" she questioned.

"Yes, the top of the stocking."

"Oh?" She was really intrigued now.

"It's known as the giggle band because if you're stroking a lady's thigh once you get past that bit, you're laughing!" He smiled.

"Ah, I see," she said, trying to be rather cool about it. "Oh, by the way, thank you for sticking up for me with that friend of yours at the table this evening!"

"Julia," he said seriously, "I would stick up for you anytime!" And he chuckled.

"Yes, I'm sure you would. How very flattering." She laughed as well.

They drove for about ten minutes when she asked him to pull over into a little parking layby just short of a cul-de-sac. As the car came to a halt, she told him that she lived in one of the houses down that road, but as it was a dead end, he would have to turn around to exit, and she didn't want to attract any attention.

"There are a dozen houses all owned by professional curtain twitchers!" she added, much to his amusement.

"Don't worry," he said, "your secret is safe with me".

He quickly followed with, "Hold still. You've got something on your eyelid. No, don't touch it. It might go into your eye. Just close your eyes for a second."

She did so, and he leaned across to give her a kiss on the lips, which took her by surprise. He stayed put, apologising and admitting he couldn't control himself.

"Hmmm, for a guy that's thirty-two and been married, is that really the best you can do?" She goaded him, looking directly into his eyes.

He moved in again to kiss her properly. Without the surprise element, she willingly returned his kiss, soft lips pressing against one another before their mouths opened in unison and their tongues danced with each other. Julia could tell he was clean-shaven with a hint of expensive after-shave, but the skin wasn't as soft and babyish as Mike's — this was a real man.

They eventually broke off the kiss, and he spoke, "Are you sure you're only eighteen? I've kissed a fair number of women in my time, and that was up there with the best of them!"

"Yeah, sure," she said cynically. He sat back and pulled out a spare business card from a compartment in the centre console and, giving it to her, said, "Look, I know I'm an old git and divorced, but I've had a great evening, more so since the dinner event finished, and if you fancy getting together again for another drink and a chat, please don't hesitate to give me a call."

"I might just do that," Julia said, looking into his eyes and trying to act cool, even though she was sure he could hear her heart beating like a timpani drum. With a quick peck on his cheek, she gathered her bag and was quickly out of the car. He watched her flounce down the road and was delighted to see her turn and wave as he drove past.

She smiled to herself as she quietly turned the key in the door lock and, removing her shoes, went to bed as silently as possible. She removed her blouse, bra, and knickers and, for once, ignored her PJs. She was thrilled at her nakedness and how her stockings and suspender belt felt as she moved in bed. Julia touched herself and was not surprised to feel that she was damp. She had masturbated before, but tonight was going to be different as she imagined Gerry skilfully seducing her and performing oral sex on her before taking her virginity.

As she massaged herself, she closed her eyes, and she could feel his experienced fingers bringing her to climax. She quickly brought the pillow to her mouth to stifle the whimpers of pleasure brought about by her own fair hand. Removing her stockings, she decided to sleep naked to experience a whole night of being unencumbered by nightclothes, and she made a promise to herself that Gerry would be the first man to fuck her. She drifted off to sleep, wondering how, when, and where.

Julia woke at her usual 'out of school' time of 8.30 am and immediately thought of the previous night's unplanned excitement. She checked her bag to make sure she still had Gerry's phone number. She fantasised that somehow, he had discovered her home number and that he would call to confess his undying love for her, then she laughed to herself, recalling that it was just one kiss! (Mmm, but what a kiss – it made her nipples hard and sent a tingle to her pussy, she had never been kissed like that before.)

Julia checked the answerphone. There were a few messages, one for her dad to remind him about golf on Saturday, others from her friends asking what she was up to over the weekend, and one from her long-term school friend, Mike. They became pals in the third year of senior school, and he was a thoroughly nice chap. She knew that he wanted it to be some great love affair. Sure, like most teenagers, they had done some kissing, heavy petting and nudity but had never gone the 'distance' to full intercourse.

She was always excited to see how she could make his penis hard and how quickly he would climax just by stroking it. Julia was intrigued by the way his semen squirted out in short bursts, how much of it there was and how she caught a whiff of the salty odour. However, as much as he tried, he could not get her to perform oral sex on him. Conversely, he never offered to go down on her either, but he, too, was fascinated by how wet she became when he fingered her, although he never had the same success when attempting to make *her* climax. They were, in essence, typical fifth-form fumblers!

Julia had to respond to Mike (who was the only one to call her JJ) because if she didn't, he'd phone her persistently until she spoke to him. As much as she liked him, she felt that she needed to move on. She knew she would purposely choose a university that was well away from his chosen path. He was good-looking enough that he would succeed with girls elsewhere, which was her escape route to gradually letting him down. She phoned him, hoping that he was out so that she could leave a message. No luck. He was home and answered. She started with, "Hey, Mike, all good with you?" Then, she responded to his quick-fire questions.

"Yes, I was working last night." She laughed. "Walk your dog? Well, as nice as he is, sorry, I'm going to be busy working for the next few days, so, unfortunately, you're going to have to walk him yourself. There are a lot of weddings coming up, and I need the money, but maybe we'll catch up in the middle of next week. Yeah, you too take care, mwah."

She smiled. Walking his dog and stroking her cat were their poor attempts at coded messages, which would hardly require the Bletchley Park Codebreakers to decipher.

She desperately wanted to phone Gerry but didn't want to sound too keen. Julia also hoped that she hadn't misread the signs, but after all, he did make a point of waiting for her. He did offer to take her home; he did suggest they go for a drink, AND…he did make the first move to kiss her. Okay, so she encouraged the proper tongue-twisting snog, but he was a willing participant, and he did give her his number, suggesting they go for another drink. So, if he was interested, there would be nothing to lose by seeing him again.

Under instructions from her mother, the morning was spent going through clothes and shoes that might go to a charity shop or for recycling, but Julia couldn't get Gerry out of her mind. She wished that she'd given him her number so that he could make the first move, but then again, what if he'd had the number and still didn't call? The uncertainty was just too much!

With the house to herself, she tried on some of her more revealing clothes and paraded around semi-naked just for the freedom of it all. She caught herself in various mirrors and wondered if she really did turn men on. Natural blonde hair, she wasn't the tallest, but she wasn't fat. Everything seemed in proportion, and her boobs were a nice shape, not like the torpedoes that her friend Melanie had. *Mel's melons,* the boys called them. Then there was sporty Leah, captain of the hockey team, with breasts like bee stings. No, she was happy with what she had and playfully cupped them in front of the full-length mirror. Again, Gerry popped into her mind, and she could visualise him standing behind her, doing exactly what her hands and fingers were doing to her boobs and hardened nipples. She was horny again. This time, she needed something to fill her while her fingers took the appropriate action.

She rarely ventured into her parents' bedroom and seriously wondered if they still had "special cuddles", as Mel would call it. They were an openly affectionate couple towards each other and never seemed fazed in front of her if anything risqué came on TV. She recalled numerous occasions when her dad would make jokes about lurid sex scenes in films and dramas, and both parents appeared to be quite broad-minded. It wouldn't be inconceivable that they still had sex.

Barefoot and just wearing her knickers, she carefully went through her mother's cupboards and drawers. Nothing, although the knickers drawer did have a few pairs of lacy panties, and the drawer below had a couple of suspender belts and stockings, so she wasn't going to give up yet. On her dad's side, in the bedside unit, there were condoms and baby oil, which was proof, and she started to wonder how often these special cuddles took place. They were damned quiet if they did it when she was in the house.

She checked the big drawer under the bed on his side - golfing jumpers, including the one she hated most, which had big red and black diamonds on it. Her last place to check was the drawer on her mum's side. Interestingly, there was a briefcase which was locked. It was one of those with a number combination lock on each side. Julia pulled it out and up onto the bed. How to open a couple of three-digit combinations? Just how many combinations can you get with three numbers times two? She would have to do it logically – three zeroes to start, then 001, 002. She sniggered to herself and thought how ridiculous this was, but she continued. After ten minutes, it flicked open on 101. She quickly tried the same number on the second lock. No good. Then she thought about it. Her mother's birthday was 10th October 1944. Excitedly, she spun the small, numbered wheels of the second set into position, 044, and pressed the catch. To her amazement and excitement, the locking arm sprang open! She hesitated and then took a deep breath before opening the case.

Her jaw dropped, and she said out loud, "Fucking hell, you dirty old sods!" And then laughed loudly as well.

4

Let's Talk About Sex

July 1988

As Julia sat on her parents' bed, she checked the time to make sure she wasn't about to be caught by one of the "dirty old sods" coming home and catching her red-handed (and red-faced). She was now pulling out several sex toys, including a big wand vibrator, a moulded penis-shaped vibrator, handcuffs, a blindfold, a hood, and an odd-looking item with a ring attached that looked like it should be pushed into an orifice. She thought, *too small to be a dildo*, and then it dawned on her!! Lastly, there was a strap-like thing with a ball in the middle of it. She then found a small catalogue from a company that supplied sex toys and found that the thing for your anus was called a butt plug, and the other item was a ball gag. Oh, wow!!! Mummy and Daddy, you are… *really naughty people!*

The revelations continued when she found several very explicit photographs of Mummy, Daddy, and a younger man engaging in lots of sexual acts. She had seen porn before when Mike had got his hands on some videos, and also at a sleepover with Mel and a couple of other girls from school when they watched a film that started off as a male strip show and ended up as an orgy. So, none of the acts portrayed in these photos were new to her, but as she flicked through them, she could see that her dear parents were heavily involved, albeit that they were about twenty years younger.

To say she was shocked was an understatement, but she was so horny and damp now that there was a more pressing requirement to relieve her wants and desires. God, she thought, if Gerry were here now, he wouldn't know what hit him.

Julia took out the two vibrators and decided she would try the butt plug another time. She closed the case, carefully putting everything else where she had found them, and put the case back in the drawer without resetting the locks so that if she was in a rush, she could pop the toys back quickly.

She went back to her bedroom to play and, using a squirt of moisturiser on the cock shaped device, she slowly pushed it in herself a little way before withdrawing it and then pushing in again a little further, allowing her pussy to stretch to welcome this new invasion. She closed her eyes with the pleasure of penetration as she did so. It was such a new sensation to feel full of something more substantial than Mike's fingers, and when she flicked the switch, her body gave an involuntary jerk forward. It was weird and blissful all at the same time. She closed her legs to keep it in place, which made the sensations even more intense. While that was buzzing away inside her, she then switched on the larger wand to a low setting. Tentatively, she brought it onto her vulva and up towards her clitoris, sighing out loud as the pulsations worked on her most sensitive spot. She lay back and held it in place, climaxing within minutes. She pulled it away immediately and quickly pulled out the ersatz cock as everything was just too intense to carry on. Within fifteen minutes of bringing the toys into her room, she was left sweating, breathing heavily and temporarily satiated.

Time was moving on, and she decided to dress in her normal casual joggers and T-shirt. She cleaned the two vibrators with a damp cloth and put them carefully back in the case, remembering to move the number dials into a randomly locked position.

She decided to phone Gerry, which again sent her heart rate skywards. Julia's fingers were shaking as she pressed the dial buttons on the phone. After a couple of rings, he answered. She tried to sound cool.

"Hi, Gerry, it's Julia. How are you?"

"Hello, Julia, yes, good, thanks. Um, look, I'm just off to a meeting. Can I phone you later or tomorrow, maybe?"

"Right, yeah, sure, tomorrow morning would be good," and she gave him her number. He confirmed that he had a note of it and would call back. She worked on the principle that her parents would be around later, and she didn't want them earwigging unless they were off to a wife-swapping party! The notion made her laugh to herself. Tomorrow morning, she would be by herself and able to chat freely, but then that nagging doubt kicked in. Was he really going to a meeting, or was he dismissing the silly little schoolgirl?

Apart from dinner, she spent the rest of the evening in her room, as she usually did. She thought that she'd carried off the social chit-chat over the evening meal quite well, although she couldn't really look either parent in the eye. Even so, the kiss goodnight for the pair of them was a bit awkward as she had this clear image in her mind of her naked mother kneeling on the floor holding a cock in one hand and smiling at the camera as she was just about to take another hard length in her mouth.

On Friday morning, she could hear the phone ringing downstairs, which was quickly answered by her father, who was about to leave for work. She looked at her alarm clock; it said 7.30 am. The call was brief, and then there was a knock on her door; it was her dad.

"Sweetheart, are you awake?"

"Yes, I've just woken up 'cos of the phone."

"Okay, it was someone for you, a guy called Gerry. I told him you weren't up yet. He said he'll phone again in an hour or so. See you later, love you."

"Okay, thanks, love you too," she replied, smiling to herself with butterflies in her stomach and a tingle in her loins. She drifted off to sleep with her hand between her legs and was startled when there was another knock on the door half an hour later. It was her mother.

"I'm just off now. See you later. Don't forget to sort out your old clothes for the charity shop. Love you, bye."

"Bye, love you too."

Julia rubbed her eyes and realised she was still naked, having slept like that for the second night in a row. She enjoyed the sensation of the cotton quilt cover touching her skin and especially her nipples. She began to stroke and pinch them. Running all of those sexy pictures of her mother and father engaged in such shameless playtime. She concluded that they had passed the libidinous gene onto her.

She stopped and got up, donning only a pair of knickers, and padded downstairs to make herself a cup of tea. She enjoyed the whole freedom of nakedness, except for her underwear. She didn't want to frighten the window cleaner or postman, so she had a T-shirt and shorts handy just in case.

As she put a slice of bread in the toaster, the phone rang. It was 8.45 am, and her heart jumped. Surely, it could only be Gerry. She nervously picked up the receiver.

"Hello."

"Hi JJ, how you doing?"

"Oh, Mike - it's you," she said, clearly deflated.

"No need to sound so keen," Mike said, picking up the disappointment in her voice.

"Sorry, I'm expecting a call about work over the weekend, and I just want to get my diary sorted," she lied but thought she sounded pretty convincing.

"Maybe if you have some time, you could come over. My parents are away now until Sunday evening." She knew he was alluding to *'walking his dog'*.

"Oh, that's nice. I just can't say at the moment, but if you have other things you could arrange for yourself, then don't wait for me to get back to you. Okay?" He would have had to have been completely impervious to the tone of her voice not to realise it was designed to put him off.

"Okay, no worries, give me a call if your plans change. You know I like to see you," he said, almost pleading. *Yes*, she thought, *and I know how much you like me tossing you off*, but concluded with, "Okay, see ya."

She put the receiver down and, stroking her nipples again, thought, *I've got bigger fish to fry and hopefully a better willy to wank*. The person attached to that willy phoned shortly afterwards.

"Hello, Julia, how's you?" came the voice at the other end of the line.

"Good, thanks,"

"I phoned earlier. I guess it was your dad that answered?"

"Yes, he told me." Her heart was thumping.

"I know it was a bit early, but I was keen to get hold of you."

"I'll bet," she said, laughing and flicking a nipple at the same time. She was starting to relax.

"Um, not like that…well, you know what I mean," he said, stumbling awkwardly through this chat.

"I'm not sure I do?" she teased.

"Well, that would be nice. But anyway, would you be available to go for lunch today?"

"Today?" he had caught her by surprise.

"Yes, I know it's short notice, but why not strike while the iron's hot and all that?" he said, regaining some composure.

"And is it?" she said, growing in confidence and trying to keep him on the back foot.

"Is what?" he queried

"Is your iron hot?" she laughed again.

"Ah…yes, very good…" He was desperately trying to get some control, but this eighteen-year-old was making him seem like a mumbling, bumbling adolescent. He wanted to say that his *iron* was perceptibly hot…and very hard.

"So, lunch?" Gerry now tried to sound like he was apathetic.

"Well, I could say I'm washing my hair. But okay," she teased again.

"Great, I'll pick you up at eleven. I need to meet a client just after that. Can you dress smart but casual - no jeans, okay?" Gerry ordered.

"Oh, okay, but before you go, can you pick me up in the layby where you dropped me last night, please?" she asked, wondering why her clothing would be an issue.

"Sure, away from prying eyes and twitching curtains. Not a problem. See you at eleven sharp!" and he hung up. She put the phone down and tweaked both nipples that were happily standing to attention. Julia wondered why this guy was having such an effect on her. It couldn't be "love" as she barely knew him. Certainly not infatuation for simply the same reason, but she felt that if he snapped his fingers, she would do anything he asked of her in the bedroom or anywhere else, come to that. She could feel how damp she was even just talking to him on the phone.

There was no time to dawdle, take a hot shower, put on make-up, and get dressed. She thought it odd that he specified the style of outfit, being rather direct about her not wearing jeans. Perhaps he was taking her to some fancy restaurant for lunch to get her drunk and then take her back to his place to seduce her and take her to bed. She questioned whether she was ready for such a big step, but the excitement, rather than nervous anticipation, succinctly answered that.

She chose a plain white skirt that came just above the knee, a soft, red, short-sleeved blouse with a round neck, a matching white bra and knickers set with white heels. She made sure not to overdo the make-up as she had seen that a lot of girls make the classic error of *'slapping on the war paint with a trowel'*, as her dad would say.

Julia was ready with time to spare and watched some TV without really watching it. Gerry was in her thoughts too much to concentrate on anything. 10.55 am, time to move. She got her key and her bag, and she was off, hoping that in the beautiful sunshine, there were no nosy neighbours tending their front gardens and wanting to chat. She was in luck; she turned the corner with a minute to spare to find the black Range Rover already parked. Her heart leapt again and she hoped she didn't look foolish balancing in her heels.

For once, he didn't open the door for her and as she got in, she wasn't sure whether she should kiss him. She decided not to and sat back in the seat, strapping herself in with the seatbelt.

"Wow, you look lovely, great outfit. You do know we're only going to a burger bar, don't you?" It was his turn to tease.

"As long as there are chips with it, I don't mind!" She was amazed at how confident she felt around him. As he drove, she had a chance to look at him properly in the daylight. His brown hair was fashionably cut in a Rick Astley style. He had a nice face, not stunningly handsome, but definitely cute. Slim in stature, again, he was well dressed in a crisp light blue shirt, smart black trousers and shoes and that hint of after-shave that she recalled from last night.

"Okay, I've picked you up a bit early because I need to meet a guy at a property I'm hoping to sell for a friend of mine. I do a bit of estate agent work when I can. It helps to keep the pennies coming in."

"Yes, you mentioned it last night," she said, thinking that there must be a decent number of pennies to pay for this expensive car.

"Hey, you can be my glamorous assistant if you like. There's a clipboard on the back seat. Just take a few notes if required," Gerry said as he drove.

"Do I get paid?" she asked, feeling a bit cheeky.

"If we sell the place, I'm sure there might be a little remuneration for your efforts," he said, focusing on the road ahead. They drove in silence. It wasn't awkward, and she never felt the need to make conversation.

"How long have you worked for the catering company?" he asked.

"Off and on since I was sixteen," she said. "It's not a bad job. I like to meet people, and money-wise, it's pretty good. I'm just trying to get an amount together now before I go to Uni."

"Oh, okay, where are you going and what are you studying?" he asked, concentrating on his driving but seemingly interested. Julia told him that she hadn't really made up her mind and that she had just been enjoying being out of the education bubble for a little while. She continued to say that her parents hadn't put her under any pressure, and she felt that she should just get out there, work hard and play hard within reason.

"Within reason?" he laughed.

"Avoid drugs!" she said. He agreed it was good advice. He regaled a story about a good friend of his, an intelligent, brilliantly funny guy. Regrettably, he was not intelligent enough to realise his dependence on heroin would be his ultimate downfall.

"Ultimate?" she queried.

"Yes, ultimate - he overdosed and died."

There was a brief silence before she spoke. "Dad says that the punishment should fit the crime. If the police catch a drug dealer, he should be asked if he's a dealer or if it's for personal use. If he admits to being a drug dealer, then it's a five-year jail term, more if it's a second offence. If the dealer says it's for personal use, the police make him take all of what he has in one go."

"There's a thought!" Gerry said with raised eyebrows at the severe consequences of such an action.

"Ha! You don't know the half of it."

"Would he be a little bit right-wing?" he asked.

"It's a close call," she said, "but as he admits to anyone, he is marginally to the right of Benito Mussolini. Mind you, you get to know when people don't agree with you when you end up hanging from a meat hook in a village square." Gerry laughed out loud, which gave her more confidence, and she began to lose those early relationship nerves of walking on eggshells, hoping not to say or do the wrong thing.

They arrived at the gated complex of some new luxury apartments overlooking a small marina. Gerry told her to grab the clipboard, and they set off to meet his client, Mr Joseph Porter. He was of medium height, middle-aged, well-dressed, balding, and too well-fed, in her opinion. Gerry introduced her as his assistant, and she desperately tried to look grown-up and business-like. The client didn't seem particularly friendly and was making negative comments about the property as he was being shown around. Gerry was extremely patient and answered even the most pernickety questions with good grace. She followed them around and said nothing.

They entered the lounge area, and she went over to the large window to take in the panoramic view of the marina below. Gerry and his client continued to talk in the background when Gerry suddenly brought her back into the room.

"Julia, yoo-hoo, are you with us?"

"Oh yes, sorry, I was just taking in the amazing view you get from this window." She was enthralled. Gerry quickly picked up on her unprompted observation.

"Yes, Julia, you're not wrong." He turned to the prospective buyer, "There you have it, Joe – the USP of this excellent property." He stepped out of the way to let the client get a better look. Gerry then spoke to Julia.

"Could you make a note there to change the carpets in the bedrooms to a plain brown colour should the customer decide to go ahead with the purchase," and he winked.

"Of course." She scribbled some notes on the notepad affixed to the clipboard.

Gerry turned back to his client and asked him what he thought. The man's negative attitude had greatly softened.

"The young lady is correct, it is very impressive, and it's *Mister* Porter to you." he paused while he scanned the view again for a few minutes, "I am very keen to go ahead, but there has to be some substantial movement on the price."

Gerry knew it was a negotiation to be conducted in private and asked Julia to go back to his car to get one of the brochures in the boot. He handed over his keys and winked again, which she took to understand that she wasn't required for this part of the deal.

"You can wait in the car," he told her.

She went back to the Range Rover and, opening the boot, shifted his golf bag and cricket bat that were covering a number of brochures. She took one out and saw Gerry and his client exiting the building, so she closed the boot and waited where she was. Julia watched them shake hands and walk towards their own cars. As Gerry got to her, he asked her to pop over to Mr Porter and give him the brochure, which she did. As she handed it over, the man asked her how long she had worked with Gerry.

"Not long," was her truthful answer.

"If you fancy a change of career, give me a call," he said, handing her his card.

"Um…Doing what?" she asked politely.

"Call me, and we can discuss it, but for now, I've got to fly," he said. As she stepped away, he got into his vehicle and quickly drove off.

"What was that all about?" Gerry asked as she got in his car.

"He gave me his card and wondered if I fancied a change of career other than working with you," she said honestly.

"Really? What a sleazy bastard."

"Oh?" Julia was surprised at his outburst.

"Steer well clear. Joey Porter is a wrong 'un. He owns a couple of bookie shops and a nightclub in the city, but for the most part, it's a front for a lot of bad stuff."

"Such as?" she innocently asked.

"How long have you got?" he laughed as he started the car and headed towards their lunch venue.

"Go on, tell me." She was quite persistent.

"He's the South Coast Porn King, and he's also into drugs, money laundering, people trafficking, and prostitution, for starters. Trust me; he is a nasty piece of work and not one to mess with."

The trafficking and prostitution thing made her shudder.

"Did you sell the apartment?" she asked, wanting to change the subject.

"No," he said and laughed.

"Oh." She was surprised. "I thought..."

Gerry interrupted her. "*You* sold it!"

"What?" She was confused.

"You sold it with your comment about the view. He was hugely negative before that."

"But he would have seen the view when he walked in," Julia said, stating the blindingly obvious.

"Yes, but his mind was set on finding fault with everything, but because you're such a head-turner, he needed telling that it was a great view."

"Head-turner?" She was still confused.

"Julia, don't be naïve. You are drop-dead gorgeous and it's something you can massively use to your advantage."

"Don't be daft. I'm short, fat, and ugly," she said, fishing for more compliments.

Gerry burst out laughing. "If you're short, fat and ugly, I'm the Pope!" he replied just as he drove into a golf club car park.

"Well, Your Holiness, is this where we're dining?" Julia said in a sharp response to his comment.

"Indeed, it is, and you've earned this!" he said, switching the engine off and taking her hand to kiss it. "Come on, I'm starving!"

They were there for two hours. She had a couple of glasses of wine over a three-course lunch, and they got on as easily as they had the night before. Any neutral observer would have said they were a natural match. Some may have gone as far as to say they were besotted, and they knew it for themselves. The real question she again asked herself was how, where and when they were going to fuck?

They got in the car to leave, and Gerry told her that he really had a lovely time and that they should do it again very soon.

"Yes, I'd like that," Julia said truthfully as he started the car and made his way back to her home. They chatted mainly about Mr Porter. Gerry explained that he was quite well known in the city, and everyone knew of his reputation as a '*hard man*'. People who crossed him did not fare well.

"The police will get him one day," Gerry said, "but hopefully not before he completes the purchase of that apartment because that would be a nice little earner," he said, mimicking a Cockney accent.

"I was happy to help," she said. "But I was just so enamoured with the view I couldn't help myself."

"Julia, you have the skill to say the right things at the right time," Gerry said with a smile.

It wasn't a long journey, and they pulled into the layby, *their* layby.

Julia undid her seat belt, turned to him and said, "Thank you very much. I've had a lovely day."

Gerry looked at her, smiled, and said, "I know I tricked you into a kiss last night, but I would very much like to kiss you again." He paused. "With your permission, of course."

For two pins, Julia would have jumped on him there and then in broad daylight but said nothing. She leaned over to him, and her left hand caressed his face as their lips met. There was no pretence of a little friendly peck; it was the kind of kiss that should lead to more, and yet they knew nothing would come of it this day. As they broke away from each other, he said, "Julia, that was the icing on the cake. Thank you."

Again, she said nothing but kissed her first two fingers and put them on his lips. "Call me," she said as she got out of the car.

"Absolutely!" he replied.

She waved as he drove off, and she took the one-minute walk home. She was on fire and cursed him for being such a gentleman. When she got in, there was an answer-phone message from her catering manager to tell her about work over the weekend, a couple more for her dad about golf, and one from Mike. She phoned the catering company to say she was available, chose to ignore Mike, but then made one other call.

Her mum was home early from work, and after the usual pleasantries, Julia asked her if she could do the usual taxi service for her work commitments on Saturday and Sunday and also run her into town on Monday for a 5.30 pm appointment.

"Of course," was the reply, "but what's of interest in town on Monday?"

"I think, as I'm off to Uni, it might be an idea to visit the FPC," Julia said, feeling that the acronym sounded more matter-of-fact than saying the Family Planning Clinic.

"Is it okay if we don't say anything to Dad?"

5

Love is in the Air

August 1988

There was no call from Gerry over the weekend, which both frustrated and annoyed her. Had she done something wrong? Was he bored of her already? Was he just playing games? Mike did call, but she told her mum to say she wasn't in. When questioned, Julia said, "Oh, mum, he's just so immature." This drew a face from her mother that said, *"That's rich, coming from a girl of the same age."*

The appointment at the FPC was fine; her medical and answers to the questionnaire were all normal, and after a chat with the doctor, she was issued with The Pill. As she walked to her mum's car armed with a couple of months' supply, she thought, "I'm on the pill, it's a licence to thrill, and if Gerry doesn't fuck me, then someone else will!" She inwardly smiled at her ad hoc piece of poetry.

Julia got in the car, and her mum said that she was really proud of her for being so sensible. Then she added some words of caution, "By all means, have fun, but also have respect for yourself and don't get a reputation!"

"Yes, mum, I understand," she said, all the while recalling the pornographic poses of both her parents in those very naughty photos. When they got home, her dad said that Gerry had phoned again he'd call back in the morning.

"Did he say what it was about?" she inquired, but already really knowing what it was about.

"No, he just said that there was a possibility of some more work if you were interested."

Her mum looked at her, and she felt that she needed to give an explanation.

"He runs another catering company, and he pays more than I'm getting at the moment."

Her mother's deadpan face said that she didn't quite believe her, but she simply said, "Okay."

Over dinner, they told her that the weekend after next, they were going to Dublin for three nights, and she would have to arrange for other transport if she was working. It was only fair that they gave her plenty of notice. Julia said it wasn't a problem; she would sort something out. She did ask why Dublin.

"We haven't been away for a long while, and the last time we were there was…1969, I think?" her mother said, looking at her husband for confirmation.

"The summer of *lurve*!" her dad interjected, wiggling his hips, to which her mum shot him a glance to warn him not to expand on that, and then she corrected him.

"It was autumn, as I recall, between the two moon landings, I think?"

"And did the earth move for you, Darling?" her dad asked, laughing, eliciting another glare from her mother, who turned back to her daughter.

"It's a lovely place to go for a break, so if you want to have some friends over, that's fine. Just make sure you don't make a mess of the place or annoy the neighbours."

"When you say some friends, how many friends?" Julia asked.

"Two or three at a real push is plenty," her dad said before her mum scowled at him and said, "Just keep it sensible. Only people you know and trust."

"So that rules out the latest intake from the Royal Navy Academy in Portsmouth!"

Both women shook their heads and smiled at his usual hyper-exaggeration.

"I'll think about it, but it'll probably just be the usual gang," Julia said, knowing that there would only be one invite for that weekend.

She watched some TV but decided to go to bed to read, wishing her parents a good night as she went. She was excited about her parents' weekend away. It was a massive opportunity for freedom, and she was hopeful one of those nights would include Gerry either staying at his place or coming there. At this point, she would have loved to borrow her mum's toys to aid her fantasy of Gerry thrusting his cock into her and making her cum, but her fingers and her imagination would have to do.

Gerry called the following morning as promised. She was disappointed to hear that he would be away for a few days, which she initially thought would mean two or three. As it transpired, it was the whole week. She asked casually if it was anywhere nice? *"Up North"* was as detailed as it was going to be. He didn't elaborate. She offered to be his "assistant" again, hoping in a moment of extreme opportunism that he would say yes and whisk her away to a paradise of endless fucking and ecstasy. He laughed and said it was a nice idea but not practical and left it at that. She hoped he could chat a bit longer, but he had clients that he was just off to meet. He did offer a crumb of comfort when saying that he would "phone her when he could" while he was away.

After the call, the same old insecurities came back to haunt her. Was he just playing games? Should she just treat it as a bit of fun and not care about how she thought he was feeling? Julia stripped off and checked herself in the mirror. Nice legs, pert bum, flat stomach, and cupping and fondling her breasts, said, "Nice firm tits. Pinky and Perky," and she laughed to herself at her silly nicknames for them. So, if he didn't like the face, her body more than compensated. Donning a loose silk top and a pair of denim shorts that were so short the bottom of her bum cheeks just peeked out, she decided on no underwear.

Julia loved how the silk brushed against her skin, especially her nipples. She pulled the shorts right up tight between her legs so that the roughness of the material rubbed against all of her sex. She snuck into her parents' room again to delve into the briefcase. She couldn't understand why she wasn't more shocked at seeing her parents en-flagrante, but they were nearly twenty years younger in the pictures and just seemed like unknown actors in an amateur threesome porn flick. She got very turned on by them enjoying themselves in various positions. What she didn't notice in her first few forays into the case was that at the bottom of one of the panels in the lid was a videotape. Her heart skipped a few beats. She was pretty sure she knew what was going to be on it. With the tape and wand vibrator in hand, she headed back downstairs. Even the act of walking down each stair was exciting as the denim rubbed against her clitoris.

She went into the front room and turned on the TV and video player. Julia took off the shorts that were already starting to get damp. The tape had already been watched as it was near the end, so she fed it into the machine and pressed the rewind button. The phone rang. It was Mike.

"Hey, you," she said, trying to sound apathetic.

"Hey, JJ, my mum has lent me the car for the day today. Are you doing anything? I thought we might go for a drive." He was as enthusiastic as usual.

Julia said that, at the moment, that would be cool unless some work was offered. She thought that at least it would kill a few hours, even if she had to give him a hand job in payment, and she still had the "get out of jail free card" using work as an excuse if she changed her mind.

It was left that he would come round just after midday, but she was keen to return to her personal playtime and in no mood for small talk - the call ended quickly enough. The tape had fully rewound, and as she sat on the floor with a deep breath, she pressed the play button.

After the initial "fog," the opening scenes showed a screen with a movie playing – so this was a camcorder video of an old super eight home movie. The video focused on illuminating the edges of the screen, and although it wasn't of great quality, it was still clear enough. It showed her young mum outside a hotel waving at the camera.

A full pan on the building showed it was flying two flags outside – one advertising the hotel name and next to it was an Irish Tricolour. So this was her parents' 1969 *'Summer (Autumn) of Lurve'* trip. Julia had seen the photos. This was the movie!

The next scene showed the plush hotel reception with her mother posing next to a young member of staff carrying their suitcase. Julia guessed his age to be around seventeen or eighteen. He was a big lad, strikingly handsome, with blonde/auburn hair, piercing blue eyes, and a wicked smile. Julia quite fancied him herself. The camera gently zoomed in on her mum's face, where she glanced at the porter. Then, she turned back to the camera, raised her eyebrows, licked her lips suggestively, smiled, and winked. Julia's heart beat heavy with excitement as she wondered what was next.

She didn't have to wait long. The video briefly went fuzzy again and then cut to show a hotel bedroom with a man on his back, spread-eagled on the bed with all four limbs tied by some long cords to the four corners of the bedstead. He was naked save for a small towel covering a substantial bulge between his legs, but she could see that he was toned with muscles in all the right places, and he obviously worked out. The camera work was a little unsteady to begin with, and she suspected the camera operator was just adjusting and stabilising the device to focus and get the best angle. There was no sound, but suddenly, a woman walked into shot. She was wearing a bandit mask, a black and red Basque with suspenders attached, holding up red fishnet stockings, a red G-string completed the ensemble. As she came into view, she turned to the camera and pointed at the man, then put a finger to her ruby red lipstick mouth in mock surprise. The woman's mask did little to hide the fact that it was her mother.

Again, Julia wasn't shocked by the sexy scene, just very turned on, anticipating what that woman was going to do to the man on the bed, who she could now see was the young man from reception. She looked closely at his well-formed torso and muscled limbs. She could just about see a tattoo on his inner left arm but couldn't make out what it was from that distance. Her mum knelt at the young man's side, making sure she didn't obstruct the camera angle, slowly taking the towel away to expose the victim's large penis and testicles. She did the pretend surprise thing again for the camera before grasping the base of his thick cock to point the tip towards and between her ruby lips. She slowly lowered her head, then lifted it and with each slow descent, his cock lengthened.

Her mother was plainly enjoying herself and slowly but surely took his member all the way into her mouth, obviously to 'deep throat' him. She seemingly had no qualms about this and managed it with aplomb, fondling the young man's balls at the same time.

The film had been edited somewhat as the next frames showed her dad standing in front of her mum, feeding his own dick into her mother's mouth as she was riding the young man's cock. This went on for a few minutes before the next scene provided a close-up of her mum now nestling beside the angry erection she had just been sitting on. She was using her right hand to make it pour forth as her left hand cradled and juggled his balls. Suddenly, the 'victim's' body tensed, then jerked, and he squirted a substantial amount of semen over her mum's face. When he finished, her mum scraped some of the excesses into her mouth with her fingers. The final shot was of her licking her digits before blowing a kiss to the camera. The tape went foggy again.

"Fuck. That was hot, you dirty sods!" Julia said to herself. She replayed that section of the tape and masturbated to climax, watching her parents in action again.

Mike came over just before midday. He was always early. It was a lovely day, and she changed into a short skirt, a t-shirt, and pumps, no bra, and just a tiny pair of knickers. She'd prepared a picnic and thought it would be a pleasant way to spend the afternoon. Mike had borrowed his mum's Nissan Micra, and they set off for Henley. Julia had never been, but her mum said it was a nice, picturesque little town in Oxfordshire on the River Thames.

The journey took just under an hour, and they wandered around the quaint little shops before finding a small, secluded area near the river to have their picnic and watch the boats go past. After eating, she lay back on the blanket, and Mike moved closer. She didn't refuse when he bent over to kiss her. She wanted to compare it to Gerry's more mature experience. It wasn't bad but too slobbery really, and she now recalled how she was forever wiping her mouth after he'd kissed her. His hand moved to her left breast, and her nipple immediately responded. He pressed into her, and he was also erect as his cock poked into her leg.

"Does your doggie need a little walk?" she teased.

"Um…I think he does," Mike replied, and he pushed harder into her leg to emphasise the point.

"Did you bring a rubber?" she asked, 'No' was the reply. Julia tutted but wasn't going to stop now. Still lying down, she made him turn his back to the river. They were shielded by quite a high hedge behind them, so no one could really see when he unzipped his shorts and pulled out his stiffening dick. Julia wrapped her fingers around it at the base and slowly started stroking it, making sure to pull the foreskin all the way forward to cover the head and then fully back again to expose the purple knob. Mike was not idle and moved his hands down to her thigh and then between her legs, which she parted for him. He was as clumsy as he usually was, but even after her earlier orgasm, she needed some attention, and his fumbling would have to do. After a few minutes and a couple of stops for some cabin cruisers to pass, she started to speed up. Julia watched his face as her manual work started to take effect. His eyes were closed, and as his breathing quickened with the occasional deep gasp of pleasure, she could see he was only moments away from his orgasmic conclusion.

"Are you going to spill the beans for me?" she asked, smiling.

He had lost all concentration with regard to her enjoyment, but she didn't mind, and then suddenly, with gritted teeth and a stifled grunt, he shot a huge burst of semen over her hand, just missing her skirt but leaving quite a deposit on the blanket. She pointed his exploding member down towards the grass and milked him to a conclusion, making sure her clothes weren't in the firing line.

"Oooh, Mike, have you been saving that up? That's an awful lot of beans, much more than usual?" she laughed, "Now you see why I insist you do it in a condom!"

He couldn't speak.

Out of the blue, she then decided to tease and surprise him. She fixed his stare and said, "Look this muck on my fingers. Hmm, clearly only one real way to clean them up…" and brought the aforementioned 'mucky' fingers to her mouth and smiled as she licked them clean. Mike's jaw dropped. He gradually recovered his composure and then tucked his messy tool away.

"Wow, JJ, that was mind-blowing, the best yet," still staring at her and getting his breathing back to normal, he asked, "What does it taste like?"

"Slightly salty and bitter but not as bad as it looks!" she laughed, "Do you know your face is an absolute picture!" Julia then took his hand and pulled him towards her for a very passionate kiss in an effort to let him taste himself. As their tongues played, Mike fondled and caressed her breasts, letting the palms of his hands excite and harden her nipples. Julia thought it was all very pleasant but just too public and broke the kiss. She held his hands and smiled, "Someone might see", and she gave him another kiss as if to compensate him.

He was visibly disappointed and said it didn't seem fair, especially as she had just tossed him off 'in public'. She told him not to be silly, and she was fine with it as they were able to keep it fairly well hidden while she did the deed. Had it been Gerry instead of Mike, she would have just let him fuck her there and then.

"It's getting late. We should be going," she said. Mike reluctantly agreed, and they set off back to the car. The journey home was quiet, although he wanted to know about her plans for university. Julia was curt and rather vague in her response, summing it up as not having made up her mind yet. It was a truthful answer. She had worked hard at school to attain her straight-A grades, and now she just wanted a break, maybe even to take a year out. When they got back to her house, he suggested that he could come in and repay her act of "mercy", as he put it. To no avail, she just gave him a peck on the lips and said, Perhaps another time, as her mother would be home shortly.

"Soon?" he added hopefully.

"Yeah, sure," was her half-hearted response.

When he left, Julia went straight to her mother's room for the vibrator and wand and put them to very good use again while watching the next section of the video. Part two had another couple of instances of the young Irishman having full intercourse with her mother. As she watched, she imagined Gerry expertly taking her virginity and was so lost in the fantasy that she climaxed and let out a loud gasp like some of the women she had seen in porn videos, surprising even herself at how loud she was.

She gave herself a few minutes to calm down and then quickly cleaned the instruments of pleasure before putting them and the tape back where they belonged. Not a moment too soon, she heard the front door open, followed by a shout up the stairs from her mother.

"Hi, Julia, I'm home. Is everything okay?" Julia quickly but silently closed her parents' bedroom door and, although a little flustered, responded with, "Hi, yes, all good. I'm just going to take a shower, and I'll be down after."

6

I Want to Be Free

July/August 1988

The days dragged, but there was plenty of catering work, which hastened the evenings. Mike was as persistent as ever, and although she was tempted, she relieved the almost constant sexual ache with frequent self-pleasuring, or *DIY,* as Mel called it. It cured the itch for a while, but surely nothing could beat being properly fucked by someone who knew what they were doing. There were the occasional calls from Gerry, which were nice, but he always seemed in a rush. She much preferred more time to chat, as conversations with him always seemed so very natural.

One call she received was not welcome. It was a Monday morning, and she was up later than usual because of working the night before. Her mother and father had long since gone to work, and she heard the phone ringing downstairs. It eventually went to answer-phone, but no message was left. A short while afterwards, it rang again. She got up, ran downstairs and picked it up, thinking it might be Gerry.

"Is that Julia?" asked the voice on the other end of the line.

"Yes, who's this?" She did not recognise the man's voice.

"I'm very disappointed that you haven't called me yet," said the stern voice.

"Sorry, who are you? Have you got the right number?" She had no idea who it was.

"Joey Porter, I gave you my card a fortnight or so ago. Do you remember when I came to look at that Marina Apartment?"

"Oh, yes." Her heart was beating hard, remembering that Gerry had said to steer clear.

"Did you like the apartment?" she asked, trying to sound business-like.

"Yes, but you impressed me more," Porter said with some authority.

"Oh?" Julia was quite flustered.

"Yes, so I'd like to have a chat with you about joining our organisation in some capacity." He spoke as if it were a done deal.

"Er–"

"Julia?" He sounded very pushy.

"Well, the thing is that I already have two part-time jobs, and it's only for the summer before I go to university," she said, embellishing her actual employment status.

"Two jobs?" he questioned as though he knew she was lying. "I could pay you much more than you're getting now for those *two* jobs." His emphasis on "two" made it clear that he had caught her out.

"Is one of those jobs with that retard, Irvine?" he continued, but she didn't answer.

"If so, I know that's a lie. You were just helping him out on the day." Porter was extremely blunt with his accusation. There was still no reply from her, but her heart was in her mouth. How could she get rid of him? Julia finally spoke.

"I work with him on an ad hoc basis, Mr Porter, and thank you for your offer, but I have worked for the catering company for quite a while, they've been very good to me."

"Good, I like loyalty, but at some point, you have to look after yourself. Why don't we have a chat and see where I can fit you in? How about today? I could send a car if you don't have transport." He didn't give her time to think. "Julia? Are you there?"

"Mr Porter, I do greatly appreciate you thinking of me, but I'm not able to consider alternate employment at the moment and I do have to go now. Thanks again." She hung up. She was extremely ruffled and wondered how he had got her number, as it was ex-directory. The phone rang again, but she didn't answer. She was shaking as it tripped over to the answer-phone - Porter left a message.

"Julia, call me. Don't waste your time with these people. I can pay you more even for the short time before you go to university. I expect you to phone me as soon as you can," he hung up.

She hadn't liked him when she'd first met him, but now he was really sounding quite menacing. She jumped when the phone rang again ten minutes later. What should she do? It went to answer-phone, and Gerry's voice was heard saying, "Julia, are you there? Pick up if you are."

She picked it up and said hello, gradually calming a little at the sound of a friendly voice.

"How's things?" he asked.

"I'm okay," she said curtly.

"You don't sound so sure," he said.

"No, it's okay."

"Porter has phoned you, hasn't he?" Gerry guessed.

"Yes, how do you know, and how did he get my number?"

"He just phoned to say that you won't talk to him," Gerry told her.

"Why is he phoning you, and how does he know where to phone you?" She was confused.

"I'm still in negotiation with him about the apartment, so he needs to talk to me about some of the finer details."

Then it dawned on her. "Did you give him my number?"

"No, but he likes you," Gerry said.

"Did. You. Give. Him. My. Number?" she asked again, pausing between each word. There was a brief silence. "You did, didn't you? Why?" She was starting to get upset.

"Julia, I didn't give him your number, but he wants me to get you to call him because he won't close the deal on the apartment until you've at least spoken to him about a job. I didn't think he would be so persistent, but you're clearly not happy about it." He tried to sound casual.

"No. I am not happy about it, especially as you said I should steer clear. Those were your very words, Gerry!" She was angry as well now.

"Julia, I'm really sorry. I'll sort it," he said unconvincingly.

"Please do!" She hung up and burst into tears. She was annoyed that he had put her in such a difficult situation, but she was now sure that their burgeoning romance was massively compromised to the point where it seemed to her that it was unlikely to continue. For the rest of the day, she willed the phone to ring so that she could hopefully hear Gerry say that he wanted to see her again and that he had put Joey Porter straight about her working for him. Just after dinner, it did ring, and although she rushed to answer it, her mum got there first.

"Hello? Hi Mikey, how are you? I haven't heard from you in a long time…Yes, she's here. She must have been expecting you because I've only just managed to get to the phone first. Hold on, I'll pass you over. Remember me to your mum." As she passed the receiver over to Julia, she whispered, "It's Mike!"

Julia tutted and mouthed silently, "I gathered that!"

She was severely underwhelmed as she said hello and explained that she thought it was a call about work. Yes, she was well. No, she wasn't doing much, and she wasn't sure what she was doing tomorrow, but she would give him a call if there was time to get together. When she hung up, her mother was hovering.

"He's such a nice boy. I think you're quite mean to him sometimes."

"Oh, Mum," was all she could come back with in a patronising way before heading off upstairs for the night. She cried again when she went to sleep, thinking of how it was all going so well and now it was all a disaster. *Men are just so fucking useless at relationships,* she thought to herself.

Julia woke in the morning, still quite flustered by Joey Porter's call, but she was determined not to let it spoil her day. She also decided that Gerry could go fuck himself as well after giving up her phone number so easily. It could only have been him because very few people knew the number. When she went downstairs, she found her mother had not left for work yet.

"Good morning to you, sleepyhead," her mum said, gathering a few things before getting ready to go.

"Hey," she answered.

"Joey Porter phoned about a job interview. I didn't know you applied for a job with him. Where did you find that? Was it in the local paper?" her mum asked while looking for her car keys. Julia didn't want to go into what she knew her mother would turn into a web of intrigue, so she replied in the affirmative.

"Anyway, can you phone him this morning, please? It's rude not to return calls." Her mother sounded insistent.

"I'm not sure about it now. I've heard he's a bit of a local gangster," Julia said, wondering if she would have to explain further.

Her mother stopped looking for her keys and said quizzically before laughing, "Where did you hear that nonsense?"

"Oh, just some of the girls had said they heard stuff about prostitution and things like that," Julia said, as though Mr Porter was public enemy number one. Her mother laughed again, responding, "What utter tripe. He owns two or three bookmakers, and I think he has a part share in one of the clubs in town, which is hardly Mafia territory. Oh, wait, perhaps they've got the wrong end of the stick because he is the founder and president of one of the local institutions that provides help, relief, and accommodation to abused women," she said. "He has a reputation of being a grouchy, miserable sod, but he isn't like that at all." And she quickly followed with, "Apparently."

"I heard he was a nasty piece of work," Julia said, quoting Gerry verbatim. Her mother was quick to reply.

"I knew him…er, of him, when he was younger, and he never stood for any nonsense, but he always seemed law-abiding, and anything he was involved in never touched people like us."

It seemed an odd thing to say, and Julia was about to question her further when her mother found her keys and said, "I've gotta get going. Phone him please. You never know, it could be a decent little job for the rest of the summer, which would leave your nights and weekends free before you go to Uni." She kissed her daughter on the forehead and was gone.

Julia decided to get it out of the way because her mother would only badger her about it as soon as she came home. When Joey Porter answered, she apologised profusely for not getting back to him sooner - he brushed it off, saying it wasn't an issue. She agreed to an interview that morning and even accepted the offer of being picked up. He sounded a lot friendlier than she had previously encountered and, although erring on the side of caution, she was more inclined to believe her mother's opinion of him than the snake in the grass, Gerry. One thing that was odd was that he hadn't asked for her address.

An hour later, she was showered, dressed (smart casual), and ready. Porter himself came to pick her up. As she sat in his large Jaguar, they exchanged pleasantries and made small talk about the weather. Joey explained that when he did interviews, he preferred to do them informally at a cafe to put everyone at ease, and he made sure she knew that included him.

The interview went well. Joey did most of the talking and even alluded to his so-called "reputation", which he explained referred to his younger days when he was making his way in the world. He laughed and added, "It is all totally unfounded, of course, but it doesn't hurt, as it makes people wary of being disrespectful." He smirked a bit as if he was recalling incidents where his perceived repute served him well.

"So, what would the job entail?" Julia asked. She was keen to get to the details because, although she wasn't as wary of him as she thought she might have been, she still didn't want to drag this out further than it needed to be.

"Yes, of course, the job. Well, one of my admin clerks has just gone on maternity leave for a few months and the work is starting to pile up. It's not difficult stuff and you would probably find it a little bit tedious, but the staff are friendly. The office manager isn't a drill sergeant, and everyone seems to get on well. I say everyone, there's only five people altogether, and basically, it's back-office paperwork covering the two bookie shops I own."

"Would I be working at the counter, taking the bets from people?" she asked, looking concerned. Joey stared at her and noted her disquiet. He laughed.

"No, it's okay, you won't be mixing with the punters," he smiled.

"How—"

"Much will you be paid?" Joey finished her question. "Five pounds per hour cash in hand, at least three days a week, but if you want to expand on that, there should be more work available." He took a sip of his coffee. "I think that's probably a pound an hour more than you're getting now. So effectively, there will be more hours available to you than the casual nature of hospitality work. Also, you'll have evenings and weekends free, so you could still do waitress work if you needed a top-up. So, it's a win-win, really."

He could see that she was genuinely interested.

"Tell you what, finish your coffee, we'll pop down to the office now, and you can meet Cheryl, the office manager, and the other girls. No obligation, and if you're worried, I would add that I'm only there a couple of times a week, if that. I have more than enough to do with my other businesses," he said casually.

"Other businesses?" She really wanted to know more now.

"Yes, I'm a joint owner of Jolly's, the nightclub. I doubt if you've been there."

"No, I was refused entry with a couple of my pals a few weeks back." Julia was a little embarrassed at her admission.

"Yes, we only allow twenty-one-year-olds and over, and it's strictly monitored."

She was beginning to take on board that he did have scruples, and this wasn't the man that Gerry had initially described. Couple that with what her mother had mentioned about the women's refuge, and really, his 'bad boy' reputation was not deserved.

It was a short journey to the main office situated behind the bookmaker's shop. She was quickly introduced to Cheryl. Cheryl was a mature, understanding woman who was very much like her mother. She appeared friendly but firm, and the general atmosphere in the office with the two other younger women seemed busy but calm and casual.

"Cheryl, Julia here is thinking of joining us. Can you run through what she'd be doing and maybe the hours that are on offer? I'm just going to the baker's," Joey said.

"Sure, Joey, no problem," Cheryl answered, shaking Julia by the hand.

"My, you're the spitting image of your mother, and no mistake," Cheryl said, which left Julia to wonder how she would know. Joey interrupted.

"I'll leave you in Cheryl's capable hands, and I'll be back in fifteen minutes, okay?" And he was gone. In the short time that he had popped out, Cheryl had given Julia an overview of the work and introduced her to the other two women. Joey returned with a box of cakes and put them on the nearest desk.

"Cakes, girls, it's my birthday!" he said to what appeared to be groans from his audience.

"Joey, you say that every time you bring cakes. You have about fifty birthdays a year and we're all getting fat," said one of the other ladies, eagerly opening up the box and snaffling a chocolate éclair.

"Stop your mumping and just enjoy!" he said and then turning to Cheryl and Julia,

"Okay, are we done?"

"Yes, I think so," Cheryl said, smiling at Julia. Julia nodded and, at Joey's behest, stood up and started to make her way to the exit when she overheard Cheryl say to Joey.

"We are drowning here with Tess away and this young lady asked all the right questions. She has the intelligence and aptitude to pick things up very quickly, AND she has keyboard skills. She would sweep through the backlog to get us back on track in short order."

Julia blushed.

"Yes, I understand—" Joey replied before Julia interrupted and said, "I'll take the job if you think I'd fit in?"

As Joey turned around, Cheryl said, "Great, when can you start?"

"I'll have to check with my mum about when I could get a lift, but maybe Monday?" Julia said.

"Tomorrow would be better!" Cheryl laughed. Julia smiled and said she would get back to her as quickly as possible. Cheryl wrote her phone number down, saying, "Welcome aboard, you're going to be a real lifeline here. By the way, give my regards to your mum. It's been a while since we met back when we were young, free and single!" She laughed.

As Joey and Julia returned to the car and got in, Joey said, "I knew you'd be a perfect fit. You'll enjoy it as well."

"I'll do my best, Mr Porter," Julia said, feeling rather pleased with herself.

"Please, Julia, only the taxman and people I don't like call me Mr Porter. Joey, okay?"

"Okay. Joey," she replied rather timidly.

"They're a good bunch, even if they are putting on weight!" he laughed, then continued, "Okay, I've just got to pop over to a gym, and then I'll take you home."

She wondered what he was doing at a gym, but it wouldn't be long before she found out. They pulled up near a boxing gymnasium, and Joey went in but was back in five minutes with an envelope.

"Sorry about that, just had to pick up some forms," he said.

"Do you have a membership there?" she asked innocently. He laughed as he shook his head.

"Now, do I look like I have a gym membership?" he smiled at her as she acknowledged that the suggestion didn't really fit with his ample frame.

"I used to box years ago, but no, I own the gym. Tell you what, if you're not in a rush, why don't you come and have a look?"

Julia said that she'd love to.

"I let my younger twin brothers run it. They're ex–Royal Navy, and they've set it up to take in kids that might otherwise be getting up to mischief on the streets. It's a good distraction for young people who may be inclined to all manner of naughtiness."

He introduced her to James and Jared and showed her around the well-equipped space. She was hugely impressed by the financial investment that had been poured into the scheme. Joey went on to explain that, between the three of them, they had also bought the hall next door.

"We're intending to hire it out to anyone interested in regular or ad hoc events, but we're going to set up some martial arts tuition – you know, judo, taekwondo, origami and bonsai, all that sort of Far East self-defence stuff."

Julia laughed at his deliberate mistakes.

"Hey, you should have a think about self-defence classes. We'll be putting an ad in the local rag and, if you're working for me, I can let you know when we start to run them, with discounts for staff, of course. Now we'd better be going – time is money."

As Julia got into the car, she said that she thought, by the size of his two brothers, that they could handle themselves well.

"Absolutely, they were very good amateur boxers in their time, but they also knew the dark arts of street-fighting as well when required. God bless the Royal Navy!" Joey laughed but left it at that.

"Hey, during the winter months, we had a lad there who went to your school. He might be the same age as you. Alan McCann?"

"Alan? Yes, I know Alan. I didn't know he boxed, though," she was surprised that Joey knew him.

"He used boxing to beef up his rugby training. We have a few evenings where people can pay to train or spar, just to keep our funds going. Young Alan was damn handy in the ring but flawed as a boxer, unfortunately." Joey sounded quite disappointed about the young man.

"Did he have a glass jaw?" she said as though she were an expert. Joey was a bit taken aback.

"What do you know about glass jaws?"

"Dad loves boxing, and I watched some big fights with him. He just told me some of the jargon."

"I see. No, he could take a punch, not that he was hit that often, because he was too fast. His flaw was that he didn't like to hurt people, although, in one particular sparring session, he was up against a real arrogant loudmouth who occasionally attended the gym to spar. Timmins, I think his name was, yes, Graham Timmins. He usually picked on people that he could hurt. My brothers always kept a watchful eye on him 'cos he was just a bully really. Anyway, he was going to spar with someone, and James asked Alan to step in at the last minute. Timmins thought he was just another patsy and hit Alan with a couple of cheap shots when he wasn't ready. I was there at the time and Alan seemed totally unmoved. He didn't get angry. Just fixed Timmins with this real focused stare and said, 'You better have something more, because if that's all you have, then I hope you can defend yourself.'

Three minutes later, Timmins wasn't so arrogant when Alan finished with him. The beating was quite severe and halfway through, James wanted to step in and bring it to a halt. I told him to let it run its course to teach Timmins a lesson." Julia could sense that Joey now spoke of Alan with some sort of fatherly pride.

"I think Timmins had to have an op to straighten his nose, and apparently, he was pissing blood for a week. Oddly enough, young Mr Timmins never came back," Joey laughed.

"Timmins' younger brother went to my school. He wasn't very nice either," Julia said, recalling her brush with the younger sibling. Just then, a question suddenly dawned on her.

"How did you know Alan went to my school?"

"You told me which school you went to, didn't you?" Joey said casually.

"No, I can't think I ever mentioned it." She was quite sure that she hadn't.

"Oh, well, I must have assumed you both went to the same school. You're both in their catchment area, so it would be logical," Joey answered rather defensively. Julia thought it odd because a private school didn't have a catchment area as such, but by that time, they had arrived at her house, so she didn't dwell on it.

"See you in the office. Give Cheryl a call as soon as you can, please," Joey said.

"Yes, I will, thanks, bye," and she smiled at him as she got out of the car and went indoors.

That short journey to the office served only to confirm that she would take the job, and she loved it from day one.

7

Amoureuse

August 1988

The day before she started part-time work at Porter's Bookmakers, Julia had one full day to herself. It was yet another beautiful summer's day, and she decided to relax in the garden to read one of her mum's books by Jackie Collins – *Rock Star*. The garden was about half an acre of blissful seclusion, and she felt sexy enough to go topless. She was horny as soon as she woke, now exacerbated by the warmth of the sun. The application of sun cream all over herself, especially her boobs and nipples, coupled with the explicit passages in the frivolous novel by the sexy wordsmith Ms Collins, now had the reader's mind working overtime.

Absentmindedly, Julia's hand stroked over her tummy and slipped into her bikini bottoms. She slowly teased herself, but not wishing to climax yet, made sure to move her fingers away from her clitoris if she started to get close. Come late morning, the sun was getting quite hot and so was she. It was time for some respite from the harmful rays and a deeper exploration of her mother's Pandora's Box of toys.

Julia picked up the vibrator, wand, and, this time, also the butt plug. She had seen how some of the women in porn videos had plugs inserted and how funny it was seeing one of the women who had a plug with a bushy, furry tail attached. *Very foxy*, she thought and smiled to herself.

Taking herself into the bathroom, Julia copiously lubricated the plug and smoothed the cold lube over her tight hole. She slowly pressed the toy forward, grasping the sink with her free hand. Breathing deeply, she tried to relax as she worked through the initial pain until it was fully in place. Julia now needed to lie down and slowly went to her bedroom, enjoying the odd sensation as she moved. As she got comfortable on her bed, Julia rubbed the dildo along her damp folds. Filling her pussy with it and working it in and out, she gasped in pleasure at how full she felt with the two objects inside of her, causing her body to quiver.

Now she really let go and was squealing and whimpering as though she was one of the louder women she had seen in the videos – it was absolute bliss. As her initial climax subsided, she went at it again. Her crescendo built more quickly this time, and she was as loud as she was with her first orgasm. This was literally breath-taking, sweaty, and tiring. It was an excellent way to spend a gorgeous summer's day. She finished the book by teatime. Come bedtime, she was horny again.

Gerry phoned early the next morning, and although the initial exchange was a tad frosty, she forgave him for passing her number on to Joey Porter. Gerry still maintained that he didn't divulge the details to anyone but profusely apologised for the whole issue. He was now home and invited her for drinks that evening. He even arranged and paid for a taxi for her to meet him in town. They met at a fashionable bar, and she was so pleased to see him again after what seemed an eternity.

He was early as usual and was sitting on a stool by the bar, having saved a second one next to him for her. Julia gave him a kiss on the cheek when she arrived and then settled herself. A drink was already waiting for her.

The evening went well, the conversation was comfortable, and they always seemed to have a lot to talk about. He made her laugh often, and if she wasn't already smitten, tonight's proceedings only enforced what she felt about him – this was the man who was going to take her virginity. Towards the end of the evening, he asked what she was doing at the weekend.

"I'm not sure yet," she teased, licking her lips and looking him directly in the eyes, trying to convey a green light.

"I see, possibly working?" he was encouraged by her body language but wasn't going to be presumptuous.

"Possibly." She still looked him in the eyes and smiled.

"Are you playing for The Saints as a stand-in for their injured goalkeeper?"

"Gerry, I wouldn't play for that lot if you paid me a fortune, and, incidentally, my dad, being a Pompey supporter, would disown me. Anyway, goalkeeper is not my position."

"Ah, a Pompey girl, yes, I can see that now, rough and ready and common as muck!"

She laughed at his cheek.

"But I'd like to think I am very good with my hands…" and resting them on his thighs, continued "…My parents are away this weekend, and I'd like to cook dinner for you at my home on Saturday evening." She tenderly kissed him on the side of the face and then leant back and waited for his reply.

He stared straight back at her with an expression that spoke volumes. The message was loud and clear. He looked away, took a sip of his drink, and then, holding her hand, said, "I would love to accept your invitation to dinner, but–" he hesitated again and took another sip of his lager.

"But?" Her smile left her lips, and she started to think she had played this all wrong.

"But I have to be in Manchester by Sunday evening," he replied and smiled.

"So, you want dinner on Saturday, breakfast and maybe lunch, on Sunday?"

"No," he said succinctly and looked at his empty glass on the bar.

"No?"

"No." He gestured to the barman for another round and was still looking away from her.

"What do you want then?" She was getting a little confused, and his facial expressions gave nothing away. Yet again, he left her to hang, contemplating his answer. Then Gerry turned to her, held both her hands in his, looked her directly in the eyes, and said simply, "You!" He squeezed her hands to emphasise the point.

It was a few seconds before she acknowledged what they both knew that meant. She clasped his hands tightly in confirmation and leaned forward to kiss him directly on the lips, firstly as an elongated peck, which then turned into a full-on passionate snog.

Julia's parents left early on Friday morning for their trip to Dublin. She worked at the bookmaker's during the afternoon and had catering work in the evening. It was a tiring day, but she did well for tips again and had a couple of phone numbers from erstwhile suitors, both were summarily binned.

Saturday, she woke early but went back to sleep and then roused properly at 10.30 am to the sound of the phone ringing downstairs. She quickly got up and hastened to answer it.

"Hello?"

"Hi, Julia, it's Gerry, all okay with you?" Gerry asked, sounding a bit hesitant.

"Yes, I've just got up as I was working late last night," She could feel her heart rate increase and hoped this wasn't going to be bad news.

"I just wanted to check that we're still on for this evening?" he sounded a bit nervous.

"Yes, of course. Why?"

"I never take anything for granted," which explained his hesitancy. "What time do you want me?" Realising the ambiguity of his question, he was about to follow that up, but Julia beat him to it.

"Well, for a guy that never takes anything for granted, I'd say that's quite presumptuous!" she laughed.

"Yes, right. I meant, what time is dinner?" He thought he'd turned that round quite well.

"Get here for six-thirty, and we'll take it from there. I hope you're not expecting à la carte. I've been known to burn toast," she said but was quite confident that whatever she served food-wise would be acceptable. Anyway, she intended to be the *main course*.

"Okay, I'll bring some wine. Do you want me to park in *our* layby?" he asked.

"Bubbly would be better," she said cheekily. "No, park in the drive on the left-hand side behind the main hedge. It won't be seen by prying eyes there. We're number ten, the fifth house on the right."

"Ooh, I am honoured. Good call, bubbly it is. I'm really looking forward to it," all his nervousness now having disappeared.

"Yeah, me too, don't be late. Mwah."

While she had been on the phone, she had been touching herself without realising. She was so horny again. She deliberated about having a little 'play' and went to her mother's divan bed drawer. The case was unlocked, and all the toys were gone!

"Dirty sods!" she said out loud. "I hope they get searched in customs at both airports. That would be funny."

Julia had breakfast and did some dusting and cleaning to make the house presentable. It was another glorious day and, sitting outside, she spent an hour just thumbing through a few of her mother's cookbooks for some ideas about something simple but showy for dinner. She decided a well-presented chicken Caesar salad and maybe some boiled potatoes would be perfect and much less hassle than proper cooking.

Her mind strayed to what should be the real event of the evening, which was her welcoming his hard cock into her for the first time to make a "woman" of her. She recalled some conversations she'd had with Melanie "Melons", who had lost her virginity to some unknown guy at a party a few months ago.

"Yeah, it was okay. We were both drunk, not much foreplay, but I was wet anyway. He didn't last long, and I was even wetter when he finished!" was the sum of it. Julia was determined that this would be a classy affair. It didn't have to be Mills and Boon romantic *de-flowering* nonsense, just something she would recall with affection forever. As Melanie said, you never forget the first time. A drunken, five-minute fuck with a guy never to be seen again was not for her.

Julia indulged herself with a long soak in a heavily perfumed bath, which included a little nap. She then shaved her armpits and legs and donned her fluffy bathrobe to go and do some prep for dinner.

She went back to her room to choose her clothes for the evening: a short grey skirt, black knickers, black hold-up stockings, no bra, and a black, heavily patterned, long-sleeved blouse that was virtually see-through, one that you should wear something underneath for the sake of modesty but tonight there was no need for modesty.

At 5.30 pm, she applied her make-up, plus a dash of perfume on her neck, wrists and upper thighs, then she dressed. Her mind was racing as to how he would react to her. She hoped there wouldn't be any awkwardness. After all, it was pretty clear from their mid-week date that, at last, they were going to consummate their desire for one another.

Julia checked herself in the mirror one last time and thought that if this didn't turn him on, nothing would. She went to her parents' room to look out of the window. From there, she could see over the high beech hedge and down the road to the junction. Heart in mouth, stomach riddled with butterflies, she stood in anticipation of his arrival. When seeing his Range Rover turn the corner, she took a deep breath and exhaled loudly. The time for the next rite of passage was upon her. Gerry manoeuvred into the drive and swept to the left behind the hedge as instructed.

She breathed deeply again as he got out of the car, dressed in a smart, light green short-sleeved shirt and white chinos. She focused on his muscled arms before staring directly at his crotch and visualising the weapon that lay in wait for her and for her pleasure.

Julia rushed downstairs and put her heels on just as the doorbell rang. After another deep breath, she opened the front door and greeted him with a kiss.

"Hi, I've brought the bubbly and some flowers." He gave her the bag with two bottles of Moet and a lovely bouquet of dark red carnations. She tried desperately not to appear nervy and quickly took the gifts before flouncing off to the kitchen.

"Thank you, gosh, they're lovely," she took the bottles of Champagne as she sniffed the flowers.

"We can open one bottle now, as they're both chilled," Gerry said as he watched her quickly walk away.

"Good idea," she called back. "I'll get the glasses."

Her nervousness was plainly obvious as she gave a running commentary on what she was doing.

"I'll put this bottle in the fridge, and you can open that one while I get the glasses and a vase. Beautiful flowers, thank you."

"You look so damned sexy!" he said, and she looked at him with such a longing in her eyes that they both knew they had to do this now. Gerry poured the fizz for them both and put that bottle in the fridge for later. He gave her one glass and raised his towards her, saying, "To us!"

Julia smiled, raised her glass, and repeated his toast. "To us!"

They both sipped from their glasses, then put them on the table as Gerry took her hand and said, "Shall we?"

She smiled, squeezed his hand, and led him up the stairs. As he walked behind her, he caught a glimpse of her stocking tops on every upward step and became distinctly aroused. When they reached the landing, he asked her which room was her parents' bedroom.

"That one," she said, pointing to the door further down the landing.

"Then come with me." He held her hand tightly and walked towards it.

"No, Gerry, we can't," she protested but reluctantly took a few steps in that direction.

"How long have you lived here?" he asked, still easing her towards the room.

"All my life, my parents have been here for over twenty years."

"Perfect," he said, bringing her into the room. "There's a good chance you were conceived here, and I think it's fitting that you become a woman in this room."

With that, he turned, his hand slipping into the hair at the back of her head, slowly bringing her to him. His lips met hers and guided them open, his tongue expertly leading hers.

"God, I want you so much," he said between more nibbling kisses. She gasped at how she responded to his touch and wrapped her arms around his head to keep him there. He kissed her neck as his hands went to her bottom and beneath her skirt, fondling the cheeks of her backside and pulling the gusset of her knickers in between them to let it stimulate her as it was pulled taut. She gasped again and squeezed her legs together to try to satisfy the burning itch between her legs.

"Julia, you are *so* sexy, but we can stop anytime if you're not sure, okay?"

She pulled his face closer to her and whispered in his ear, "I'm yours. I need you now."

They kissed passionately, and her hands stroked his back before she moved them to frantically undo the buttons on his shirt. He continued to kiss her neck and throat while his fingers undid the zip of her skirt. As it loosened and fell to the floor, she stepped out and kicked it away. The kissing and fondling became more urgent, and as she undid the belt and zip of his trousers, he pulled off his shirt.

Her hands grabbed the back of his chinos and pulled them down, revealing his snug-fitting boxers and the hardened treasure within them. Julia licked her lips as the fingers of her right hand traced and stroked along the obvious length of his cock and the bulge of his balls. She said, "Ooh, is that all for me? I am such a lucky girl!" She giggled. She amazed herself at how at ease she felt.

His hands went under her blouse and caressed and cupped her breasts, her nipples pebbling beneath his touch and the friction of his palms.

"These are gorgeous. Are they for me as well?" He kissed her again, and they both aided one another in taking off her top.

"These are my *girls*," Julia said proudly, thrusting out her chest. "Let me introduce you to Pinky and Perky!" she smiled.

"Hello, Pinky. Hello, Perky." He kissed each nipple in turn before saying how beautiful they were.

"Get on the bed," he ordered as he removed his socks and shoes and kicked away his trousers.

"But–" she made one last pitiful effort to stop them from desecrating her parents' bed, but the want in her was too strong.

His whispered "shush" saw all of her resistance swept away, and she lay back. He knelt between her legs and lightly caressed her body, starting at her neck and shoulders, over her breasts and nipples with wide-fingered hands sweeping over her, trying to touch as much of her as possible as he did so. He pushed a knee firmly against her nylon-covered pussy, feeling how hot and damp she was. Her eyes were closed, but she rubbed herself against his knee as her hands stroked his arms in encouragement.

Gerry pulled away slightly to drink in the sight of this beautiful girl with her firm breasts, hard nipples and flat stomach, which he stroked lightly to the point of it being almost ticklish. He leaned forward and ardently kissed her again as her arms went around his neck and her legs widened. Leaning back again, he hooked his index fingers into each side of her knickers and pulled them down, with Julia lifting her bum to help. The soaking garment came over her ankles and away.

Her legs were wide open, and he could take in the glorious sight and smell of her engorged, wet orifice neatly framed by her trimmed pubis. He leant forward again and, propping himself up on his hands, kissed her and then trailed his tongue between her boobs. Her stomach was heaving with anticipation as he moved towards his ultimate goal.

Gerry settled himself and lay between her thighs, millimetres away from her welcoming slit. He wasted no time in sliding his arms under her legs to bring his hands back to her breasts and tummy as his tongue and mouth made contact with her sex. Although she knew it was going to happen, the bliss of his tongue licking along the full length of her vulva made her sigh with pleasure, and her body jerked when, at last, he touched her clitoris. She had often masturbated with thoughts of a man giving her oral pleasure, but the delight she felt now was unlike anything she'd had before.

Julia hitched her knees up towards her stomach, hopefully to widen herself to allow him even more access. Gerry brought his right hand down under her and massaged the area around her perineum, anus and the sensitive entrance to her vagina. It was all so intense that she didn't think she could bear it any longer. She then brought both her hands to the back of his head, imploring him to press harder. She climaxed in minutes, and the resulting powerful sensitivity forced her to push his head from her, allowing her to close her legs, writhing to get away. She lay on her side, breathing heavily. He moved up her body to hold her close from behind, and as she calmed, she was able to take in what had happened.

"Are you okay?" he asked in all sincerity but was secretly quite pleased with himself for having gotten her to orgasm so quickly.

"Fuck," she gasped. "That was fantastic."

She was still breathing deeply but became aware of his prick jabbing into her thigh. She reached behind herself and massaged it through his boxers.

"Would you like to take a break while I get us a drink?" he asked as he stroked her arm.

"No, I just want you," was her quiet response.

Julia lay on her back again as he pulled off his boxers. She closed her eyes as he positioned himself.

"Yes. Gerry, please," then she gasped as she felt the hot, hard knob rubbing against her sex, back and forth, slipping between but not inside. She urgently pulled him onto her, hoping his cock would slip into her, but it had the opposite effect as the pressure caused the shaft to slip externally upwards. Gerry eased backwards and, fingering her, found the entrance.

"Stay still," was all he said as she felt the arrowhead nudging at her again, but this time, he followed his fingers into her, just an inch to start with.

"Oh, yes," she sighed, and then couldn't help herself again, urging him on.

He held her thighs and said, "Slowly, you gorgeous girl, take it slow. It's all yours," and he controlled the glacial pace of penetration. Julia's hands grabbed his shoulders to steady herself. His penis felt ridiculously thick, so much bigger than her mother's dildo, and yet there was no pain - just an immense feeling of being filled. He stopped and pulled slightly away, almost to the point of complete withdrawal, then began to push into her again, just a little further this time. She gasped with the pleasure of it and thrilled at the thought of literally being taken.

Gerry withdrew and re-entered three or four times until, eventually, he was fully inside her. He stayed still and let her squirm to enjoy the moment, almost imploring him to fuck her. She gasped again and then, out of the blue, said, "Gerry, I need it now! *Do it!*"

He required no second bidding and began moving in and out of her. Julia sighed with each thrust, not realising she was even making a noise. Gerry kept up a steady rhythm for a few minutes, but to his dismay, it was reaching a crisis point for him. This beautiful young girl with her gorgeous body and her hot, slippery cunt wrapped around his rock-like dick was heaven. He slowed and stopped to kiss her to give him some time to get a second wind. She still wriggled to keep up the feeling, but he managed to keep some control.

He started again, so slowly, and she was in ecstasy. Minutes later, she felt the tell-tale build-up again, and she clawed at his back and arse to urge more vigorous action - it was just too much. He succumbed to the hair trigger.

"Oh, fuck," he grunted and managed to pull out, even though she was still pushing against him. His cock was poking at her pussy lips, and he ejaculated over her. "Shit," he grunted again through gritted teeth as another jet of hot jizz joined the first, now trickling down her furrow. More spasms of semen pooled and trickled on her and on the bed while she came to her senses and realised what had happened.

"Oh, wow," she paused and thought better of saying something sarcastic so as not to ruin a lovely start. "That was fucking hot."

Julia loved every second of their copulation and wanted it to carry on to bring her to orgasm. She knew it would have to wait. They were both breathing hard as he flopped down on top of her, and she planted a number of kisses on his face and neck.

"You could have stayed inside me. I wanted you to fill me up," she whispered in his ear.

"Sorry, we hadn't talked about contraception, so I wasn't sure." He was still out of breath.

"Silly. I'm on the pill, but you're right. That little detail seemed to get lost in the heat of the moment," she laughed. "But it was fabulous. Thank you for such a special moment."

"Moment? You saucy mare, I lasted as long as I could," he smiled as he kissed her cheek." She laughed again. "But—" she kissed him deeply before he broke off and repeated, "But?"

"But. Gerry, it was wonderful. I will remember this forever!" She kissed him again.

They hugged, and then he told her that he had a legitimate excuse.

"Oh?" she queried. "What would that be exactly?" She ran her fingers through his hair and stared at him.

"It's been quite a while since I had a girlfriend, and, well, you are so sexy that just hearing your sighs was more than enough. I couldn't help myself," he offered by way of explanation.

"It might be something you'll have to get used to, though, don't you think?" She smiled at him with wide, loving eyes.

"I very much hope so." They embraced passionately.

"I don't want to be too forward, but are we dining, or shall I pop out and get us a couple of kebabs?" he asked rather cheekily.

And that was the real start of their love affair. Julia could not believe her luck at meeting such an amazing man. They fucked again early the following morning and lay in bed for a couple of hours afterwards, drifting off to sleep in each other's arms. When she woke with her lover next to her, she thought nothing could be as perfect as this.

The phone rang and thinking it was her parents telling her of their travel arrangements, she picked up the receiver from her mother's side of the bed.

"Hello?"

"Hey JJ, how's you?" It was Mike asking if she'd fancy going out for a picnic today. Gerry listened intently as Julia explained that she had a lot to do as her parents were returning on Monday from a weekend away. She then had to justify why he hadn't been invited to come over to the empty house. She offered the excuse that she had been working. Gerry was not amused at the interruption and Julia cut Mike rudely short.

"Who the fuck was that?" Gerry asked irritably, rubbing the sleep from his eyes and sitting up.

"My long-term good friend, Mikey," she said, as though it was a given that she had friends from school.

"Oh, you have a boyfriend?" Gerry sounded a bit tetchy. Julia was unhappy with the call but wasn't keen on the perceived resentment from Gerry either.

"Yes, I think I do have a boyfriend," and before he could respond, she added, "You!" She could see that he was rather taken aback by that.

"So, who is Mikey?" he said, trying to seem nonchalant as he picked up his watch from the side and proceeded to put it on.

"As I said, he is a long-time friend of mine from school, okay?" She tried to emphasise the 'okay' but continued, "He isn't my boyfriend, although, in the last year, I think he would like to be."

"Ah, so you're not a virgin then?" he said, almost sarcastically.

"Not now, thank you!" She slapped him playfully on the back. "I was before last night!"

He nodded a few times and then said, "So you've never had sex with him then?"

"No!" she said emphatically. "We've petted a bit as kids do, but since we met, you were the only one I wanted to give myself to." She hoped that would assuage his apparent growing animosity.

"Define 'petting?'" he asked.

"Gerry, does it matter?" She was getting tetchy now. "It was school stuff in the last few months. It was nothing."

"So, define it then!" He was persistent but wouldn't look at her.

"We kissed. He fondled my boobs a few times. You know."

"No, I don't know. What else?" He wouldn't let up.

"Oh, Gerry, for God's sake, I tossed him off a couple of times, and he fingered me, so what? And to be honest, he wasn't very good, so it's no big deal, okay? Please, don't concern yourself with him." She stroked his back as if to confirm that he was number one in the farmyard. He was silent for half a minute, which seemed like an hour. He nodded and said, "Yes, of course. I shouldn't be concerned about stuff you've done before we got together."

"Gerry, this has been the best weekend of my life. I want you. Mike is just a friend." She kissed him again in reassurance of her desire for him.

"Okay, but I don't want you to see him again, right?" He was still unsettled by it all.

"Of course, you don't need to worry," she said, trying to pacify him as he lay back.

But Julia was the one who was worried. Why was he so determined to get upset about someone who really didn't mean much to her sexually or emotionally? She was almost flattered that he appeared to be quite jealous but then felt guilty about her friendship with Mike and wanted to make it up to her new lover.

She moved down his body and stroked his flaccid penis, delighting in the fact that he stiffened so quickly. She kissed his stomach as her fingers toyed with his growing length. Still working his cock with her hand, he groaned as she took the helmet into her mouth. She wasn't massively keen, but she knew it would please him.

Julia enjoyed the warmth and smooth texture of his knob end. Still stroking him, her mouth bobbing up and down, he was evidently relishing it. Suddenly, he held his breath, and his hand came around the back of her head. She realised too late that he was going to shoot all of his 'muck' into her mouth. She tried to pull away, but Gerry firmly denied her retreat. His loud grunt was immediately followed by several hard squirts of thick cum. Her eyes squeezed shut, and the only way she could deal with it after initially gagging was to let it fall from her mouth. He still held her in place as he started to go limp.

"Sorry," he gasped. "It was just too good to stop." He sounded apologetic, but was he exacting some kind of punishment for her casual view of Mike? Julia said nothing but pulled out what excess there was in her mouth using a finger. It wasn't so much the salty taste but the viscosity. A drink of water was called for, and she made a hasty retreat to the toilet, offering an urgent need for a wee as an excuse, where, in fact, she spat the rest of his ejaculation into the sink.

Breakfast was a quiet affair, but the farewell kiss was passionate enough. She cried when he left that morning.

8

Smalltown Boy

September 1988

Like his elder brother, Alan McCann loved his parents dearly but couldn't wait to get away from their overbearing influence, especially from his father. Academically, Alan was top of the class and yet, he felt, that was never good enough. His brother, who was really a mentor to him, told him not to worry - once he left school and went to university, he would, in essence, be free. His sibling's advice, half-jokingly, was to move away as far as possible.

Alan had received unconditional offers from three universities, but Glasgow won the day. It was a logical choice; it was a vibrant, exciting metropolis and a world away from small-town Hampshire. He felt a massive emancipation when he moved into a house with a couple of other guys. Gone was that awful daily parental pressure of having to live up to unattainable expectations or having to account for all of his actions outside of the family environment. He was now fully liberated from psychological bullying and control.

Even at the age of eighteen, he was a confident young man and was sure that he was well-equipped to deal with whatever university life could throw at him. One thing he was also quite certain about was his sexuality. Alan knew that he was bisexual but erred towards his own gender. He couldn't explain it and never felt the need to perform an in-depth examination of why. He just knew what turned him on, and the beautiful face and body of a man would get him aroused as easily as that of a pretty girl, if not more so.

Alan was also sure he was not going to post his sexual orientation on the side of a bus. People could make up their own minds about him, but he was never one to take the lead or initiate sexual activity with either sex. If it happened, then so be it. He hated watching pushy guys be rude or try to coerce girls into going to bed with them. It showed a huge lack of respect just for the sake of a shag.

He had taken a room in a small house in Kelvinside; his other two housemates were 'Doric' Donny, from the *'wilds'* of Aberdeenshire, and Palvinder (aka Pally), from the big city bustle of Birmingham. After the shenanigans of Fresher's Week, Alan joined the Rugby Club and the Chess Club, which his new buddies thought was quite incongruous. It appeared to Alan that Donny and Pally only seemed to be at Uni for alcohol, sex, and pleasure-seeking in any form. Their ethos was that if they got a degree of any reasonable grade, then that would be a bonus. Neither Alan nor Pally could quite get to grips with Donny's bewildering dialect or why he called everybody 'Ken', but if they managed to understand one word in three, they were doing well. Even so, the three of them gelled and looked out for each other.

As Alan settled into the routine of lectures, studying, club activities, and the odd party or two, he suddenly found that he had developed a massive crush on one of his lecturers. Charles Corbiere, a man in his late fifties or early sixties, could have an audience eating out of his hand. Even in his introductory lecture of every first semester, he would flounce into the lecture hall and write on the big whiteboard, *"Professor Charles Oliver Corbiere – Senior Lecturer in Anything You Want to Know,"* much to the amusement of his spectators. He would then underline each of his three initials and, sweeping his hand across his handiwork, he would boldly state, "By name and by nature - sorry, ladies!" And he would laugh loudly before adding, "However, your persuasion is irrelevant. Our modus operandi is to make education fun. If it's fun, then you will engage. If you engage and enjoy, then you will go far. I don't stand on ceremony here; don't call me Professor or Sir or Mr Corbiere or even Charles – I answer to the name of Corby!"

Corby was extremely posh, perfectly coiffured, with short, grey hair and a trimmed goatee beard. He was always dressed in a fashionable, light-coloured suit with a bright white shirt, a gaudy bow tie, and he always had a pair of glasses on a chain around his neck. On Saint Andrew's Day and any Robert Burns' celebrations, he donned a kilt, together with a dark grey Braemar jacket and a matching waistcoat. He would also have a rabbit's fur sporran and would joke that he usually preferred to wear it on the inside of his kilt. He would add that there was a dirk tucked into the top of his woollen sock, even if he would like something sounding very similar to reach that far.

Charles Corbiere lectured in Politics and Business Management and, not least, *"Anything You Want To Know"* but appeared to have no particular political persuasion, either left, right, or middle of the road. The dark side of this vivacious, gay man was that he was a very selective predator. He knew how to spot a likely target and would skilfully groom a vulnerable young man into virtually all and any legal act of sexual depravity, casting the taboo of staff/student relationships aside. His personal modus operandi was to pick one young man for the university year and dispense with him after the exams in the following May. He had no desire or need for a long-term relationship.

Alan was marked as soon as he stepped into the lecture hall. The fact that Corby, the "queer boy" as he was known behind his back, also ran the chess club just added to the inevitability.

Alan ignored other derogatory comments about Corby, although he did find a couple of them very amusing, courtesy of a fellow student from the East End of London. Barry (the barrow boy) sometimes called him a "chutney ferret" or a "turd burglar", which Alan had never heard of before, but it did make him laugh. Barry's cockney rhyming slang term calling Corby an "iron", which translates to iron hoof (poof), was another amusing moniker. The "irony"(!) was that Barry was also an "iron" and could be found in some of Glasgow's seediest public conveniences, dolling out blow jobs and hand jobs for five quid a time to fund his various addictions. He was dubbed *the Cockney Sperm Bank* by the local gay community.

Alan's visits to the Chess Club initially drew some polite conversation with the older man regarding games he played against more experienced students. Alan was enthusiastic but considerably out of his depth. He did have an off-the-cuff style about his play and made some outrageous moves that fascinated Corby, who couldn't work out if Alan was carelessly naïve or outrageously stupid. Getting Alan alone, he asked him about his maverick style and what his tactics were when starting a game.

"Absolutely no idea!" Was Alan's honest response.

"Do you prefer defence or attack?" Corby asked him.

"I prefer to attack, but defence can be fun as well."

"Yes, it's quite thrilling to attack, but you must never leave yourself exposed at the back, or people will take advantage," he said with such an obvious innuendo that wasn't entirely lost on the young man.

"I'm not in the class of all these guys here, but I enjoy rattling their cages a bit when they think there's an ulterior motive to some of my nonsensical moves. But they are exactly that, totally nonsensical, because I think I'm reactive rather than proactive. These guys think many moves ahead, and I wouldn't mind getting to that standard," Alan stated confidently.

"Yes, I can see that, despite the fact you don't win, your unorthodox style does unsettle people. You do seem to be an interesting challenge to several players here." Corby was keen to sound complimentary.

"I don't want to appear unkind, but you play like a semi-gifted schoolboy where it's all about percentages. If you're fortunate enough to get a piece ahead, then you'll trade at every opportunity. No bad thing, but you can get undone by not seeing how the game is developing while you concentrate on that strategy."

"Constantly losing is depressing, though," Alan added, and Corby pounced on that to set the trap.

"I'm always keen to see people improve themselves in everything they do. I love chess myself and fully understand that continual defeat weakens the spirit. If you have time on an occasional evening, I could show you a few pointers. I run an extra-curricular chess group at my home once a fortnight that might help. I know you'll be studying hard and probably have a thousand and one things to immerse yourself in, but the offer is there should you so choose."

Alan was overjoyed that this magnetic man showed such an interest in him, but maybe worldly-wise cynics would be pressing the alarm button.

"That would be great, thanks. When is your next group?" Alan asked, closing the trap on himself.

Corby acted fast. "Monday next week, 7.30 pm, there's another chap who is also interested, so you can learn together. Here's my address." He handed Alan a card with his name, contact details, and address. He lived alone in a two-bed apartment provided by the university, not far from the campus.

That following Monday, Alan turned up on the dot and Corby ushered him in. He casually added that the "other chap" couldn't make it, so it would just be the two of them. Alan wasn't unduly concerned and, in fact, preferred the idea of one-on-one tutelage. In further conversation with his mentor, he said that he wanted to learn more because he had never beaten his father at the game, and his parent wouldn't let him forget it. Corby sensed some friction and offered some strategies that would surprise any previous opponents. Alan was hooked.

They met every fortnight, and Alan was very comfortable around Corby. He knew that Corby was gay, but at no point did he ever feel threatened or worried about the time they spent alone together. He never even considered that he was being groomed. But being groomed, he was.

Corby would often be dressed very casually in a polo shirt and loose-fitting track bottoms. He was fit for his age with no hint of middle-aged spread, which he put down to a lot of jogging. He would often be seen doing a circuit of the campus in the early evening or at weekends.

A month into their 'study group' sessions, on one specific evening, it was clear that Corby had just returned from a run and, letting Alan in, told him to get himself a beer and set the pieces up while he grabbed a quick shower. Alan had just placed the last pawn on the board when Corby called out down the hall.

"Alan, could you bring me a towel from the tumble dryer in the kitchen, please? Stupidly, I forgot to get one."

It was no problem, although when he got to the bathroom door, he hesitated.

"Where do you want it?" Alan asked.

"Right here, dear boy, right here," Corby replied, pulling open the bathroom door.

As Alan walked in, Corby turned around stark-naked, sporting his semi-erect penis.

"Oh, thanks," Corby said as though it was no big deal and took the towel from Alan.

He stared at the boy, who in turn was staring at the hardening appendage before quickly turning away and walking down the hall. The crucial tipping point of whether Alan would go or stay was imminent. Alan was sitting by the chessboard when Corby came through, wearing just a bathrobe.

"Shall I start?" Corby asked and, not waiting for the answer, spun the board around so that he was ready to move the white pieces. Alan said nothing and didn't divert his attention away from the board or the pieces. They played a few moves, and Corby went for the jugular.

"Did you like what you saw?" he asked, staring at Alan.

"Um–" Alan wasn't sure what to say.

"My penis and testicles. Did you like what you saw?" Corby was persistent.

"Ye–er… Yes, um, sorry, I didn't realise you would be– er…" Alan was quite flustered, more through the line of direct questioning.

"Naked?" Corby laughed at Alan's embarrassment. "I have nothing to be ashamed of. Men should not be embarrassed about their bodies, especially if they are fit and handsome like yourself."

Alan continued to stare at the board and said nothing.

"I am sorry, my dear boy. I did not mean to humiliate or embarrass you. I think we're friends, and it just did not occur to me that you wouldn't be comfortable with my nudity. I do apologise."

He tried to sound remorseful, but he knew exactly what he was doing and what he was saying. It was engineered to the point where any perceived shame was Alan's for being embarrassed about something he wouldn't think twice about in a rugby changing room.

"No, no, it's okay. I just didn't expect you standing there…er…you know." He sounded a bit confused.

"My dear boy, I think it was obvious I'd be there naked, which is why I required the towel, but please don't worry about it."

Alan drank his beer and played the game of chess badly, losing in a shorter space of time than normal. Corby commented on it and said that they should probably wind this session up for the night, as he

(Alan) was seemingly distracted. Alan looked away and Corby asked him what he was thinking about.

"I really don't know, yes, I was shocked but—" Alan falteringly tried to explain.

"But? I know what you thought," Corby said convincingly.

"You do?"

"Yes, you were shocked, but something in your head clicked, and you found my semi-aroused state quite exciting. Totally different to catching occasional glimpses of flaccid appendages of teammates in the shower to see how big they are and how you might measure up. He laughed as though it was all quite natural. Alan now realised that this blatant homosexual was coming on to him, and he was falling under this man's spell. Unknowingly, he had been stalked for weeks, and just like a chess match, it was now moving to the endgame. Corby was not going to let him off the hook.

"Do you know, I think the thing that bothers most humans is being naked around other people. Clothes cover a multitude of sins, and we try to hide our little imperfections as though we're deformed. When I'm here by myself, I'm usually *au naturel* or just wear a small pair of slips as I love the feel of material like these." He stood up, opened his robe, and took it off, revealing his naked body except for a tiny pair of yellow briefs with the tell-tale bulge obviously showing his growing arousal.

"There, don't you think the human body is attractive? Both the male and female form does something to us to make us desire one another regardless of anyone's sexual persuasion."

Alan was fascinated as Corby stood there in front of him. He could hardly divert his gaze from the swelling in Corby's inadequate underwear that was now struggling to cover it. Corby kept talking

"I realise your discomfort because all you've ever done is cover up except for showering with friends after football—"

"Rugby," Alan corrected him.

"Ah, rugby. Well, there's a game of all shapes and sizes!" he laughed at the double entendre.

"Tell me honestly, Alan, have you ever been exposed to another person in a sexual way?" Corby asked, pulling his briefs up a bit to cover his stiffened cock.

"No. I guess I'm too shy," Alan said truthfully.

"Well, I've seen some girls look at you, and let me tell you, they like what they see…" There was a brief pause before he added, "As I do."

Alan's head was swimming, almost drowning. He liked girls but always felt shy around them and always missed the obvious green lights they offered. But now there was this very attractive man who was easily old enough to be his father or grandfather, saying how he, too, found him attractive. Alan always felt much more comfortable around men. He was a man's man, but it never dawned on him that one would find *him* sexually desirable even if he himself had accepted that he found men physically attractive. Corby stared at him and casually fondled his own penis over the material. As a result, Alan was hugely stimulated. The older man spoke in a manner that almost seemed like an ultimatum.

"I'm going to go to the kitchen to get another couple of beers. I also need to tidy up the bathroom, I'll be about ten minutes. If you want to leave, we'll talk no more about this situation. I will bow to your conviction and accept that I have possibly misjudged you. However, if you want to throw off this puritanical view of clothes and, even more, of bottled-up sexual desire, then I'd like you to strip to your underwear, and we'll have a beer together and see what comes up," he laughed at his own innuendo.

"If you wish to go home, then my feelings for you as a friend and student will remain unchanged, and I hope you would just look at this as a stitch in life's rich tapestry." Corby smiled at him reassuringly and left the room, fondling his cock and enjoying what he was doing to himself.

Within three minutes, Corby heard the front door of the apartment open. There was a brief pause, and then it was closed. To say he was disappointed would put it mildly. Rarely in his time of seducing young virgin men to the great gay way was he wrong about someone. Ah, well, he would need to start again with someone else. University was a target-rich environment.

When he walked back into the lounge, he was delighted to see Alan sitting on the couch, totally naked and fondling his own semi-erect penis.

"I heard the door," he said.

"Yes," Alan hesitated. "I was going to leave, but I realised this was the now or never moment. It's something I've agonised over for quite a while now. You have made things very clear to me in one direction, although how I feel about girls is far from certain." Alan seemed calm and eloquent.

"My dear boy, you can like men *and* women, you know. My feeling is that you're a dyed-in-the-wool homosexual, and you're just coming to terms with that," Corby said, kneeling in front of Alan and reaching out to take his cock and balls in his hands.

"The thing is, I just like men, young beautiful men with young beautiful cocks!" He leant forward to take Alan's stiffening tool in his mouth.

Alan gave in to the exquisite fondling, caressing, and oral work provided by Corby's experienced mouth and fingers. He cradled Alan's balls as the other hand stroked up and down his shaft in time with his mouth bobbing and sucking hard when he reached the tip. It was so good that he tried to force more of his cock into Corby's mouth, but the older man had it all under control. As the hard shaft became more lubricated, Corby gently eased back the tight foreskin to increase the pleasurable sensations on the exposed glans. Alan gasped at this previously unknown bliss and hesitated to touch Corby, but he couldn't resist putting one hand on his shoulder and the other on the back of his head to keep it in place as his orgasm built.

Corby recognised the tell-tale signs of heavy, laboured breathing and how the penis he was almost devouring got harder as the balls tightened. As Alan climaxed for the very first time with someone else, Corby grunted in approval when the hot, thick fluid jetted into his mouth. Eventually, as he felt the last dribble join the initial flood, Corby pulled away and opened his mouth to show his new young charge how much he had unloaded. He pushed his tongue out slightly and curled up the tip to prevent it all from sliding out, although inevitably, some did escape to run down his chin. He watched Alan's fascinated expression before swallowing the lot with a complimentary, "Mmm, we will do that again soon." He tapped Alan's thigh and said, "Get dressed. I think that's enough for your first outing."

"But…" Alan was disappointed. He wanted to indulge in further play.

"No buts," Corby said in a kindly but authoritative manner. "You've taken a huge step on a long voyage of sexual discovery. You've done very well." Then he laughed and said, "And your juice was… particularly sweet. I shall enjoy more of that in the time to come." He touched the corners of his mouth as if to wipe any excess away before he got up and donned his bathrobe.

He watched Alan dress quietly, admiring the young man's toned body and handsome but now flaccid penis and testicles, somewhat shrouded by a dark, hairy bush.

"I think you need to trim that significantly," he said, pointing to the growth around Alan's tackle. "You have a lovely set there; show it off, and besides, it'll make your beautiful cock look even bigger in the showers!" he laughed. Alan smiled and said, 'okay.'

"We can look into various aspects of personal grooming and hygiene in due course." Corby sounded quite strict in a manner similar to his father, but Alan knew this was for his benefit rather than the criticism he persistently endured at home.

"When can we?" Alan began to ask as they headed for the front door.

Corby held up his finger and said, "When I'm available. Probably in a fortnight's time, our usual time for chess. Which, by the way, we shall still continue with. But I can't say for certain. I will let you know, dear boy." He hugged Alan and whispered in his ear, "You're mine now, and you're in very safe hands."

All week, Alan had heard nothing from Corby since his inauguration into the world of same-sex play, and he was very disappointed that his big crush had not been in touch. He felt that having taken such a momentous step in his life warranted something more than silence. Corby deliberately played it cool – *'treat 'em mean…and keep 'em keen.'*

The following weekend, there was an inevitable party at a house a few miles away. In effect, there were parties almost every night of the week to start with, but the novelty wore off along with the realisation that there did need to be some work done. As far as Alan was concerned, only the weekends were dedicated to hardcore downtime.

It was a good autumn Saturday. The rugby team had won handsomely against a bunch of bruisers and there was much celebrating to be done. Generally, though, the level of celebration was indistinguishable between defeat and victory, except that the beer tasted so much better when they won.

On this particular Saturday, he seemed to be very popular with everyone, especially the ladies who always hung about the team. Modestly, he shrugged off the adulation, passing it off as a massive team effort. As he would tell people, rugby teams are split into two camps: piano players (the backs) and piano shifters (forwards). He just happened to be a piano shifter.

Alan consumed a few more beers than normal. The drinks were flowing, and he'd exceeded his normal self-imposed limit but realised it a bit too late. Even so, he was enjoying the adoration and resigned himself to a hangover in the morning. One young lady, Bailey Bunson from Hartlepool, was particularly persistent in wanting to talk. She was on the same course as Alan but a couple of years ahead. She joked about being the older woman and how it was her doing all the chatting up. He was flattered, of course and welcomed her interest in him.

As the evening wore on, the conversation dried a little, so she insisted that they dance. Alan was initially reluctant, but it was a slow one and all he had to do was hold her and shuffle around in a circle, hopefully in time to the music.

She snuggled in close and although he was usually slow on the uptake, even he couldn't miss the signs that she wanted him to kiss her. It was inevitable, as were the subsequent kisses, and she eventually whispered in his ear that she thought they should find somewhere to be alone. He was consumed with temporary infatuation and let her steer him upstairs to find a small bedroom with a single divan. They kissed again, but her hands were not idle in undoing his shirt and trousers. In less than a minute, they were both naked, and she pushed him on his back on the bed and straddled him.

Alan thought this was all a bit of a rush, but conversely, he was the virgin here, so why not let her take control as she appeared to know what she was doing. They said nothing, but she dribbled some spit onto her hand before applying it to his shaft, which wasn't very enthusiastic. Bailey sat on his thighs, and he could feel how hot and wet she was. His hands went to her small, pert breasts. Her nipples were extremely responsive, which thrilled to his touch even as clumsy and inexpert as he was. She stroked his cock, hoping for a response which wasn't forthcoming.

"What's wrong, don't you like me?"

"You're gorgeous, it's just being a bit lazy, is all." Alan was a bit flustered as to the dysfunction below.

"Think of how much fun we'll have when you're nice and hard." She enthused and continued to work on him.

Alan tried to think of some pornographic scenarios he'd seen on a recent video of Donny's, but to no avail. His mind then drifted to Corby's blow job and that did the trick.

"Oh yes, that's my lad," Bailey sighed in approval and moved into position to sit on him. As she slowly impaled herself, he grunted, his body jerked, and he climaxed.

"What the fuck?" She exclaimed in disappointment. He was fully in her now, but the deed was done!

"You've cum!" she said, looking decidedly disappointed. "That was quick!" She felt his cock begin to wilt and eventually slip out of her, along with a puddle of jizz.

"Ye– yes…Oh, sorry." He really didn't know what to say.

She cuddled up to him, stroking his stomach and inner thighs, hoping against hope for some miraculous recovery.

"Do you have a girlfriend at home?" she asked while continuing her intimate massage.

"No, I didn't think it would be fair if I was coming away for a few years," he said truthfully, although he'd never asked a girl out in his life, mainly through shyness but also for fear of rejection.

"What about you, have you got a boyfriend at home back in Hartlepool?" he asked.

"Aye, well, he thinks he's my boyfriend. You guys are funny, though," she said with a smirk.

"Oh, how so?" he quizzed.

"A couple of shags, and they think you're theirs for a lifetime. By fuck, I couldn't wait to get away," she said, now wrapping her fingers around his penis, still slippery with her lubrication. She now realised he was done for the evening – effectively DOA!

"It's your first time, isn't it, Pet?" she guessed with a bit of a frown. "I do get 'em, the bonniest lad at the party, and he's a virgin!" she laughed.

"Sorry," was all he could muster.

"Oh, don't worry, we all have to start somewhere," and she kissed him, but the disappointment was written on her face.

Alan knew she was frustrated but hoped she wouldn't think too badly of his lack of sexual talent. They said nothing, but after about five minutes, Bailey told him that she'd better get going, her friends would wonder where she was. He watched her get dressed in an awkward silence, not knowing what to say.

"Okay," she bent over and gave him a quick kiss, "See ya, bonny lad."

"See you Monday?" He asked in a semi-suggestive way of a date.

"I'll be around, I'm sure. Take care." And she was gone.

Alan sat up and then got dressed himself, thinking that was it. He'd lost his virginity in a few seconds and felt very little emotion about it. He went downstairs looking for Bailey, but she had gone. Bish, a rugby teammate of his, pointed out that he'd been missing for a while, and Alan just smiled.

"Oh, wait, you were talking to Bailey, weren't you? Don't tell me you went upstairs with her?"

Alan just smiled again. His raised eyebrows were all the confirmation that was required. His flatmate Donny came over.

"Aye-aye min, an far hiv ye been?" Donny asked innocently in his Aberdonian accent, which seemed to get stronger the more he drank.

"He's been upstairs with Bailey," Bish added constructively.

"Nae, not Bailey the Bike? Wow, brave mon! A bangin' bosie with Bailey the Bike!" Donny said enthusiastically and then laughed.

"I heard she bangs like a shit-house door in a gale. Bunk-up Bunson Burner, they call her!" said Bish.

"I need a drink," Alan said, trying to change the subject.

"I'll bet you do. She must have sucked all the goodness out of you," said Bish. Donny shared the sentiment.

The following morning, Alan woke with a hammer drill going off inside his head. He began to recall the events of the night before and was very underwhelmed by the whole experience of losing his virginity, not least because Bailey seemed quite dismissive, as he clearly had not lived up to her expectations.

On Monday lunch break in the Uni canteen, he saw her sitting with a couple of her friends near the window. She saw him at the same time and briefly raised her head in acknowledgement before turning back to chat with her friends, who then both looked around at him before giggling. It was obvious they were laughing at him, and he blushed. His mind was racing. Should he go over and say hello once he'd got his lunch or turn away? He paid for his food and looked back at her table. She sort of half-smiled at him and then turned back to keep talking to her friends as though embarrassed to see him. He got the message and looked for a table by himself, hoping his embarrassment wouldn't be obvious to anyone else.

Donny, in a short space of time, had become a good mate, but he was also like the proverbial bad penny.

"Hey, pal, ah didnae hear ye ging oot the morn, fit like?" he asked.

"Yeah, all good," Alan replied when it was clear he was anything but.

"Noo, ye are nae frettin aboot yon wee quine, are ye?" Donny hit the nail on the head. Alan gave a half smile.

"Oh, pal," Donny looked at him, trying to read his face. And he did so very accurately. "Jist tak it fae fhat it wis. A shag, ya ken! Ah wis speakin tae Bish last nicht aboot her, an she's had mair pricks than a second haun dart board. Seems she hae a monthly tally o foo, fhat, wen an farr. Pal, she's a cock hound ken."

"To be fair, Donny, that doesn't sound overly respectful," Alan pointed out, thinking that whatever she was, she didn't deserve to be insulted in such a way.

"Pal, ah ken ye're posh an led a sheltered lyffe, bit welcome tae the rale warld o Uni. It's een fuckin' great knockin shop, an' the quines are jis as bad as the lunes, sae if ye are gaun tae be here a while yee'd better get used tae it. Fin ye see her neixt, jis smile say aye-aye min, an leave it aat aat, ya ken?" Donny was the urban Scottish Guru, even if most people, including lowlanders and central belt Scots, didn't understand a word.

Alan, now almost accustomed to Donny's Doric dialect, took it on board and nodded. He also hoped that she didn't put him on her supposed monthly tally. One thing was for certain: he would not be so gullible next time.

Shortly after lunch, Alan was buoyed as he'd received a note in his locker from Corby confirming Monday evening's chess class was on. His heart rate increased as he read the simple note.

9

It's a Shame

Monday evening couldn't come quick enough. Alan was welcomed at the door by Corby, wearing just his bathrobe.

"Come in, dear boy. Drink?"

"Yes, please. A beer, thanks," Alan responded. Corby led him into the lounge.

"I took the liberty of getting one in advance," Corby said, sitting in his favourite chair and allowing his robe to spill open.

He watched the young man carefully.

"Alan, you look a tad worried. We don't have to do anything if you don't want to. We can just play chess. There is no pressure here."

"No, it isn't that. In fact, I am quite looking forward to more–" Alan struggled for the word.

"Exploration?" Corby suggested helpfully.

"Yes, exploration."

"Then what troubles thee, my young friend?"

"Oh, I don't know," Alan sighed. He did know but couldn't think how to put it and then it came to him. "Expectation."

"Expectation?" Corby asked. "Are you having difficulty with some assignments? I'd be glad to assist."

"No, the studies are fine, and I'm enjoying it," he said truthfully.

"Then speak up, dear boy. I'm sure I can help." Corby sounded very sincere.

"I was at a party on Saturday, and there was a girl…"

"Ah, the sexual card!" Corby announced. "Who chased who?" Corby asked.

"I'd had a few drinks, and I was flattered by her attention," Alan admitted. "I thought she was interested in me personally, but it appears otherwise," he said, rather downcast.

"Ah, I see. Did it end up with sexual intercourse?" Corby asked as though it was just a matter of fact, although he could see that Alan was quite embarrassed about it. Alan nodded.

"And you just felt used afterwards?" Corby continued with his accurate assessment.

"It was my first time," Alan blurted out, "and I–"

"Wanted it to be a great romance?" Corby interrupted again.

"Maybe not that, but I wanted it to mean something to me and her," Alan said.

"Yes, of course, and you're so right. There has to be a meaning and cerebral connection to anything concerning the human spirit; otherwise, we may as well be animals. It's a sad fact, however, that many young people, when they reach puberty, are only interested in fucking and don't consider the feelings and emotions of the person they are doing it with."

Corby let him consider that for the moment and then continued, "You are not so shallow and that is a huge plus in your make-up. However, it's a fine line between physical pleasure and emotional pain, and it's something you will need to come to terms with when considering future escapades. No one wants to be used, but then again, should you deny yourself mutual pleasure with another person because you're aware there won't be a long-term commitment?"

Alan said nothing but took a sip of his beer.

"I can only offer my thoughts on the subject and that is it boils down to one word, which I believe Aretha Franklin put quite succinctly – respect!"

Alan nodded, and Corby continued. "You have to respect the other person, appreciate their motives, don't push them for more than they want to give and however it goes, don't talk about them to anyone afterwards. It's a word that applies to everyday life, really, when you come to think of it."

"Yes, that makes sense, and I realise now that that is the problem," Alan said as Corby listened intently. Alan continued, "She was a bit quick to want to leave afterwards and I saw her in the canteen with her friends today, where she barely acknowledged me. It was obvious that I was just a big joke to them."

Corby could see he was upset about it.

"And I'm guessing that it didn't go so well. ED or PE?" Corby asked, suggesting that he knew what the answer was.

"ED or PE?" Alan queried the acronyms.

"Erectile dysfunction or premature ejaculation!"

"Both…ED…PE and ED again," was Alan's embarrassed and hesitant response.

"Of course, very understandable. All of this would have been extremely nervy but massively exciting for you. Was she experienced?"

"Yes, she's older than me," Alan said.

"Did you wear a condom?" Corby asked, a little concerned.

Alan hesitated again. "No," was the guilty admission.

"Tut, tut, tut." Corby was now in fine schoolmaster mode.

"You must carry a packet with you everywhere. Sexually Transmitted Diseases are rife in institutions like universities. I get the impression that the young lady has no concerns about who, where, or when, and I think if you have escaped infection, you will have dodged a bullet."

Corby got up, went over to his desk in the corner of the room and started scribbling a short note before placing it in an envelope and sealing it.

"Remember, a second skin, while providing protection, will help to desensitise the whole experience. Ha, wear two, and you could fuck all night!" Corby handed the envelope to Alan.

"Tomorrow, before your first lecture, pop along to the Medical Unit and give this to the Head Nurse, Mrs McIver. Hopefully, she'll have time to take some blood and do some tests as a favour to me. If you are infected, the quicker you have treatment, the faster you'll be cured."

Alan could detect a note of disappointment in Corby, although the older man tried not to make his feelings obvious until he said, "Unfortunately, until we know the result, it does rather put the kibosh on any exploration. They played chess instead, with very little further conversation. Alan lost again.

The following morning, the Head Nurse did have some time to read Corby's note and act on it. Within forty-eight hours, Alan received a note in his locker, effectively saying that he had *dodged a bullet.* At the Wednesday lecture, Corby assailed him afterwards and simply asked if he was well. Alan confirmed that he was, and within an hour, there was a note from the older man to say that the fortnightly Monday evening chess session could be brought forward a week to this coming Monday and was on for 7.30 pm. Alan was more than excited.

This time, there would be no disappointment. Alan spent a good hour in the bathroom on the Sunday before tidying up his pubic area. He'd already had a lot of stick from his teammates when they saw how manicured it was recently, but he'd decided that Corby's opinion mattered more and just hit them with, "Lads, the girls love it. They don't want a face full of fuzz when they're going down on you. Anyway, it makes my dick look even bigger than the monster it already is!" He had practised his "ad-lib" quip to the point where he was perfect in word and delivery.

Monday evening came, and after an early dinner, he showered, making sure all of his important little places, including his anus, were scrubbed and meticulously clean. His heart was in his mouth as he turned up at Corby's apartment.

"Come in, dear boy." Corby was his usual effervescent self.

"How are you?" he asked without waiting for an answer. "Are you looking forward to tonight's game? Or would you rather just play chess?" he laughed at his own ambiguity.

"I'm ready," Alan said, a bit croakily as his throat had suddenly gone dry.

"Good, good. You will not regret this. Lust, passion, desire, and sexual joy are the great gifts of life. Too many want to hide it away, keep it behind closed doors, and yet the human body is an instrument to be played for pure sexual gratification. Come with me." He led Alan to the master bedroom.

"Have you ever kissed a man, I mean a proper French kiss, not just a peck on the lips?" Corby asked him as he turned to face him.

"Girls only," Alan answered.

"So, we are starting from scratch, then, good. You won't have any bad habits that need to be corrected. It's a bit like golf, really!" he laughed his infectious laugh.

Corby took Alan's face between his hands, and they kissed with open mouths and twirling tongues. He then held him close and said, "What we do now and what we may do in the future is between us. Homosexuality is not illegal between consenting adults, although in some quarters, it is frowned upon. I am damned sure your compadres in the rugby team wouldn't ever let you forget about it should you come out of the closet, so to speak. Personally, I believe we are all bisexual in varying degrees, and if people accepted that, then the world would be a better place," Corby said profoundly.

"Now, you will undress me. I'm not wearing a great deal, so it won't take long, but dwell on the flesh as it's exposed. Stroke it, kiss it if you feel the desire. Don't forget that it is all part of the seduction process. The more excited your partner becomes, the more you'll enjoy giving pleasure."

Alan did as he was asked, starting with Corby's shirt and slowly undoing the buttons before slipping his hands inside to stroke the older man's skin and hairy chest. When he'd undone the last button, he pushed the shirt back from Corby's shoulders and took it off.

"Okay," Corby said. "Not bad, but now I'm going to take your shirt off, take mental notes as I go and feel free to close your eyes and just dwell on the sensations."

Corby undid the first couple of buttons on Alan's short-sleeved shirt, and he closed his eyes as requested. Corby's hands were inside the open area and stroking Alan's upper chest and shoulders before pulling him close and kissing and nibbling his throat and neck. He continued to undo buttons and ran his hands around Alan's back to stroke him at the same time as nibbling along his collar bones. The shirt was then pushed off without Alan even realising it and he was already erect.

The two men were roughly the same height, and Corby asked Alan to turn around to face away from him. As he did so, Corby stroked the young man's back before moving closer to him and hugging him from behind. Corby stroked his chest and stomach with both hands. Alan could feel Corby's impressive hardness against his backside, and now Corby's hands moved to undo the belt and top button on Alan's jeans - then the zip, reaching inside to find Alan's bare cock and balls.

"Very good. Prepared indeed and suitably hard. I can see that you are going to be a star pupil, and you never know, you might even get good at chess," Corby said playfully, tweaking one of Alan's nipples. Alan simply responding with, "Mmm."

Within moments, Alan had kicked off his trainers and was barefoot. His jeans hit the floor, and he stepped out of them. Corby still stood behind him, stroking his stomach with one hand and manipulating his cock with the other.

"Turn around, my boy, kneel down and remove my shorts. Feel my hard member in your mouth. Don't worry, I won't cum. You're not ready for that."

Alan did as he was asked, kneeling before his mentor and allowing himself to be tutored by this expert in something other than academia. He unzipped Corby's shorts, and he, too, was naked underneath. Alan stroked Corby's bum cheeks while watching his penis jerk spasmodically as if to seek attention. He looked at the length of it and his low dangling balls.

His immediate attention was drawn to the fact that his pubic area was entirely shaven and smooth, and it just seemed the most natural thing in the world to want to take the swollen shaft into his mouth. Before he did so, he looked up at Corby, who stared back and said, "Yes, take it. I've wanted this moment for weeks."

Alan did not hesitate any longer, opening his mouth to take the bulbous, circumcised head of Corby's penis into his mouth. He tentatively ran his tongue around, eliciting a gasp of delight from the older man. Then he held the stem at its base and tried to see how much he could take in before gagging.

"No teeth, my boy, no teeth," Corby said as a warning that he needed to be aware of scraping or damaging the skin. He took his time enjoying the firm, hot flesh, and his other hand now came round to fondle Corby's heavy balls.

"Mmm, yes, you will be my gold-star pupil. Slowly feel it touch the back of your throat, and then, little by little, take it just that tiny bit further… Slowly now," Corby instructed.

Alan made another gagging noise but was not put off, and then Corby held his face and slowly moved his cock in and out of Alan's slippery orifice.

"Fuck yes, make your lips tight around my penis. Mmm," Corby encouraged before withdrawing fully after five minutes or so, leaving Alan on his haunches.

"Bend over the bed and spread your legs wide. I have something eminently enjoyable for you," Corby ordered. Alan eagerly did so, although he wasn't sure if he was ready to be sodomised just yet.

"I've only tried a finger up there, and it was very tight," Alan said worriedly.

"What?" Corby was momentarily confused. "Oh no, dear boy, that's a long way off. Now do as I say, please."

Alan bent over and propped his head on his arms, resting on the side of the bed, but he wasn't sure what "pleasures" awaited him. He felt Corby stand between his legs and then heard the cap of a bottle click and some cool, oily liquid squirted on the top of the crack of his buttocks. As it dribbled down, he felt Corby smooth it in the valley before he felt what he thought was Corby's thumb slowly push into his anus. Alan let out an involuntary sigh of bliss as Corby gently rotated his thumb.

"Mmm, yes, you are very tight here, and it will take time, but you will love the experience of being properly buggered in the true sense of the word when the opportunity arises." Alan's cock jerked in response to Corby removing his thumb and carefully, with more lubrication, inserting two fingers to go a bit deeper and stretch his sphincter a bit wider.

"Yes?" Corby asked without elaborating.

"Hell yes," Alan responded enthusiastically. Corby withdrew his fingers and knelt behind Alan.

The next thing he knew, Corby was kissing and nibbling his buttocks but steadily working towards his bum hole. Alan was hoping he wouldn't kiss such a forbidden place, but his body was screaming for it to happen as he spread his legs wider.

"Good boy," Corby said before the tip of his tongue encircled Alan's anus and then, joy of joys, probed, pushed, and penetrated the opening, which again made Alan sigh with pleasure. The older man pulled Alan's cheeks wider apart to gain more access, and Alan's cock jerked fiercely in response. Corby's mouth and tongue were firmly between Alan's butt cheeks, working their magic when Corby grasped Alan's hardness and determinedly wanked it with long, slow strokes.

Without realising it, Alan was so close to orgasm that by the time he shouted, "Stop, stop!" it was too late, and he gushed all over Corby's hand and the side of the bed. Corby didn't stop what he was doing immediately but instead slowly squeezed the last few drops from the now spent appendage and finished rimming Alan's arsehole. Corby leaned back and, licking his fingers, asked Alan to lie fully on the bed. He did so and was fascinated by the older man continuing to clean his fingers with his mouth before eventually reaching for a towel.

"I knew you'd like that. I didn't realise that you'd like it that quickly!" Corby said, chuckling. Alan realised he meant it in a non-judgemental way and laughed a little with him. He tried to apologise for being too quick.

"No need to apologise, dear boy. I take it as a compliment that my skills have been so welcome and so effective."

"It was just so…just so…" Alan struggled for the right words.

"Beautiful is the word you're struggling for. Beautiful, and so are you, dear boy."

Then Corby climbed onto the bed and, cuddling Alan to him, kissed him fully on the lips, pushing his tongue into Alan's mouth to meet its counterpart. Alan didn't care that that tongue had been in his anus moments before. It was all too…*beautiful.* He had kissed girls, and they had kissed him back, but there was something different here. He felt a real desire for and from this more experienced man. It became clear to Alan what passion and lust meant. He couldn't explain it, but he understood.

Corby was delighted when this young man embraced him back and even more so when he forced the older man onto his back, barely breaking the kiss. Alan had no thoughts that they were of the same sex as he licked down Corby's body. He knelt to move directly to Corby's semi-hard appendage.

"Take your time, laddie. There's so much to be gained by stalking your prey; it's a delicious, agonising anticipation before you get there, and the coup-de-grace is just the next step to further ecstasy." Corby murmured, enjoying how the young man listened to every word and took it on board.

By the time Alan's mouth had reached its target, Corby was virtually fully hard. A simple grip of his shaft with Alan's right hand while the other clasped the balls below was the final step to rigidity.

Corby enjoyed the attention, although he was a little put off by the over-exuberant slobbering noises. It was noted, Alan would need to be told how to do this naturally without adding his own soundtrack.

Corby allowed it to go on for several minutes and then held Alan's right wrist as if to say stop.

"Mmm, laddie, you're learning fast," he said as a compliment, but he knew there was much to do in Alan's education.

"We've come a long way, but now you will manually finish me off. Kneel beside me and give me hand relief. While you're doing it, recognise how my breathing changes as the climax approaches, how my cock gets even harder as that moment gets nearer and how my whole body reacts when the trigger is pulled. It will stand you in very good stead in the future.

Alan settled to his task and liberally squirted baby oil on his hands before massaging all of Corby's genital area and then taking hold of his fully hard dick, stroking it up and down, applying the same sort of pressure that he did when masturbating. As Corby's breathing quickened and became louder, he was eager to bring about the climax and quickened the pace of his wanking. Corby groaned noisily, and Alan was surprised how the older man's body convulsed as a skein of semen erupted into the air and over both of their bodies. That eruption was followed by two or three more before the force lessened, and the emission subsided to a few thick dribbles of cum. Corby smiled and told his young charge to scoop up some of the semen and examine it.

"Don't be frightened or disgusted by it. It is, after all, the elixir of life!"

Alan left an hour later with Corby's praise ringing in his ears. When he got home, he masturbated, allowing the hot liquid to shoot into the palm of his left hand so that he could examine his own "elixir." He played with it between his fingers, smelt its salty aroma and even tasted it.

At that moment, the young man firmly believed he was a confirmed *'dyed-in-the-wool'* homosexual. He remembered the joke about a guy saying to his friend, "My mother made me a homosexual!"

To which his not-so-bright friend replied, "If I gave her the wool, would she make me one too?"

He thought he should present a ball of wool to Corby and chuckled to himself.

10

All Night Long

May 1989

The final week of term was casual and easy-going. A fair number of students were packing and leaving, but quite a number just enjoyed the party atmosphere of nothing to do but attend a few laissez-faire lectures that were no more than post-mortems of the year or insights into what was to come next semester. The rest of the time was for pubs, clubs and parties.

Corby told him to keep Thursday evening free for an end-of-year farewell – Alan was really excited about that. At the weekend before Corby's special evening, the rugby team sealed the league title with an easy win over mid-table also-rans. There was an impromptu celebration in the clubhouse afterwards, followed by a party at fellow student Aileen McConnell's home, not too far from the sports ground. Most of the team and supporters were there, and Alan was just enjoying the feel-good factor of winning such a hard-fought campaign.

A couple of girls approached and started a fairly innocent conversation with him.

"Hey, you're Alan McCann, aren't you? You got the man of the match for the game today?" One of them said. Alan shrugged it off, saying it was a team game.

"We came down this afternoon to watch. My name is Anna, and this is Iona. We thought it was a great game."

"Hello to you both, I'm glad you enjoyed it. Do you watch the matches often, or was this a one-off?"

"We come as often as we can. I love rugby," Anna said.

"My dad was a Scottish International", Iona said, "Rugby does it for me."

"Ok, it was a good result, but it was a bloody hard game." Alan said, trying to stick to his old physical education teacher's mantra of *'Modest in victory, magnanimous in defeat.'*

"Aye, but you were brilliant. You're the player of the season as well, aren't you?" Iona said.

He replied that yes, he had been awarded that prestigious trophy, but the league title was the one he valued most. It was then that he was stumped for something to say. These girls were maybe a year or more likely two years older than him, and as much as he loved the perceived adulation, he was too naïve to continue the chat. The girls fired banal questions at him about rugby before Iona drifted off to chat with someone else. Anna started to talk about his course at Uni, but he switched it around to ask her a few questions and let her talk about herself. Doric Donny, his worldly-wise Scottish housemate, had given him that useful advice, and he was surprised at how effective it was.

"Wind 'em up and let 'em go! Quines love speakin' aboot 'emselves, all you hae to do is nod and laugh in the richt places and jist throw in another question if you think they're losing interest."

The rest of the evening was a complete blur. In the pre-dawn hours of the following morning, he woke up in bed with a stinking hangover. Very slowly, he tried to gather his thoughts and desperately attempted to recall the events of the night before. Fuck…putting the pneumatic jackhammer headache to one side…or as much as he could, he tried to go through the evening's chronology.

Deep breath – Clubhouse piss-up. Walk to a house party, …where though? Chatted to a few people about rugby. Oh yes, the rugby…we won, and now his battered ribs, back, and face reminded him of just how physically demanding it had been.

Chatted with a couple of girls…oh, what were their names…?

One whose dad played for Scotland…and the other one…fuck… pass… it'll come to me, he thought. The first one had bigger eyes and boobs than the other one.

He danced with one of them…fuck, what was her name? He got drinks for them and himself - often.

He recalled talking to Pally, who had appeared to try to get in on the act with the girls.

He remembered having another slow dance with the second one because she made him. He snogged her…because she made him. The first one reappeared, and he danced with her…because she made him.

 He now started to panic because he didn't remember anything else.

Suddenly, he realised that the bed he was in was not his own and it felt like a rat trap. But was he in that trap with another rat, maybe one of the nameless ones? He didn't move but listened intently to hear if there was any sound of breathing. His head was thumping, and with bleary and beery eyes, he looked in the half-light just before dawn to see if he had brought a glass of water to bed with him…FUCK, no, he hadn't, and his mouth was as dry as a well-chalked snooker cue.

He was now reminded that his bladder was at bursting point, and there was no margin of error. His mind turned to mush, where was he? Giving in to the immediate urgency, he sat up slowly so as not to rattle his throbbing brain too much. He swallowed hard, peeled his tongue from the roof of his mouth and exhaled in a big puff. It was so pungent it could curdle milk at ten yards. Even he could smell it. Alan looked around the floor for his clothes, and thankfully, most of them were in the vicinity, quite near the bed. He grabbed his boxers, put them on and tentatively walked towards the door. It wasn't a big room and as he got to the point of opening it, he looked back at the bed.

On the other side of where he had been sleeping was the top of a head with long hair draped over the quilt; whoever was there was still asleep, and he panicked as to who it might have been. The call of nature for the moment was too desperate to worry about the mysterious woman, and he found that this strange bedroom had an en-suite bathroom…thank fuck!

As the relief of emptying his bladder down the pan swept over him, he glanced around the room. As far as he could tell in the pre-dawn light, it was all very pink with lots of toiletries that his mother would use. There was a bowl of potpourri on the window sill and a pink, fluffy bathrobe hanging on the door. Even in his sub-normal state, he could tell this was a female's choice of décor, but who the fuck was in the bed?

He washed his hands and face and took advantage of a swig of mouthwash from the bottle on the shelf above the sink; that was a relief unto itself. He didn't flush the toilet but put some toilet paper loosely down the pan to cover his excess waste, but now he needed an escape plan.

He quietly slipped out of the bathroom, and while the body in the bed kept still, he grabbed his clothes and shoes and tiptoed out of the room, quietly closing the door behind him. He dressed on the landing and slowly made his way downstairs. A quick glance around the front room and large open-plan kitchen, together with the carnage of party detritus – glasses, beer cans, general mess and a couple of comatosed bodies told him that he was still at the house where the party had been the night before…but who was in the bed upstairs next to him?

He had a two mile walk back to his house, which allowed him to gather his thoughts and clear his head. Regrettably, it didn't give him any further insight into the last hours of the party, where he ended up with some anonymous female.

Alan arrived 'home' just after 9.30 am and all was quiet. He downed a glass of water in one go and went to his room. He stripped and had a quick examination of his wedding tackle to see if there were any tell-tale signs of activity from the night before. There were no bite marks, scratches or open wounds, although he wasn't sure what he might expect to find, but everything appeared to be normal – until he saw something at the top of his right thigh. He checked the mirror to get a better look. Someone had written 'A+I xx' in lipstick, and he wondered how on earth that got there. However, he was too hungover to give it much thought, apart from thinking it must have been his bedmate from last night. He drank some more water, hopped into bed and slept until noon.

When he woke, he downed even more water and headed off to the bathroom for a shower, plus further inspection of his tackle AND the inscription on his upper thigh - 'A+I xx'. What did that mean? He surmised that the xx were kisses, so was it 'A' for Alan, plus the initial of the female in bed with him, or that he was an A1 lover? His brain hurt too much to delve further and he hoped his memory would return as he sobered up properly. He could hear movement in the kitchen and guessed that at least one of his buddies had made it home, perhaps either of them could enlighten him as to the previous night's activities.

Alan entered the kitchen to see Pally.

"Wow, here he is - the lady-killer. How was it with the old dear?" his housemate said. Just behind him, his personal bad penny, Donny, had just come down the stairs.

"Git tae fock Alan, ye dirty dug," Donny said and then laughed. Then he sang a little song to the tune of Scotland the Brave…

"He shagged a Scottish Mammy, great big tits and a hairy fanny…la, la, la la la, la la la la…" and he burst into hysterical laughter along with Pally. Then he swapped the lyrics around, and Pally linked arms with him to do a little jig in a small circle.

"Alan shagged a Heelan Granny, hairy nips and a mile wide fanny…" and they both nearly wet themselves.

Alan looked at both of them blankly as they stopped and laughed at him. Pally said, "Surely you got your end away. The last time you were seen, you were being dragged upstairs by Aileen's mum," he stood and waited for Alan's response.

"Aye, she wis like a lioness wi her prey bein dragged up a trie ya ken," Donny said descriptively.

"Leopards, Donny, leopards," corrected Pally.

"Leopards, fit wye nae lions?" queried Donny.

"Leopards drag their kill up trees to stop other predators from taking them. Lionesses kill mob-handed and are quite able to defend their dinner except from male lions 'cos they get first dibs!" said Pally.

"Quite richt too, but listen tae David Attenborough yon!" teased Donny, "anys hoo, ye got oot alive – jist!"

"Yes, looks like a couple of flesh wounds, though," said Pally, pointing at Alan's neck.

"Woah, far else has she had her clays and moo I wunner?" asked Donny and, pulling up Alan's tee-shirt, exclaimed, "focking hell see the howk marks Pally she had sharp clays and nae mistak ken!"

"Wow, look at that love bite on your neck – was she a vampire?" Pally said, looking seriously concerned at the damage.

"Lads, you're going to have to fill me in with some details because I don't remember any of that."

"You're not serious?" Pally said, looking at him as though he was lying.

"I remember us being at the clubhouse and then going on to a party."

"Aye– Aileen's party at her ma's hoose," Donny added.

"You were talking to a bunch of girls," Pally said.

"Aye, Iona's posse…," said Donny.

"And her pussy…" Pally chipped in, laughing.

"Yes, I was talking to her and another one, I think," said Alan.

"Anna," Donny said.

"Yes, that was her – Anna," Alan was relieved that those blanks had been filled in.

"A bonny hoose it wis too wi jis Aileen an her ma's there sin her dah buggered aff wi his secretary," said Donny. "Did ye see the size o yon gairden ken? It was huge mon!"

"All I remember after chatting to them was just lots of people, I don't recall seeing Aileen at all."

"Really, that's all you remember?" asked Pally, taking a swift glance at Donny.

"Yes, but I know the drink was going down very well, though," Alan added.

"Well, yes, you were talking to those girls, then I joined you, then Iona and me went to get a drink and left you with Anna. She was very interested in you," Pally continued.

"She can certainly talk a lot," Alan said.

"Well, late on, gone midnight anyway, Anna disappeared, and you were briefly talking to Aileen."

"Aileen? Really?" Alan asked.

"Yes, she was banging on about the rugby because she went to watch the game yesterday afternoon. Then, as luck would have it, her mum arrived with a couple of her marauding MILFs terrorising the guys. It was hilarious; all three were pretty much tanked up, and the boys were running for their lives," said Pally.

"Nae youz though pal!" said Donny, patting him on the back, "ye stelled up fur us lunes richt eneuch literally ken!" They sang their little song again as Pally linked arms, and they did their little jig. Alan shrugged his shoulders as if to say it was all a blank.

Pally continued, "Aileen introduced you to her mum and then left you to it because she was getting the other ladies a drink each, and then she got side-tracked by someone throwing up in the hallway." they all pulled a disgusted face.

"Anyway - her mum, what's her name?" Pally asked Alan. He got a blank stare back.

"Oh!" Pally exclaimed, "So you met, chatted, snogged, went upstairs to look at her stamp collection, then slept with her…and you don't know her name?" Pally shook his head and then laughed.

"Mrs McConnell", Donny chipped in, "Isabel McConnell!!" and then he laughed before adding, "Knock knock."

"Who's there?" asked Pally.

"Isabel."

"Isabel, who?"

"Isabel necessary on a bicycle!" and both Pally and Donny burst out laughing again.

"Yeah, that was it, naughty Isabel had you pinned in the corner talking about the match, supposedly, but you could see the way she was looking at you – there was no escape!"

"You were doomed!" Donny said in his best Private Fraser (From Dad's Army) Scottish accent, "Sae fhat wis she like in flechie mon?" Donny asked.

"I told you I don't remember any of this," Alan said and then asked them both for a description of her.

"You, my friend, got up close and personal for a first-degree woofty-shufty. Wow, if anyone knows how she's built, it would be you, wouldn't it?" Pally said logically, and he got a shrug of the shoulders from Alan.

"Fhat the fock is een woofty-shufty?" Donny asked, "Is aat Punjabi fur stirring the porritch?"

"Stirring the porridge? You mean a shag? Yes, pretty much. But hark at you pronouncing every WH word with an F!" Pally replied.

Donny laughed. "Aye, ahm a reid blooded teuchter fae Torphins Aberdeenshire aye an prood o it ya ken! Focking lowlanders from the Central Belt, call us sheep shagging bastards. Ma reply as – don't knock it 'til you've tried it, ken!"

Both Alan and Pally stared at him as though he was an alien and then looked at each other as if to say, "What the fuck is he saying," before Pally followed up with a description of Aileen's mum.

"She's like Aileen but more mature and curvier, and she was a bit obvious with that choice of dress, wasn't she…it wasn't leaving much to the imagination."

"But Aileen's not exactly skinny," Alan said, trying to imagine an older, rounder version of his fellow student.

"Mate, she's hot and curvy, yes, bordering on curvy plus, but like Aileen, she has a lovely face and laughs a lot. What more could you want if you want to get your end away, eh? Anyway, you'll probably see her this week. She'll be at the informal farewell bash on Wednesday. You can get reacquainted with your new squeeze." Pally then gave him a playful punch on the arm.

Alan was mortified.

"We aff tae the pub ah cwid dae wi a hair o the howkit," Donny said.

"I'm going to do some bacon sandwiches first and then we'll go," Pally said.

"Nae agwen yer religion like alcohol?" Donny said, laughing.

"For the millionth time, you hairy-arsed jock, I'm Sikh, not a Muslim or Hindu! I can eat bacon even if it is frowned upon and can drink alcohol but only for medicinal purposes!"

Donny gave him a wry smile and added, "Ahm thinking ye are as muckle o a FEB or Guffy as anyone sooth o the border ken." Donny said and nudged his buddy good-humouredly.

"FEB?" Pally questioned. Donny laughed and looked at Alan.

"Focking Anglish Bastard!" and he laughed again as Alan smiled and shook his head.

With bacon sandwiches devoured and washed down with cans of Red Bull, they sauntered off to the pub, with Alan wondering if his second sexual excursion with a woman was with someone old enough to be his mother. One thing was for sure, he thought, the 'A+Ixx' equalled 'Alan + Isabel, which now made sense. He vowed never to get that drunk again.

On Wednesday, Corby was doing a final short and sweet speech in the main lecture hall, encouraging students not to be lazy during the summer recess, and he hoped that their exam results reflected the 'huge' amount of work they put in during the year.

"Fock ah hope nae ah ve hardly opent a buik," said Donny to a few sniggers around him from people who could well identify with that. As Corby was finishing his address, a rather rotund lady with a flowery-patterned dress came into the room and stood in the corner.

"Ooh, Alan, there she is, it's Isabel!" said Pally, nudging Alan.

"Where?" asked Alan.

"Over there by the door with all of those forms. The cuddly woman with the bleached blonde hair. You must remember her now, surely?" Pally said.

Alan took a deep breath and started to perspire.

"Knock knock," Donny said and sniggered. Corby continued with the sermon.

"And finally, Mrs McConnell from Administration over here to my left will be issuing you all with a personal information form for you to complete and hand in before you leave these hallowed halls. She will also be able to provide you with details of the local Alcoholics Anonymous Meetings and, probably just as relevant, the STD Clinic!" he smiled to raucous laughter before adding, "And if you have acquired a drug addiction, then you're on your own with that one. Glasgow University disavows all knowledge or responsibility for such a shameful vice," he then sniffed, rubbed his nostrils between thumb and forefinger and laughed as did his audience. He finished to rapturous applause and took a very theatrical bow to what he thought was well-deserved acclaim.

There was a bit of a queue as the forms were slowly handed out. Mrs McConnell relayed the names, as they were given to her by each student, to one of her minions to tick a checklist so that they knew who had received the form. Alan stood in line. Pally was behind him.

"I hope she doesn't make a scene about how you just left her wallowing in bed without a kiss goodbye or thanks for the fuck or your confession of undying love," Pally whispered, digging him in the back.

"Fit if she s fu up, ken?" Donny said unhelpfully.

"What?" Alan didn't understand.

"In fulpie ye ken, up the duff, bun in the oven… Tut… the nine-month wytin list… ach fur fock s sake – PREGNANT!" Donny said, raising his eyebrows.

"Wow, you could be Aileen's stepdad!" offered Pally and he and Donny both giggled.

Alan shook his head, hoping this would all go away. As the queue shuffled forward, it was now his turn. She looked at him, or rather looked through him and said:

"Name?"

"Alan McConnell," Alan said, and Pally sniggered behind him. She looked at him properly now with a quizzical look on her face.

"We only have one McConnell, and that's a girl!" She was rather officious.

"Yes, yes, sorry…McCann, Alan McCann," he corrected himself.

She handed the form over, asking him to please complete it and get it back to the office today. She then went on to ask Pally for his name. Alan was relieved and confused in equal measure.

"Well, pal, ye got away light there," said Donny.

As they got outside, Pally asked him if seeing her again rang any bells.

"None, and I didn't seem to ring any bells with her either," Alan added, and deep down, he was beginning to smell a rat.

"Perhaps she was as drunk as you and is suffering from the same alcohol-induced amnesia?" Pally said. They went to the Students' Union bar, which was crowded.

"You seem confused again, Alan, and it's not a good look, you know," said Pally as they sat down with their pints. "What troubles you, my comrade?"

"The thing is, Mrs McConnell doesn't resemble the shape and size of the woman that was lying in bed next to me," Alan said perceptibly, still quite confused.

"Really, aye aat ll be richt!" Donny said, barely able to keep a straight face.

"And she has short bleached blonde hair, and now I know who she is, Mrs McConnell has always had short, bleached blonde hair. The person next to me had long brown hair," Alan added.

"You said she was covered up, didn't you?" Pally asked as though he were an interviewing police officer.

"Yes, but her hair was draped over the pillow," he had that quizzical look about him again.

"Mebbe ye had een o her sexy pals instead o mebbe een was her muff?" Offered Donny, laughing, which to Alan sounded deeply suspicious.

"You said you saw me going upstairs with Aileen's mum?" Alan said.

"Ach weel ah had a fair bucket mesen sae it might hiv been een o her pals, ken." Donny wasn't very convincing.

"But you said I was snogging Aileen's mum?" Alan quizzed his Scottish friend and was now staring directly into his face. Donny didn't return his gaze, but just then, Aileen herself arrived at their table.

"Hi, Guys, I hope you all had a good time on Saturday?" She was as bubbly as ever.

"Brilliant, Aileen," said Pally.

"Rocking!" enthused Donny.

"The place must have been a bit of a mess on Sunday, though?" Pally added, recalling how most party venues looked like the aftermath of a war-torn city.

"Aye, it was a bit," Aileen laughed. "Luckily, Mam wasn't hame 'til Monday evening, so I had plenty of time to get it ship-shape," she smiled.

"Not home until Monday?" Alan asked, looking directly at Pally and Donny.

"Naw, she'd gone for a pampering weekend with one of her pals to that poncy Health Club near Loch Lomond." Alan still stared at his two buddies.

"Anyway, guys, I came over to ask if any of you knew anything about these…" and she reached into the bag she was carrying and pulled out a T-shirt and a wig of long brown hair. That almost did for Donny, he was fit to burst. Alan realised now that he'd been had.

"And where were they found?" he asked Aileen, although he knew the answer.

"In Mam's bed, the T-shirt had been screwed up in a ball, and the wig was on that with some pillows below to make it look like someone was sleeping there, I think, but it's all a bit odd. The thing is, it was obvious someone had been sleeping on the other side of the bed, and the dirty dug used the loo and ne'er flushed it."

Alan blushed before saying, "What's on the T-shirt?" as he spied some sort of slogan.

"Villans Victorious!" she said, opening it out. "I have no idea what that's about."

"Villans Victorious?" said Alan, staring at Pally, who was a fanatical supporter of Aston Villa Football Club, whose nickname just happened to be 'The Villans'.

Alan still stared at Pally. "But you've got no clues as to who was in the bed?" he continued.

"No, they must have just got up, used the toilet and gone, but anyway, I'm just trying to find the owner of these so that I can give them back."

"Ok, well, good luck, but thanks again for a great party!" Pally added.

"Nae worries, will you be at Malkie's next Friday?" she asked all of them.

"Dist the sun rise, Aileen?" asked Donny.

She laughed and said that she would probably see them there. As she moved on to another table, Pally and Donny lost it entirely while Alan just stared at them, trying to bite his tongue for a good ten seconds before saying…

"You cunts!"

They were still helpless with laughter as he continued, "You fucking pair of card-carrying cunts… You are two cheeks of the same fucking arse!"

He let them enjoy their moment and did see the funny side, sitting there half-smiling and shaking his head more at how they had managed to dupe him so effectively.

"A Caledonian cretin and a Bhangra Brummie boy… fucking twin twats!" He puffed out his cheeks, accepted that no real damage had been done and laughed at himself as well as laughing with them.

They looked at him, barely able to control themselves. Alan drew a finger across his throat and sneeringly said, "You were my best friends, but you are dead to me now…" trying to say it in an Italian Mafia accent…and then they all laughed again.

"Mate, you were so out of it we couldn't resist," Pally said, still laughing.

"Where did you get the wig?" Alan asked.

"In a joke shop ages ago, I was going to wear it later at the party just for a laugh, but then there was the glorious opportunity to set you up," Pally added.

"'Cos, you were so blutered," Donny said between bouts of uncontrollable laughter.

"Cunts!" It was the only viable response.

When the pair of them settled down, Pally told him the truth.

"Mate, you missed a real trick at the party. The two girls you were talking to both took you upstairs for a threesome."

Alan shook his head in disbelief.

"Honest Alan, it's true. You were snogging the pair of them in the kitchen, and then all three of you went upstairs. No wonder, really. Think of their bragging rights, both shagging the player of the season! Then Anna and Iona came back down ten minutes later, saying that you fell asleep as soon as your head hit the pillow. Buddy, they were sorely disappointed in you!"

Pally could see the realisation on Alan's face, but continued.

"That's when me and Donny hatched our little plan!"

"So where did the love bite come from and the lipstick message on my thigh?" Alan asked, staring at them.

After a pregnant pause, Donny smiled and showed his teeth.

"Biting you was ene thing but fhat lipstick message, ken?" Donny was confused.

"All the other marks on your body must have come from the rugby match," Pally added. Alan didn't elaborate but realised only the girls would have had lipstick on them.

"Fhat a stonker, eh, pal?" Donny added, chinking his glass of beer with Pally before Pally went to retrieve his stuff from Aileen.

"I'm going to need a tetanus jab now!" Alan said, feeling the bite marks and shaking his head.

Alan now knew that the 'A+Ixx" made sense. He must have gotten naked with the girls and then fallen asleep, allowing them to leave their mark.

He became great long-term friends with Donny and Palvinder and made regular contact with both of them after they all left Glasgow.

He was overjoyed to hear that Donny and Aileen became an item, and he attended their wedding in the *'wilds of Aberdeenshire'* in 1996. Donny still called him 'Ken'.

Some years later, he was devastated to hear that Palvinder had been stabbed to death in a racist attack in London. He recalled the prank that Donny and Pally played on him at Uni, and he laughed through the tears.

11
What's Love Got to Do With It?

October 1988 – May 1989

Alan's sexual education developed all through the winter of 1988 into the New Year and up to the early Spring of 1989, mostly at the hands of Charles 'Corby' Corbiere. They usually met once every two or three weeks at Corby's insistence – *'To maintain the excitement and anticipation'*. No new experience was ever rushed, and the older man was determined that Alan would always remember with exhilaration and fondness when he (Alan) indulged in a specific sexual act for the first time. One such instance took place in February as the new semester started.

After a number of drinks and a game of chess, Corby took Alan by the hand and led him to his bedroom. They indulged in their usual foreplay of stripping each other, long embraces, kissing, fondling and general building of pleasure. Corby took some strawberry-flavoured lube and stroked his own anus with it. He had Alan lying on his back a little way down the bed, and Corby straddled him on his chest, facing Alan's feet.

"You are going to rim me now. I'm unequivocally sure you are ready for anything I can throw at you."

Alan was pleased that his sexual mentor had so much faith in him and emboldened by the alcohol, grabbed Corby's thighs and steered Corby's arse towards his mouth. "Pull my cheeks apart as much as you can and let me feel that beautiful tongue on me and in me."

Alan tentatively poked his tongue towards the elder man's anal orifice while parting his cheeks with his hands. He tasted the strawberry lube, and when he heard Corby sigh with pleasure, he threw himself into the mission before him. It was not an onerous one as Corby was always immaculately clean and well-perfumed with expensive aftershave. Corby often moaned with delight and was pleasantly surprised when his young student started licking his perineum while slipping a finger into his (Corby's) anus.

"Oh yes, you are my gold-star pupil", Corby said in encouragement (on quite a regular basis).

After a good fifteen minutes, Corby moved away from Alan's mouth and straddled him further down. He asked Alan to pass him the normal lube and squeeze a large glob of it onto his hands. He then smothered Alan's semi-erect penis, bringing it to full attention.

"Time for a reward, my boy", and with another squirt of lube on his fingers, which he then smeared on his own arsehole, he shifted onto Alan's cock and slowly impaled himself on it with a groan of pleasure as it penetrated him.

"No need for condoms. I am regularly tested, and I trust you haven't fucked anyone of late?" Corby said and he rode Alan with purpose, not waiting for an answer. He caressed Alan's testicles as he did so. After a short while, Alan held on to Corby's thighs, and Corby knew Alan was about to orgasm when the younger man's hands and fingers tensed, gripping his thighs tightly. Alan climaxed with a loud grunt, shooting his semen into Corby's slippery anal cavity.

"Oooh yes… unload it all into me, breed me, you wicked boy," Corby sighed, slowing his riding to milk the last few drops and massaging Alan's testicles at the same time. He could feel Alan's cock wilting and then quickly lifted himself up and backed up again to Alan's face.

"Now, clean up the mess you've made, dear boy."

Alan was surprised but really had no choice as Corby's rear end, awash with semen, was now firmly planted on his mouth, with Corby himself pulling his own arse cheeks apart. Corby again groaned with the ecstasy of having his arsehole rimmed by his enthusiastic apprentice. Alan was just lost in the bliss of giving pleasure that he was oblivious to how distasteful it might appear to anyone not fully involved in their mutual desire to please one another. Corby eventually moved away and lay down next to Alan, turning toward him to kiss him deeply.

"I desperately need you to take my seed in your mouth, my boy, to taste all of me. You will do that for me, won't you? I just know that you are going to love having my gift."

Alan was too drunk to object, not just through alcohol but by the whole licentious experience. He sat up, then turned to kiss Corby. As he moved down the older man's body, forgetting how to increase the anticipation by doing it slowly, he held Corby's shaft and said,

"I cannot wait. Empty yourself into my mouth."

Corby breathed deeply and waited for that first oral contact…and then the angry head of his cock was engulfed. Alan's tongue initially swirled around the crown, but he seemed to be in a hurry. Alan had made up his mind that his mentor had asked him to accept his semen orally, so he was not going to disappoint him. His head bobbed up and down on the helmet while his hands massaged the swollen shaft. He knew he was having a big effect as Corby started to thrash about on the bed, culminating in the older man cupping the back of Alan's head and then grasping roughly at his hair prior to flooding his mouth with his salty cum.

"Don't swallow or spit," was the groaned command, "keep it in your mouth and bring it to me," then, with a loud exclamation, he let loose several waves of hot spunk.

Alan thought it would never stop and had to let the overflow seep out of the side of his mouth as he continued to slowly stroke the softening stem. He then sat up with a mouthful of sperm.

"That was marvellous, dear boy," Colby said, breathing quite heavily, "bring it to me and drop it into my mouth, it may be winter outside, but this is the best snowball that there is!" And he laughed.

Alan moved up towards Corby's face and leaned down towards the expectant opening to let the entire spend dribble into Colby's waiting orifice. He watched Colby toss it about and saw his tongue almost wiping all of his teeth and gums with it before he put his hands on Alan's face to pull him back for a kiss to play and share the semen. When both had swallowed it all, Corby said that this session was the best yet.

Alan was allowed to sleep with him that night, and they slept soundly with Alan cradled in Corby's arms – "You've done so well, my boy. I am very proud of you."

Over the next three months, Corby fully initiated Alan into many aspects of sexual activity, including such deviations as BDSM, toys, fetish wear and cross-dressing. He introduced him to sniffing poppers – a recreational drug of sorts popular in the gay community to relax the smooth muscles in the body, specifically the sphincter. Alan learned how to be a willing 'sub' to Corby's domination.

The older man tenderly broke him in anally while Alan was tethered to a purpose-built frame. And occasionally, the young man was also allowed to sodomise his "Dom" to experience what it was like to be a 'top' rather than a 'bottom'. Corby explained that his personal preference was to be versatile so that he got the best of both worlds; he added that a *'queer'* friend of his always said that he preferred to be the train rather than the tunnel!

The ad-hoc chess sessions were now just a front, and the only pawn that was ever moved was Alan. Play sessions were curtailed for the exam period as they would be far too busy, but Corby promised Alan that he was ready for something special, so special that he would remember it for the rest of his life. Alan wondered what it could be, as Corby had already introduced him to so many incredible experiences, and the more they enjoyed each other, the more devoted Alan was.

Their rendezvous was to be on the last Thursday of the college year. Corby knew that the final weekend was always full of parties, and he didn't want his subordinate to be otherwise engaged or maybe undecided as to where he would be for these last few days at Uni in this first year.

"You will love every moment, dear boy," Corby assured Alan on their penultimate coming together the week before. "You have put your trust in me, and I just know that you understand that I would never do you any harm. Be here at 7.30 pm on Thursday next week, oh and save up all of your gentleman juice, no sex or masturbating or if you do, no climax!"

It wasn't an unusual request as Corby loved to indulge in watching and enjoying the huge amount of semen Alan would release when 'forced' to save it up. He often filmed these orgasms and was thrilled not just by the amount but also by the smell and taste.

"Now away with you, you are filling a large space in my bed that I need to spread out in," before smacking his arse in a playful manner. Alan knew when to take his cue and leave. Corby was quirky and jokey, but many a true word was spoken in jest.

When the 'special evening' arrived, Alan reached Corby's apartment on the dot as usual. It had been a warm day, and Corby greeted him at the door in just a scanty pair of shorts.

"Good evening, Mr McCann, you're on time as usual," Corby said, hugging him closely before holding Alan's face to fervently kiss him. He led him into the master bedroom.

"This is going to be sublime," he said, kissing him again.

"You know I have a penchant for you dressing, so please wear these…" Corby pointed to the black crotchless leather chaps and thong lying on the bed.

"When you're dressed, sit on the bed, and I'll be back shortly."

It was an instruction that required no questions or further information. Alan was well-trained in subordination and just replied, "Yes, sir."

He stripped and dressed as required. He was aroused as his semi-erect penis would testify, although there was a modicum of uncertainty that added a nervous excitement to the whole proceedings. He sat on the bed to ponder how the evening would pan out. Corby came back to the room ten minutes later.

"Oh yes, dear boy, you will definitely do!" Corby said and then told Alan to stand up. He then gave him some poppers to sniff with the instruction, "Breathe deeply, dear boy – breathe deeply."

Corby then told him to turn around so that he was facing the bed. Corby stood directly behind him and stroked Alan's smooth back before moving his hands around to Alan's front and then caressing his stomach and moving down to his thong-clad cock. Alan threw his head back to enjoy the sensations as Corby kissed his neck sensuously.

"You truly are a beautiful specimen of humankind, my boy," Corby said as he then took Alan's hands and cuffed his wrists behind his back in a pair of fluffy handcuffs.

"Turn around," Corby commanded, and Alan looked intently at Corby as he did so.

Corby pulled his face close to his and kissed him again.

"Sit down on the bed here," Corby said, pushing him backwards so that sitting was unavoidable.

"Close your eyes," Alan obeyed, and a few seconds later, a leather hood was pulled over his head, pulled tight and tied at the back. It covered everything except his mouth and nose. He was now deprived of sight, and he suddenly became very concerned. The whole outfit was completed with a leather dog collar and lead.

Corby sensed Alan's disquiet. He moved closely to his ear and whispered, "It's all ok, relax, you are mine. Remember, there are special rules, and you will now be silent unless you are asked questions, yes?"

"Yes, sir," was the immediate and appropriate response.

He then sensed Corby standing in front of him and then felt the older man's hot, hard cock pushing into his mouth. He knew what to do with that and immediately relaxed as the shaft moved gently backwards and forwards a few times before being withdrawn completely. He felt Corby move away and then heard him leave. Alan heard movement again coming from the hall, and there was undoubtedly more than one person entering the room.

"Oh, he is beautiful. This one is the best for a long time," an unfamiliar voice said.

"Mmm, has he been this year's plaything since September?" another voice said.

"October," Corby said, correcting the other man, "he was a complete virgin and needed time."

Alan was dumbstruck. It was beginning to dawn on him that this 'special evening' was going to involve more than Corby. Three others, to be precise, no names - they used trees as their code names. Mr Oak, Mr Elm and Mr Ash. Corby introduced them to Alan and added that they had plenty of wood to satisfy him, the others laughed.

"Let's see what he's made of!" said Mr Elm, who asked Alan to stand up. Alan waited for Corby to give him the command, and he then responded immediately.

"Oh yes…one of the best, Charles – can I?" the voice asked. Alan then heard Corby speak.

"My dear friends, he is ours for the whole evening. My rules are the same as they are every year. You treat my subordinates with respect. He is here for your complete pleasure, but you will not inflict any pain on him, and you will all abide by my rules as usual. You all agree?"

The three guests all agreed.

"You all swear that you are disease and drug-free?" he waited for their individual response. They all confirmed that they were and had recently been tested.

"Then I see no reason why we shouldn't play bareback," Corby said.

"Your boys get taller every year, Charles, but they also get more muscular, and he is so sexy in that outfit!" exclaimed Mr Oak, who then started to stroke Alan before pulling his thong to one side to expose Alan's penis and testicles. The 'assailant' grabbed the hardening cock and started stroking it slowly.

"He is fully broken in?" asked Mr Ash.

"Yes, of course, but be gentle. He is a tight fit, ok?" Corby said.

Alan now knew he was just Corby's piece of meat and not the lover he hoped for. He was not so much frightened for his safety, given Corby's words, but was more crushed by the fact that his love for Corby appeared to mean very little in the realms of monogamy. Here he was trussed up like a Christmas turkey, available for others to use him. And use him they did…

First, they had him on his knees, and Alan performed oral sex on each of them for five minutes per person. His head was spinning, but he was excited by the varying sizes of cocks he serviced. He enjoyed the welcoming groans and sighs of pleasure and commentary provided by those waiting their turn, especially when Corby told them how good he was at fellatio. Alan could imagine the men encircling him wanking themselves to keep hard.

"I think we should spit-roast him now," Corby said, undoing the cuffs, and they made him crawl on the bed. He was told to get on all fours and felt someone kneel in front of him.

Something was put to his nose, and he was told to sniff deeply. A large penis was then thrust into his mouth as the owner held his head to assist his face-fucking. One of the others got behind him and smeared a copious amount of cold lube to his arsehole before he then felt his anus being probed, at first with a finger, then two fingers, before they were removed and the real weapon slowly but methodically penetrated him. As his orifice relaxed, the perpetrator slowly fucked him. Further instructions came from Corby, and it was clear that he was filming the whole occasion.

As he was being rocked backwards and forwards by his two 'assailants', he heard Corby tell them to stop to allow him (Corby) and the other guy to have their turn. He knew it was Corby who was buggering him as his mentor spoke gently to him to enjoy what was happening. A smaller penis was poked into his mouth, but the owner was much more frantic in his prodding than the last one, and it wasn't long before he heard the man grunt that he was going to cum. Alan tensed as the hot fluid squirted into his mouth. He tried to swallow quickly, but some of it escaped and dribbled out, especially as the man was still thrusting. Corby withdrew, and someone else replaced him; he also had a smaller dick, and it was a lot more manageable. His mouth was fully engaged again, and this was Corby as he complimented Alan on his oral skills.

And this assault continued for what seemed like hours and he was made to take cocks in his mouth and arse and, of course, their semen when it was fired at him and in him. He was kissed often by all of the men, some of them passionate, some of them sloppy, and one of them not very good at all. Finally, Corby suggested a group ejaculation over Alan "for those that still had any jizz left," and he laughed.

They made Alan kneel, and he could feel himself being encircled by the four men. Only two managed it, but by that time, he was past caring. Corby suggested one final act as a reward for his subordinate.

"Who wants his juice? It's a lot first time, thick as rope, and quite tasty," Corby said to his excited friends. Two of them volunteered, and they stood Alan up and kneeled in front of him before both mouths descended on his semi-erect penis. Corby stood behind him and brought his right hand around to start wanking him to full attention. He persisted until Alan started to shake and, with a deep breath, tensed and climaxed over the men's faces and into their mouths.

Alan was thoroughly used and abused, and by the time they had finished with him, he was sore and exhausted. He was left to sit on the bed as Corby's guests departed, and he was emotionally numb. As Alan heard the last one leave Corby then came back and was full of praise for being *the best subordinate ever.*

"You were superb, Darling..." and as he pulled off the hood, he embraced him and kissed him ardently, "Now strip off and have a good long shower to wash off their nasty ministrations. You will be staying with me tonight."

When he returned to Corby's bed, he was embraced again and showered with compliments in between being told that he was effectively this year's model, but that was now at an end. Sensing Alan's heartfelt disappointment, Corby said.

"Don't be sad. This is something I do each year because I don't want to become too emotionally involved with anyone," he paused, "although you, my dear boy, have been very close to being a keeper". He kissed Alan again, "Please understand that you're very young and our age difference would eventually see you despise and detest me if this became anything more than what it is."

"And what is it?" Alan asked, trying to hold back the tears. Corby replied in an instant.

"Why, it's been momentous fun as it should be, and you have learned a huge amount about relationships, love, lust, passion, oh and chess, I hope."

"But…" Alan was stopped immediately when Corby put his hand up as a gesture to discontinue his protest.

"No buts. In the next few days, you will feel sad, but don't dwell on that. Think of all of the positives."

Alan was only minimally consoled by Corby's words, but deep down, he knew he would have to accept that this would be the last time. He was heartbroken.

He spent the next three years knuckling down to studying. He continued with his rugby but gave up chess. Alan still idolised Charles Oliver Corbiere but accepted his mentor's rules and was happy that the object of his affection still acknowledged him on the occasions that they were ever at the same social events.

Alan never came '*out*' but did visit male-only saunas on rare occasions to satisfy his homosexual urges.

12
Love is a Battlefield

1988/90

Julia and Gerry's love affair blossomed from their very own *"summer of lurve,"* and within a couple of months, she invited him home to meet her parents. Her dad didn't like him, but she expected that. Her mum was lukewarm but just wanted to make sure Julia was happy. Julia's parents concluded that he was too much of a "Flash Harry," but, in time-honoured fashion, the more they railed against him, the more she was pushed into his arms and his bed.

Gerry swept Julia off her feet. He was often very kind, generous, and spontaneous, surprising her with gifts of flowers and jewellery. She was caught up in his fast-lane lifestyle with access to fancy dinners and parties, outings to sporting events paid for by corporate sponsors and, inevitably, rubbing shoulders with dignitaries, business people and the occasional celebrity.

At Christmas, he arranged for a surprise weekend in Paris, where, with cliché upon cliché, he proposed. Julia agreed without hesitation and could hardly wait to phone her parents with the news. She was sorely disappointed with their reaction and saw the inquisition of *'aren't you a bit young?'* as a slur on her maturity. In private, her dad was seething but kept it to himself. When the couple returned from Paris, Gerry was invited to dinner to "celebrate" with her parents. It was as near to an engagement party as they were going to get, even if Julia had hoped for something more lavish. Gerry played it down, saying that it just wasn't his thing.

The glamorous lifestyle continued, although he was away a lot of the time during the week. At weekends, they lived to the max, burning the candle at both ends to indulge in sex, drinking, and rock and roll. Her parents found solace in the fact that drugs were not on the agenda. They were happy that she lived with them when he was away and had to accept that she stayed at his poky little flat when he returned.

Julia kept herself busy with her job at Joey Porter's Bookmakers' office. The pay was okay, the people were nice, and it killed time between each exciting weekend. University was canned - she was too busy enjoying life to worry about further education.

Gerry had told her that when they got married, she could take on the administration of his new business venture and could leave Porter's 'sweatshop'. Julia felt she should be excited but there were nagging doubts, he never ventured much detail. After one of his trips away, he picked her up at her home early on Friday evening. As Julia got in the car, he could see she was beaming.

"You look pleased with yourself," he said with a slight frown. "Have you been promoted in that dingy betting office?"

"Better than that," she said.

"You've left?" he guessed, in a disturbingly positive manner.

"No. Don't be silly, I like it there. The people are nice." She was rather scornful of his comment.

"I have passed my driving test!" and she did a little sitting down dance in his car.

"Isn't that great?" she said, hoping he would be just as proud and delighted as she was.

"Oh, okay. Well done, but you never told me you were even learning to drive!" he said as though he didn't think it was the greatest news he'd ever heard.

"I wanted to surprise you, and now I'll be able to drive you to places, and you can have a drink instead of you driving all the time or us using expensive cabs." She was rightly proud of herself.

"What are you going to drive?" he questioned, although he knew what was coming.

"Well, this, of course. Ronnie the Range Rover!" She patted the dashboard as though the car was a friendly pet, but she was a bit put out that he wasn't very enthusiastic.

"You are joking, aren't you? And what's with the name Ronnie?" he sneered.

"No, I'm not joking. Why do you say that, and what's wrong with naming the car?" She was quite confused.

"Julia, you're not eight years old that you have to give a name to something, especially a car. You are not driving this!" He was quite terse.

"Why not? We'll be sharing everything when we're married, won't we?" She was starting to get upset.

"Maybe so but you're not driving this car. That's the end of the conversation!" He was abruptly dismissive, and although she was put out, she knew not to pursue the point.

"C'mon, let's get back to the flat. I've had a tiring week, and I just need a good soak in the bath."

Gerry knew he'd upset her and started some idle chit-chat, asking how everyone was without really giving a toss. She picked up on the apathy in his voice and kept the conversation brief. When they got back to the flat, he said he was too tired to go out, but he had bought a couple of microwave dinners, which would have to do.

Julia was very disappointed. She desperately looked forward to the weekends, especially to see him but also to let her hair down. His indifference to her achievement was, to her mind, a spiteful snub.

Gerry had a bath and a short snooze for ten minutes before they had their nuked dinners on their laps with a couple of glasses of wine. They had an early night but any thoughts she had of the usual Friday night fuck would have to wait as he fobbed her off, saying that he was too exhausted and too stressed. She wanted to understand this change in his usual temperament but could see that her efforts to help him were in vain.

In the morning, he was back to his usual self and brought her some coffee and toast in bed.

"Look, I am very pleased for you that you have passed your test and I'm sorry if I was a bit tetchy last night. I've got a lot on my mind at the moment," he offered as some sort of apology.

"Okay, I just thought it would be nice if I drove you around for a change." She was still perceptibly upset.

"Yes, of course. Tell you what, nearer the time of setting up the business, we'll get you a little car. There, a *company* car, no less. How about that?"

"Can I choose what sort?" she perked up a bit.

"Yes, you can - and name it what you like. Later, I'll put you down as a named driver on the Range Rover insurance."

"Ronnie?"

"Yes," he tutted, "Ronnie, but not just now because it would be astronomical as you've only just passed your test, okay?" It seemed logical but she made up her mind to do some homework on that.

Julia and Gerry got married a few months later. He insisted on a registry office with less than twenty people in attendance – he just didn't want a fuss. The one real bonus was that he had managed to rent the luxury Marina apartment from Joey Porter, so Julia was confident that he was doing okay financially to be able to afford it.

However, even in the early part of their marriage, he liked to be in control of her movements. Julia had gone full-time at the Bookmakers and quickly became an integral part of the management team. When Gerry wasn't working away, he would always take her to work and be there dead on five o'clock to pick her up. At first, she thought about how protective he was of her. Little by little, though, it started to grate, and his constant suffocation was increasingly worrying. The promised new business venture was put on hold as he said he needed more capital to get it off the ground. Her income seemed to be more important than ever.

It wasn't long before Gerry started to badger her about having children. She initially put him off, saying that their current lifestyle would drastically change but, anyway, what was the rush? She was still only eighteen and he was hardly an old man, even at thirty-two. Julia talked him into getting a kitten to hopefully focus his attention away from the patter of tiny feet - tiny paws worked for a short while. The affectionate little feline was called Abbi - Abbi the Tabby, and they both took to its funny little ways of playing with toy mice and ping-pong balls. Gerry wasn't happy with its total lack of respect for the furniture but tolerated it because Julia was happy.

After a month, the pestering for children recommenced and it was relentless, with his temperament becoming ever more erratic. Three months into their marriage, they attended an event at a local hotel. Gerry was never slow to mingle, as he would see this as a glorious opportunity to stalk potential clients. At similar occasions, he would often leave Julia in the capable hands of unwitting chaperones.

This event in particular saw him disappear for quite a while and she decided to get herself a drink. To her very pleasant surprise, she bumped into a guy she hadn't seen in almost a year – Alan McCann, the boy who had rescued her from the evil clutches of the school bully. He had matured greatly in his short time away at university and she saw, probably for the first time, that he really was a handsome chap. They made the usual small talk about his studies at Glasgow University, and she felt rather embarrassed that she presented herself as just a humble office clerk. Alan was rather surprised to hear that but added that she was still young and there were several routes back into further education.

Out of nowhere, Gerry appeared and did not look best pleased. Julia started the formalities of introductions.

"Hey, you're back. Alan, this is my husband, Gerry."

Alan smiled and extended his hand as a gesture to shake Gerry's hand.

"Gerry, this is an old school–"

"I don't give a fuck who he is. Why are you not talking with Karen?" Gerry said, grabbing her by the arm, digging his fingernails into her flesh and steering her away. Julia was too shocked to say anything, as she had never seen him like this.

"Come on, we're going home," he growled.

"But it's only ten o'clock!" she protested.

"Don't *but* me, get your coat, we are leaving!" he said through gritted teeth. She decided this wasn't the place to cause a scene.

They said nothing in the cab home and Gerry was quite rude to the taxi driver when he paid and got out, so much so that she apologised for his behaviour to the young guy.

"It's okay, I've had him in my cab before and, sorry for the language, but he's an ignorant cunt!" Julia was astounded at his profanity but was more confused and concerned about Gerry's unprecedented behaviour. On entering the apartment, he flew into a rage, accusing her of flirting with Alan and then remonstrating with her about apologising to the "scumbag" taxi driver.

"Are you drunk? You're behaving like a Timmy Tantrum!" she said, getting rather angry herself.

That was the last straw. He swiftly turned and came at her, his chest heaving with anger. He harshly grabbed her by the throat. Julia was almost paralysed with terror.

"Don't you ever talk to me like that again!" He was almost spitting each word at her, "I catch you chatting up some guy and you accuse me of having a tantrum? You fucking bitch…" and then he pushed her away, leaving her to hold her throat, gasping for breath. In a state of shock, she stumbled off to the toilet and locked the door.

Half an hour later, Gerry knocked on the bathroom door, full of apologies and excuses about why he was angry. Seemingly, it was all to do with a deal that hadn't gone to plan and that he'd been cheated out of a lot of money by someone at the party. He added that it was also the frustration of her unwillingness to have children just yet that he said had been too much for him. He swore he would never do that again and begged and pleaded with her to forgive him. Although Julia was still confused and upset, there was something in his tone that made her believe him. He heard the key turn in the lock, and she opened the door. He was slumped on the floor and was crying with his head in his hands.

Julia wasn't quite in the mood to forgive him and just told him that she was going to bed. He got up and followed her into the room, still pleading for forgiveness. He kept emphasising that she would know that this was totally out of character, it was just down to stress. She continued to undress and was down to her underwear when he came up and stood behind her. He pleaded with her again and held her to him, kissing her neck and shoulders. His face was still wet with tears, but as he pressed into her, she could feel that he was fully erect. He then cupped both her breasts before slipping one hand down and into her knickers to massage her pussy.

He held her firmly and she, too, became aroused. Her nipples hardened, and his fingers were wet with her own essence. Her mood changed as he played with her, working her body like the expert he was, knowing exactly what to touch.

"I want you so much," he said and bent her over the bed. She wanted to make love, to feel like he was truly sorry for what he'd done. All he wanted was to fuck her.

Her request to cuddle and make love fell on deaf ears as he dropped his trousers and pants and, pulling her knickers down, roughly penetrated her. All their previous "quickie" sexual encounters were usually urgent but passionate. It was all she'd known up to this point but now he was like some frenzied animal. He grabbed her hair and pulled it hard. She heard him grunt every time he pushed into her with short jabbing strokes. He was mumbling incoherently, but often she would hear him say, "Take it, you slut", or "bitch", or "common little slag". The last one he'd repeat over and over. Then, when it seemed like he was going to orgasm, he pulled out of her and told her to sit on the floor in front of him. He manually brought himself to climax as he harshly held her hair to keep her head in place.

"If you don't want to get pregnant, you'll take my cum over your face," and he shot his hot, salty jizz into her hair, over her face and into her mouth. Again, she was shocked, as he had never forced the issue like this before. He still appeared to be angry when he told her to clean herself up because she looked like a common whore.

She barely slept that night, wondering who this man was who was sleeping next to her like an innocent child. At some point, she drifted off to sleep and was awakened in the morning with, "Hey, come on, Miss Dozy, I've made us breakfast."

She came to her senses slowly and gradually, last night's events came flooding back. And yet here was the calm, faithful Gerry, being nice and attentive.

Over breakfast, he profusely apologised again, blaming his wrath on a deal that was scuppered by a so-called friend who had cost him a substantial amount of money. The amount? She was told that she didn't need to know. A more pressing concern was regarding his repeated frustration at not yet becoming a father. He told her that he was happy to give up the fast lane for a speedy road into parenthood. Julia didn't want to annoy him while he looked to be back to normal, and she said she'd have a good think about it.

"Julia, I won't nag you, but I'd like us to have kids while I'm fit enough to enjoy them." He lied. The pressure was unrelenting, and their social activities diminished as he knew this was Julia's prime reason for her reluctance. She realised this was his main tactic and it just wore her down. Finally, she succumbed and told Gerry that her supply of pills was finished; she wouldn't get any more.

He was delighted, and they went to bed to "rejoice." She told him that it was quite unlikely to happen straight away. They really didn't have to change the way they made love or the frequency; it would all happen naturally. Julia was wasting her breath, the new routine was to fuck with very little foreplay, at least once a day when he was home. Sex was a regimented chore - a means to an end.

Nearly three months passed with no result, and she could see that he was getting more and more exasperated. One Friday, after a week away, Gerry picked her up from her parents' home as usual. He rarely went in because he knew he wasn't particularly welcome. When she got in the car to go home, he was quite surly. She asked him if he was okay and he grunted. Julia knew when to keep quiet. They got indoors and she asked him again if he was all right.

"I'm just frustrated that you're not pregnant yet," he scowled at her. She could sense there was more to come.

"I mean, I've pumped gallons of sperm into you and nothing," he was getting more agitated as he spoke. She laughed at his exaggerated analogy of why she should be pregnant, it was a bad move.

"Oh, you think it's funny, do you?" He was about to snap like he had before. Julia said nothing.

"Do you know why you're not pregnant?" he said, raising his voice.

"Look, Gerry, I'm sure it will happen in its own good time. We're just putting pressure on ourselves. Why not just make love like we used to and relax?" He wasn't listening and asked her again.

"Do– you– know– why– you're– not– pregnant?" he said through gritted teeth, with an emphasis on each word.

"No," she said, and she was getting angry with this interrogation. "Perhaps you're firing blanks!"

That was all the trigger he needed, and he slapped her hard across the face, her head jolted to the side with the force of it. As she held her cheek, she could see the anger in his eyes. Julia now feared for her safety. Gerry then reached into the large drawer in the kitchen where she stored her baking ingredients and pulled out a small, unmarked tin. He took the lid off, pulled out the contents and threw them at her quickly, followed by the tin itself, which hit her in the face, cutting her near her left eye. The pain was immediate.

"You fucking deceitful bitch, you never came off the pill, did you? DID YOU???" He was incandescent with rage now. Julia was still holding her face when he grabbed her by the hair and dragged her into the bedroom. She reached up to his hands, but he threw her to the floor and kicked her in the thigh.

"Strip off, you useless slag," he ordered and stood in front of her. Unsteadily, she stood up, and while she was crying, she slowly stripped off and kept saying how sorry she was. She pleaded and begged as she wept because she just wasn't ready and told him so.

"If you can bleed, you can give birth. Now bend over!" Her pleas for him not to hurt her went unheard as he smacked her hard on the buttocks, and with every slap, he shouted insults at her.

He must have hit her a dozen times before he quickly stripped, and then he fucked her. It was rough, but thankfully, he came quickly. He withdrew and smacked her hard again, leaving her to cry, curled up on the bed. Gerry then made her watch as he popped all the pills from their blister packs and flushed them down the toilet.

"From now on, we're going to fuck twice a day!" he snarled. "Now, get my dinner ready!" He was seething but left her there.

She said nothing but got dressed and went to prepare the food. He was not apologetic this time, and she blamed herself for her duplicity. Julia quickly grew to resent the coldness of his bi-daily injection of seed, and as inconspicuously as possible, she would quickly go to the toilet to try to wash it out of herself. She succeeded for the first month, much to his continued frustration and anger, and she found herself on the end of a tirade of insults when it was obvious that she hadn't conceived. Her self-esteem sank to the point where she was barely able to function at work. She rarely visited her parents, making excuses and preferring to talk to them on the phone.

In the second month, her period was late. She hoped against hope that that was all it was, but to no avail. A week went by, and she just knew. Gerry kept asking her as he had the dates clearly marked on the calendar, and in the end, he brought home a pregnancy testing kit. She did it alone and when the result was confirmed, she cried. She told him that it was through happiness, but she lied. Of course, he was overjoyed, not just because it could be a son and heir to carry on his name, but it was also another level of control over her.

During the pregnancy, their relationship became more consistent, and not in a good way for Julia. When she wasn't at work, she was expected to stay at home all the time with only a few excursions to see her parents. This was the pre-Internet era, and mobile phones were the privilege of stockbrokers who could afford to use those house bricks with aerials. Gerry did all the food shopping and, of course, she wouldn't be allowed to have an alcoholic drink.

Her life was not her own anymore, made worse by the fact that he wasn't away as much as he was previously. Regrettably, his cruelty was ever-present. Her mother realised what was going on, although Julia did not admit to the full extent of his control and passed it off as him being overly cautious with her condition.

Sex for her now was non-existent, except for having to give him a blow job whenever he was home. She found the whole act distasteful in more ways than one.

Gerry allowed her mother to take her for her regular hospital check-ups and at thirty-six weeks, she was admitted to the hospital with the potentially dangerous condition of pre-eclampsia. The doctor explained that it would enable medical staff to carefully monitor her symptoms of high blood pressure and excess protein in her urine. It was certainly a concern, but she felt so much safer away from her husband.

When he learned of her confinement, he came to visit her. Of course, to the medical staff, he was charm personified. However, when he got her to himself, he flung all sorts of allegations at her about manufacturing this to get away from him. As usual, she said nothing to avoid a scene but knew it was the stress she was under, living with this overbearing bully that caused her to be there in the first place. A nurse came in to do one of her checks and could see that all was not well and made a comment about the monitors showing quite high readings and suggested to Gerry that it might be a good idea to let his wife rest. She could see that caused some irritation but, thankfully, he didn't press the matter and, kissing Julia on the forehead, said, "Good Night," and left.

His subsequent visits were deliberately irregular, citing work issues as an excuse. Thankfully, her mother came on a daily basis, bringing "supplies", as she called them, which consisted of magazines, books, and a little contraband such as chocolate.

The medical staff decided to keep her until she got to full term, and at forty weeks, she was induced. Only her mother was present at the birth of a gorgeous baby girl weighing in at 8 pounds, 2 ounces. Gerry came in the next day with flowers for Julia and a cute teddy bear for the baby, who was to be called Kirstie after his Scottish Grandmother. Julia had no say in the matter.

Mother and baby were kept in for a few more days to ensure there were no after-effects from the birth or the pre-eclampsia, and she eventually accepted that she had to go home to Gerry. She hoped now that, as he had the child he longed for, he would go back to how he used to be when they first got together.

Her mother took her home to an empty flat and reluctantly left her after Julia insisted that she should go. She looked around for Abbi, but the cat was nowhere to be seen. The litter tray had gone from its usual place in the utility room and so had the food pouches. In her fragile state, she was heartbroken.

He came home late that evening, a bit worse for wear through drink and she was horrified that he could have driven in that condition. He stumbled into the bedroom, and she asked him to be quiet as she had just gotten the baby off to sleep.

"It's my child. I'll see it whenever I want!" he said, turning on the light, which caused little Kirstie to stir. Julia watched him closely. There was no fatherly pride, which he confirmed with a grunt followed by, "You couldn't have been a boy, could you?" as he stared down at the tot, who started to cry.

"You'd better sort your daughter out. What's for dinner?" he said coldly. Julia was annoyed with him.

"What have you got in? I mean, I couldn't even find any cat food, let alone something for our dinner. Where have you been eating since I was in hospital?"

"Cat food? What the fuck are you on about?" Then it dawned on him. "Oh, that thing, I got rid of it. I thought it might be dangerous for the baby." Julia was distraught.

"It was just a kitten. What did you do with it?"

"I took it back to the RSPCA. Now, what are you doing about my dinner?" He appeared to be getting more and more enraged.

"If we don't have anything in, we'll have to go to the supermarket. But you can't drive in your condition, and you still haven't insured me for the Range Rover."

"Oh, fuck you…" was his parting shot as he left the flat. Julia didn't see him again for two days.

The next couple of months saw an uneasy truce between them, but he wasn't interested in the baby. Thankfully, his absences made it easier for her to concentrate on Kirstie. When he was there, he still demanded sex, and she just lay back and let him use her. She made damn sure she hid her pills properly this time.

She realised far too late that he was a "user" of women and a brutal man. The mental and physical pain he caused her was unforgivable and would, no doubt, scar her for life. Regrettably, like so many women, she felt powerless and too frightened to leave him. She had no money of her own and relied on his "generosity" to make up the shortfall from her wages to get all that was required to run the household.

Her mother regularly topped up the housekeeping to keep them afloat, but it was a real struggle. She often told Julia that if she wanted to leave, she and Kirstie could move back home with them. Julia felt that she had to try to turn things around and not admit that her parents were right in the first place.

She told Gerry that she would like to go out for her upcoming birthday and had arranged for her mother to babysit. For once, he appeared to be quite amenable and said he would arrange for dinner at the Waterfront Restaurant that they used to frequent before Kirstie came along. The day duly arrived, and her mum came early afternoon to pick Kirstie up together with all of her paraphernalia, commenting that she should really buy a van to cope with the amount of clothes, equipment, and toys that came with a baby for a one-night sleepover.

Julia had a bath and a long soak before Gerry, who was home unusually early, caught her there. He stared at her with a hateful look in his eyes and shook his head.

"Look at what's happened to you, you fat bitch. You're expecting me to fuck you when you look like that?" She could see the disdain in his eyes. She openly started to weep.

"Your cunt is like a fucking horse's collar and you're a mess. Get yourself in shape if you expect me to fuck you again." With that, he left and didn't return until the following day.

This was now to be the new normal. He made her go back to part-time work with the "sleazy" Joey Porter, and little Kirstie was minded by Granny while she was there.

At the bookmaker's office, Joey and Cheryl were disappointed that she was reducing her hours but accepted that full-time working was difficult to balance with childcare responsibilities. Cheryl mentioned to Joey that she was concerned about the change in Julia since she got married, citing how down and worried she always seemed to be when at work.

It was only a matter of weeks after her birthday before Gerry insisted that they have another child. Julia laughed and then stood up to him. Slowly but angrily, she said, "Do you think I would bring another child into this relationship when you behave like you do? I've realised that I'm living with an absolute monster. This is the real you, a complete and utter cunt, and I've heard people call you a prick, so I guess, legitimately, you can go fuck yourself. I absolutely despise you and I'm leaving you to keep me and Kirstie safe."

It would be to her cost. His facial expression didn't change, and she was shocked when he suddenly punched her full in the face, splitting her lip and knocking her to the floor. As she gathered herself, she slowly got up, dabbing at her mouth and shouted at him.

"You're so brave, aren't you? I fucking hate you!" Julia was enraged and as he went for her again, she slapped him, scratched his face and tried to claw and kick at her assailant. With flailing arms and legs, she landed a few blows, including a kick in the groin, which stalled his attack. As he overcame that pain, he really went for her. Julia was no match for him and her beating was so severe that when she phoned her mother to come and help her look after Kirstie, her mum could barely understand what she was saying. When she arrived, she immediately called the police despite Julia begging her not to. He had already disappeared.

Gerry was summarily arrested the next day and interviewed under caution by two officers at the local police station. He flatly denied beating Julia but refused to give an account of how she had two black eyes, a split lip, a dislocated jaw, and multiple bruises to her face and body. He sneeringly suggested that she had fallen down some stairs when she was drunk. She had, at this time, already refused to press charges and without his confession or hard evidence of him committing the alleged assault, the police were virtually powerless to take it further. The tape of the interview was terminated by one of the officers and the old sergeant, who mainly conducted the interview, said calmly but sternly, "Mr Irvine, please remain seated. I'd like a word."

Gerry was about to say something when the policeman banged his fist hard on the table.

"Unfortunately, we often get cocky, bully boy cunts like you in here who think they're so macho, beating up defenceless women. You may have got away with it this time but you're on our radar."

Gerry shrugged his shoulders and shook his head. "You can't touch me. You've got no evidence. She ain't gonna press charges!"

"I find that quite interesting. Given your earlier statement, why suggest she wouldn't press charges if nothing happened?"

Gerry kept quiet. The police sergeant stared at him and finished up with, "Go on, fuck off, you despicable prick!"

As Gerry neared the door, he felt an almighty slap on the side of his face, causing his head to hit the door frame.

"Oh, mind how you go there, Mr Irvine. The floor looks a bit slippery," said the sergeant from behind.

"A damn good job you weren't at the top of a flight of stairs, don't you think?" Followed up with, "The exit is through there. I do hope we never see you in here again."

Gerry rubbed the side of his head and checked for blood. He turned to the policeman and glowered at him, but it was obvious that the sergeant was goading him and it would not end well.

After being released from hospital, Julia stayed with her parents for a few days so that they could provide care not only for her but more especially for Kirstie. Thankfully, Gerry did not make contact, although Julia's dad was itching to get his hands on him. Mr Fulton adhered to his daughter's wishes to "*let it go.*" She was determined to divorce her spouse and did not want any legal complications regarding retaliatory acts of violence.

13

I Will Survive

August 1999

Just over three weeks after the event, Julia returned to work in the betting office. She tried to cover up the lingering facial damage with heavy makeup, but it was clear to anyone who looked closely enough. All of her friends and co-workers asked how she was after her "accident", and although they suspected otherwise, they kept up the pretence that she had fallen down the stairs, as had been reported by her mother. She kept herself to herself as much as possible and got on with the work. On the Wednesday of that week, Julia was called into the meeting room by Cheryl.

"Come in, Julia, and take a seat. Would you like some coffee?" Cheryl asked.

Julia was nervous. "I'm sorry I was off sick for so long. I…" She found it difficult to speak as her jaw had not yet completely healed.

"Julia, stop it please, you're not in any trouble–" Cheryl was then interrupted by the door opening and in stepped Joey Porter.

"Ah, Joe, you're here. Would you like a coffee?" Cheryl asked.

"I'd love one, thanks. Usual, white, no sugar."

"Joe, I've been making your coffee for the last thirty years. I think I know how you want it."

"Maybe," he replied as he sat down and turned to Julia. "How are you, Julia? I hear you've been under the weather." He focused intently on the damage to her face. Julia gave him a brief look and said nervously that she'd had an accident.

"It was very clumsy of me. I missed my footing at the top of the stairs and—" Joey interrupted her.

"Yes, very nasty. By the way, which stairs did you fall down?" he wondered, still staring at the semi-concealed fading bruises.

"Um, sorry?" she hesitated.

"Which stairs did you fall down?" He sounded rather abrupt.

"Joe!" Cheryl interrupted as she set the coffee down next to him. He stared at her with a look that said, "don't interfere." Julia hesitated.

"It was the stairs outside of our apartment," she stammered, still trying not to catch his eye.

"Wow," he said in a way that was rather patronising. "That's a nasty set of stairs to come a cropper on, if I may say so. You were fortunate that you only came away with the damage you sustained. Why didn't you put your hands out to protect yourself?" he questioned.

"Um… I was carrying some of my little girl's stuff and took the stairs because the lift didn't appear to be working," she offered, but her heart was pounding now, and she knew by the way he was looking at her that he didn't believe her.

"Okay," he said and took a deliberate break in his examination of her testimony like a barrister in court.

"Lovely coffee, Cheryl. You always make a damn fine cup of coffee. Bloody useless at everything else but coffee is your forte," he said, staring at the cup and stirring the contents.

Cheryl laughed in a way that suggested she'd heard that line a million times and added, "You couldn't do without me, you old fraud!"

Julia was surprised at the way she spoke to him. After all, he was the boss. But she watched him nod his head in proper recognition of Cheryl's matter-of-fact statement. He took another sip of his drink and turned back to Julia.

"The stairs outside of your apartment, you said?" He was staring at her again.

"Yes."

"You're sure?"

"Yes."

"It's just that when your mother phoned in to tell of your…" he hesitated, trying to find the right word, "accident, she said you had fallen down the stairs at her house, isn't that right, Cheryl?" He said, tilting his head and narrowing his eyes as though he didn't understand the anomaly.

"Yes, I have the notes here. Judy at reception took the message, and Julia's mother clearly stated that the accident occurred at her house, and she had taken Julia to hospital directly afterwards," Cheryl confirmed. Julia was nonplussed and had to think fast.

"Well, she's got that wrong. She must have been confused."

"Or maybe you are Julia," Joe said. Julia said nothing.

"Cheryl, can you make sure Julia gets all the medical back-up she needs, including more time off if required–"

Julia interrupted, "No, I'm fine. I need to get back to work. There's a lot to catch up on." Joe held his hand up to stop her from speaking.

"I can see speaking is painful for you and I'm sure you do want to get back to work. We need to make sure you're well enough to do that, okay?" He then looked at Cheryl and said, "If you could just leave us for a minute. By the way, there's cakes in the kitchen. It's my birthday." Cheryl nodded, smiled and took her cue to leave the room, asking Julia to pop in and see her before returning to her desk. As Cheryl closed the door, Joe took another sip of his coffee and said to no one, "Damn fine coffee, that." He looked at Julia, who briefly glanced back at him.

"Now, I know I have a bit of a reputation for being a bit of a hard man, but people who work for me are important. And, as Cheryl would hopefully testify, I am as loyal to them as they are to me."

"Yes," she said, her heart pounding at what he might say next.

"I also have a reputation for being blunt and the thing is, there is an awful stink of cubs here."

"Cubs?" she queried.

"Cubs. Complete and Utter Bullshit!" Joe took another sip of his coffee as he continued to stare at her. He went on to say, "You'll remember some time ago when I was trying to get you to work for me. I called that low-life husband of yours a retard?"

Julia nodded timidly and fought to stem the tide of tears waiting to fall.

"What I should have added was that he was, and clearly is, a dangerous retard. Did he ever tell you why he got divorced from his first wife?"

"Yes," she didn't elaborate.

"Go on…" Joey pressed her for more.

"He said he caught her in bed with someone - well, two other men." She wondered where this was going.

"Hmm, well that's true up to a point," he said with a sneer.

"Do you know, if I thought there was any semblance of accuracy in your story about falling downstairs, I'd let this go, but, Julia, you are lying. There's no other word for it. I'm not going to ask you for a reason, but I suspect it's in some mistaken loyalty to little Kirstie's shit-bag of a father."

She started to cry, fearing that not only was she humiliated because he knew she was untruthful, but she was also going to be sacked because of it.

Joey continued, "You're probably not going to want to hear this, but I think you should have been made aware of Mr Irvine's former activities before you became involved with him and I will forever blame myself for that. I had hoped when you first started seeing him that he had changed and that, somehow, it was down to you. I try to take care of people who work for me, and I keep a careful eye on how things are going. I was surprised to see that all seemed to be good for you, so I kept quiet about his previous history. Give him a second chance if you like," he paused. "I was daft for being so gullible. Leopards like Gerry Irvine do not change their spots."

Julia sat there grim-faced, dabbing her eyes with a tissue, expecting the worst regarding her job but also morbidly intrigued about Gerry's former life.

"Gerry Irvine is a narcissistic chancer and a bully. Oh, he's charming enough with the ladies and gets what he wants but they don't mean anything to him. His first wife, Laura, was a lovely girl, but she was as dim as a dodgy light bulb. She never had an ounce of brains compared to you, but in her blind devotion to him, the more she gave, the more he took advantage of her. He had a string of affairs with married women, some of which she knew about. The very few times she took exception, she got a beating for her insolence, so she just accepted that it was her fault." Joe finished his coffee.

"The incident where he supposedly found her with two other guys was engineered by him. What he didn't tell you was that through an adult contact magazine, he had arranged for two guys to come and shag her while he filmed the whole thing and then he was going to try to sell the video. Now, as you may or may not know, I do have some dealings in the adult video market but it's all legal and above board. In any event, he wondered if I'd be interested in some amateur offerings, to which I told him to fuck off, even though I was sure he would find some sleazy outlet for his crap."

"Anyway, the particular night in question, the two guys turned up, and she was to be tied up and used by them in whatever way they wanted, and I mean really used. I'm sure you don't need me to expand on that." Julia shook her head.

"By all accounts, it started okay, but then she decided enough was enough and wanted to stop. The two guys, to their credit, did stop, but Gerry was insistent. Then a row broke out where the guys said they were not going to do anything against her will, they got dressed and left. Our little charmer, Gerry went berserk and beat her up so badly that she was hospitalised for over six weeks."

"To cover his tracks, he poured a lot of whiskey down her throat, then got her partially dressed and dumped her unconscious in an alley not far from where they lived in Brighton. She was found a few hours later and it was assumed by the police that she had been attacked on her way home from wherever she had been. When she came out of her coma, she said she couldn't remember anything about where she'd been or who had assaulted her. Part of it was true as she had suffered such a trauma that her brain blanked out anything before she came round."

Julia asked how he knew all of this was true.

"The assault, or rather, supposed attempted rape, was in all of the local papers, but the amateur filming incident was told to me by one of the guys who was there because he is one of the male strippers that perform in my club on Ladies' evenings. He was horrified when he found out that she had been beaten up and didn't know whether he should report it to the police. I advised him not to."

"Why?" she asked.

"Julia, you have such blind faith in our justice system. If he had come forward with his story, he and his buddy would have been the prime suspects. As it was, she couldn't remember who had attacked her or probably didn't want to remember and you could bet your life Gerry would have found some alibi to make sure he wasn't connected. After she left hospital, Laura went back up North, where she originally came from and divorced him soon after."

Julia was stunned but his words resonated with her and her experience with the abusive man she was married to.

"I guess that thug doesn't treat you or the baby very well, but that aside, I would stake my life on the fact that he did this to you, and you will have to convince me in no uncertain terms that I'm wrong. Am I?" He looked directly at her and as much as she tried to restrain herself, she completely broke down and wept. Joey got up and crouched down beside her, holding her hands.

"Julia, I assure you he will not do this again." There was a genuine sincerity in his voice that she drew from to help her compose herself.

"Now then, I can't bandy words with you all day. We both have work to be getting on with," and he stood up.

"You're not going to sack me?" she asked, almost disbelievingly.

"What for?" He looked rather surprised at the idea of it.

"For…for lying," she stammered. He shook his head as if he didn't understand the concept of dismissing her for something he knew wasn't her fault.

"Julia, get back to work, and don't forget to see Cheryl," he said, trying to be the gruff misery he usually seemed to be.

The day continued, and she welcomed work as a huge distraction. Her visit to Cheryl's office was just to confirm that she could take any time off that she needed and any financial help would be forthcoming. Julia felt buoyed by the support from everyone in the office, but as home time drew near, her anxiety increased in case Gerry was waiting for her outside.

After his chat with Julia, Joey stayed around for an hour or so, making a number of phone calls and then disappeared until just after four o'clock. On his return, he went straight into Cheryl's office, closing the door behind him and then came back out and over to Julia's desk.

"Okay, Julia, get your stuff. I'll give you a lift home," he said as a matter of fact.

She was surprised as she still had another half hour of her time to work but said, "Thank you, but my mum is picking me up with Kirstie."

"No, Cheryl has spoken to her and she's bringing the little one home to you later. I'm taking you back to the flat."

Julia was confused and even more anxious, but Joey hurried her along, giving no time to dwell on the change of arrangements. Nothing was said on the short journey to the apartment but when they arrived, Joey said that he would see her indoors. He was out of the car and off in his business-like way, again not allowing any questions or discussion. She could barely keep up but her heart rate and anxiety were increasing by the second. They took the lift to the first floor and were then in the apartment in a few minutes.

"I've never known these lifts to break down…ever!" Joey said randomly.

Julia nervously opened the apartment door, watched carefully by Joe. She went in cautiously, and Joe said calmly, "Don't worry, he's gone."

"What?" She was now apprehensive *and* confused.

"Your cunt of a husband has gone, packed his stuff and vacated the premises!" Joey was still very calm. She quickly walked to the bedroom, and sure enough, all of Gerry's clothes were gone from the wardrobe and his chest of drawers. She came back to find Joey looking out through the panoramic view of the Marina. "You were right, you know, it is an amazing view."

"But where has he gone?" she asked. It was only one of a dozen questions that she now needed answers to.

"I neither know nor care. What I do know is that he won't bother you or Kirstie again," he said.

"But how am I going to afford this place? And I won't have anything to get food for us and…" She started to cry when the enormity of her new financial situation hit her.

Joey took her in his arms and said, "Julia, it's all taken care of. I don't know what Gerry told you about this apartment, but he wasn't paying me any rent for it. When I bought it through the Estate Agent he was working for, I planned to rent it out as a long-term investment. He knew that I hadn't found a tenant and offered me a small rent so that he could move in with you when you got married. It was a pitiful amount, but he gave the impression that he cared a lot about making this marriage work and, like the altruistic arse that I am, I fell for it."

"Over the last year, he hadn't paid a bean. He did say that when he could afford it, he'd be moving out to a house of your own, which I took to mean a few months, not the length of time it turned out to be. So, you can live here as long as you like. Just keep the place in good order and, of course, any repairs or maintenance work is down to me. It's already making me money as the market improves and anyway, I don't need the cash."

She tried to take that in and asked about housekeeping and direct debits and stuff. He continued, "All the direct debits and standing orders were coming out of his bank account. He was the registered tenant up until today and any debts accrued and/or outstanding are his and his alone. You are now the registered tenant and Cheryl has, since our chat this morning, opened a new bank account in your name, which has been topped up with a loan. She's also been sorting out all of the new direct debits and standing orders for this place, also in your name. She'll run you to the bank in the morning to do the necessary paperwork. We'll deduct a small amount from your wages to pay the loan off over time. Your mother is doing some shopping at the moment, so you'll be okay for food and supplies until you get the relevant debit cards and all of that malarkey. So, you see, there's nothing to worry about. He's gone, and he's taken all of his nasty shit with him. Oh, and a locksmith will be here by 5.00 pm to change the locks."

She cried uncontrollably with relief. Joey held her for a long time before asking for a cup of coffee to keep her distracted enough to bring her back to normality. At last, she could get off Gerry Irvine's treadmill of brutality.

"Hmm, not a bad cup of coffee but have a word with Cheryl to see what brand she uses, there's a Love," Joey said as he admired the view yet again.

14

I'm Still Standing

Spring 1999

Julia was diligently working through some daily tasks at the bookmaker's office when her phone rang.

"Julia, I need you to stand in for me at a charity event coming up shortly. Cheryl would normally do the honours, but we've got the VAT Vultures due at roughly the same time to make sure we're not on the hey diddle, diddle," there was a pause. "If you could…" It was Joey with not so much of a request, more a polite if unspecified instruction.

"Yes, of course, Joe, when and where?" Julia was always happy to oblige.

"It's a fundraiser for the MacMillan Nurses people. It'll be a nice afternoon hosted by some good friends of mine. The thing is, I'm not a great one for being thanked and all that back-slapping, self-congratulatory nonsense, only we need to keep up appearances in order to raise awareness. Unfortunately, I will be out of town on that day."

"Yes, Joe, not a problem but when and where?" Julia asked again.

"When and where? Do you know that is a damn fine question!" he said, as though *he* was asking for the details. She waited for his answer.

"I have no idea. You'll get the details from Cheryl. Thanks, Julia," and he ended the call. He wasn't the sort of person to engage in unnecessary chit-chat or too many pleasantries like "hello" or "goodbye". As she got up and went to find Cheryl, she wondered how Mr Porter wasn't going to be available for the fundraiser if he didn't know when it was.

Cheryl saw her coming and gave her the usual beaming *Cheryl* smile, followed by, "Joey's been on the phone, hasn't he?"

"Yes, he's asked me to stand in for him at…"

"MacMillan Cancer Support Fund Raiser. Yes, I have the details here. Did he tell you that the VAT Inspectors are coming as well?"

"Yes."

"VAT Vultures, he calls them," Cheryl said, and they both chuckled as Julia nodded.

"Our Mr Porter doesn't do charity events or tax inspectors, regardless if he's available or not."

"Ah, I see," Julia fully understood.

A week later, Julia was shaking hands with some of the great and the good around mid-Hampshire. It was a much larger affair than she had imagined it would be and, to her great delight, she recognised a friendly face from school all those years ago. That friendly face also recognised her and spontaneously broke out into a huge smile before making some rapid excuses to the people he had been talking with. He then swiftly made his way over to her. He kissed her on both cheeks and just said, "Wow! Julia Fulton the Head Girl of one of the most prestigious private schools in the district. What's a lovely lady like you doing in a place like this?"

Even in those first few minutes, he appeared to her to be an outgoing, exuberant man, as opposed to the quietly confident student who saved her from the school bully's evil clutches in their final year at school.

"Alan McCann. I haven't seen you since…"

"Since your husband rudely interrupted us at that bun struggle in Southampton, when was that, nine years ago?" he asked, hoping she would remember the year.

"Ten, I think. Yes, I am so sorry about that." Her apology was genuine.

"He's not around now, is he?" Alan asked, comically looking around the assembled throng, expecting the madman to come bursting onto the scene. Julia laughed.

"No, he's long gone, and I am well rid," she said with a smile. Alan said he was sorry to hear that, but she replied that she wasn't sorry in the slightest.

"Well, here's to the single life!" Alan raised his glass and then said, "Oh, sorry, you may well be spoken for a second time round?" He rather hoped she wasn't.

"No, not at all and I'm very happy that way, thank you very much," Julia said emphatically.

They smiled at each other. She liked the change in him that had come about over those years since school. This pleasant but tepid function was suddenly very interesting, and she was intrigued by the handsome fellow who stood before her. Julia had a million questions for him but her initial excitement at seeing her old school friend was cut short when he said that he had another engagement to attend to forthwith.

"Oh, that's a shame," she said, unable to hide her disappointment.

He gave her hand a squeeze and apologised before he enthusiastically said.

"Hey, maybe we could go for a drink, or if I push my luck, might I even ask you to dinner to catch up for old times' sake?"

"Yes, I'd love to!" She gave him a big, cheerful smile and a peck on the cheek. They exchanged contact details and, within a couple of days, arranged dinner. Julia was elated and, if she did but know it, so was Alan.

They met at a local Italian restaurant. He was the perfect gent and even more charming and funny than he was when they met days before. For a man nearing thirty, he had physically aged, but with that came a worldly, wise maturity. The dinner went well; it was as if she had chatted to him only last week and yet the rich vein of stories and experiences made him even more enthralling. She was embarrassed that she had virtually done nothing with her life.

He didn't elaborate too much on his university experience; suffice to say that he told her he was a typical student. "Wine, women, and song. And to quote a favourite lecturer of mine, *If you can get through four years without a drink or drug dependency, or a dose of the clap and earn a reasonable degree, then you're doing well.* You know the sort of thing." He was relieved that Julia didn't delve into detail as she pointed out, "No, unfortunately, she didn't know what typical students did."

He was sad to learn that she never made it to university because of *"that man."* She also didn't go into the specifics of her cruel relationship, but she did add that the only real positive to come from it was her enchanting little girl, Kirstie. Alan was genuinely pleased for her and held her hand across the table all the time she talked about her nine-year-old daughter. He was so amiable that he seemed to be equally captivated by her dedication as a single mother working full-time.

"My parents have helped me enormously," she offered as an explanation and then asked him about his life, his loves and his children.

"I am a lone wolf!" he laughed. "I've always been far too busy with work to burden a long-term partner with my single-minded enthusiasm," and he left it at that. Julia decided not to pry. She was hopeful that there would be other opportunities for him to open up.

The more dates she went on with him, the more she looked forward to seeing him and yet he seemed so ambivalent to physical contact over and above a kiss on each cheek and a hug. She wasn't unduly concerned and put it down to how shy he always was with girls. In her own mind, she was still not ready to introduce a physical aspect into any relationship. Gerry had turned off any teenage burgeoning libido with his brutality and she often wondered if she could ever get it back.

Julia decided not to stress about it. She enjoyed being with Alan immensely and decided whatever would be would be. After years of avoiding male company on a social level, Alan now breezed into her life and cared nothing about the barriers she had put up to protect herself. Perhaps it was because of his calm, friendly manner, or maybe she recalled that at a moment of danger, he was the knight in shining armour who rescued her and wanted nothing more than to see that she was safe. Over the next couple of months, they met numerous times and spoke or messaged each other on the phone on a daily basis; Julia loved their friendship.

Their next dinner engagement was a shift away from the norm. Alan invited her to his house, where he promised to cook for her. It was a casual request with no suggestion of anything other than dinner. Even so, she couldn't help reminding herself of how her own dinner invitation to Gerry Irvine so long ago was so sexually charged that the dinner itself was superfluous to the main aim of the evening, which was to lose her virginity, she recalled how wonderfully sexy it all was before the walls of their newly built relationship swiftly came tumbling down.

She readily accepted Alan's invitation and was fairly relaxed about his motives, if he had any. He was always very open, and she trusted him implicitly. There was a slight nagging in her mind that maybe he might steer things towards a more physical engagement, which she was not ready for. However, she had the perfect excuse that she had to get home for Kirstie should anything become awkward.

Alan lived in a beautiful four-bed house near Beaulieu, on the edge of the New Forest. It was immaculate and as she parked in the drive, Alan was at the door to greet her with the usual hug and a peck on each cheek. He gave her a quick tour downstairs, including the wow-factor contemporary kitchen, where pots were already simmering and plates were ready. She accepted a half glass of fizz, explaining that she was driving. He didn't seem particularly perturbed by that, she thought, so he wasn't expecting her to stay anyway. She relaxed at that point, there was no hidden agenda, and she scolded herself for being so suspicious.

They went into the dining room; there was an enormous painting of an elephant, an original by David Shepherd.

"Wow," Julia was enthralled by the beauty of it.

"Yes…" Alan looked very serious, "There is something we need to talk about."

Julia smiled and got the joke immediately — "Would that be the elephant in the room by any chance?"

He laughed and then pulled out her chair at the table and asked her to sit. He disappeared and came back with starters. Something simple, he told her, but it appeared to be anything but. Scallops in garlic butter with a small apple salad, all very well presented, and it was delicious.

"Gosh, you've learnt some very decent culinary skills," she complimented him, but he waved it away as just being able to RTFM, which he did for much of his work.

"RTFM?" she queried.

"Yes, Read the Manual," and he smiled, waiting for the inevitable follow-up question.

"But you said RTFM?" and then it dawned on her what the F was for, and she laughed.

The conversation was as fluffy as their previous dates. He was interested to hear about her day and how Kirstie was doing at school. Julia was usually happy to answer anything, but again, she was a little frustrated that he rarely went into personal detail about himself. Alan just glossed over her questions, saying that to the ordinary man in the street, his job would "Bore them rigid, even if they understood the in-depth technical aspect of digital technology."

"Alan, you're always so enthusiastic about my tedious days, and I like how you are interested in Kirstie, but you never say much about yourself," she said, not wishing to put him on the spot but, in essence, doing exactly that. She continued, "The thing is, my ex was always rather coy about his daily doings and used to get very tetchy if I pressed him on it and I guess I'm just a little wary of people who... who don't want to elaborate about anything, especially when I am genuinely interested."

Alan laughed, "Jules, I could tell you as much as you'd ever want to know about digital technology, but we would need several lifetimes just to explain the nuts and bolts of it and I'd say that we are only scratching the surface of what it will do for the world."

Julia smiled, "I love your whole-hearted dedication to your job, but..." She wasn't going to let this go.

"But?"

"But what about you? All I really know is that you went to university in Glasgow and moved into the world of computing and telecommunications and travelled around a bit, but that's it really. We've been on quite a number of dates, which have been lovely and brought me back to a world of social enjoyment that I had given up on and yet I sat at home the other night after we had been to the theatre and realised, I know so little about you!" She stared at him and tilted her head to one side as if to say, "That's it, the ball is in your court."

"Ah, I see. Of course, you would be interested. You were the same at school. You made everyone feel like you could be a friend because you always showed an interest in them. I always marvelled at how you did that, and I'm surprised that you haven't taken up a role in counselling of some sort," Alan said profoundly, but indulging in the dark art of deflection.

"It's probably something I would have found had I gone to Uni but what with work and Kirstie to concentrate on, I don't really have time to look into it now. It's a very good observation, though. Well done," she said, taking a sip of her bubbly.

"You undoubtedly should. You'd be brilliant at it." Alan left it at that. "I'll get the main course," and he quickly took his opportunity to evade further questioning. After a minute or so, she suddenly realised that he had skilfully sidestepped her initial interrogation.

"Beef Wellington, Madame!" he said as he proudly put the dish before her.

"Gosh, that looks amazing!" she said admiringly, and as he sat down, she was on the case again. "So, where were we, Mr McCann? The counsel for the prosecution has not finished our cross-examination," Julia said, trying to sound like Tom Cruise in "A Few Good Men."

"Is it an examination or cross-examination?" Alan smiled as he corrected her.

"Examination, I think?" she said, looking confused.

"Yes, examination. It would only be a cross-examination where the opposing counsel can ask me questions about the testimony I have given to the counsel who called me. So, your initial question, i.e., what I have done with myself over the last number of years, is you examining my testimony… or lack of," he laughed.

There was no hint of trying to belittle her and she knew that. They had got on so well in the last few weeks that their sense of humour was as one. Julia laughed as well before saying, "I think the defendant needs to consider his position and answer the question truthfully without further distraction or deflection before I jab this fork into his right thigh, where the blood won't show. Well, not for at least a few minutes."

Alan smiled and then said something about client/witness intimidation before she picked up a fork and stared at him.

"Am I under oath?" he chuckled.

"Very much so."

He suddenly became quite serious before saying, "Do you know, even in this short time since I've been back in Hampshire and met up with you again, I think we are just so in tune with each other. I was going to tell you a lot about me and, as random as this might sound, discuss a proposition with you." He looked at her, trying to gauge how this might be received. She was poker-faced.

Alan went on to elaborate. The fact was, he was essentially a solitary animal but adored her company and always had, even from a young age. They had both matured into responsible adults, which just made the attraction so much stronger for him. He explained that he felt that sexual attraction wasn't high on both their agendas, but their cerebral chemistry was second to none. They made each other laugh, they enjoyed the same cultural pursuits and although they had never been away together, he was sure they would enjoy the same type of holidays.

He let her dwell on that for a few seconds and then continued to say that he had set out a work plan, which would eventually get him to where he felt his real chosen path was.

"Which is?" she queried.

"Local politics and also charitable work," he told her. He was about to start another job which didn't involve so much travelling or living abroad that he had to endure now and, if it all worked out, this would carry him through the next ten years. He could then give up the world of technology and all the globe-trotting that went with it. By which time he could indulge in his real passion of doing things for the local community on a government level and then who knew? Onto something bigger and better.

Alan continued to open up. Since he'd left Uni, he hadn't had time for a social life. Yes, he had travelled the world but rarely had time to explore countries and cities due to the volume of work. He felt that he now needed to introduce a little work/life balance before he burned out. This new job would offer an opportunity for that. Even so, he said that he just didn't have time to go looking for the perfect partner and then suddenly, as if by some God-given plan, Julia appeared in his life again. He added, "It has to be fate!"

Julia thought about what he said for a good number of seconds.

"Is this a roundabout way of proposing… Something long-term?" she asked with a smile, although she was still not entirely sure if she had picked up exactly what Alan was offering.

"Do you know, I could address a thousand people in Paris in fluent French, about the benefits of free digital technology in every home in the world? I could do the same in Madrid in Spanish and yet you make me so tongue-tied that I just don't know the right words to make this proposition attractive and beneficial to you. I guess the crux of the matter is that I really don't know what you want for yourself?"

She thought about that for a few moments. Finishing her last sip of fizz, she said, "The truth is, Alan, I don't know either." She paused. "I could be the conventional single mother, so desperate for a surrogate father for my child that I would marry any half-decent guy that came along, who was reasonably attractive, had a job, didn't beat me up and didn't molest my daughter." He nodded and knew there was more to come.

"I would say that if I wanted to do that, I would have been married and divorced several times over by now, but I am far too fussy. No man I have ever met ticks all the boxes. I know it's wrong of me to expect that they should, but it is the reason I have stayed single for so long after my divorce. I have switched off any thoughts of having a partner. Kirstie is my life, my heart, and my being. I have convinced myself that I don't need anything for myself and then you come back into my life after all this time, and I am now in complete turmoil!"

Julia started to well up, but after a few deep breaths, she falteringly continued.

"Up to now, it's been fairly easy to avoid any form of a relationship and I'm happy about that," she paused. "No, not happy. That's the wrong word. I've been content. I don't need anyone for me. Until you came along. You are exactly as unassuming as you were at school. You are as endearing now as you ever were and unless you're a first-rate actor with a cupboard full of skeletons since school all those years ago, you are, my great friend, one in a million."

He looked very surprised, but in a positive way.

"Oh, Jules." He looked down at the table, struggling for a response but nodded again and took her hand, then spoke softly.

"I fully understand, probably more than you think. I've done the career thing and been dedicated to work at the cost of being married and having children. But now I need the sort of support that only a family can give me, you know, something and someone to work *for* other than for the work itself. I want to be a happily married man with a home life that conforms to the norm." He hesitated, thinking this could be a make-or-break admission, but then continued.

"I am going to be honest and up front with you because we are, I think, really good friends."

He took a deep breath and said calmly, "I am not a sexual person. I don't base importance on the physical side of a relationship–" He paused.

"People would think it sad that the few relationships I've had only ever lasted more than a few months." He pondered for a moment. "Well, weeks, really. My apathy towards the physical aspect and my devotion to the job were too stressful for anyone to deal with. So much so that they rightly assumed I was ignoring them."

He looked slightly ashamed of his apparent inability to keep a relationship going and, tightening his lips, looked anywhere but in her direction. She reached across the table and held his other hand.

"I get the picture. You're an intense individual when you concentrate on something. You always were. It's not something that ever made you less of a friend to me, even if others thought you were a bit too focused sometimes. So, carry on with your 'proposal'– oops, Freudian slip. Proposition, I'm all ears!" she smirked.

"And lovely they are, too!" he smiled. "Julia, you are the loveliest all-around human being I have ever met. I love being with you. I love the fact that silences are not awkward. I know I am not God's gift to women but I think we could enjoy being together for as long as we live. I have a very comfortable lifestyle. I wouldn't ask you for anything except your companionship and respect and I wouldn't do anything to hurt you. I would be as protective and loving as anyone could be to you and Kirstie. You won't know this, but I loved you even at school. I was thrilled when you found time for me, and you always did." He paused.

Julia pondered on his words and was about to say something, but before she spoke another word, he added, "As I mentioned just now, I have no need for the physical aspect of lovemaking. It might sound odd. I know it does to a lot of people, but I don't. You may not be like me, though. All I would say to that is I don't have any problem with you satisfying your desires elsewhere as long as you are thoroughly discreet and I know nothing about it." He paused momentarily and, with tears in his eyes, asked her to marry him.

She was also very close to tears. His heartfelt proposition was going so well, except for this revelation and yet the cold, hard fact was that she had become like him – ambivalent and apathetic to sex. He could see she was wrestling with the thought of this proposition.

"No need to decide now, just have a think about it. I'll get the desserts."

He quickly had the dinner plates in his hands, and he was away. She needed to think. She was as secure as she could be, but a full-time companion would be stupendous, especially if it was someone who adored and cared for her and, more especially, her daughter.

Could she love and admire him, though, if he allowed her to do her own thing sexually? But conversely, that wasn't a priority anyway. Maybe, in time, she could turn their huge affection for one another into something more physical if, and when, they were both ready. The enormous first hurdle was whether she could ever overcome her own lack of sexual "want", which she had so successfully suppressed because of what she had endured.

Something clicked in her brain. She had nothing to lose. Alan had met Kirstie quite a few times and they got on well. Even her daughter told her what a *"nice ma*n" he was and how he made her laugh. Julia wouldn't let him stew any longer and went to the kitchen. She was surprised to find Alan fussing over some plates while a fully uniformed chef, whose face she was sure she had seen on TV, was clearing up some of his equipment.

"Er, Alan…" the chef said, looking at Julia.

"What?" he looked up and saw Julia staring at the celebrity professional cook.

"Oh, bollocks. Busted!" He stood there like a rabbit in the headlights.

Julia burst out laughing and said, "With regard to your proposal, it's a *yes* from me. And it's a good job I can cook. I want to hear more about your intriguing proposition."

Julia and Alan were married in a civil ceremony in Alton three months later. For Julia, it was a wedding attended by yet another small gathering which included her mum and dad, friends, workmates and Joey and Cheryl. Alan's parents and brother were also in attendance. Her beautiful daughter, Kirstie, was as pleased as punch to be the bridesmaid, and Joey told her how delighted he was that she had found a real, solid, reliable man.

15

I Want That Man

May 2007

Julia and Alan's platonic marriage had worked so far and neither of them asked for anything more than loving companionship. Kirstie was officially adopted by Alan within six months of the marriage, providing a stable environment for her. Now she was seventeen and a year from flying the nest.

Julia and Alan shared a bedroom with two three-quarter-sized double beds. Alan was always very tactile in his unprompted desire for a cuddle, but full-on, blood-pumping intimacy was never an option for either of them.

Julia knew what she was signing up for, and after her brutal sexual treatment at the hands of her ex-husband, she was happy for the years of a peaceful, non-sexual comfort zone. She didn't seem able to disassociate the act of lovemaking from violence and abuse, and she froze at the thought of another man touching her in that way.

Lately, she had thought a lot more about that comfort zone - something inside her made her question her arrangement with Alan. In her mind, she often rolled back the years to how it was when she was eighteen and newly in love with Gerry and, of course, the lustful, tender passion they enjoyed before the demon in him surfaced. Over the last year, she began to masturbate on a regular basis. Once a month escalated to three or four times a month and then as much again in a week. Her hormones were on the march and the need in her was as strong as it ever was before her ex-husband suppressed it with his cruelty. Julia found herself surfing the World Wide Web for free porn sites and was excited at the entertaining, sexy scenarios that couples (and moresomes) engaged in. For some reason, the cougar/toy boy genre was of particular interest. The raw sexual enthusiasm of the handsome, athletic young men was beguiling. The real question she could not answer was, could she go the extra mile to become intimate with a man again?

Alan had been back a few days from yet another long, exhausting trip and, although they were few and far between, it was perceptibly taking its toll. Julia looked at the fatigue that engulfed him as he sat in the kitchen while she prepared dinner. She poured a couple of glasses of wine and decided enough was enough.

"Sweetheart, you're working too hard. You're gaunt, and you've lost a lot of weight. You need to take a break," Julia said to him. Alan insisted he was fine, but he wasn't very convincing.

"I'll get on the internet now and have a look for a two-week break, somewhere, long-haul, just the two of us. Bali, the Maldives, or somewhere like that. You need the rest and I'm not taking no for an answer. That company will always work a willing horse, and they definitely get more than their pound of flesh!"

"Christ, I didn't know you were related to Shakespeare. Have you got any more clichés you want to throw in there?" said Alan, paying lip service. "But what about Kirstie?" he asked, hoping that would put a dampener on the whole suggestion.

"She's virtually a young woman and can take care of herself. In any event, my mother would oblige if she wanted to stay there for a couple of weeks," Julia said emphatically.

"Come on, Alan, I mean it. You need to get away from work for a while. What would you fancy as a holiday?"

He was warming to the idea as Julia topped up his glass. He tutted and thought for a couple of seconds.

"Don't know." He thought again for a minute while Julia fussed over some plates and cutlery. "I've always wanted to go on a safari in South Africa. I've been to Jo'burg and Cape Town but that was all work. I'd like to get out in the wilderness but with some comfort, if you know what I mean. I think my idea of camping is a three-star hotel." He was quite deadpan with the delivery. Julia smiled and understood - creature comforts were paramount.

"Great idea! Tell you what, I'll look at some stuff and will give you the details before we book."

"Okay, Love," he said, resigning himself to his fate.

The following day, Julia had found the ideal vacation. She chose an all-inclusive two-centre holiday, the first week in the African bush under canvas (!), the second in a complex of luxury beach huts in an exclusive resort on the Indian Ocean.

Julia didn't give Alan time to back out and, checking his diary, found a two-week slot for much-needed R and R. A couple of months later, they were on their way. In the whole time they had been together, this was their first long-haul trip just as a couple. Previously, vacations were centred around school holidays, mainly to Spain or Portugal. There was also the almost compulsory trip to Florida and the delights of Disney World and Universal Studios, which featured twice over a six-year period. The first time in 2001, when Kirstie was eleven, Alan described it as *enchanting* to see the delight in his adopted daughter's eyes. Julia remembered weeping at the time because of that pure magic. Alan was the real magic that had been brought to her and Kirstie's lives by creating such a safe, secure but more especially a loving family environment.

The safari was fabulous, and even the lack of all mod cons couldn't detract from the magnificence of the animals on show in their natural habitat. However, at the end of the week of waking before dawn and endless creepy crawlies, they were both ready for the following week's relaxation in luxury.

It was a trip Julia would either have to do alone or ultimately forego. When they returned to some level of civilisation and messages and calls were received, it was obvious that Alan was urgently required back at work. She was quite dismayed, although she acknowledged that he resisted as much as possible by making and receiving endless phone calls to negate the requirement to fly home. Eventually, his loyalty to the company and his work got the better of him.

Julia grudgingly understood and said she would return with him, but he insisted she stay. Why go back to an empty house when he would be off to Edinburgh, he reasoned. And although she felt quite disloyal to him, she reluctantly agreed. She was very upset when he left, she had hoped that the luxurious second week in a five-star resort might enable her to, maybe, light some previously unlit fire within him… and her. Julia wished him a safe trip, and she would see him at home when she got back.

The adults-only resort boasted a small but palatial complex of a dozen quite luxurious one-bed beach huts, a hotel of approximately twenty rooms, two bars, a restaurant, miles of white sand, and the beautiful blue ocean. The food was delicious, the staff friendly and helpful (persistently so), and the other guests were mainly there for the same reason that she was - relaxing solitude, convalescing from rat-race stress, mostly as couples with a few singles.

A young American couple, in their mid to late twenties, were in the hut next to hers. Larry and Joanne were on their honeymoon. They were friendly and polite; that was when they surfaced of a day because, by night, all they wanted to do was fuck. Actually, night-time had nothing to do with it. They were the "Martini" couple - anytime, anyplace, anywhere, and in any position. Julia enjoyed their enthusiasm for physically pleasuring each other and she hoped against hope that for them, it would last a lifetime. She somehow knew it wouldn't.

Their first morning on the beach, when they thought Julia was reading, she caught Joanne with her hand down his Speedos, massaging him to lift off before they went for a dip in the sea, where they cuddled in deeper water and Joanne must have impaled herself on him there and then. Sunglasses could almost make you invisible if your head is tilted one way, but your eyes are looking elsewhere. She amused herself by imagining Joanne would wear his prick away to a stub, but they were in love and there was nothing wrong with their lust and passion for each other.

That evening in the restaurant, she sat down for dinner, totally comfortable with the reality of her being the only single female present. Shortly after, a tall, strikingly handsome man, possibly in his mid-fifties, suddenly appeared at her table. He was well built, had neatly cut greying hair, and wore a well-tailored light-blue short-sleeved shirt over a pair of navy-blue chinos and boat shoes. She noticed that on the inside of his left arm, he had a tattoo of a sprig of shamrock with some words underneath that Julia guessed were Gaelic. She was sure she had seen that tattoo somewhere before.

"Would you mind if I joined you? It seems so lonely dining alone in such beautiful surroundings," he asked in a soft Irish accent. He stood patiently waiting while she struggled to overcome her initial surprise at his sudden appearance before she hesitantly said, "Er…no, not at all, please sit." He did so and called the waiter over.

He introduced himself to her specifically as Patrick, not Pat, Paddy, or any other variation of the name. They exchanged pleasantries and after she explained that her hubby had been called back to work, he said with an odd twinkle in his piercing blue eyes, "Madam Fate has a beguiling sense of humour, doesn't she?"

Julia thought for a second or two. "Why would you assume that Fate is a woman?"

"Because only a woman could conjure up such delicious opportunities in life," he said confidently before ordering a bottle of Moet.

"Is the bubbly on the all-inclusive list?" she asked, knowing it wasn't.

"No, but I can't drink any more of their pish that they call white wine, so why not be hungover for a sheep as a lamb?" he said succinctly. She laughed.

"I'm sure you could help me with it, couldn't you? I couldn't drink a whole bottle myself," he smiled.

Julia smiled back and thought to herself that he was just so bloody obvious, and he knew it. He also knew that she knew it, and he smiled as he stared at her.

"Ach sure, it's all one bloody big game, isn't it?" he said, sampling the small offering given to him by the waiter before saying, "Yes, that will do, pour the lady's glass first please, and could you make sure there's another bottle chilled? Thank you."

The waiter nodded.

"What's a game?" Julia asked as she thanked the waiter.

"Life, love, relationships," he took a swig of his bubbly. "Birth, marriage, death – it's all one bloody big game and God himself has the best seat in the house," and he laughed. Julia liked his laugh and his black-and-white theory of life.

"I'm guessing you don't have kids?" she said, regretting that she sounded like she was Mrs Killjoy.

"None that I know of!" He laughed again. "And the thing is, if you really want to enjoy the game to its fullest, it's probably the only way to be…it's better not to know."

Julia nodded and then, pointing to his arm, asked him about his tattoo. Patrick opened his left hand to take hers gently and display the legend in full. She accepted the contact with pleasure.

"What does it say?" she asked as she stared at the words. He spoke it softly and perfectly in Gaelic without reading it.

"Is clann de chine troda sinn, Nár aithin aithrighe riamh fós,

Agus sinn ag máirseáil, an namhaid le h-aghaidh, Canfaidh muid amhrán saighdiúra."

She smiled, shook her head, and then looked at him as if to say, *'It's all Greek to me,'* and he smiled.

"I would have been hugely impressed if you understood any of that. It means, *'We're children of a fighting race that never yet has known disgrace. And as we march, the foe to face, we'll chant a soldier's song.'* It's a sort of unofficial verse or very loose translation of a few lines of one of the Irish national anthems. Basically, it's about standing up to you, nasty British people, invading our homeland," he laughed again. "Walter and Oliver should have stayed at home!" he added.

Julia understood the reference to Oliver Cromwell but asked about Walter.

"Walter Raleigh, the man who started the British Empire and decided Ireland would be first in the 16th Century. Oliver just carried on his nasty work during the 17th.

"Oh," History was never a favourite subject, but she was enjoying his company even if he did seem a little too cheeky and forward for her liking, but it was better than dining alone. Patrick went on to explain that he was a hotelier in Dublin and just occasionally liked to get away to see how other people ran their establishments.

"It's a bit of a tax fiddle too. Now, you won't be telling our Revenue Commissioners, will you? You wouldn't want to see a hard-working man condemned to slave labour for depriving the government of a euro or two?" he confided. "But apart from that, it's grand to get some sun on the old bones."

"Could I ask why Ireland has two national anthems?" she queried.

"The reason is unity. Ireland's Call was penned in 1995 as an anthem that would bring together every corner of the country and wouldn't have political undertones. Amhrán na bhFiann - The Soldier's Song is the national anthem of the Republic of Ireland, first written in 1912 but sung properly at the Easter Rising in 1916. Still, its use arouses... um... sensitivities among those with Unionist sympathies in the North."

"There is a lovely song I enjoy hearing, and that's The Fields of Athenry!" she said. He gave her a huge, beaming smile.

"'Tis no word of a lie; that was my mother's favourite. 'Tis beautiful indeed, but so sad. It's about a young man being sent off to Botany Bay for stealing some corn from a rich British landowner so that he could feed his children during the Great Potato Famine around 1845, oddly though it was written in the 1970s. Jaysus, your ancestors were real shockers!" and he laughed again.

Julia enjoyed listening to him talk about Ireland. He never questioned her about anything personal, yet the small talk was amusing and entertaining. So, when he offered, she indulged in a slow dance with him at the end of the evening.

"I'm no Michael Flatley, but if I only tread on one of your feet, you'll still have another one to hobble about on," was his retail strategy. She could hardly refuse and not for one minute wanted to. As they danced closely, he said to her that he was sure he knew her face from somewhere, but just couldn't place it. He asked if she had ever been to Ireland. She replied honestly that she hadn't.

"I might forget names, but I never forget a beautiful face, and yours looks so familiar. Ach, must have been another life," he said, but let it go. The evening was drawing to a close and it had sped by with this garrulous, charming Irishman.

"Well, Julia, I have to say this has been a lovely finale to my holiday. Thank you for allowing me to spend time with you before I go."

She was a little disappointed. "Oh, are you going home soon?"

"Sadly, I am. I have a taxi picking me up within the hour to speed me to the airport and a flight back to Dub. I would be delighted if you would let me escort you back to your abode," he offered, holding her hand and staring at her with his alluring blue eyes. She smiled, and as they walked back, he said rather cheekily that it was a shame he had to leave so soon, as he would have loved to see what Madam Fate really had in store for them both.

Julia chuckled at his presumptuousness. "You are a real cheeky chappie. I'll bet there's many a lady that can't resist your charms. As for me, you and what Madam Fate may or may not have had in store, we shall never know!"

"Now, why would I rest my cap on just the ladies, pray tell? There's many a beautiful man to dally with when the opportunity arises. But you, my lovely lady, will be the one that got away and I shall be forever doomed to wonder what you are like in the throes of ecstasy!" He laughed at his own unbelievable impudence. She smiled a smile that said, *you boys and your games.*

"Good night and goodbye, Patrick. It has been an illuminating, if lightning encounter." She held out her hand to shake his when suddenly, he took her face into both of his big hands and kissed her fervently. She was both shocked and thrilled in equal measure. She had not been kissed like that in over seventeen years.

"There, a lover's kiss for you, Julia. I believe we are fated to meet again!" Then he whispered, "Here's my card, just in case Madam Fate is a bit slow to bring you to me. Good night, my Lovely," and he was gone. She was still rather stunned as he walked into the darkness, and she eventually went into her hut to dwell on the evening. She went to bed naked and, in the darkness, masturbated, thinking of Patrick taking control of her and her pleasure. She was 18 again.

Another beautiful morning followed and after breakfast, she went to the beach again to read and watch the capers of the honeymoon couple. As she surreptitiously watched, she imagined herself with Patrick and knew she would have let him fuck her given the opportunity. For some reason, she really started to look forward to bedtime. The couple's beach hut was very adjacent to hers and with windows wide open, she grew accustomed to getting off on hearing their sighs as Joanne built to a screaming climax before he would grunt in ecstasy as his orgasm flooded from him.

On the fourth night, Julia watched them leave the bar and, giving them ample time to get down to it, she wandered past their hut, much nearer to their bedroom than was necessary. Sure enough, by the noises, they were already getting to grips with each other, and she was nervously overjoyed to see that they hadn't quite closed the shutters, affording her quite a view of their antics. She watched with a gorgeous, sexy tingle as she found them in the classic 69 position, with Joanne on top. They tongued and sucked noisily at each other's sex, and she felt compelled to lift the hem of her short skirt in the darkness and frig herself through her thin knickers, which were already damp.

It was delightful for her to watch as the young lady stopped what she was doing to him and began whimpering and moaning louder and louder while pushing her pussy harder onto his features. He assisted her face fucking by holding onto her hips to enable him to bring her off before she slumped onto him.

He allowed her a few seconds to come back to earth before he stroked her back and bum as a signal for her to get onto all fours. She duly obliged, her breasts swaying as she moved. Julia could see Larry position himself behind his gorgeous wife. He steered his average-sized, rock-hard cock all the way into her, causing her to grunt at each inward stroke. As he held Joanne's hips, Julia could hear her encourage him to *'Fuck her brains out'* and also saw her reach between her legs to caress his balls as he pistoned in and out.

Suddenly, Joanne pulled away from him, turned, but remained bent with her arse in the air. She took his dick in her hands and stroked him slowly from tip to base. Joanne then ordered him to *'finish in my mouth'* before putting her pouty lips around the tip whilst picking up speed with her hand. He held her head quite tenderly, but then he suddenly jerked, sighed and with fingers clenched tightly in her hair, he slumped forward and ejaculated. His wife lovingly swallowed his outpouring and then finally kissed him enthusiastically as she knelt upright to cuddle him.

Julia's sex was on fire, and she slipped away to her hut to relieve her reawakened desire, unrealistically wondering whether they fancied a threesome. Her brain was swamped with visions of the young man's erect penis. Not just fingers, this night could satisfy her lust, though. She needed something more, something to stretch her cunt so that she could imagine being fucked. She quickly grabbed a straight-ish banana, heavily lubricated it with her expensive moisturiser, pulled down her damp knickers, lay down and slowly pushed it all the way 'home'. If anyone could see her now, masturbating with a banana, they would have thought she was mad. She didn't care; she was lost in lust and frantically fucked herself while caressing her clitoris with her free hand, squeezing the knub between thumb and forefinger. Julia convulsed several times and moaned out loud as she exploded into a glorious climax. As her pounding heart gradually slowed, she withdrew her 'toy' and placed it back in the bowl before retiring for the night. When she drifted off, she realised that this young couple revived long-suppressed memories of how beautiful sex was when she took Gerry as her first and only lover, with no commitment other than to the gratification that it provided. Oh, why did Patrick have to go home?

In the morning, she awoke to a knock on the door.

"Who is it?" Julia asked.

"Michael, ma'am. I have fresh fruit for you today."

It was the young man who supplied the huts with fruit, tea, coffee, fresh towels, and other items.

"Hold on," she said and threw on a long T-shirt, which just about covered her modesty, before letting him in.

"Good morning," he said brightly. "How are you today?"

"Fine, thank you, Michael," she said, turning away to return to the bedroom. He was a friendly chap, always smiling and always pleased to help. He sang to himself as he replenished the fruit. Julia watched him through the half-open door. He was only about eighteen or nineteen, with the build of an athlete, his bright white smile a complete contrast to his ebony skin. As usual, he wore the hotel uniform of a white polo shirt with the hotel logo and a pair of baggy blue shorts, and she wondered what he thought of the wealthy clientele that stayed at the complex.

He came to the door, disturbing her daydream.

"Does the beautiful ma'am wish to keep her toy?" he asked, holding the used banana to his nose. "The lovely lady smell wonderful!"

He continued sniffing it with his eyes closed as if to block all other senses from detracting from his perceived enjoyment. Julia was mortified. She could feel herself blushing with embarrassment. He stared right at her and, still smiling, said, "I see my lovely lady last night. Sad to see alone, beautiful lady, no need to be alone. I come to you tonight and we make jig-a-jig. I make you cum pretty good. Michael plenty experienced. Last long, long time, many, many mature ladies take big cock. Make you cum pretty good!"

He was unabashed with his sales pitch, and with that, he dropped his shorts to reveal a flaccid but enormous penis and a large ball sac beneath. His hand grasped the base of his shaft to lift and point it at her as if to show it off further.

"See, big cock. Please many ladies."

"Get out!" she shouted, more in embarrassment than anger. Michael still smiled at her.

"I come tonight, no one see me. We make jig-a-jig. You cum pretty good."

"OUT!" she screamed, waving her hand at him in a gesture to enforce her words and he smiled, pulled up his shorts, and left.

She felt she could've died of shame. As she had spied on the honeymoon couple, so she too had been spied upon. At first, she tried to dismiss it, but the vision of that exceptionally sized equipment kept coming back to her, as did his words – *make jig-a-jig, make cum pretty good*– and again and again, that beautiful big black penis. Even through her unease at being seen last night, she played with herself again, imagining him stretching her vagina wide and nudging at the gateway to her womb but this time she did it with the blinds tightly shut.

She spent the rest of the day on the beach, just soaking up the sun and reading. Even so, her mind would not let the mental picture of

Michael's flaccid prick go and then her imagination ran riot, wondering how big it would get when fully erect. She got horny as hell. It didn't help that the honeymooners were back in the ocean "cuddling" again. As the sun cooled, she returned to her hut to shower and dress for dinner. Concentrating on getting ready, she momentarily dismissed thoughts of Michael and his *"many mature ladies"*. For God's sake, she thought, he was little more than a boy. Then dismantled her own argument when she countered with– *a boy, perhaps, but with a horse's cock.* With all the recent sexy events, she really did fancy a proper fuck now. Julia had been in self-denial for too long but now it was her time to rediscover desire and physical passion.

How she wished Madam Fate had been kinder and allowed Patrick a few more nights to seduce and take her to bed. However, since he left, there was only one realistic target. A single, middle-aged Frenchman, who seemed to be a bit of a bore and who, up to now, hadn't shown too much interest in her other than a polite *Bonjour*. But she needed a loving human touch, and he would have to do. She donned her sexy, yellow short-sleeved dress, which buttoned all the way up the front. Underneath, she wore white knickers and no bra. She felt really good about herself. She hadn't been this sexually confident in years.

The best-laid plans of mice, men, and this horny female were cast to the four winds as her womanly wiles were rejected by her target. He much preferred a clandestine liaison with one of the "in-your-face" homosexual entertainers.

After dinner, she watched the honeymooners retire early again. She finished her drink, went back to her hut, and resigned herself to another night of finger-fucking to the sounds of Larry and Joanne making out. Julia reckoned without Michael…

Moments after she had locked up and started to undo the buttons on her dress, there came a tap at the door. She knew immediately who it was. Thoughts flooded her brain. Correction, one thought flooded her brain – his cock, his long cock. His long, black cock, his many mature ladies, his jig-a-jig, his make cum pretty good long, black cock.

Her pulse rate went through the roof as she opened the door to be greeted by his bright, white, knowing grin. She said nothing but stepped aside to allow him in. As she closed the door, he turned to face her and held her hands. His beautiful, smiling eyes met hers.

"Beautiful lady not need toy tonight. Michael shower, then make lady cum pretty good. You see." He stepped nearer to her to kiss her and slipped his hands into the opening of her dress, fondling and cupping her breasts, causing the nipples to harden and pebble with the touch of his rough, calloused hands. His large tongue filled her mouth, and he prodded with it; it wasn't good, but his hands more than made up for it. Julia sighed heavily, and although he pulled away from the kiss, she still stood there, eyes closed, anticipating more attention.

"Come, pretty lady, wash Michael's huge stick, then we play."

He stripped on the way to the bathroom, stepped into the shower and, without words, started to wash away the exertions of his day. She was barely able to take her eyes off his gorgeous weapon. She pulled down her knickers in anticipation.

"Pretty lady wash Michael's cock, yes?"

Oh yes, she thought and standing away from the water, Julia took the soap from him, lathered around his prick and balls and meticulously cleaned every square inch of his genital area, occasionally allowing her hands and fingers to stray over his arse cheeks and between them, and then to return to his growing penis. She desperately wanted to see this amazing tool angry and so concentrated solely on his length. She was thrilled to see how quickly it responded, and although not fully erect yet, it was easily nine inches long with a relative girth to match.

She rinsed him off and just had to take him in her mouth. It was a struggle, but she was determined. This cock was the first one she had willingly taken onto her tongue in nearly two decades. She just wanted to devour it, spending ages licking up and down the whole length, rolling her tongue around the knob end, massaging him and sucking on it, hoping to make him flood her mouth with his seed. She stroked his full balls and again caressed his buttocks.

"Lady give good cock-sucking, but we fuck now, yes?"

"Yes."

She eventually removed her dress as he sat on a stool near the bath and she straddled him. Initially standing up, she carefully, cautiously, lowered herself onto his incredible missile. Julia was soaking and he grinned as he looked up at her, occasionally teasing her nipples with his tongue. As she gradually took all of him intimately, she was a wanton slut, stabbing her sopping wet pussy with his invading shaft. Suddenly, and with strength that belied his age, he stood, lifted her up, still joined, and carried her into the bedroom, where they fell onto the bed. He was on top of her now and in complete control.

"I fuck you good now, my beautiful lady. Feel my cock stretch you. I make you cum real good."

Julia wrapped her legs around his waist, hooking her ankles at his firm arse as if to lock him in place and keep herself in this moment of ecstasy forever. Michael began moving again, guiding his cock painfully slow out, her hips lifting and gyrating against him before he'd slam back into her swollen cunt. Her breasts bounced as he thrust forward. Her breath came quick and between each one, she whimpered or moaned or swore. It was euphoric and she was now grunting like a stuck pig as he thrust his meat in and out of her, varying the speed and rhythm.

"Oh, fuck me, fuck me, fuck me. Fill me up, Michael." Julia could scarcely believe she was actually talking dirty. "Make me cum real good."

He was driving her into an absolute frenzy. She clawed at his back and arse to get even more of him inside her and then she climaxed, amidst a gorgeous spasm of sheer pleasure, she climaxed, and she was sure he ejaculated, feeling the hot liquid rifle into her, which Michael used as extra lubrication. However, he continued to pump away at her, planting kisses on her face and neck and slowing his rhythm slightly, bending to flick his lizard-like tongue across her stiff nipples.

He built up speed again and she had barely come down from one orgasm before starting that inevitable path to another. This was no boy. He was literally a *fucking* superman. She heard screams from herself that seemed like they belonged to someone else. Her mind floated. Randomly, she thought of a line in a song about the rainfall on another planet, and she knew exactly what the singer meant, and she climaxed again. Julia eventually became almost breathless and needed him to complete the coup-de-gras. She was desperate to have the searing white heat of his semen inside her to complete her renaissance.

"Come, Michael. Give me your seed, please fill my womb up with it all. Do it now!" she urged between her joyous moans and sighs. He increased the pace of his perpetual thrusts, then slowed, lifting himself up slightly to stare directly into her eyes.

"Take my hot cum, lady. Michael safe – no babies," he purred as one final full-length injection caused the most amazing scouring spurts of his love juice to pour into her, burning the hot honey walls of her sleeve.

She held him tightly and reached as far down his back as she could to stroke his balls as if to make him give her the last few drops. Her cunt throbbed in unison with his pulsating muscle. She squeezed him with it as if to keep him there for eternity, but he was not done with her just yet.

Disappointingly, he slowly withdrew and then kissed and tongued his way down her body to the centre of her well-fucked being. He began to lap at her saturated crotch and, after a couple of minutes, came back to dribble his recycled spunk over Julia's breasts and nipples. She ground herself against his groin and resolved to take his juice in her mouth next time. Incredibly, in the space of less than ten minutes, his re-awakened snake-like prick nudged urgently against her sex and yet again, they were off on the heavenly ride to nowhere.

Over the next few nights, he restored her faith in men and, more importantly, her desire for sex. Fleetingly, she considered his "no babies" comment to mean he was sterile but only when she returned to the UK did her thoughts centre on the lack of contraception and protection. She berated herself for the stupidity of her besotted behaviour and visited her doctor at the earliest opportunity, where it was found that she was clear of any nasty diseases or additional "baggage." Julia decided that, given her willingness to indulge in "opportunities", it may be best to visit the local family planning clinic. It was still the same place she had first attended nineteen years ago, although it had been redecorated and all the staff was newer and younger.

PART 2

MY GENERATION

16
The First Time Ever
I Saw Your Face

July 2012

Kirstie could hardly wait to tell her friends about Matthew, and tonight was the night.

Matthew was *The One!*

He stood just shy of 6' tall, had a great personality and was practical and intelligent. Matthew was attractive without being stunningly handsome but something about him said *SEX*. Her mum was delighted when Kirstie first brought him home. Weird Auntie Crystal, a self-confessed clairvoyant, said. *"You'd better watch that one, he has a very experienced soul,"* which gave her a few shivers. Her mum made light of the comment in response.

"Don't let it put the willies up you!" Then, realising what she'd said, burst out laughing.

The gang of four - Kirstie, Sarah, Mia, and Samantha- hadn't got together for almost two years, with interruptions from university and Sarah living and working in Ireland for a while. The gathering was long overdue. Their excitement at meeting again was joyous and affectionate and as they settled down with their drinks, they were keen to quiz Kirstie on her new boyfriend. She was full of pride in herself, landing what she thought was a real 'keeper', and they teased her mercilessly about him.

"What's his name?"

"Where did you meet him?"

"What does he do for a living?"

And almost inevitably from Sarah, "What's he like in bed and how big is his cock?"

Kirstie could barely conceal how smug she was and revealed that they had met in Liverpool in the last few months of their final year at Uni. She was amazed that he came from South London and was only a forty-minute drive away from her parental home. They had been at the same university but only got together at the end of their respective courses when meeting at a party in the Student Union Bar. She glossed over Matt's rather tragic background, where he was born only a few weeks after his father had been killed in the "Troubles" in Northern Ireland.

Kirstie remembered being rather emotional when he showed her his father's military medals, which were the only tangible reminders of a man adored by his mother and hailed as an impressive, loyal, funny guy and revered by the men who served under him in his regiment. Matthew told her how his mum drilled home his father's mantra when it came to manners and respect for others, regardless of who they were or wherever they came from.

"We are all equal in God's eyes, and you should do unto others as you would want them to do unto you." Matt went on to tell her that they were obvious Bible quotes, part of which was from the Gospel of Matthew 7:12, which is how he got his name.

Back to the inquisition, she continued to say that he'd landed an IT job with a nearby engineering company, so he had moved to Eastleigh, which was virtually on her doorstep.

"He shares a rented flat with a friend of his, but we've now found a flat of our own and we're moving in together in a couple of weeks." Kirstie enthused. She was positively beaming.

Mia put her hand to her ear and said she thought she could hear wedding bells and hummed the tune of the Wedding March. As for Sarah's question, Kirstie laughed and said,

"He's the best of my less-than-outstanding total of three, and as for the other question, standard issue but knows how to use it!"

"Ooooh, don't leave it at that. We want chapter and verse of the complete roll of dishonour!" demanded Sarah. Kirstie laughed again and shook her head but having been bullied into a confession, she divulged, "Okay, my first was a one-night stand in a Ford Focus in Ducks Wood Car Park," she said, almost embarrassed at how meaningless that was.

Sarah laughed, "A Ford Fuck Us, oh the irony!"

"Ducks Wood Disco!" the others said in unison about a notorious public car park adjacent to some woods that always had more cars in it after dark than during the day.

"Then there was Manny. This was a two-year liaison at university and looking back, he was a real bore. My mum wasn't keen, but he had great teeth and outstanding prospects in the world of accounting. So much so, he could even shag by numbers!" They all laughed.

"He was a nice guy, but there was something a bit odd about him, which I couldn't fathom until I caught him at a party with his willy in someone else's mouth."

"Oh, wow, that must have been a surprise," Mia said, understating the shock.

"Yes, it was. Especially as it one of our best friends," Kirstie added calmly.

"What a bitch!" Sam said.

"Well, that was the thing I couldn't quite get to grips with him. Was he the bitch or was it the other guy whose mouth he was filling at the time?" Then she laughed at the surprise on everyone's faces. The table went silent for a minute as no one really knew what to say before Sarah broke the silence.

"Awks!" And they all sniggered.

"Come on then, girls, what has everyone else been up to? Let's start with you, Mia," prompted Kirstie.

"You went to Uni in Newcastle, didn't you? Party Central!" shouted Sarah.

"Yeah, after being accepted there, I picked a course at random, business-related, what a waste of time," and she yawned to prove the point. On the plus side, I had well-manicured nails; such was the interminable boredom of the lectures. However, I joined the Amateur Dramatics Club and loved it. I loved it so much that I applied to RADA and also the Royal Central School of Speech and Drama Performance in London."

"And?" Kirstie pressed.

"Not a peep from RADA, but after an interview and acting workshop at the RCS, I was amazed when they took me on. Girls, I am made up. There's so much opportunity for black people in performing arts now."

Sarah told her it wasn't luck. "You saw something. You took the chance and went for it. Girl Power!" She raised her fist to symbolise it. The girls nodded.

"I've always meant to ask you, which Caribbean Island your family comes from?" asked Sam.

Mia looked at her rather oddly and said, "Which Island?"

"Yes, which island?" Sam repeated her question.

"Canvey Island, near Southend!" Mia said and laughed loudly. "I'm a second-generation black British bitch!"

Sam laughed, too, along with Sarah and Kirstie.

"It's okay. I know what you mean. My grandparents came to the UK from Saint Kitts in the Fifties. They called it the Windrush Generation because that was the name of the ship that brought a lot of West Indians here to work."

"They used to tell me how hard it was with so much open prejudice and racism. A generation on, my parents themselves had it tough as kids growing up in the sixties and seventies, but thankfully, my dad was left a fair bit of money by a relative in Saint Kitts. He worked hard at school and university and became a lawyer. My mum was studying to be a solicitor when he met her, and he found that her parents came from Antigua. Antigua is a neighbouring island in the Caribbean. They got married and moved to a nice house in Hampshire and sent me and my sister to a great school where I met you lovely people!"

"Aww, and you're such a great friend as well. *But* what about a love interest, Mia? Any luck in that direction?" Kirstie asked.

Mia looked at her drink before taking a sip and then said, "I had a few short-term boyfriends at Uni and drama school, but they never floated my boat. I thought it was me, you know? I didn't turn them on enough; they did nothing for me either. I just gave up on the whole thing for a while. Then, six months ago, BANG!"

"Oh, Mia! Go on, who is he? When do we get to meet him?" asked Sam.

"Wow, secret squirrel, tell us more?" asked Sarah.

Mia smiled, "I realised when I met and made love with…Jenny, men were not for me!"

A couple of jaws dropped, but Kirstie hugged her and said, "Good for you. Nobody's going to judge you these days. So, how did you meet?"

"I was working part-time at a law firm, you know, shuffling papers from one desk to another, and one of the paralegal girls took me under her wing. We just hit it off. I thought nothing of it when she said we should go out for a drink one evening, which then turned into dinner and then a nightcap back at her flat. We were just sitting on her settee facing one another, talking, then she leant in and kissed me. I was so shocked and a bit tipsy that I didn't resist and, well… God, it was terrific, she then led me to the bedroom, and we made love. She was just so tender and enthusiastic, and she made me cum, which no guy ever did. The only times I ever achieved a big O before that was to do it myself!" They all sniggered knowingly.

Sarah agreed, "Young guys are so fucking useless. How old is she?"

"She's thirty-five. She's been married before, but she realised that women turned her on more."

Sam said it seemed to be a bit of an age difference. Sarah replied, "Oh, Sam, have you never heard the phrase – many a great tune played on an old fiddle?"

They all laughed before Kirstie asked what she would know about it, fully aware of Sarah's track record.

"Kayzee, we all know, most young guys are just out to satisfy themselves. I can't tell you how many twats I've been to bed with that have wanted to press the 'GETRID' button on the headboard as soon as they've cleared their custard!"

"GETRID button, what's that?" asked Sam.

"A lot of guys would like this imaginary button on the headboard that, as soon as they're satisfied, they wish they could press to make us girls disappear; we've served our purpose and are surplus to any further contact like a kiss goodbye or anything more than a one-minute cuddle. I've never wanted them to confess undying love but there must be a bit more respect afterwards than *wham, bam, thank you, ma'am, now fuck off!*"

Sarah was agitated but took a sip of her drink and calmed down before interrupting the silence that she had just created.

"Have a guess at the age of the best lover I've ever had…so far."

"Forty-three," Mia tried, diving in first.

"Maybe someone in their early fifties and knowing you, probably married," Kirstie said.

Sarah pretended to be insulted and laughingly responded to her best friend, "How catty!" She smiled, then turned towards the bar, "Barman, a saucer of milk here for my ex-friend, please."

"Fourteen!" Mia said, giggling. "Or is that when *you* lost your virginity?"

Sarah pulled a face at Mia, then laughed. "Way off the mark, all of you!"

"Go on then, don't keep us in suspense." Mia was desperate to know.

"Early sixties!" Sarah said with a smile before taking a sip of her drink.

They all gasped in shock, although Kirstie knew of the guy Sarah was talking about but didn't realise he was as old as that.

"Yep, early sixties, and what a fantastic fuck he was too. Wow, he could really make me sweat!" She laughed at how her friends were so flabbergasted. It was quiet for a good minute as they tried to digest how such a gorgeous young woman would happily be taken to bed by a grandad. Sam broke the silence.

"Women don't sweat; we glow!"

"Glow? If I had glowed anymore, I would have burst into flames!" Sarah replied. The girls laughed.

"And one of the classiest things about him was that he was never in a rush to sod off afterwards. He always said that the '*afterglow*' was the icing on the cake and sleeping with me when he had the chance was the cherry on top." Sarah was quite wistful as she said it, the girls just stared at her for several seconds.

"Why did it end?" Mia asked.

"Why does any affair end? He could snore for Britain!" They all found that highly amusing.

"And he was married, maybe?" guessed Kirstie.

"Ah, yes, that as well!" Sarah replied with a wry smile.

There was a minute of reflection from the group before Sam spoke.

"So, Sarah, what's your background? I don't think I've ever asked you. Where do you get your gorgeous dusky skin and good looks from?"

"The clue is in the surname – Sangamenetha," Sarah said. "I am the product of an Irish mother and a Sri Lankan father who met my mother in Southampton when his ship was docked there for a few weeks in 1989. They had a whirlwind romance, got married and nine months later, I was born."

"Wow, you never told me that before," Kirstie said, quite a bit surprised.

"Well, my father died in an accident on the ship a few months later and although my mum received a fair amount of compensation, I always felt that there was a bit of a stigma attached to the fact that she was effectively a single parent to a tanned sprog.

After primary school, I went to the local comprehensive, but my colour seemed to be a magnet for bullies…um, how did they put it? I was *'a half caste'* or *'Pakky-shit'* or *'wog'* as some of the nastier kids called me. The teachers only seemed to pay lip service to their anti-bullying protocols, and I recall one of the department heads saying, in front of everyone in the class, "Oh look, here comes Sarah Sangamenetha, what a tan she has. She must spend most of her life on a sunbed".

"What a bastard!" Sam said indignantly. Sarah shrugged her shoulders and carried on.

"I remember one girl, who was a real cow, always surrounded herself with her minger mates. She used to chant *'sunbed Sarah, sunbed Sarah'* whenever I was within earshot."

"Probably because she couldn't say Sangawotsyourname", Sam said, and they all chuckled at the irony of her not being able to say it either.

Sarah continued, "But I did get her back when I caught her alone one time".

The girls were captivated by what was to come.

"She was tidying up in one of the stockrooms when I confronted her…isn't it funny how bullies are so pathetic when they're on their own."

"What did you do?"

"I just said to her, ok, you bitch, just you and me now, so what's that you keep calling me? She never answered. So, I prompted her again, but she just told me to fuck off back to Pakky-land and, unfortunately for her, that lit the blue touch paper…"

"You hit her, didn't you? Please say you hit her?" Sam said, clenching her fist and willing her mate to deliver the coup de gras.

"You bet I fucking hit her. I may be only five foot five but there was a lot of pent-up emotion in that one punch, which splattered her nose all over her ugly face," Sarah said with no little pride in herself.

They all said, "Girl power!" again.

Sarah nodded, "Yes, she was bleeding all over the floor, and I warned her that there would be more if she continued insulting me. Just then, the teacher walked in and must have realised what was going on. He was a nice guy and knew about my situation.

He told me to scoot and as I left, I heard him say to her – *'you had that coming, didn't you but you're going to tell people it was an accident or there will be serious repercussions about your persistent bullying…'*"

"Good man," Mia said.

"But all in all, it wasn't much fun, and Mum got me out of there before I was expelled. It was easier for them to blame me for provocation than to stop the bullies. Thankfully, she found our lovely school where, luckily, most people had a different opinion on the colour of my skin."

Kirstie laughed, "Yes, especially the boys!"

Mia chipped in, "The boys? What about the teachers!" They all laughed, knowing Sarah's alleged reputation but left it at that.

"So why did you go to Ireland over the last eighteen months?" asked Sam.

"I just needed a break. Work was shit and I split up from a boyfriend at the time. Mum got in touch with a cousin of hers in Dublin and I got a job working in the hotel industry for a while. It was good fun and a really good experience. So much so that I've now set up my own little Events Management company, so, engagement parties or even a wedding would be no problem," she looked directly at Kirstie. "I'm your girl, mates rates, of course!" They all complimented her on her new venture and said they'd be after more details.

"Come on, Sam. Your turn. Background, life, work, love and boys?" Kirstie asked.

"Nothing to tell, really. I'm from good old-fashioned Anglo-Saxon stock, my mum and dad run an estate agency and unlike me, they seem to be real party animals."

"You worked at an Estate Agent's for a while, didn't you?" Kirstie said to Sarah, trying to put her on the spot.

"Briefly!" Sarah glared at Kirstie. "Go on, Sam."

Sam continued, "I went to Loughborough University to study Sports Science, and you know I always liked hockey, so got heavily into that. I've just been temping at various companies so that I can concentrate on hockey. I've been in the England elite squad for six months now, but haven't made the breakthrough yet," she said, drinking her lemonade.

"Oh, Sam, it'll happen. You just need a little bit of luck, and we'll all be there to support you when you get picked," said Mia.

"Here's hoping." Sam crossed her fingers.

"Oh, come on, get to the juicy stuff. Boys!" Sarah said enthusiastically.

"Or girls," Mia chipped in, much to the others' amusement. Sam looked at the table and said quietly that there wasn't much to report on that score.

Mia was incredulous when she said, "You spent four years at Loughborough with all of those athletes and never got a shag?"

"I was friendly with a guy for a little while, but he was a virgin as well and had about as much idea as I did. You could write what both of us knew on the back of an iPhone SIM card."

"Other mobile phones are available but what's there to know?" Sarah added incredulously. "You just do what you feel, surely?"

"We did try a couple of times but on both occasions, he was too quick off the mark and just made a mess."

Sarah laughed loudly and then apologised.

"See, young guys – no fucking idea. So, there you were, covered in cum and Two-Stroke Tommy was out of the game?" she said sarcastically.

"Tommy? No, surely his name must have been Justin. *Just in.* See what I did there?" Kirstie said as they all groaned.

"I wouldn't mind, but he never even touched me apart from kissing. It was like a different form of spontaneous combustion when we got undressed," Sam said disappointedly.

"Bloody hell, Sam, that's almost a religious experience, making him cum hands-free. You might be some sort of Messiah bringing guys to the boil just by taking your clothes off!" Sarah added, and they all sniggered.

"Ha ha." Sam was smiling but they could see it had severely knocked her confidence.

"Get on the other bus, Sam. It's so much easier and a lot less mess!" Mia said, giving her a cuddle.

"So, what you're saying is that at twenty-three, you're still…" Sarah prodded.

Mia interrupted, "Okay, Sarah, you don't have to paint a picture. I think that's pretty clear."

"Yes, I'm an old dear and still not broken in. Ha, it's probably healed up by now," Sam said, laughing at her own synopsis.

"Who needs guys, anyway?" Mia said.

As they ordered another round of drinks, Sarah began staring at a young couple sitting in the corner before announcing to the girls.

"Don't make it obvious but see that fella over there in the corner?"

The other three made it immediately obvious when they all tilted their heads around Sarah to look. Mia said, "The gorgeous guy sitting with that blonde girl?"

"Yes, that's the one. I've decided I'm going to marry him!" Sarah announced as though it was a done deal. The other three started laughing and Mia asked how she knew that this was going to happen.

Sarah shrugged and said, "Because I'm going to make it happen. Easy-peasy, lemon-squeeezy, Japaneezy, bright and breezy, and any other fucking eezy you want to add to it."

They all laughed again just as the guy got up.

"He's a big lad!" said Mia, taking in how well-built he was.

"Bloody fit, though," said Sam.

He walked past their table without noticing them on his way to the toilets. Sarah wasted her bright, beaming smile.

"That went well!" Kirstie said sarcastically to Sarah.

"Don't worry, he's mine. He's too gorgeous to let go and he is packing some serious weaponry!" Sarah said, waving her hand in front of her face to simulate how hot she felt after looking at him.

"How can you tell?" Sam asked.

"A little tip from a cabin crew friend of mine. They call it *the chopper check!*"

The girls laughed. "No, it's true. It's easier to tell when guys are sitting down, but that guy fills a pair of jeans like few others and I'm going to have him! Tell you what, I'll put my money where my mouth is!"

Sarah reached into her purse to pull out three five-pound notes before putting them on the table.

"I'll bet you a fiver each that I'll be going home with him tonight. I'll collect my winnings when I see you next. Message me in the morning for the SP!"

"Define '*going home*?" Sam asked.

Sarah smiled, raised her eyebrows and said, "Use your imagination. Goodnight, girls. Mwah."

With that, she took her drink, grabbed her handbag, stood up and went over to speak to the blonde still sitting at the table. The girls just stared in awe at how decisive she was.

Sam said, "She's pissed, isn't she?"

Mia responded with, "Ooh, she's a terrible flirt!"

"I think you'll find that she's very good at it," was Kirstie's reply.

They watched as Sarah sat down with the girl and after a few minutes, "Blondie" stood up and stormed past her returning boyfriend, loudly calling him a bastard for most of the clientele to hear. He then watched his date for the evening leave in a huff. He turned back to look at the uninvited guest.

"What was that all about?" he said to Sarah, who was innocently sitting there. She spoke calmly.

"I'm not quite sure. We were having a little chit-chat, and she got a bit upset."

Sarah continued, "I think… It may have been when I told her that you were my fiancé."

His jaw dropped, his brow furrowed and he said, "Why on earth would you say that?"

Sarah held out her hand and said, "Hello, my name is Sarah, and you can thank me later for saving you from a lifetime of interminable boredom with Dull Doris, who just wants to live the dull dream of a dull marriage, living in a dull semi with dull snotty kids, a dull job, a dull car and turn a fine fellow like you into Mr fucking Dull living in Dullsville and the only excitement you'd have is the Wednesday night wank watching some porn when the kids are in bed while Dull Doris has fucked off to her yoga class," Sarah smiled at him again.

"You're fucking mad!" he said, staring at her.

"Yes, I am rather partial to great sex, that's very intuitive of you. I'll bet you could make the earth move, too!" She smiled that engaging smile of hers and asked him to sit.

He still seemed very confused but did as she requested, just as his phone pinged and then pinged again shortly afterwards. He checked the messages.

"They're from Doris, aren't they?" Sarah said as his mobile pinged a couple of more times.

"Amy. But yes, they're from her," he said, alarmed at what he was reading.

"I'm thinking that she's not best pleased."

"No, not very."

"Are there many nasty names?"

"A few."

"F-word?"

"Several."

"I'm hoping the C-word isn't there. It's not nice for a lady to use the C-word," Sarah queried.

"No, there are no C-words." Just then, his phone pinged again. "Oh…wait, the C-word has just arrived. All by itself." He shook his head before putting his phone down.

"Ouch, very succinct. She must be quite miffed," Sarah mused, rather understating Amy's anger.

"So, what's your name?" Sarah asked cheerfully, changing the subject.

"Dan."

"Well, Dan the Man, are you going to buy me a drink, or shall we go somewhere else?"

"You've wrecked my evening. It'll be a real arse to get her back," Dan was most definitely very irritated but all the while starting to appreciate the seductive beauty sitting before him.

"She *was* a real arse and be honest, you don't want her back. I was watching you. You were bored to tears while she was, no doubt, prattling on about all of her married friends and suggesting dinner with her parents and stuff."

Dan nodded. Amy had indeed hinted at meeting her mum and dad and only a few days before, they'd had dinner with a couple that had just got married.

"See? Why have Accrington Stanley when you can have Real Milan?"

He sat and watched her smiling face and then corrected her.

"Madrid."

"Madrid?"

"Yes, it's Real Madrid, not Real Milan. Milan has two clubs – Inter Milan and A.C. Milan, and they're Italian. Madrid, which, as you probably know, is in Spain, has four clubs. Real Madrid and Atletico Madrid are the two largest."

"I stand corrected and rather patronised!" Sarah said, still smiling at him.

"It's just that if you're going to use that analogy, citing one of the most famous football teams in the world, it's best to get it right, don't you think?" Dan said pointedly.

"Of course, um… sorry, which one of the two is the most famous? No, wait, don't worry. All that aside, you'll see that I am for Re-al!" She chuckled to herself when emphasising the name of the team but enjoying her own pun.

"Yes, very good. So, I guess you're a Chelsea supporter?"

"Oh, why?" Sarah was intrigued.

"I don't know, maybe it's because you look as though you should be on the set of *Made in Chelsea*," Dan said, admiring her gorgeous face and shapely body, the curves of which were accentuated by her flimsy figure-hugging dress.

"I'll take that as a compliment. And I think if I had to support a team, it would be Chelsea because they just sound so fashionable. But I cannot stand those so-called reality TV shows."

"Me neither," Dan agreed, recalling that Amy was a huge fan of that mind-numbing genre and soap operas as well.

"So, you seem to know a lot about football. Do you play?" Sarah said, looking at him and blatantly flirting as she fished out the lemon slice of her G&T and started sucking on it.

"Play?" Dan asked, picking up the hint of ambiguity.

She smiled. "Yes, football. You look more to have the build of a rugby man?"

"I played rugby at school and Uni but got a severe kick to the 'particulars', so I decided not to risk my prospects of becoming a father later on in life, so now I play football."

"Ooh, I'll bet that hurt. Everything in order now?" She sounded quite concerned.

"Yes, fully functional, thank you." He was almost smiling now.

"So, what's your favourite position?" she asked without dressing it up.

He hesitated before saying what he thought was an excellent response.

"I don't have a particular favourite. I am equally adept at any position you care to name."

Grinning, she held his gaze and gave a slight nod.

"Yes, I'll bet you are!" She licked her lips.

"Well, Daniel, the fates have decided that you will marry me, and I am anything but dull." She stood up and, gently placing her hand on his face, whispered in his ear, "I am going to rock your world. Shall we go somewhere and consummate our newfound friendship?"

Dan could barely take in what was happening, but if this beautiful girl wanted him, then who was he to refuse? He finished his beer and as they stood up, she looked over at her pals, who were glued to the unfolding scene. She gave them a cheeky wink before rubbing her thumb and forefinger together, symbolising money. Kirstie winked back, then turned to the others and said, "And that's how it's done! Ladies, you have just witnessed one of the greatest man-eaters of all time doing what she does best!"

She raised her glass and said, "To Sarah Sanga-Maneater!" They laughed and toasted their friend before Mia pointed out that "*Maneater*" was a Hall and Oates song.

"As was '*Sara Smile*,'" Sam said.

"Spooky," Kirstie added, "her surname should have been Dix, then she could have had a middle name of '*Loves.*'"

As they left the bar, Sarah seemed to be dwarfed by Dan's six-foot-two frame, she held his hand when they took the short walk to the taxi rank. Although it was a lovely summer's evening, there was a slight chill in the air, and Dan noticed how prominent her braless breasts and nipples were.

They grabbed a taxi, and as Dan gave his address to the driver. Sarah cuddled up close to warm herself and rested a hand on his upper thigh. It only took ten minutes to get to Dan's flat, and he noticed that there was a light on.

"Looks like my flatmate is home," Dan said.

"Oh, you share a flat?" Sarah said with a hint of disappointment.

Dan picked up on it and reassuringly said, "It's okay. He'll probably be in bed."

Sarah didn't say anything, but she wasn't unduly fazed by the possibility of someone hearing what they were about to get up to. In fact, it appealed to her exhibitionist tendencies.

When they arrived, Dan paid the driver, who gave him a smile and pointedly said, "Enjoy your evening!" Dan wryly smiled back. They entered the small but tastefully decorated apartment where Dan's flatmate was packing some books into a box. Dan introduced him to Sarah.

"This is my very best friend, Matt. Matt, this is Sarah."

"Hello, Sarah," Matt said before shaking her hand and then looking quizzically at Dan, who mouthed, "Don't ask!" away from Sarah's view.

"Matt is busy packing up his stuff because he's leaving me for someone else," Dan said, as though he was heartbroken.

Matt smiled and said, "Yes, I'm moving in with my girlfriend in a few weeks' time. I cannot bear this slovenly slob any longer."

"Mate, I don't need any 'slovenly slob' lectures from you!" Dan laughed. Matt smiled, then, realising that he was playing gooseberry, said he was off to bed and bade them goodnight.

"He's well trained," Sarah said, turning towards Dan and looking up at him, almost imploring him to kiss her. He didn't respond to her comment but took the hint with regard to the kiss. They broke away briefly before she commented, "Wow, that's a very good start." And she pulled him in for another go.

"Mm, even better." She started to undo his shirt and ran her fingers over the exposed flesh.

"I think it might be an idea if we went to my bedroom. You can have a look at my boy scout badges if you like," Dan said between kisses, which she seemed increasingly more desperate for.

"Yes," she said briefly. "I'm guessing you have one for lighting fires - or why don't we forget the badges and... How about we fuck each other's brains out instead?"

Dan said nothing but, to her surprise, lifted her up and carried her into his room. He had already tidied it in anticipation of Amy sleeping with him that night. Matt heard Dan's door close and took the opportunity to use the bathroom while he correctly assumed that the happy couple would be otherwise engaged. By the time he returned, he could hear a lot of giggling from Sarah through the wafer-thin walls separating the two bedrooms. That was followed by some unmistakable sighs of pleasure from her. He lay down in the dark and listened to the "performance".

He knew exactly when Sarah encountered Dan's penis for the first time and smiled to himself when he heard her say, "Wow, for fuck's sake, that is impressive!" And he heard her giggle again. He continued to listen and thought to himself that Amy was nowhere near as loud as this one. The "soundtrack" was so erotic that he was fully erect and lay there stroking himself until sleep took over, despite the noise.

The following morning, he was awakened early by yet another bout of rhythmical plaster removal and accompanying squeals, grunts and giggling. He made a visit to the bathroom and could still hear the "show" as Sarah was almost reaching her peak, judging by the gasps, sighs, and profanities that were coming from that direction. It was almost like the scene out of *"The Secret of My Success"* but without the fizzy drink.

"What a lucky bugger he is," he said to himself. Matt showered, brushed his teeth and, wrapping a small towel around himself, left the bathroom only to literally bump into Sarah, who was naked except for being swamped by one of Dan's shirts, completely open at the front.

"Morning," she said brightly, smiling at him. Unabashed that he could see her firm, round boobs, erect nipples and shaped landing strip as she stepped into the bathroom and shut the door.

Dan's door was ajar, and Matt took the opportunity to tackle his mate about his latest conquest.

"Wow, she's a stunner. But what happened to Amy?"

"You wouldn't believe it, mate but I'll tell you later."

Matt looked around the room and said, "Christ, this looks like a cyclone has hit it."

"You're not wrong. She shags like she's plugged into the mains. I am fucking drained."

"She's a bit vocal with it as well," Matt said, smiling.

"Yeah, sorry about that," Dan grimaced a little and tried to straighten the bed up a bit.

"Don't worry, it was a lot more entertaining than your usual prey."

"Mate, there was only one predator in this bed last night, and it wasn't me," they both chuckled. Matt heard the toilet flush and quickly returned to his room.

As he dressed, he could hear them talking and laughing before it went quiet, and then he could just about hear Dan sighing, which was unusual. He quietly made the bed, listening to Dan's sighs get a bit louder before a surprise elongated gasp followed by a grunting exclamation of, "Fuck… Stop, stop," from his buddy.

"Jammy sod. Well, if he wasn't drained before, he sure is now!" Matt thought, fully aware of why his best mate needed her to stop.

Matt texted his girlfriend to say he would be over to pick her up in half an hour before they went into town to buy a few bits for the flat that they were going to share. As he left, he called out to Dan, "I'll be out with Kirstie for most of the day."

"Okay," was the response. Then Matt said, "Nice to meet you, Sarah." He smiled to himself at their accidental contact, where he got a good view of his mate's latest squeeze.

"You too," was her reply.

As the front door closed, Sarah said to Dan that he seemed like a nice guy.

"Yeah, we were at school together. He's a top bloke. He's heavily in love with his girlfriend and I reckon marriage is on the cards there."

"What is her name again?" she asked, wondering if she had heard it correctly.

"Kirstie, although most times he calls her Kay for short."

The name registered immediately, and then she recalled that her best friend had said that her new boyfriend was called Matthew and he lived in Eastleigh with his flatmate.

"One of my friends is called Kirstie. She was there last night."

"Really? And there's me thinking that you were an angel that had fallen to earth from heaven," he cuddled her to him.

"Hmm, a fallen angel at best. Anyway, did you see her?" Sarah asked.

"I have to say I was so mesmerised by you that I really didn't notice anyone else."

"Flattery will get you everywhere, Daniel, but you didn't recognise her in the bar?" Sarah said inquisitively.

"I've never met her. I've been working in California for the last four months on a secondment from the company. I only got back a couple of weeks ago, and our paths haven't crossed yet."

Sarah sat up, displaying her stunning breasts before leaning forward to reach for her bag and grab her phone. After a brief scan of a number of messages from her posse asking about her evening, she messaged Kirstie.

"Hey K, one question I need answering quickly. You said last night your Matthew shared a flat with a friend, what's his friend's name? xxxx"

"Whereabouts are we?" she asked Dan.

"Paradise…or Eastleigh to other mere mortals around here."

A minute later, her phone pinged with a message from Kirstie.

"Odd question, but his mate's name is Dan. Hope you had a good evening did you win your bet? LY Kxxx"

Sarah replied with, *"The bet was never in doubt but OMG it's a small world !!!!!!!!!!!!!!!!!!! lol LY2xxxx"*

The response: *"Maybe, but I wouldn't want to paint it x"*

17

The End of the Innocence

January 2013

Dan breezed into the pub in his normal fashion. There were a couple of regulars propping up the bar at one end. Matt was at the other end, just about to make some inroads into his first pint of Guinness. Donald, the landlord, topped up the other one meant for Dan. The unwritten law of the land is that the finest pint of Guinness takes two minutes to serve.

"Game of pool?" Dan asked.

"Yeah, shortly. You owe me a tenner, so I'd better give you a chance to get your money back. Let's have a beer first, I'm gasping!" Matt said, wiping his top lip of froth. Dan sat on the stool next to him.

"All good with you, Donald?" Matt asked the landlord as he paid for the drinks.

"Ach, jist hinging together," was the Irishman's reply and he wandered into the back room to get some peanuts and crisps to put onto the bar for nibbles.

They sipped at their drinks before Dan spoke.

"Do you know Matt, you have to be the luckiest guy alive!"

"How so?" Matt asked, seemingly uninterested in his friend's assessment.

"Well, not only are you going to marry one of the most beautiful women this side of the Universe, apart from my Sarah, of course, *but* you also have the bestest best friend and bestest Best Man that any best friend could ever have or best come to that!"

"Really?" Matt said. "Who might that be then?"

"Me! You ungrateful knob," said Dan, taking a good slurp of his pint.

"Okay, mush, I'm guessing this is news about the stag weekend. So, what's your plan?"

Dan smiled and took another sip of his beer.

"All sorted mi compadre. All sorted – dates, location, residence, participants, transport, and the full intinererary," Dan said, stumbling over the last word deliberately.

"Itinerary," Matt corrected him.

"Yes, that as well!" Dan replied.

There was silence as Matt expected to hear the master plan, which wasn't forthcoming.

"So, do I get to know any of it, oh bestest Best Man?"

"Of course, there's no expense to you, though. It's my treat!"

"Don't be daft!" Matt said quite indignantly.

"Well, whatever but first the dates, twenty-first to twenty-third, March, as previously discussed."

"Yep, where are we going?" Matt was full of anticipation.

"The venue, you ask?" said Dan, looking like he was gathering his thoughts, ready to launch his monologue.

"Yes, the venue. Will I need my passport?" Matt said sarcastically.

"Very intuitive!" Dan countered, grinning, "It is…Las Vegas!" Dan said dramatically in an American accent, opening his arms only to turn his right hand and point towards Matt and say, "But wait!" He was really bigging this up to his totally unmoved buddy.

"I know what you're going to say," he paused. "You're going to say that it will be too expensive for all the usual suspects to afford.

More importantly, why waste valuable drinking time flying thousands of miles somewhere?" Dan didn't wait for the inquisition. "It is the Las Vegas of the North…The North of England, that is!" Dan quickly studied Matt's poker face. There was no comment, so he continued. "It's Blackpool, home of the Golden Mile, the poor man's Eiffel Tower, and Strictly Come Dancing!" he announced with such fanfare that he smiled widely and again spread his arms wide as if he was presenting the new iPhone to an adoring public. Donald laughed and shook his head before serving another customer further down the bar. Dan waited for the massively supportive reaction from Matt that he was sure would come.

It didn't. And as his arms dropped, so did his smile.

"What d'ya think?" Dan asked, hoping for some affirmation.

"Did you have a brain freeze at the moment you thought that it would be a good idea to travel nearly three hundred miles to a town in the North of England? Especially in winter?" Matt asked him with a sort of incredulous look.

"It's only two hundred and fifty miles and it's not winter, it's officially spring. We had a consensus around the team," Dan said.

"Oh, really and how many came up with Blackpool?" asked Matt.

"Mate, it's not a fucking democracy. I'm the Best Man, I'm in charge and anyway, none of the other suggestions met with my approval. Don't worry, you'll love it!" Dan assured him.

"Have you been before?" Matt asked, stony-faced.

"Yeah, it was brilliant."

Deeply suspicious, Matt questioned, "When?"

"A while back." Dan was too vague, and Matt wasn't letting him off the hook.

"How long of a while back is *'a while back'* then – you know specifically?"

"Okay, so I was ten. But my cousin's brother's best mate's sister said it's brilliant, there's only one thing wrong with it."

Matt looked confused and said, "Your cousin said that their brother, who by definition is also your cousin, his best mate's sister, thought there was only one thing wrong with it, a dump, maybe?" Matt said, totally underwhelmed.

"No, listen carefully. It was my cousin's half-brother, so not technically a blood relative. His best mate's sister said there's not enough blokes and the ones that are there are Northern Monkeys."

Matt shook his head. "Jeez, Blackpool, Lancashire. Full of Northern Monkeys. Who'd have thought?"

"Mate, you miss the point," Dan said and then, to emphasis his stance, went on to say, "Women outnumber guys there by two to one. Northern women might slag off Southerners because their parents tell them we are the Ante-Christ, but *they love us* cos we're different and we don't treat them like shit!" Dan said emphatically.

"Danny, Blackpool is not Afghanistan, I think you're making a massive generalisation about the under-thirty male population of Northern England, and, by the way, you seem to say, *'Love It'* a lot, which makes me think quite the opposite."

"Matt, come on. You're my best mate. Would I lie to you?" Dan said with all the sincerity of a Member of Parliament.

"Yes, you would. But get on with it," Matt said with a smile of recognition and resignation. To be fair, he really didn't care. It was just a weekend away with some good guys from the football team, and it was only two nights.

"Okay, residence?" Matt asked.

"A very palatial hotel not too far from the Tower," Dan said, hoping to quickly move on to the next subject.

"How many stars?" Matt knew he had Dan on the ropes and was enjoying giving his friend a rough ride. Dan mumbled something.

"Sorry, I didn't quite catch that?" Matt asked.

"Three…well, nearly three," Dan whispered. Matt looked at him open-mouthed.

"Nearly three? What's that… oh *two*, then?" Matt repeated, taking a sip of his Guinness.

"Two bordering on three…I think," Dan said.

"It's basically a Bed & Breakfast in a tent?"

"Very harsh - no. Every room has an en-suite shower, and it has a licensed bar. What more could you want?"

"Okay, it's basically a B&B in a tent, with an en-suite and a bar?" said Matt as a matter of fact.

"Oh, what's in a title? Anyway, the participants consist of most of the footie team, including our glorious manager, Ian. There's you, me, Ian, Cliff, Billy, Steve, GG, Cream Bun, Gump, Dwayne, Rudy, and Ollie. I've booked a minibus with a driver and that's it. We're all sorted."

"I'm surprised Stevie's got permission from Her Majesty, being pussy whipped and all," Matt said.

"Me too, but he's adamant that he's coming. He's paid the deposit, so we'll have to take his word for it."

"That's a good turnout, though. I thought it would only be half a dozen of us. I'm well pleased with that," Matt said, surprised at the uptake.

"Ian persuaded the League Committee to postpone our match for that weekend, so we won't lose any points. We're well-placed to win the division, so that's good."

"True," Matt replied. "So, the other five couldn't make it?"

"Nah, Phil and Peter are skint. Roger is even more bird-bullied than Steve. Lofty is already away that weekend, and Jonah hates your guts," Dan said with a chuckle. There was a pause.

"Jonah hates everyone's guts," Matt said pointedly. "He could start a fight in a phone box by himself. To be honest, I don't know why Ian still picks him."

"Yeah, that's true. He is a miserable git and never really had a whale of a time, but Ian picks him 'cos he doesn't mind being sub and ain't a bad, almost unbiased linesman, almost." Matt groaned at the well-worn pun. "We're better off without him. You've done well, mush!" Matt conceded that his pal had put in a lot of effort, told him so and patted him on the back.

"Cheers, Buddy," Dan said, smiling, acknowledging Matt's gratitude before calling Don over for another round.

Matt was delighted that Dan had gone to a lot of trouble, but he had already confided to Kirstie that he wasn't fussed about going anywhere. He would go through the motions for the lads because that's what was expected but running amok for a weekend didn't sound like fun. However, he doubted there was much mischief to be had in a northern town in mid-March.

"Hey, you'll never guess who I bumped into the other day," Matt said to Dan as Don did the honours with their pints of Guinness.

"Go on?"

"Jenna Crumplin!" Matt said with a nod, "Her mum and dad run that portable homes business in Gosport."

"Not Jenna Crumplin with the mighty crumple zones, all the poise, grace, and charm of a JCB. She's a sturdy thing and no mistake. A free spirit who loved…um…shagged whoever she wanted, whether they liked it or not. In love or lust one day and gone the next," Dan said, picturing the last time he saw her, which was in the back of a Ford Transit with the rear doors wide open. Between her legs was a local builder rogering her senseless while she squealed like a greased pig. He was about to tell Matt that very fact but was stopped in his tracks when Matt confessed that she was his *'first'*.

"Nooo, really? When was that?" Dan asked.

"2005, the summer holidays after our first year of sixth form. We were at Kenny Smith's party when his parents were away. Do you remember?" Matt asked.

"Hell, I remember going to the party. I don't remember the six hours of boozing, but I do recall spending most of Sunday shouting at the floor with a thumping headache to match. So, what happened?" Dan wanted to know.

"I'm not really sure. We got talking and then the next thing I knew, she was dragging me off to find a bedroom, which were all fully occupied, so we went out to the garage."

"How romantic!" Dan said.

"Hmm, well, we had a heavy-duty snog and there was a lot of fumbling, mostly on my part. Then she gave me a condom, pulled down her granny pants and bending over, supported herself on an old chair... and told me to fuck her."

"Wow, she wasn't taking any prisoners then?" Dan interrupted again.

"Or no for an answer, but at that point, she let Percy out of prison!"

Dan nearly choked on his mouthful of Guinness as Matt smiled at how he remembered the whole scenario developing into a farce.

"She did what?" Dan said incredulously.

"She bent over, and botty burped!"

Dan laughed out loud and was speechless, conjuring up the scene in his mind. When he was able to speak, he said, "Are you sure it wasn't a fanny fart? You know, when it sounds like they're blowing a raspberry?"

"Nope, it was a proper windjammer. She sounded like Sooty's mate Sweep, you know, that kazoo type of sound."

Dan laughed out loud again. "I loved Sooty and Sweep when I was a kid but anyway, that must have caused a bit of a recoil on your part?"

"Recoil? Fuck me, she nearly blew me out of the door. She didn't even apologise, just said, *'Oops… better out than in!'*"

Dan was beside himself with mirth but told Matt to carry on.

"Anyway, I dropped the gear, rolled on the rubber, she steered it in and off we went…for about five minutes. Thankfully, she didn't fart again!"

"Christ, that long?" Dan said with genuine surprise at Matt's first time. "I thought a rutting deer would have lasted longer. You know – 4 seconds!"

"Yeah, well, I thought it seemed like five minutes, although she wasn't very impressed when I'd done. She just said, *'You useless fucker,'* pulled up her enormous bangers and left." Matt looked a little embarrassed but could see the funny side.

Dan nearly spilt his Guinness; he was laughing so much.

"What about you?" Matt asked.

Dan immediately became quite thoughtful and, after an elongated pause, said, "Do you remember Mrs Malin at school, used to teach Maths? Curvy woman with short, dark curly hair. Always immaculately dressed and smelt great?" he said.

Matt thought for a few seconds. "Yeah, Mrs MMM… Monica Malin. She was quite short but had nice legs. Posh speaking and always seemed quite aloof. Must have been in her mid-thirties."

"Thirty-nine," Dan said.

"Jeez, that's specific!" Matt was quizzical but Dan didn't elaborate, so Matt continued. "There were rumours she was having it off with the flashy PE teacher. What was his name? The Welsh guy who coached the First 15 rugby team. You'd know him 'cos you were playing rugby at that time. You were in that side, weren't you, even though you were a year younger than most of them?" Matt asked.

"Yes, Harris, Rod Harris. Yeah, nice guy, he was in the under-twenty Welsh Team as a flanker, but it turned out that he was more wanker than flanker, so he turned to teaching. The rumours came about because the lovely Mrs Malin often came to matches against other schools as part of the kitchen staff, doing the coffees and bacon butties, etcetera. She would then hang about afterwards, and Rod the Prod could give her a lift home. Allegedly."

"Lucky man!" Matt said, picturing Mrs Malin sampling Rod the Prod's rugby tackle and smiling to himself.

"She must have been the subject of many a wank fest. She definitely filled a few of my fantasies. Anyway, what about her?" Matt asked, almost forgetting the original question. Dan sipped at his beer and again looked thoughtful, then hit Matt with a revelation.

"Well, when you're talking about saddling up for the first time, she was *my* first proper indulgence. I don't think you can count being tossed off by my mum's best buddy at a party a month before."

Matt was confused at this double disclosure and wasn't sure what he meant. "How do you mean? As in a fantasy woman to get off to and what's that about being wanked off by your mum's friend?"

Dan took another sip of his beer and spoke a little quieter, "Just between us, Mrs Malin was my first ever... friend with benefits." He had another sip of his Guinness as he let that sink in.

"As in rumpy-pumpy?" Matt looked at him aghast.

Dan nodded and then said, "The other incident doesn't count."

"*No, really?* Nah, you're winding me up. Anyway, she left when we were sixteen."

Dan corrected him. "Seventeen 2005, same as you."

"Jeez, go on then. Paint me the picture of your nefarious sexual activity with a woman who should have known better. And one I would have loved to have known better."

Dan took a good swig of his Guinness and called Don to get another round in. Don acknowledged him with a nod, grabbed a couple of Guinness glasses and began to pour.

Matt was impatient for a continuation.

"And?"

"It was the last day of term before the summer holidays, her last full day because she was leaving, although none of us knew at the time. We always broke up early on the end of term Friday, if you remember, hers was the last lesson. About ten minutes before the end, she was handing out our homework journals but didn't seem to have mine, so she told me to wait at the end, and she would go and find it."

"As everyone left, she went off to get the journal and came back with it fifteen minutes later. She was a bit surprised that everyone had gone, saying she needed two strong lads to move some furniture at her house. Paid, of course."

"Of course!" Matt agreed, smiling and wondering whether "payment" meant the same for Mrs M as it did for his buddy.

"Then she said that as I was a big, strong boy, I'd be able to manage it by myself if I was interested but she really needed it done that afternoon. I wasn't doing anything and all that was waiting for me at home was a porno mag with the pages stuck together."

Matt laughed but then urged his friend to get on with the story. Dan waited for Donald to bring the pints over and paid him with the exact amount of cash.

"I said I'd be happy to help, and she replied that she'd give me a lift home afterwards."

"Didn't you suspect anything?" Matt asked.

"Well, you always hope in your fantasies that something like that would transpire into something out of a porn flick, but she was so sort of casual about it all that I took her at her word. Looking back, the only tiny clue was that she thought it best that she picked me up from the lay-by at Seaton Park rather than her being seen taking a schoolboy directly away from school. I remember to this day that she said, '*We don't want people to get silly notions of anything untoward.*' God, I can still recall that posh accent of hers. Anyway, I thought nothing of it and agreed to meet her in about fifteen minutes. She had some things to tidy up first, and it would take me a good ten minutes to walk there, anyway."

"It was a lovely day, and when I got there, I sat on the bench near the park and just enjoyed the sunshine. She was late and I was just about to bugger off home when she drove into the lay-by and waved at me to join her. She apologised for her '*tardiness*' as she put it; she had been waylaid by the headmaster but was glad that I'd waited. We hardly spoke at all on the way to her house."

"She had that nice BMW Z4, didn't she?" Matt said.

"Yes, and I kept glancing at her hemline gradually riding up as she drove…so damn sexy."

Matt nodded, "At that age, I'd have been bricking it with an older woman, however innocent she made it sound."

"Anyway, she took me to her house, a big place on the outskirts of Richmond. She parked in her secluded drive and switched off the engine. I thought it was a bit odd that she stared out of the window for a few seconds before turning to me and saying, '*You know why you're here, don't you?*' She never let me answer before repeating it, emphasising the point, '*You do know why you're REALLY here?*'"

"I was a bit confused but innocently said that she wanted me to move some furniture. I remember her looking at me with those mesmerising, big brown eyes and smiling. Then she said, '*Daniel, the only furniture that I want you to move is my king-sized bed…with us in it. Do you understand?*' I just gawped and I started shaking, fuck I remember like it was yesterday."

"You jammy bugger!" Matt shook his head, incredulous that these things actually happened, but he knew his mate wasn't lying. "Bloody hell, I would have run a mile!" he added.

Dan continued, "She was still looking at me and leaning slightly across, put her hand on my upper thigh. She was half-whispering and said that if I didn't want to do this, she would take me back to the park and it wouldn't be mentioned again. But if I entered the house, she was going to take me upstairs to her bedroom and we were going to fuck. Mate, I was hard in that instant. It was just the way she was looking at me and the way she said '*fuck*'. It seems to be so much naughtier when a posh woman says that word."

Matt nodded and hung on to everything Dan was saying.

"She swore me to secrecy, saying I must never tell anyone. EVER, then she leaned closer and kissed me. Her tongue just invaded my mouth, it was awesome. Then she put her hand between my legs, just touching my groin, before lightly stroking the bulge. She pulled away a bit and brought her hand up to my cheek to stroke it and then she pushed my chin up so that she could kiss and nibble my throat. I'll tell you now, as simple as it was, it was the sexiest thing that ever happened to me. It seemed like ages before she sat back but still looking me straight in the eyes, she said, '*What's it going to be, Daniel, off to the park with the boys, or learn how to be a man?*'"

"My mind was mush. I was seventeen, just sitting there and here was this gorgeous, mature woman offering herself to me. She held my hand and then said that we were wasting time adding, '*I so want you.*' I just went blank, but I closed my eyes and my mind and let my animal instincts take over. I mean, who wouldn't?"

Matt sneered. "You lucky bugger!"

"I got out of the car, and she told me to put my bag and blazer in the boot before taking me round to the back of the house. We were hardly through the door when she was at me again, kissing and pawing at me. I remember she used the same perfume as my mum, Rive Gauche. Her breath smelled of mint and to this day and forever, I just remember the desire in her eyes. God, I was so hard. She shut the back door, locked it, took my hand and led me upstairs to her bedroom. I cannot for the life of me remember how it was decorated but even though she was fully dressed, she had me stripped naked in no time and when she grabbed my cock, I was seconds from unloading.

She said, '*Mmm, I'm going to enjoy you,*' and she kissed me again before ushering me into the shower, telling me to get cleaned up before we were going to get down and dirty. And she laughed a real dirty laugh. I remember that vividly because I'd never heard her laugh before."

"No, as lovely as she was, she was never very approachable," Matt said, picturing the scene...

"Mate, she couldn't have been any more approachable without me being *in* her and that was imminent. Anyway, it was a walk-in type of shower, more of a wet room really. I had my eyes closed, washing my hair, when I felt her come up behind me, reaching up to stroke and kiss my shoulders. She held me close, and I could feel her tits and nipples pushing into my back as her hands came around and grabbed my cock and balls. She said, '*Clear your mind, dismiss thoughts of me as a teacher. You are male, I am a female, regardless of our years on this earth. You are of lawful age and there is nothing to prevent our union and intimacy. Just enjoy the pleasure we can give each other.*' She kissed and hugged me again." Dan paused to recall the bliss of that situation.

"She took the soap and started soaping my upper body before working lower. Then she went to work on '*Monty and the boys.*'"

"Wait, Monty and the boys?" Matt interrupted. Dan laughed.

"Yeah, Monty and the boys!"

Matt looked at him quizzically.

"Well, ever since puberty, my lodger seems to have a life of its own, so I thought I'd give it a name; Monty...Monty Python, and 'the boys' are my danglers!"

"Oh. I get it." Matt also laughed.

"Anyway, what she was doing was fucking fantastic. Again, I was right on the edge before I turned around and leaned down to kiss her.

She was even shorter without her heels. Lovely boobs, a bit of a tummy and a dark hairy growler. Fuck, I'm hard now just thinking about her."

"Me too," said Matt, shifting on his barstool.

"She soaped her hands again and washed my bum cheeks, and sliding her hands between them to wash my crack, she even slipped a finger in my chutney channel, which caused a real reaction. She had Monty back in her hands and was giving it the five-knuckle shuffle before I shot all over her tummy and legs and there was even a huge dollop of it in her muff." Matt laughed out loud, and Don and the two guys at the end of the bar turned in surprise at such a loud shriek.

"She kissed me and said, '*Mmm, good boy, well, that's got that first one out of the way,*' she laughed and muttered something about the exuberance of youth and laughed again. Then she pointed to the towels. '*Be off with you and get in my bed while I get myself ready for you.*'"

"My legs were shaking, but I took a towel and went into the bedroom to dry myself. She took a while, so I just pulled the covers back and got in. She came out a good few minutes later with a big towel around her and a smaller one around her head. She wanted me to pull the covers back because she wanted to look at me while she dried off. She told me not to be shy because I had a beautiful body.

"So, as I pulled the covers back, I already had half a lob on. I remember her licking her lips. She sat down on the edge of the bed next to me and let the towel fall off her shoulders. She just had this command about her. We were about to have sex and yet she was still the schoolteacher. '*Massage my shoulders, Daniel,*' she ordered, so I knelt behind her, stroked her neck and attempted to massage her bare shoulders. She rested her head on my chest, and I did my best. She asked me if I had a girlfriend, which I didn't, as you know. Then she just came out with it and asked if I'd ever had sex with a girl. I remember hesitating but she told me not to be embarrassed if I hadn't. I said that I'd kissed a couple of girls - not at the same time, which made her laugh, but no, I hadn't. I didn't mention my mum's friend Christine. She suddenly stood up, turned around to face me, and dropped the towels to the floor. She was roughly the same height standing up as I was kneeling on the bed, and she threw her arms around my neck and kissed me. She said, '*So I will be your very first and you will remember me forever, how delicious,*' and then she kissed me again."

"You lucky bastard!" Matt said, shaking his head again. It was now his stock reaction to this major revelation.

"We spent ages just kissing and fondling each other, then she lay on her back and said that she wanted me inside her. I got between her legs, and she held the old chap, which couldn't have been harder, before positioning it at her gash. '*Push nice and slow and look me in the eyes as you do it. I want to see the ecstasy on your face as you become intimate with a woman for the first time.*' Well, a man's gotta do what the lady asks, and she sighed loudly before smiling and licking her lips as it went in. God, her cockpit was hot and soaking and it was all I could do to stop firing off again!"

Matt grinned at his buddy and thought how different it all was from his five-minute fiasco.

"When I was all the way in, she held me tightly and told me to pause just to feel how blissful it was. '*I can feel all of you in me, and it's wonderful,*' she said and wrapped her legs around my arse before whispering in my ear to make love to her slowly, with long strokes. Mate, it was literally fucking amazing. Her sighs of pleasure were such a turn-on."

Matt smiled again and said, "I'll bet. Abracadabra!"

"What?" Dan looked at Matt quizzically.

"Magic eyes and sighs - Abracadabra, The Steve Miller Band."

"Oh, right, yeah, magic indeed. The rest of the afternoon, we spent fucking in different positions interspersed with lots of oral sex. She showed me how to go down on her and which bits needed more attention than others. I can now understand why a woman's sex is called a beaver. Her pelt went from her 'beard' right around to her bum-fluffed arsehole. I wasn't sure whether to lick it, pet it, or give it a biscuit!" They both laughed loudly again.

"In between, we talked about school and what I hoped to achieve ambitions-wise. It was a lovely way to spend four hours, and I could barely walk afterwards. Have to say, I was quite concerned when she climaxed the first time. She was so loud I thought she was having a seizure!" Matt chuckled again.

"Another thing I recall her saying to me was that the whole sex thing was totally absurd. Animals do it to procreate. Only humans and dolphins do it for the fun of it. Sex is a requirement to perpetuate the human race, but God really had a sense of humour with the desire and lust thing, and of course, jealousy and possessiveness just cause so many issues."

"Wow, that is profound!" Matt replied.

"I didn't take it all in at the time, but I just loved hearing her talk in that posh accent but mainly talking to me like I was an adult, not the boy sitting at the back, bored to tears with fucking algebra and all that bollocks. And the main thing was that when I spoke, she looked at me so intently, like she was really interested. I could have fallen in love with her, given half a chance."

"Dan, you are one spawny git. Women just flock to you, don't they, even then!" Matt just shook his head at the apparent injustice of desire and lust that women have for some guys and for his best mate in particular. Dan wasn't done.

"As the time was getting on, she demanded that I finish off by putting my cock between her tits as she pushed them together, squirting a little baby oil there for lube. She wanted me to give her a *'pearl necklace'* and had to explain that I was to use her breasts as a surrogate pussy and shoot my cum on her neck. There wasn't much, given she'd had two loads already, one in the shower and one over her fingers from another hand job. When I did the deed, she just sighed and smiled and told me to always remember her as a very sexy lady, not the stuffy, stuck-up teacher boring kids to death."

"Christ, Danny, I think she was well and truly stuck up when you finished with her. Did you see her again during the holidays?" Matt asked, hoping for some more juicy stories.

"As she drove me home, she asked if I was doing anything on Sunday. Unfortunately, I was off on the family holiday the next day. She said it was a shame as her husband was coming home Saturday night, and he would have enjoyed me as well!"

Matt's jaw dropped. "What, as in…?"

"She said he was bisexual but didn't elaborate further. I wasn't sure what would have gone on, but I was gutted that being with her was a one-off, as she told me that they were moving to the US before I got back. It was the only disappointment apart from…"

Matt looked at him quizzically.

"She never paid me for moving the furniture!" And they both laughed loudly. Dan continued, "She emigrated just before I got back from holiday, Houston, I think. I guess she'll be kiddy-fiddling Americans now," Dan said wistfully.

"Oh, mate, don't you know what happened to her?" Matt's face was quite stern now.

"No, what?" Dan asked quizzically.

"I was in the dentist's for a check-up a couple of months back and was just browsing through the local paper in the waiting room. There was a small article on their 'World News' page that usually tells you that some British tourist has been savagely dismantled by a goat in the West Indies or some other *major* scoop, but this one headlined that a local teacher who had moved to the US had been murdered. In the article, it named Monica Malin and her husband and said they were shot dead by one of her students from the local High School. It didn't say why, but apparently, he called the police to confess and when they arrived, he turned the gun on himself."

Dan looked shocked. "Oh, fuck! Why didn't the cunt do that first and just leave them alone?" The breath seemed to leave him as he was distraught about her tragic death.

"Their gun laws are a joke – as a nation, they all think the OK Corral is at the end of High Street, USA. They carry a gun to make sure they get to the shops safely just to buy a loaf of bread or more fucking bullets!" Matt said.

They didn't bother with a game of pool and as they finished their pints, they sat in silence as if to pay some sort of homage to the sexy maths teacher they had the privilege of knowing.

When Matt settled down in bed that night with Kirstie, cuddling up, he was sad to recall Mrs Malin's demise. He was shocked when he read about it the first time but now knowing his bestest, best, Best Man was emotionally involved made it all the more saddening. He then recalled his own personal, unspectacular cherry-picking. He had a pre-arranged overnight stay at the party and came home the following morning. His mum was cleaning; she was always very house-proud, even if it was only rented accommodation. She would die of shame if people thought she lived in a pigsty.

"Good morning" was his mother's reply to his chirpy "Hi, Mum," then she stopped what she was doing and looked at him before very pointedly and profoundly saying, "So the boy has become a man!" She looked him up and down and then, nodding slightly, said, "Well, it had to happen at some point." She turned and carried on with what she was doing before continuing with her words of wisdom. "Be very responsible with your newfound superpower. At the very least, always remember their names and don't use girls, especially if they're vulnerable and think they're getting more from you than you're willing to give. What was it Michael Jackson sang about? Breaking girls' hearts." She went on to fuss about straightening a few cushions.

Matt was embarrassed that he was so transparent, or was it his mother who really had the superpower? He watched her for a few moments, not knowing if she was going to add anything else to pile on the humiliation. He thought about questioning her accusation and couldn't think of anything to say that wouldn't incriminate himself further. As he stood there, she stopped what she was doing and came over to him. As big as he was to her tiny frame, she cuddled him to her and told him, "It's all about respect, okay? Don't use or abuse, and don't allow yourself to be used or abused just for the sake of fleeting gratification. Meaningless shenanigans are demeaning and embarrassing."

"Yes, Mum," he remembered saying to her all those years ago, and in the darkness, he shed a tear, although he wasn't sure why.

18
Jailbreak

Friday morning, 21ˢᵗ March 2013

"Behave yourself! Love you," Kirstie smiled and gave Matt a peck on the lips before he grabbed his bag and let her drive off to work.

It was 7.50 am at the car park of the football team's home ground. He waved at her as she drove away before he chatted with some of the other early arrivals. Kirstie had no concerns about him, and she was looking forward to her last day at work before starting her new job on Monday. She also had a night out planned that evening with her best friends, Sarah, Mia, and Sam, to catch up and have some fun.

The minibus arrived punctually at 8.00 am. All twelve lads were buzzing and ready to go. Overnight bags stowed, beer loaded, everyone present and correct, and they were off on the 250-mile trip to Blackpool, which would take around six hours, including a short break near Crewe, all traffic dependent.

They had barely driven out of the car park before Cliff tackled GG on his evening excursion to a local club.

"How did you get on with that hippo you were talking to last Saturday night?"

"Hippo?" GG questioned, a bit put out by the inference.

"Yeah, that big girly, the one with an arse that could block the Blackwall tunnel. What was her name, Large Marge?"

"Flabby Gabby" was a random suggestion from the back, as was "Burly Shirley."

"Sturdy, Cliff. Sturdy," Billy said helpfully.

"Sturdy? What, as in Sturdy Gerdy?" Cliff said in a mimicking tone.

"No, just sturdy," Billy said. "People can be sturdy rather than large or a weeny bit heavy," he chose his words carefully, but the bus was silent, waiting for pearls of wisdom.

"So *sturdy* is a nice word. Don't you think?" Unfortunately, these were pearls before swine.

"Billy, self-appointed professor of the English language, I know the difference between *sturdy* and downright fucking obese. Mate, this girl could have taken on Tonga's rugby forwards in a scrum by herself and won. There's sturdy and there are people who abuse the privilege of being fat. She was the type where there's a fuck in every fold and you could smack her arse and ride on the ripples."

He stared at Billy with an added shrug and raised eyebrows that signified that he expected Billy to know exactly what he meant. Billy did acknowledge that with a nod of resignation. As chance would have it, the bus was held up by a truck towing a horse box, which clearly was not fit for the purpose of transporting a huge Shire horse whose hind quarters were almost spilling out the back.

"Fucking hell, does her arse look big in that?" shouted Rudy.

"Is that Large Marge?" asked Ollie. GG leaned to one side to look through the front and thought about it for a second or two. "No, the proportions are about right, but it can't be her 'cos her pubes aren't that long." The majority of the passengers were absorbed in the comedic value of this unfolding farce.

Cliff turned his attention back to GG.

"So, having established that it is not her in the box in front, GG, how did it go when you got to grips with her? Did you love the lard? Was beauty just a light switch away?" Cliff was persistent.

"Fuck off, Cliff, she wasn't that big."

Cliff responded. "Okay, I'm prepared to concede she wasn't as big as the behemoth in front but we're all desperate to know how it went when you took her home last week." There was silence, and all eyes fell back on GG. It was like a tennis match.

"Well, I'm quite sure I have never gone to bed with an ugly woman. Although I might have woken up with a few. If you must know, we're getting engaged when I get back!" GG said almost defiantly. A big roar of laughter from the lads, who then momentarily wondered if he was joking. Cliff asked if he could be the best man.

"Sorry, mate," GG said. "Her brother, who is an Earl or something, would have to be best man, as it's their family tradition. Of course, you'll all be invited to the wedding, but you'll need to be vetted by some MI5 people because of her links with the Dutch Royal Family. But hey, if you don't have a criminal record or a lock-up full of illicit contraband, you'll be fine!" GG said confidently.

"That's half of you lot fucked, then!" Ian said seriously. The bus was totally silent, with the guys trying to work out who this girl was that GG had managed to snare.

GG called out to the driver, "Chris, roughly when do you think we'll be stopping for a cuppa? I need to phone Lady Lydia Van Der Shaggan to tell her I'm okay. I can't do it in front of this bunch of hyenas with their ears flapping." He purposely pronounced the word *Shaggan* in a French accent.

"Is she posh, then?" Asked Gump.

"Mate, she is so posh she doesn't cum - she arrives!" GG said.

Again, momentary silence before Ollie said sarcastically, "Lady Lydia Van Der Shaggan," and started to laugh at the obvious yarn, as did the rest of the ensemble, including Cliff, who enjoyed the riposte.

"Lydia, Lydia riddled with chlamydia," shouted somebody at the back.

"Is chlamydia her twin sister and does she really come from Holland?" asked Gump.

"I'm not sure, mate but she really liked my Nether Lands!" said GG, casually looking out of the window as everyone got the joke.

"So…How did you get on with lardy Lydia, then?" Cliff asked. GG looked out of the window again before turning to Cliff and saying in a matter-of-fact way.

"Well, when we got back to her flat and she stripped off, she had tits like torpedoes, a bush like a used Brillo pad and with legs akimbo, I'm faced with the great divide and a minge like a badly packed kebab. Even though it was like chucking a sausage up Oxford Street, I bashed the gash and fucked her senseless…for a good three minutes. Then she turned over, and I smashed her back doors in. I'll tell you something, you don't know you've had a great shag until you've got shit under your fingernails and your foreskin. She loves me. What more can I say?"

The boys cheered loudly. GG took a bow, and no one cared what part, if any, of the story was true.

Long-distance trips never change. They start with the initial excitement, lots of chat, followed by the resignation of how tedious travel can be. During the inevitable lull, some guys were on their phones or playing cards, and others slept to pass the time. It took nearly four hours to get near Crewe and a break for lunch. Seventy-five miles to go, back on the coach, it was time to break out the beer. Under strict instructions from Chris, they were not to be seen from the road, drinking out of cans. Plastic cups were issued to all participants; weak bladders could be catered for by reusing the empty tins. These "toilet receptacles" were to be kept separate from cans that still had beer in them.

Chris added, "I know some lager tastes like piss but for fuck's sake, don't mix them up and don't knock 'em over. I have to clean this bus, and I don't want it smelling like a conga in an old people's home."

They were all on keen alert now to count down the miles to their pilgrimage and just after Preston, they merged from the M6 onto the M55, and it was full steam ahead. Or it would have been as it appeared that POETS Day (Piss Off Early Tomorrow's Saturday) was not just the privilege of Southern commuters.

The delay caused some disquiet in the group eager to get to their destination. They sat in silence for the next thirty minutes as the traffic crawled along the motorway. Cliff, the team captain, felt he needed to get the guys back on track. He handed each of them a new can of beer and said, "Right, boys, anyone know any good jokes?

"Matt, it's your weekend. You can kick it off!" Cliff ordered.

"Thanks, Cliff," Matt said indignantly.

"If you don't want to be chained naked to one of the trams on the Golden Mile, you'll start," Cliff said with a laugh. Matt thought for a minute and said he didn't have a joke, but he did have a Limerick. Gump asked what a Limerick was and was swiftly told to listen.

"It's a little poem, mate," said one of the more helpful travellers.

Matt presented his offering as though he were a Shakespearean actor, which included some overblown armography.

"There was a gay Countess of Bray,
And you may think it odd when I say,
That in spite of high station,
Rank and education,
She always spelt Cunt with a K."

There were a few laughs and Dan's submission was short and sweet: "What's the difference between a prostitute and a Kit Kat?" Silence for a few seconds, before Dan delivered the punch line with aplomb, "You can only get four figures in a Kit Kat!"

Billy told the audience that his offering was another Limerick. He cleared his throat and went for it.

"There was a young lady from Dallas,
Who used a dynamite stick as a phallus,
They found her vagina,
in North Carolina,
And her arsehole at Buckingham Palace."

Steve was next. "How do you turn a fox into an elephant?" No response and then said, "Marry it." That drew a lot of laughs and a few comments. One rather pointedly asked, "You're not speaking from personal experience, are you, Stevie?"

"Might be," Steve said and then added, "I bought her flowers for Valentine's Day, she thanked me but then said, 'I suppose this means I've got to spend the weekend on my back with my legs in the air.' I replied that I thought we had a vase in the cupboard."

The whole audience dissolved in laughter before he continued, "It's her birthday soon and I'm going to buy her a bracelet and a dildo, 'cos if she don't like the bracelet, she can go fuck herself!" There were quite a few smirks and chuckles for the ad hoc extras.

Ian then chipped in with his effort, "As we're on a poetry kick, here's one about *love*!" The throng groaned in unison.

"The love from a boy for a beautiful maid,
The love of a woman for her man,
The love of a baby unafraid,
Have existed since time began.

But the most wonderful love,
The strongest of loves,
Even greater than a son for his mother,
Is the all-consuming, undying love,
Of one drunken sod for another."

The polite applause was indicative of their feeling of cringe. Cliff said, "This is going from bad to verse!" resulting in more groans from the captive audience.

"Okay, my turn," he announced. "This old couple are driving down a country lane. It's dark and it's pissing down. They just get around a bend when some animal runs out in front of them. The bloke brakes and nearly stops in time but does hit the creature. They get out and see a badger lying in front of the car. The guy finds that it's only stunned. He then says to his wife, 'I think it's in shock. Quick, put its head between your legs to keep it warm. His wife grimaces and says, 'but it's all wet and smelly.' Her husband snaps back, 'Well, hold its fucking nose, then!'"

They all knew Cliff would steal the limelight with what they thought was the best joke so far. Cliff bowed in acknowledgement of their acclaim and then pointed at Dwayne.

Dwayne said, "I'm useless with jokes, but here goes. We call our Granddad Superman," he paused. "Cos he can't get out of the bath." There was silence, and he couldn't work out why, then realised, "Oh, wait, that should be Spiderman, not Superman, sorry."

Ollie nipped in with his effort. "Why does Edward Woodward have so many Ds in his name?" No reply. "Otherwise, he'd be called Ewar Woowar!" Spontaneous laughter from all but one. Gump asked who Edward Woodward was. Cliff heard him and, shaking his head, just said, "Oh, Gumpy boy, you are priceless, but we do love you."

Cliff looked at Gump's feet. "Mate, why are you wearing odd socks?" Gump checked to see and then said, "That's weird. I've got another pair like that." The rest of the bunch just smiled at how absurd he sounded.

Billy, who was sitting behind the driver, asked him if he'd put the CD on that he was handing to him. Chris said it wasn't a problem and also agreed to turn the music up. There was a bit of hubbub in the bus until the opening chords flooded the van.

Who's Sorry Now - Connie Francis. Somehow, this was the team's song. No one knew why but they all loved it and sang along like pub singers because it had to be done in that style. There was a bit of chat when it finished before the distinctive opening riffs of "*Layla*", which stopped everyone talking and by now, with the beer taking effect, they all joined in, including an air guitar from Gump.

No Woman, No Cry followed, which brought about some high fives from Rudy and Dwayne, the West Indian contingent. Billy told them he didn't want them to feel left out. Next:

Bruce Springsteen (The Boss) – Born To Run

Dire Straits – Sultans Of Swing

Bob Seger – Hollywood Nights

Thin Lizzy – The Boys Are Back In Town

Jeff Beck - Hi Ho Silver Lining

Cockney Rebel – Come Up And See Me

Rolling Stones – Can't Get No Satisfaction, where Paul (aka Cream Bun) did a very passable impression of Mick Jagger, strutting up and down the very short aisle of the minibus with his hands on his hips and an exaggerated pout.

Queen - Bohemian Rhapsody, with Cliff conducting sections of the group to do the quirky verses before bringing them all together for the full finale.

The Who – Can't Explain one side of the bus singing the lyric with the other side singing "Can't Explain" and all joining in the chorus.

David Bowie – Queen Bitch

Neil Diamond – Sweet Caroline

Lastly, *Queen – We are the Champions*

The CD finished with a huge round of applause.

"Well done Billy, great stuff." Cliff was lavish with his praise, and it killed a good hour of crawling traffic.

Steve, who was the self-appointed tour scout and entertainment manager, got the SAT Nav operating as they neared Blackpool. It was raining heavily and with the wind blowing off the Irish Sea, it made it feel ten times worse. Despite the weather, they were all in high spirits as the bus drove along the esplanade, past the empty cafés, bars, restaurants and amusement arcades. Matt turned and looked at Dan.

"Not exactly rocking, is it? A northern town in Winter!"

Dan smiled and said, "Today is the first day of spring, buddy and it's what we make of it. You'll see!"

As they neared the Tower, they turned into one of the narrower streets full of big terraced Victorian houses, where virtually every other one was a bed-and-breakfast establishment. Luckily, they managed to park fairly near to theirs and, braving the elements, grabbed their bags and hurried in.

They were met by the overly friendly landlady, standing five-foot-seven, with bobbed, bleached blonde hair and a low-cut top displaying ample-sized boobs in a sheepdog bra (rounds 'em up and points them in the right direction). She was about fifty years old, with a mummy tummy and a short skirt showing off a very nice pair of legs. She smelt of inexpensive perfume and wore a lot of cheap jewellery, including an ankle chain, but there was something undeniably very sexy about her.

"Come in, lads. Go into the bar, and we'll get you sorted with a complimentary drink, then I'll get you checked in." She ushered them through to the big bar area and went behind the counter.

"Okay, lads, first drink is on the house while I give you the lecture," she said to a big cheer from her new guests.

"My name is Barbara, and I expect you to treat my establishment properly. You all get one set of keys each. The front door is locked at midnight because I need my beauty sleep."

"Never!" shouted Cliff. "You are lovely enough."

Barbara looked over at him and, with disdain, said, "I didn't realise I'd taken a booking from a footie team with impaired vision, but I would appreciate not being interrupted again. Think of it as the safety drill you get on an aircraft. Now you say, *yes, Barbara!*" She had an aura of authority, which you challenged at your own peril. She then conducted them in what was a half-hearted response of, "Yes, Barbara." She puffed out her cheeks in disgust at their apathy.

"We'll try that again because you don't all seem to be singing from the same hymn sheet. One, two, three…"

"Yes, Barbara!" they all said loudly.

"To repeat, you get one set of keys each. The front door is locked at midnight, but you'll have a front door key and your room key. *Do not lose them*; you will be charged fifty pounds to have them replaced." She paused, held her hands out to urge their reply.

"Yes, Barbara!"

She continued to pour drinks while carrying on with her well-rehearsed monologue.

"I and my neighbours would appreciate quiet when you arrive back after your evening's entertainment, but as you're from down south, I am sure you're so well-mannered that you don't really need to be told."

Again, she gestured and received the unanimous response, "Yes, Barbara!"

"*And*, lastly, your bed is for you and you alone. Do not bring outsiders back here for your little holiday romance. That means women… or men if you're on t'other bus. *Got it?*"

To a man, they responded with, "Yes, Barbara!"

"Good, I hope you all have a lovely time here in Blackpool," was her final response before allocating keys to the group.

Matt took his beer when Barbara offered it and thanked her before saying, "That doesn't sound like a Northwest accent. It's more Geordie, I think?"

"Oh, we have a Doctor Higgins among us," she said, smiling at him. "What's your name, bonny lad?"

"Matt," he said, smiling back at her and surreptitiously glancing at her cleavage, although it didn't go unnoticed. "Who is Doctor Higgins?" he added.

"The professor in My Fair Lady who was an expert in linguistics and regional accents." Barbara could see he was confused.

"Doesn't matter but well done, young man, you are spot on. I'm originally from Scarborough. Barbara from Scarborough but was brought up just south of Newcastle."

"Well, here's to Newcastle and Scarborough. Hopefully, their footie teams will win something again soon," Matt said, smiling at her and still trying to subtly take in her figure.

"Aye, 'howay the lads!" she said, taking a sip of her hastily poured glass of wine, and then she made her excuses and went into the back room.

Some of the boys made short work of their freebie drinks and drifted off to their rooms to get ready for the evening. Matt was last to finish his beer, along with Dan, with whom he was sharing a room, and they looked outside to watch the horizontal rain drilling against the windows.

"It's forecast to stop by the end of May," a voice was heard behind them. It was Barbara, making light of the appalling weather. "But I'm guessing you're not here to get a suntan?" she added in a tone suggesting she required an answer.

"Barbara, you are correct. Matt here is getting married in the summer and this is his stag weekend," Dan said.

"Ah, I see," Barbara replied, looking Matt up and down. "Well, you look very young to be throwing your life away on long-term commitment, but I'm sure you love the young lady and all the very best of luck to you, Pet…and to her, of course," she said, raising her near-empty glass of wine to him.

"I keep telling him he's too young," said Dan. "But he won't listen. To be fair, his bride-to-be is stunningly beautiful, and he is massively punching above his weight!" Dan said.

"They will make a handsome couple and have lots of beautiful children. Here's to you, Matthew," Barbara said, looking him straight in the eye, lingering with intent.

As young as Matt was, the message was received and understood.

Within an hour, everyone was showered, shaved, and dressed to party the night away. They decided on a quick pint in the bar before heading out and Ian took an opportunity to tackle Steve about how he had managed to get away for the weekend.

"How d'ya mean?" Steve replied, looking a bit put out that his presence on the trip was being questioned.

"Oh, come on, the *'war office'*, aka your missus, won't even let you go to Tesco by yourself." Ian put him on the spot.

"Other supermarkets are available!" shouted one wag.

Quietly at first, Stevie said, "I haven't told her." There was a bit of confusion before someone asked what he said. He repeated it, louder this time. "I haven't told her. Well, I did say last night I was going on Matt's stag do. I wasn't massively specific about how long it was going on or where it was. Anyway, she was moaning about how I never listen to her, and then she started banging on about some other shit, so I left it at that. I sent her a text this morning saying I'd be a bit late coming home."

This caused absolute bedlam, and then GG said, "A couple of hours late is a smidge different from a couple of days, don't you think, Steve?"

"Well, possibly, but it's easier to ask for forgiveness than permission!" There was more uproar. Behind the bar, Barbara smiled and shook her head.

"If my husband did that to me, I'd take a knife to his gentleman parts and re-arrange him."

Ian asked where her husband was, Barbara was quick to respond. "I should say my ex-husband and he's under the patio." More laughter before the attention turned back to Steve, who said, "It's all gone pear-shaped, as she has, literally. The last time I got my hand in her knickers was when I was hanging the washing out. Over the last year or so, she's become a miserable cow," he said wistfully. "I've come to the conclusion that women live with guys hoping to change them; men live with women hoping for the opposite of that."

It rather killed the mood, but Cliff piped up and told everyone to drink up and get going for something to eat and then meet up again in the Tower Ballroom at 8.30 pm. Last one buys the drinks.

Matt returned to his room and tried to phone Kirstie but then remembered she was going out with the girls, so he just sent her a text to say that they had arrived safely and they could chat tomorrow, adding in a "Love You" and a few kisses.

19

I Kissed a Girl

March 2013

Having left the light and love of her life in the car park for his stag weekend, Kirstie drove to work for her final day at that company. She contemplated that this was the first time since living with Matt that they were apart. She felt a little empty but today would be a huge distraction with a little celebration at work with her colleagues, followed by an evening out with the "gang."

Kirstie loved working at the publishing company she was at but always knew it would be a stepping stone to a large media company. She would be working in a new team of human resources specialists headed up by someone from a legal background and she could hardly wait, even if the prospect was very daunting. Time to get nervous about that on Sunday night, she thought. Today and the weekend were for fun.

Most of the morning was spent clearing out what was left in her desk. She was cajoled into a lunchtime gathering of close co-workers just to say farewell. Mid-afternoon, there was a large congregation for a presentation, where she received a card signed by everyone, together with a John Lewis voucher for a substantial amount of money. This wasn't just a leaving present but also a gift for her wedding in four months' time. She was quite upset as she left for good but the excitement of seeing her pals that night more than compensated.

In the evening, the gang of four reconvened in the same small pub where Sarah had met Dan eight months previously. Sarah was as bubbly as ever, so much so she was positively radiant.

"*Wow*, Saz, living with Dan seems to have done you no harm at all," Kirstie said as the four of them sat down with their drinks.

"Obviously getting it regular!" Mia said with a wink.

"I know. To think it was only last summer when I met him and we've been living together since November," Sarah said. "So how are we all doing?" she asked. Kirstie said that she had left her job today and was starting her new job on Monday. There was quite a substantial pay hike and the possibility of some European and domestic travel, plus other benefits – private health care, final salary pension and a cheap car loan for starters. She was asked about the wedding and said it was all going according to plan but she would be consulting with Sarah on a few things.

"I'll let you all know when you'll be required for the final fitting of the bridesmaid dresses, but so far, so good.

"Oh, and while I remember, I've arranged the hens' weekend," Kirstie added.

"Don't tell me we're all off to some sexy European city where the men are gorgeous and we can fuck who we want without getting caught!" Sarah said, laughing.

Kirstie smiled at her. "Not quite, as my lovely mum is coming as well," she said.

"Oh, brilliant!" Mia said. "I love your mum. She's always a good laugh and you look so alike that you could be sisters."

"That's super. I'd go along with that as well," said Sam.

"Even if your mum's coming and let me say I am very pleased that she is, she can still find a gigolo to keep her entertained for forty-eight hours, couldn't she?" Sarah suggested.

Kirstie stared at Sarah and shook her head, resigned to the fact that Sarah would always steer any subject around to sex.

"Okay, so last time we got together, it was only Kirstie and Mia who were in love," Sarah said. "How do we all stand now? Put your hands up if you have a full-time partner that's jumping your bones!"

Kirstie and Mia were the first to raise theirs.

"Come on, Sarah, don't be shy. We were here that night you snared Dan, and you haven't stopped jumping *his* bones since. In fact, I'm surprised you found enough time to get out this evening," Kirstie said sarcastically.

"Ha, Ha," Sarah sneered and added, "as you well know, Danny is sleeping with Matt tonight under the bright lights of Blackpool Illuminations. Let's hope it doesn't end up like something out of Brokeback Mountain, although two cocks at the same time is a nice idea," and she raised her arm together with the other two.

They all turned to Sam, who sat there quite demurely but her face broke into a wide smile, and she raised her arm to join them.

"That's awesome, each and every one of us is all loved up," Sarah succinctly put it, "even Sam!"

They were thrilled when she told them that at last, she had found a steady partner and that she was very content.

"Very content?" said Sarah, quite amazed at how ambivalent she sounded. "Very content is when you're eighty and can just about control your bladder, let alone manage a half-decent shag. Not when you're in your twenties and nowhere near your prime yet."

They all chuckled but they were delighted for Sam after hearing her harrowing tale of trying to lose her virginity to Two-Stroke Tommy at university. None of them were in the least bit surprised to find out that Sam's new intimate friend was a girl who was apparently very similar to herself, dedicated to her hockey and not overtly sexual.

"So, you're officially a todger-dodger. Hmm, a bully-off in the bedroom. It makes you wonder what you could do with those hockey sticks, doesn't it?" Sarah said, chuckling to herself.

"Just shows you how out of date you are, Saz. You don't bully off in hockey anymore and they haven't since 1981," Sam corrected her.

"I was never into hockey anyway. Too many butch girls trying to whack you with their sticks, present company excepted, of course Sam, no offence," Sarah said in mitigation.

"None taken!" Sam tutted and smiled.

Mia hugged Sam and said, "Sapphic love is just the best, isn't it? We can be the Sapphic sisters!"

Sam reminded her that she had nothing to compare it to but just said that she felt wonderful making love with her partner and left it at that. Her other good news was that she had at last been selected to play for the full England side in an international friendly against Spain in two weeks' time. From there, she was hoping to make the full squad for the Commonwealth Games in Glasgow in August 2014.

The other girls congratulated her and asked where the game was being played.

"Madrid!" Sam said, much to their disappointment, except Sarah, who then said that they could all have Kirstie's hens' weekend in Spain and sample the tall, dark and handsome talent there. They all knew the logistics of organising that so quickly wasn't on but Sam told them the match would be on TV, so they could support from their armchairs.

"I am so made up for you, Sam. In love and the hockey is going well too. What's your partner's name and are you living with her yet? Or is it early days?" Kirstie asked, squeezing Sam's hand.

"Her name is Olivia and we're planning on moving in together. The only thing is that she's from Norwich, so we only see each other at weekends at the moment," Sam said with a twinkle in her eye.

"Mmm, shagging all weekend. What fun!" Sarah said.

"Bloody hell, Sarah, is that all you think about?" Mia said, laughing at her. Sarah pondered for a second or two before saying, "Um, pretty much but it's so hot getting to know someone by spending all day getting down to it."

"You're right!" Sam said enthusiastically as the others turned to Sam and looked quite shocked at their usually demure pal extolling the virtues of protracted lovemaking.

"That's my girl!" said Sarah and they all clinked their glasses together to toast her.

"To Sam!"

"Look at us, four sex-mad nymphos," Sarah added.

"Speak for yourself!" laughed Kirstie.

"Oh, come on, Kayzee, we all love nookie, especially when it's with a lover that cares about pleasing their partner and vice versa," was Sarah's smiley rebuke.

"So Sarah, if you didn't like hockey, what sport did you get into at school?" Mia asked.

"Tossing off boys behind the bike sheds for a pound a wank," Kirstie quickly said, poking fun at her mate.

"Two pounds, actually and it went towards my CD collection. The last week of one summer term, I made over fifty quid!" replied Sarah, smiling, but again the others weren't sure that she was joking.

They all nodded, drawing on mental images of their own experiences with their "forever" other half. Sarah didn't want to let the loose talk stray from carnal coupling, though and, taking advantage of the fact that they'd had a few drinks by now, asked the group what they loved the best and what they didn't like.

Kirstie shot her a glance and said, "I think some things should remain private!"

Sam agreed, but Sarah wasn't letting them get out of it.

"Oh, come on, we're all girls together, maybe what you might think isn't so great can be worked on to enhance playtime. I'll start. I love all of it – I love it when Dan takes control and won't take no for an answer."

"Gosh, that must be rare!" said Sam. "I didn't think 'No' was in your vocabulary."

"Ooh, Meow," Sarah said, smiling. "You're probably right, though," she sipped at her wine. "But sometimes I just say no to wind him up." She laughed, then continued, "I love it when I have him tied up and he's at my mercy and conversely, when he has me tethered to the bed and performs oral on me for ages, mmm."

"What don't you like then?" asked Mia.

"When he says no, or he's not feeling up to it," Sarah chuckled again.

"What do you do then?" asked Kirstie.

"Go out and find someone that will."

They all laughed at how brazen she was with a joke like that, but Kirstie wondered if there wasn't some truth in it.

"Come on Sam, you next."

"I love when we're orally pleasing one another at the same time," she said quietly as if the whole pub was trying to earwig the conversation. "It almost becomes a battle of wills sometimes but just occasionally - we hit it off at the same time."

"God, yes, a mutual climax is special," Mia said.

Kirstie nodded in agreement, although she had never achieved that with Matt, or anyone, come to that.

"I'm not keen on Olivia playing with my bum, though. It's strictly exit only. She likes me to play with hers, which I'm not keen on either," Sam said.

"Oh, you don't know what you're missing," Sarah interrupted. "When he's doing me doggie style, he times it just right to pull my hair hard and push his thumb up my arse and that always tips me over the edge."

Kirstie thought she'd better add something before Sarah latched on to her and accused her of being a bit of a prude. "Yes, that works for me too," she said unconvincingly.

"And me," said Mia and the other three looked at her quizzically. "Well, that's when Jenny uses a strap-on."

"Ooh, I'll bet that's *so* sexy," said Sarah, knowing full well what it was like being penetrated from behind by another woman wearing a strap-on dildo.

"Enough talk about shagging, it's making me fucking horny," Sarah added. "Tell us more about the Hen weekend, Kay."

"The weekend is arranged, ladies. Like it or lump it!" Kirstie said. "I've provisionally booked a two-night stay for five of us in a Health Club and Spa resort just outside of Birmingham. When we're fed up with being pampered, we can go into the city and shop 'til we drop!"

"Gosh, I can't remember the last time I went shopping," Sam said. "What weekend are you thinking of? I'll check that it doesn't clash with the England Hockey Camps."

Kirstie gave them the dates, and they all seemed to be available and happy to meet their share of the cost, much to Kirstie's relief.

"I'm sure they'll have some fit-looking masseurs there, so I'll make do with a couple of those," Sarah laughed.

"So, Kirstie's got a new job. How's your business going, Sarah?" Mia asked.

Sarah said that her business was going well, although it was causing a little bit of friction at home because some events that were being booked by local individuals and businesses weren't always being held locally, which meant that sometimes she had to travel and stay overnight away from home.

"Hey, but the money is so good that him indoors really shouldn't complain. We're thinking about moving to a house soon with a garden, so we need every penny we can get. Although I did treat myself to a new car a couple of weeks back," Sarah said with some pride in her new purchase.

"Gosh, what did you buy?" asked Sam.

"A nearly new Freelander 2 in black to match my favourite colour underwear!" Sarah laughed. "Top of the range spec, heated leather seats, sunroof, Sat Nav, the works."

"Have you christened it yet?" Mia asked, fully expecting to hear a positive answer.

"Of course, I've called him Freddie, Freddie the Freelander," and she laughed. "I always give my cars names," she added.

"Yes, I've called mine a few names before now as well! Fucking bastard was one for an old Citroen I had," Mia laughingly said before continuing, "You know what I mean, though!"

Sarah smiled. "I picked Dan and Matt up from football on the Saturday I collected it. I only had my stockings and sussies on and a teensy-weensy pair of knickers."

"In black," Kirstie added helpfully.

"Yes, of course," Sarah said. "And I just wore my big camel-hair coat over the top, strolled into the bar to collect them and I'm sure some of the guys thought it was a bit odd that the coat was done right up, although it might have been the killer heels that got their attention!"

She laughed again. "Anyway, Matt went off to the loo as we left and I gave Dan a flash outside. We dropped Matt off and then went to Ducks Wood Disco car park and fucked there for an hour or so."

The others smiled and shook their heads, thinking Sarah was the epitome of exhibitionism.

"Bloody good job, they were leather seats!" said Mia as the others giggled.

"You are not wrong!" Sarah replied, laughing with them. "I nearly slid off them once!"

"Good for you, Saz. How's Dan and his job? Is everything good there?" asked Kirstie.

"As far as I know and he shouldn't moan about me going away for an evening or two because he has had the occasional secondment to America before now and there is always a chance he'd be called over there again."

"And him and Matt are running wild in Blackpool tonight and tomorrow night!" added Kirstie.

"Did Dan speak to you tonight before you came out?" Kirstie asked Sarah.

"No, I just got a text saying that they had got there safely and he was having a quick kip before going out. They have already been on the lash!" she laughed. Kirstie smiled but wasn't overly impressed because she had got roughly the same message.

"But it's okay. I shall punish him when he gets back," Sarah said menacingly.

"Oh, go on, do tell. Are you going to withdraw his conjugal rights?" Kirstie said.

"Hell no, he's too good in bed for that. No, I shall handcuff him to the bed and tie my wand vibrator to his knob with a pop sock and my bullet vibro to his balls and switch them on."

The girls all laughed at how absurd that sounded but Sarah added, "You can laugh but believe me – it's a punishment. I've done it to him before, just as an experiment."

The three others stopped laughing and looked at her quite curiously.

"You start with the vibro on the balls 'cos they can withstand that for a while but if you tie the wand to their cock with the business bit specifically massaging the bell end, he will climax in less than two minutes. After that, it's all far too sensitive and he'll be begging for it to be switched off. It's exquisite torture and if you really want to go to town, switch it off just before he cums. Do that a few times and he'll be putty in your hands!"

"Ooh, you sadist," Sam said, recalling how, in her limited experience with Two-Stroke Tommy, his penis was so sensitive even he couldn't touch it after orgasm.

"Hmm, I might have to try that on Matt," Kirstie said. "But I'll need to buy some toys first, though."

"You don't have any toys?" Sarah said, almost incredulously.

"Why would I need toys when I've got Matt?" Kirstie asked.

The other three looked at her with an expression that said, "*Why wouldn't you have toys?*"

"Gosh, Kay, even I've got a vibro!" Sam said and then blushed a little, thinking how outspoken she was on such an intimate subject.

"See!" Sarah said. "Even our sweet virgin has got a vibrator. Come on, Kayzee, get with it! What about you, Mia?"

"We have quite a selection," she laughed loudly. "In fact, we've got more toys than Hamleys!"

Mia was briefly quizzed about how things were going with her live-in lover. She said it was phenomenal, then suggested they all go back to hers for a nightcap, then they could at last meet Jennifer, as she was sure they would all adore her just as she did.

"We can check out your toy collection as well!" Sarah said, chuckling.

"Why don't we go now? Time's getting on and it'll be cheaper than drinking here unless you've got your eye on anyone, Sarah?" Mia said, looking around for prospective prey for her friend.

"There were two guys at the bar around the corner who were smiling at me when I came back from the Ladies," said Sarah, half-joking.

"Are you sure you didn't have your skirt tucked into the back of your knickers?" asked Kirstie, smiling.

"I can categorically say I did not have my skirt tucked in my knickers. One, the skirt is too short and two, I'm not wearing any!" They all laughed loudly.

A few minutes later, they were in a taxi heading to Mia's for a nightcap. Sarah sat up front and was jokingly trying to blag a free trip by offering the old boy payment in 'kind'.

The girls shook their heads again and then started laughing when the driver said, "You are a lovely-looking girl but I'm a happily married man. My wife tells me I am."

"I'm not superstitious," Sarah said, smiling her sexy smile at him.

"That's as may be but I'm on medication, which puts a dampener on such enjoyment."

Sarah persisted. "I have healing hands, and I'd be willing to bet I could bring it back to former glories."

"Love, I don't think even Jesus could manage it, despite his alleged success with Lazarus but thank you for the offer. It's been a very long while since a beautiful girl took a fancy to me!" and as he pulled up at their destination, he said, "That'll be eight pounds, fifty pence, please."

Sarah gave him a ten-pound note, a kiss on the cheek and followed up with, "Betcha that tenner I could make it work!" The driver just smiled and said, *"Thank you and have a very good evening!"*

As the girls walked to the house, Kirstie put her arm around Sarah and laughingly told her that she was being outrageous this evening.

"I know Kayzee. I am just so fucking horny lately. Well, even more horny than normal!" and they linked arms and joined the others. Mia had texted home to say they were on their way for a few drinks. Jenny was waiting for them at the door when they arrived.

She enthusiastically hugged and kissed the girls on both cheeks as they came into the house. She told them that she had already poured the fizz in the lounge - they should go on through. Sarah whispered to

Kirstie that she looked so damn sexy she could quite fancy her herself. Kirstie told her to behave but she could see what Sarah meant.

Kirstie was surprised as Jenny wasn't how she imagined her at all. She had short, brushed back, dyed blonde hair, quite sharp features but a friendly face, nonetheless. Standing around a slender but shapely five-foot-nine tall, with big boobs that were braless and shown off to good effect. She wore a short, low-cut woollen dress, cream-coloured, with a loose black belt and black knee-length boots to match. She had perfect makeup, wore Coco Chanel Mademoiselle perfume and very expensive gold jewellery – earrings, with a matching necklace, a number of bracelets and bangles and a stunning Cartier watch. (Later on, as they sat on the luxurious leather sofas, Jenny removed her boots and Kirstie noticed she had a gold anklet with alphabet charms attached – a 'J' and an 'M'.)

They chatted easily and Jenny wanted to learn more about the girls' friendship and their time at school before the subject drifted on to each of their personal relationships with their other halves. Mia sat close to Jenny as the more mature woman put her arm around her and caressed her neck.

The fizz flowed well, and Jenny said she was off to the kitchen to get another bottle. She asked Mia to give her a hand with some fresh glasses because it was a different brand of champers. Mia was just off to the toilet, but Sarah offered to help.

After a number of minutes, Kirstie wondered why they were taking a while and went into the kitchen only to find Jenny and Sarah tucked in the corner, fully engaged in an enthusiastic French kiss with Jenny's hand under the front of Sarah's short skirt, visibly indulging in some stroke play while Sarah was cupping and fondling Jenny's breasts and nipples. She was enthralled at how erotic the scene was but gathered herself and, despite her shock, she left them to it. She waited outside the toilet and when Mia came out, she said quite loudly, "I thought you were stuck in there!" Hopefully, this would give the erstwhile "*lovers*" an early warning in case they were so engrossed with each other. Mia laughed and went to the kitchen.

Kirstie delayed shutting the door, but she could hear the conversation between Mia and Jenny and decided they must have broken off their entanglement in time not to be caught with sticky fingers.

As she sat down, she could not get that picture out of her mind. Two very sexy women kissing and fondling one another but then she thought of Mia and how it would break her heart if she knew.

The next morning, she phoned Sarah and if she was shocked the previous evening, she was even more so when Sarah said she knew Jennifer from a while back. The kiss, she said, was that they were just catching up for old time's sake. Sarah went on to say that girls were not usually her thing, but Jenny was always hot. She assured Kirstie that there was nothing more in it, but Kirstie was rather cynical and added that she wondered what Mia would have made of it.

"Kay, it was just a kiss and that's how we would have put it to Mia. Anyway, you could see that Jenny rules the roost in that house, so maybe Mia knows what she's like," Sarah added.

Kirstie was almost incredulous but left it at that and decided that she may not have seen what she thought she saw. But that vision, imaginary or not, was very, very stimulating.

"By the way," Sarah continued, "you know we had the same cab driver on the way home?"

Kirstie said yes, and Sarah pointed out that she was again chatting up the old boy to try to get a freebie fare.

"True!" Kirstie agreed.

"Well, he dropped me off last, as you know and I won my bet in less than seven minutes!" Sarah laughed. "It's amazing what a few compliments, dirty talk and eye contact can do together with dextrous fingers and a hot mouth!" she laughed again.

Kirstie was up early on Monday. She showered, did her makeup and dressed in white underwear that was simple but sexy. Matt had the day off to recover from the Blackpool excursion and woke to see her just about to put on her smart grey suit with a knee-length skirt and white silk blouse.

"Kay, could you make me a cup of coffee, please and then join me back in bed for a quickie, 'cos you look damn hot!" She knew he was joking.

"Later, Darling. You know I'm starting my new job today, so I'm in a rush."

"Oh, yeah, maybe a shag for luck then?" he suggested without meaning it.

"Later, Babes, let's see how it goes."

She kissed Matt on the lips and thought he really needed the mouthwash today as he smelled like a brewery. She went downstairs to finish off getting ready. She was too nervous for breakfast but had a quick cup of coffee and put on a modest pair of black, heeled shoes.

Kirstie took her time with the extra twenty-minute commute but still arrived a good fifteen minutes before she was due to meet her new boss. She sat in the car in the car park for five minutes and then decided to show that she was keen if she arrived a little early. She went to the reception and explained that she was due to start work there and had a meeting with M/s J. Marinello.

"Ah, yes, you are Miss McCann? Good, please take a seat and I'll let her know that you're here."

As she went to sit down, she heard the receptionist say on the phone, "Hi, Miss McCann is here for you," and as she hung up, she told Kirstie that M/s Marinello would be down shortly. Kirstie was checking her phone when she was aware that a very well-dressed woman was standing in front of her, with black heels, dark hosiery, black skirt, and a similar silk blouse to the one she was wearing. There were a couple of buttons undone, showing a decent amount of cleavage and there before her stood Jenny with a huge smile. Kirstie was dumbfounded but as she stood, Jenny pulled her close for a hug and a kiss on each cheek and said, "Oh, how super! We are going to have so much fun." She steered Kirstie to the security door, thanking the receptionist on the way. As they walked to Jenny's office, Jenny said how much she enjoyed meeting the gang on Friday and followed with, "I know Sarah from a while back, and if you saw anything in the kitchen, it was just a little kiss hello as we hadn't seen each other in a while. Nothing to concern yourself with."

"Oh, I only saw you giving each other a little hug, so I didn't think anything of it and Sarah told me later that she knew you from a couple of years ago," Kirstie lied but again conjured up that sensual image in her mind. As they got into Jenny's office, she turned and held Kirstie's hands, then leaned in towards her to kiss her fully on the lips before saying, "I can see we are going to get on famously!"

20

The Boys are Back in Town

March 2013

Stags continued

Matt, Dan, Dwayne, Cliff and Rudy were first at The Tower Ballroom and to Matt's surprise, the place was heaving. They were served their pints in plastic glasses - this was a whole different world from the glitz and glamour of television's Strictly Come Dancing. Dan mentioned that he hadn't seen Ollie since they arrived, but Cliff got a text from GG to say Ollie had "*shot his bolt*" and was speaking to God on the great white telephone just before they were due to go out. Apparently, not only was he drinking beer on the bus, but also had a hip flask full of whiskey.

As they surveyed the scene and talked amongst themselves, they hadn't realised that a group of six forty-something women were standing a few yards away who, just by their body language, were plainly interested in the lads.

"Watch out, I think we're being stalked here, boys. There's a pack of cougars on the hunt," Rudy said, evidently up for the challenge.

"And on the lash," said Dan, "and I think we're their prey!"

"They all look like they're married," Rudy said.

"Oh, like we give a fuck!" replied Cliff.

"I think that's exactly what they're hoping for!" said Ian, who had just joined them together with Paul. "And I think they're after you two," Ian added, looking at Rudy and Dwayne, "They'll have heard the rumours about Windies 'wonder willies' and I don't know if you guys have noticed, but there's not too many people of a darker persuasion in here."

"Good point," said Dwayne. "But the rumours, man, they're all true."

"Fuck off, you forget we've seen you in the showers. Those todgers are literally nothing to get excited about," Cliff said disparagingly.

Rudy chipped in with, "Until the todgers get excited, my friend, that's what sorts the men from the boys. I'm not from Australia but I'm big down under!"

"I'm not an Estate Agent but I do have a semi that the ladies can look at," Dwayne added.

"Hmm, don't look now but I think that lot wouldn't mind finding out," Ian said.

The women made a move and stood near the bar to get a round in and, of course, they could now hear the boys' accents.

"Ee, they're soft Southerners, girls," said one, laughing to her friends.

"Cockney bastards!" said another.

"There is nothing soft about me, darlin'. Especially where it counts and my parentage has only been called into question by people who didn't like me much!"

"Cheeky fooker," said cougar number two. "You're just a Cockney poser."

"A…Cockney poser…?" Cliff said indignantly. "Madam, I am not *A* Cockney Poser, I am *The* Cockney Poser!" He stuck out his chin and his chest to prove it, which made all the women laugh. A couple of the really attractive ones started some banter with the lads when the DJ's heavily advertised seventies erection section kicked in with Gladys Knight's *"Help Me Make It Through The Night."*

Out of the blue, the shy, short, very curvy woman with an attractive moon face asked Matt if he'd like to dance. The taller woman who kept in shape looked rather astonished, especially when a startled Matt thought for a second or two, then said, "Yeah, I'd love to." He took her by the hand onto the dance floor.

"Hello, I'm Matthew. What's your name?" he asked.

"Rachel," she said and then went on, "Jeepers, I don't know what came over me. I have never, ever asked a man to dance before."

"Well, in these days of equal opportunities, why shouldn't you? And I am flattered."

"Fook, you're flattered? Look at the herd of jealous cows over there."

"Why?" he asked naively.

"Why? I'm telling you, Debs, the one with the long dark hair, had her eyes on you as soon as she walked in. She's not going to be happy with me."

"Oh, is my zip undone?"

Rachel laughed, "I think she wishes it was."

"Does she always get what she wants?" Matt asked, glancing at Debs.

"Usually. We'd better just have the one dance," she said, stealing sly looks at her friend, who was pretending not to care but returned a glance and a scowl anyway.

"Rubbish!" Matt replied, and she laughed again, which he could see made Debs a little tetchy. The music merged into *"Let's Get It On"* by Marvin Gaye.

Rachel told him that they'd all come from Chorley, but she herself was originally from Gateshead, south of Newcastle. She lost her Geordie accent when she moved across the Pennines before she got married. She went on to say that there were usually a couple of coaches that came to Blackpool on a Friday and Saturday every week. He now understood why the place was so busy if they bused people in from all over the north.

Rachel was candid about her situation. She was recently divorced after marrying young, but the guy was a bullying, control freak, and she was better off without him. Matt got the impression that there was a lot of pain and heartache behind that lovely face.

They were now into the third slow dance and Debs was not a happy bunny.

"*Love Won't Let Me Wait*" by Major Harris was next up.

"Ooh, this is a saucy one," Matt said and, picking up the negative vibes from Debs, whispered into Rachel's ear. Rachel held him closer.

"What do you think Debs might do if I kissed you?" he said confidently.

"Who cares what she thinks. Aye, you carry on me lad if you want to but kiss me for *me* not to spite her, okay?" she said, looking up at him expectantly.

"Where do you want it?" Matt said, smiling at her.

"Naughty boy." She had a real dirty laugh. It was a tentative touch of lips at first but then they snogged. She might have seemed to be a bit of a shrinking violet when they first started talking but she was no stranger to quality kissing.

"Jeez," he said, "no wonder your old man was the jealous sort."

She laughed and held him even closer. Matt could feel Rachel's boobs in his front and Deb's daggers in his back. The mood music changed to something he would only dance to, given a real surfeit of alcohol. He gave her a quick kiss, said thank you and asked her if she would like to go to a bar that was less noisy. He really preferred to find out more about her without having to shout.

Matt also had the ulterior motive of distancing himself from the boys. He worried that they had plans of chaining him naked to a lamppost on the seafront, where he could die of exposure. She looked a bit surprised but seeing that he was serious, gleefully accepted.

They both explained to a member of their respective groups that they were disappearing. Rachel was reminded of the coach's departure time and, more importantly, that *"it wouldn't wait."* Matt was told to *"fill his boots"*, to which he smiled and said, "It's not like that, this place is too loud, too busy and it's a ruck waiting to happen. Keep Cliff and Rudy under control if you can."

As he moved away, Debs tugged his sleeve and said something. He leaned into her and, putting a hand gently on her upper arm, said, "Sorry, Love. I didn't hear what you said."

She also leaned towards him and, putting her opposite hand on his waist, whispered very close to his ear, "You don't know what you're missing," and nibbled it before she stood back, staring at him. It was serious eye-to-eye contact. Momentarily, he paused, then kissed her on the cheek and said, "Neither do you, but you are gorgeous. Hips that pass in the night, I think." She smiled at him in some sort of agreement, and he stepped away, quite amazed by his own display of confidence. Where on earth had that come from, he wondered?

He escorted Rachel outside and instinctively kissed her with no restrictive audience. As they broke away, she looked up at him and said, "God, you're lovely," and before he could respond, she pulled him down to kiss him again. When they surfaced for air, he said, "The night is young and so are we. Come on, let's find a bar that doesn't blow our ears off." She gave him a squeeze in confirmation, and they moved off.

Spoilt for choice, they found a decent-sized pub with a George Michael tribute act. As they made their way to the busy bar, "George" was performing a great impression of his peerless hero with *I Don't Want Your Freedom*. The bar was rocking, but at least it wasn't as loud as the previous venue and the pair of them found a corner that was a bit quieter so that they could chat without bellowing at one another. They spent a good hour slow-dancing, chatting, drinking…and kissing.

"I think we should run away to some South Pacific Island and live on the beach. We'll open a little rum shack or something and make love at every given opportunity!" Matt offered.

"Soppy sod!" Then, looking at her watch, she realised she had to go. Deb's warning that the coach wouldn't wait was ringing in her ears. They drank up and Matt held her coat up for her to put on.

"Ever the gentleman!" she said. They hugged and quickly left. As they walked, she linked her arm into his and said she would love to have been able to invite him back to her home. But the "bairns" were there, and the neighbours would talk. She laughed at her own absurd notion of wishful thinking. They stopped about twenty yards short of the coach that was waiting for her and Matt turned to kiss her.

"I'd bet Debs would be beside herself if she found out I stopped for the night." Matt laughed. "But I'd choose you first every time, thank you for a lovely evening."

"Oh yes, I've got that interrogation to come. I'd better go and face the music."

They kissed again.

"Farewell, sweet prince, thank you for a rare, lovely evening," she said, and after stepping a few yards, turned and blew him a kiss, which he returned.

The coach driver was out of the bus talking to Debs, who saw Rachel and shouted, "Shift yoursen' you silly mare. You're late, and he was going to go without you, he'll expect a hand-job as compensation!"

Rachel picked up the pace and apologised to the driver as she got on the coach. Debs watched her and then turned to Matt and gave him a little wave. He put his hand on his heart and then put it to his lips to blow her a kiss as well and thought that life was just so full of missed opportunities.

As the coach pulled away, he could see some women's faces peering at him from the back window, all waving at him. He blew kisses to them from alternate hands and laughed to himself, thinking it was all a bit surreal, before turning around and as the bus disappeared into the distance, he wondered where the hell he was.

Sheltering from the wind and rain on the built-up side of the sea front, he really, really needed to answer the call of nature, a Jimmy Riddle, pointing Percy at the porcelain, bleed the bladder, a wee, a slash…The urge to urinate was the only thing occupying his thoughts, as were all the different phrases and words to describe the fact that he was beyond desperate. He looked around for somewhere to go and thought about crossing the road and going down on the beach but decided against it. It was far too exposed - it would have to be a doorway.

He slipped into one of the shop entrances and, with his zip undone, he had just got the old fella out when he was tapped on the shoulder. He spun around in surprise to see two mature, short, sturdy women police constables.

"We've been following you, young man, and your mode of travel suggests you're not completely in control of your limbs. What were you going to do here, might I ask?" One of them said, quickly followed by the other, "You're not thinking of relieving yourself there, are you?"

"Sorry, officer, I was desperate," he said, just about to stuff his todger back into his trousers.

"Hands away from your pockets, get them up in the air. We need to make sure you're not carrying anything that could harm us or you." They wanted to prolong his complete embarrassment, along with the excruciating pain of trying to hold it in.

"What's your name and have you got anything on you that you shouldn't have?" One of them asked, as the other failed to stifle a snigger. He told them his name and answered, "No, officer."

"So Matthew, what are you doing staggering about alone at this time of night?" the first one asked.

"I'm on my stag weekend and I wanted to get away from the other lads because I think they've got something very embarrassing lined up for me." Despite feeling drunk, the cold weather and his current predicament were sobering him up fast. He regained a bit of composure in spite of his willy just hanging there.

"I thought I could get back to the B&B without any of them knowing and I just got caught a bit short. I am really sorry. I couldn't find any bars or public conveniences."

"The public conveniences are shut at this time of night, lad but pubs and bars? Get real, there are hundreds!" The other one said.

"Hmm, there are a number of charges we could bring against you, couldn't we, Constable Fairbrother?"

"Aye, Constable Smith, urinating in a public place for one. Or indecent exposure," said Fairbrother.

"But, officers, I haven't done anything," he pleaded.

"Well, unless that's a half-sized saveloy sticking out of your zip, then it would appear that you have indecently exposed yourself to two police officers!" said Smith. He said nothing. He could see they were dragging this out to make it more uncomfortable for him.

"Anyway, there are other charges. Drunk and disorderly," said Smith.

"Or going equipped," said Fairbrother, sniggering.

"In possession of an offensive weapon!" said Smith, which they both found hilarious.

"Oddly enough, it's quite a cute one as dicks go, not very big though, so hardly offensive," said Smith.

"In mitigation officers, it is rather cold, but could I put it away now, please, before it disappears of its own accord?" Matt asked, almost pleading with them.

Smith giggled, turned to her colleague said, "Ooh, hark at Rumpole here. In mitigation, aye? This lad's far too posh to piss in a doorway, Alice. I think we should direct him to a local hostelry where he can relieve himself to his little heart's content, should he need to do so, don't you think?" She paused, "Churchill's?"

WPC Alice Smith agreed. "Aye, Churchill's," and nodded to Matt to conceal his "inoffensive weapon."

As he fumbled to tuck it away with his cold fingers, he got the lecture.

"Now, talking of dicks, just a little word of warning to you, young man. We don't take very kindly to barmpots like you decorating shopfronts with your excesses. It's not very nice for shopkeepers to have to wash down their premises of a morning when people have used it like a public toilet. Do you understand?"

"Yes, Officer, I am really sorry."

The policewomen decided to drag out his agony a little longer.

"So, a stag weekend up from the 'Smoke' and when do you get married?" asked Smith.

"In July, and we're up here from Hampshire, not London," said Matthew, who suddenly felt an idiot volunteering such irrelevant information.

"Oh, *Hempshire?*" said Fairbrother in her best imitation of the Queen, "See Alice, definitely a posh twat."

"Okay, we're going to let you go with a warning and frankly, I cannot be arsed to go back to the station to do the paperwork for an idiot like you." Fairbrother pointed down the road and said, "See that junction there?"

"Yes," he said, almost hopping from one foot to another.

"Go along that road and there's a bar called Churchill's. Buy yourself a drink and use their facilities," she said sternly.

"Yes, officer, thank you," he held out his hand to shake theirs. With a look of horror, Fairbrother said, "I don't think so after what you've been playing with, on your way, lad." She gave a contemptuous flick of her hand.

"A kiss for luck then, as I'm getting married?" He was emboldened by his success so far that evening.

There was a few seconds' hesitation as they looked at him.

"Aye, go on then," said Smith to his surprise and as he leaned down to give her a peck, she pulled him in close and just went for a full-on tongue twister.

"Is that not assaulting a police officer?" said Fairbrother, and as soon as he'd finished, she moved in for her turn. Cold lips, he thought on first contact, but more open-mouthed and what a tonsil tingler.

"Resisting arrest?" Smith questioned.

"Hardly Alice. He doesn't seem to be able to resist anything," replied Fairbrother, wiping her mouth. "Go, lad, on your way!" she said dismissively. He shuffled off quickly.

The two police officers smiled at one another.

"If I didn't have that lazy fat arse of a husband occupying my little house, I would have taken young Matthew home and handcuffed him to my bed until he sobered up," Smith said.

"And then what?" asked her colleague.

"Wendy, do you really want me to go into detail? Just think Fifty Shades of Grey!"

"You're a dirty cow, Alice…but he was rather tidy."

Matt sped up as the issue at hand was even more fraught. Turning the corner, he could see the bright lights of the pub. The bouncers paid him no mind and luckily, as he entered, there was a barman to hand to order a pint of Guinness. He did so and left a fiver on the counter, explaining he was nipping off to the toilets. The facilities were well signposted and, thankfully, not far. Those last few steps to the urinal were the most painful and he thought of the unwritten scientific law that the nearer you are to getting relief from a full bladder, the more desperate you become. Unzipped and out, he had Percy pointing at the porcelain to his great relief.

He then suddenly realised that a guy from nowhere stood next to him at the adjacent urinal and was also readying himself for a slash. Matt thought that was a bit odd, as the other eight urinals were empty. Blokes always adhere to the etiquette of leaving the bare minimum of at least one basin free before occupying the next one. He became a bit more unnerved when the guy spoke to him.

"How's it going, lah?" the guy asked in a Scouse accent.

"Good, thanks," said Matthew, looking back at the wall and desperate to finish urinating.

"You here for the weekend?" said the Scouser.

"Yes, my stag weekend."

"Oh. Okay, no worries," the guy zipped up and left.

That was odd, he thought, the guy never had a piss but after washing his hands, Matthew went back to the bar. It was a busy place with loud music and lots of people. Wait, lots of people, but no women. Not one single woman in the pub. It then dawned on him. He was so desperate to get to a toilet that he hadn't noticed that the clientele and also some of the erotic art on the walls were dedicated to all things male.

He returned to his pint of Guinness and the shrapnel of change left there. He tried not to make eye contact with anyone. It was an excellent pint of the black stuff, though, and he really wanted to people-watch for a little while. He was particularly fascinated by four transvestites that were so convincing he thought he could quite fancy any of them – Team Tranny! Matt was definitely wasted - it was time to leave.

Outside, the cold air hit him again and he knew he was totally lost. He wandered slowly along a few streets, but he was getting very tired.

He managed to flag down a cab and the driver asked him the 64,000-dollar question, "Where to, pal?"

"That's a tricky one," Matt slurred. "I have no idea."

The driver just shook his head and drove away and a few minutes down the road, he saw two police officers on the beat. He knew them both and told them he was worried about a young guy who was lost and particularly worse for wear. Fairbrother and Smith looked at one another and both nodded in resignation as to who it might be before asking the cabbie to take them to him. He was happy to oblige.

"There he is, large as life," Alice said, pointing to the lone figure a little way down the road.

"And twice as drunk," Wendy agreed just as the car pulled up next to him.

"Oh my word, Matthew, you're looking worse now than you did when we saw you last!" said Fairbrother. Matt looked up and spoke slowly, trying not to sound as drunk as he was.

"Ah, my two favourite policemen…er…police-people…umm police…constables. Ladies, it's just possible that… you have… saved…my life because it's got…very cold out here… Oh, and I need to speak to you both about that pub you sent me to."

"Yes, yes, now look, Matthew, we need you to concentrate because if we can't get you back to your hotel, we're going to have to arrest you for your own safety," Smith told him.

"Nope. No. No, nope. I didn't piss in a doorway, sorry… I didn't wee, urinate, leak, or slash in the doorway…I am innocent. Free the Hampshire One!" he began to shout.

The cabbie then said they should at least sit him in the car before he died of hypothermia.

"C'mon, m'lad, sit in this nice warm car and we'll find out where you're staying." Ordered Fairbrother.

They helped him to get in the back, and Fairbrother sat with him while Smith sat in the front with the driver.

"Now, do you know the name of the hotel that you're staying in?" Smith asked him slowly so that he would understand.

"No… but it's a B&B, two star…nearly three. I can't think what would get it to three stars, but it's very nice," slurred Matt.

"That's narrowed it down to about seven hundred, then. This could be a long night. Can I put the meter on?" The cabbie had seen all of this before.

"Gotta do a bit better than that, me lad, c'mon, don't fall asleep. Is it near the Tower?"

He desperately tried to keep his eyes open. "Yes, about a ten-minute walk."

"Great, that's slashed the number to look for to about three hundred," the cabbie was getting bored now.

"Can you think of any part of the name? What might it begin with?"

He was rocking backwards and forwards, trying to concentrate and yawning often.

"Maybe the name of the street. If we could get that, you could probably recognise the building."

"It had nice windows. Yes, nice windows…F, it began with F," Matt said, still struggling to stay awake.

"Good, is that for the name of the street or the B&B?" Fairbrother asked.

"Yes. F."

The cabbie looked in his mirror and said, "I know something else that begins with F."

"Give the lad a break, Charlie. It's his stag weekend," Smith said sympathetically.

"Poor bugger, there you go. You can arrest him!" Charlie replied.

"On what grounds, Charlie?"

"On the grounds of being monumentally stupid!" he added. The two WPCs looked at each other and shook their heads.

"Not everyone marries the local 'brass' and then takes ten years to find out before getting divorced, Charlie!"

"Well, I was young and didn't know she had more customers of an evening than I did in my taxi!" Charlie mused. The WPCS smiled.

Matt started to point as though he were conducting an orchestra. "Name some football teams in the northeast."

The ladies looked at one another and shrugged. Alice said, "I think we'll have to give up on this. Sorry, Charlie, for wasting your time."

"Wait," Charlie said, "Middlesborough?"

"No bigger than that."

"Sunderland?"

"Nope," Matt waved his hand about. "*Much* bigger than that, they've won nothing for years, zebras - black and white."

"Newcastle United?" Charlie suggested.

"Yeah, that's them. Bloody useless."

Charlie clapped his hands and smiled, the ladies still shrugged, and one of them said, "Newcastle United, good, but pray tell, Charlie, where has that actually got us?"

Charlie nodded and said it was a valid point.

Matt took a deep breath and said, "Yes, not Newcastle United, not Newcastle. Scarborough."

The other three occupants in the car said in unison, "Scarborough?"

Matt sat back smugly and said, "Yeah, Scarborough," and he took a deep breath and closed his eyes for a few seconds.

Alice sighed, looked at Wendy, and shook her head. She switched her radio on. "Tango-two-five, tango-two-five." The radio crackled into life, "Go ahead two-five".

"Yes, yes, can we have a wagon, please to…"

Matt suddenly woke up and said, "Barbara from Scarborough!" Then nodded to himself, "Yes, Barbara!" and chuckled. Alice looked at him and then went back to her radio.

"Tango-Two-five, sorry, cancel the van, false alarm. Yes, yes, confirm, please cancel, out."

"Set your meter, Charlie. We're off to Farnshaw B&B, Livingstone Road," and they all strapped themselves in with Wendy Fairbrother assisting Matt with his belt. Matt put his arm around her.

"Did you want another kiss?" he asked.

"No, I'm putting your seat belt on," Fairbrother said dismissively.

"But I could kiss you as a thank you for making me safe!" He puckered up expectantly. Fairbrother told him to sit quietly; he would be at his B&B soon.

As they pulled away, Alice explained that she knew Barbara because their kids went to the same school. It was a two-minute drive and as they parked, the lights in the bar were on.

"That's the one driver, Bab's B&B, well done, thank you," Matt said, pulling out the set of keys for the door, which had the B&B name emblazoned on the key fob. Wendy tutted, thinking of the time wasted when he had keys all along.

"How much do I owe you?" and he fumbled for his wallet. As he did that, Alice phoned Barbara.

"Hi Babs, it's Alice, Alice Smith, no, nothing wrong. I think we have one of your little lambs in the car outside. Actually, he's more like a waif and stray. I don't want to wheel him inside in front of other people you've got there. Could you pop out and just check, and then we'll take him round the back?" They could hear Babs laughing.

"Only got a tenner mate… but keep the…change… you've been… e e especional, exccspesh…great, thank you so much," Matt said, waving the ten-pound note about.

"Lad, it's only £3.60, let's not worry about it. Get to bed," Charlie said, just wanting him out of the cab.

"*No*, I insist, thank you. I want to pay you and give you a tip. Don't get off a moving bus!" and Matt laughed loudly at his own inane comment. "Or, how about this one: sharks will only attack you if you're wet." Matt was still the only one laughing.

Babs was at the car now with a raincoat pulled over her head. She leaned in and recognised him immediately.

"Oh, Matthew, what have you been up to?" she said, as though she was his surrogate mum.

Charlie helped Alice to get him around the back. The policewoman explained to Babs that he was very close to being caged for the night for his own safety and as they pushed him into the kitchen, the cabbie gave Barbara the ten-pound note to give back to him.

"He hasn't been any trouble," and he and Alice quickly left.

Babs knew that Dan and some of the other lads were back in the bar for a nightcap. It was time to be protective.

"Matthew, you need to listen to me. Some of your pals are in the bar, so you had better hide for the moment. Use that bedroom down the hall and I'll let you know when it's all clear". She made him a cup of instant coffee, then let him into the room. Babs set the cup down on the small table, told him to take a seat and drink it while it was hot. She quickly returned to the bar.

The room was quite dimly lit, and his scrambled brain and tiredness got the better of him. He just stripped off, putting everything on a nearby sideboard and got into her cosy double bed. He was half asleep when she came in a bit later and locked the door. She was very surprised to find him in *her* bed.

"Now, Matthew, when I let you in here, it was just a temporary hiding place to keep you away from those canny lads of yours," she said sternly.

Matt took a number of seconds to deal with the simple sentence presented to him. He answered slowly.

"I know… but this is just…so comfortable," he said, slurring a bit. "And I love… the smell of you here."

She sat on the edge next to him, stroking his hair as though he were a little lost boy.

"My but you're as bonny as a bunny in a bow tie," and in what little light there was in the room, looking at all of his clothes, she realised he was naked under the quilt.

"But, Pet, it's *my* bedroom." She was almost pleading with him to get up and go to his own bed.

"Sorry, sorry, Babs. Barbara from Scarborough. Yes, Barbara," he chuckled to himself. "I didn't know but this bed is just so nice, I'd go so far as to say…it's the best bed in the world and I'm… cattled. I don't think I could make it up the stairs," he mumbled with his eyes now closed and almost asleep.

"That is very naughty, young man. Matt, please, you must get up!" She waited, then hesitated, as if deciding on what course of action to take. She was hoping that Matt would just get up and go but he looked so rested there and worse, she could see how vulnerable he was.

She took a deep sigh. She was also very tired. Babs reasoned with herself that it would take more time to try to get him up and out than to just sleep with him in the literal sense. He had already dozed off.

"Oh well, you're here now and anyway it's cold outside so you can keep me warm," she said out loud, though she knew he was out of it. She stripped off and climbed into bed next to him. There were only a few seconds of hesitation before she got much closer and put an arm around him. In his light slumber, he sighed at her touch, and she just relaxed in the heat of his young body, keeping her warm on a cold, wild, wet evening. She just about managed to resist "copping a feel" of his dormant todger and they both slept soundly.

21

What's the Story Morning Glory

March 2013

Early the next morning, Matt gradually woke up, mouth parched, head thumping, and the half-light was like lasers to the eyeballs. He blinked slowly and often as his pupils adjusted to the gloom. He looked around at very unfamiliar surroundings and realised that this was not his room, but his first concern was his phone. "Fuck it," he knew he had to get his brain into some form of working order first and hope that things might fall into place. He formed the words in his grey matter to tell himself to stop the 'white noise of pain' and concentrate on the series of events that got him to be lying in an unfamiliar bed.

Some minutes later, he had managed to work out the timeline of events up to the police escort back to base. He then slept the sleep of the dead, thankfully not literally, but he was awake now. But where?

An arm reached over him and stroked his chest. "Mmm, you're awake," was whispered into his ear and the hand then moved down over his stomach and continued until encountering his fully erect cock.

"Ooh, you *are* awake!" the voice said seductively. He then felt the warmth of a woman's cuddly body press into his back.

He still couldn't immediately think who it was, but it was so damn comfortable and quite sensual, snuggling up to him. Her accent was familiar and at least he could feel the comfy pillows of ample breasts, so it couldn't have been one of Team Tranny, to his great relief. Was it Rachel? He desperately tried not to sound as hungover as he felt and he said, "Um, I know this is going to sound a bit odd, but I think there may have been a bit of confusion last night. Could I ask…"

"Did we fuck? Is what you want to know, isn't it Pet?" the voice said.

"Um, as we appear to both be…as we are… did we take advantage of each other?"

"Did we fuck? Is the phrase you're looking for Pet?" the voice was now very familiar.

"Yes, Barbara, that is my question," he said.

"I've known a few men in my time but you, Matthew, have to be the most naïve I've ever had in my bed. But let me ask you, would it trouble you one way or the other?"

His head hurt and he asked for a timeout. She chuckled and offered him a glass of water and a couple of paracetamol. He accepted both gratefully, sat up, swallowed the capsules and finished the full glass in one hit. She stroked his back as he did so. He took a couple of deep breaths and lay down on his back so that she could continue her intimate massage more easily. He hoped that distraction might ease the brain pain.

"Okay, my answer to your question is… no, it wouldn't bother me as long as I didn't force you to or make a complete idiot of myself." His eyes were still trying to adjust to the dim light without setting off the pneumatic drill of a headache again.

She laughed. "Matthew, as strong as you are, I'm not sure you're capable of the first option and as for the second, we all do silly things when we're ten sheets to the wind."

"So did we?"

She embraced him and said, "Sweetheart, if we had, it would be something you would remember for a lifetime." She felt really horny having this young man in her bed.

"But this delightful plaything of yours is getting me extremely frisky." She continued to stroke up and down its length. Suddenly, there was a knock at the door.

"Ma'am, it's 6.30, I'm going to get stuff ready for breakfasts." It was Barbara's eldest daughter who helped part-time at the B&B.

Barbara put a finger to his lips to make sure Matt said nothing.

"Okay, I'll be there shortly."

They heard her daughter move away and Babs whispered that they would have to make this just a quickie. Matt lay there and realised he wasn't going to get a say in this, and it was all so sexually charged that he closed his eyes and let her take control. She pulled back the quilt to admire her handiwork.

"Mmm." She sat up and straddled him before she slowly fed him into her. Babs circled her hips with her warm, wet pussy, stimulating every inch of his cock, just enjoying the intimacy. He briefly opened his eyes to see her smiling at him with her big boobs swaying back and forth as she moved. She took his hands and placed them on her breasts to let him fondle them and feel their heavy weight. She then started to move up and down, sighing every time she was on the down stroke.

"Oh, that is *so* good!" Babs said as she rocked backwards and forwards and up and down. "Pinch my nipples, you naughty boy." He did so and she squealed quite loudly.

Matt looked at her and said, "Shush." worried that her daughter might hear.

Babs didn't seem to care, and her sighs and gasps became a bit louder. She moved her right hand to her clitoris and massaged it, which caused more exclamations of pleasure. His eyes dropped to watch her stroke herself, and it turned him on even more.

"You'll have to stop, Babs," Matt said, looking a little concerned.

"Why? This is *so* lovely."

"Because. It's far too lovely," Matt groaned, moving his hands to her hips to slow her down.

"Ooh, just fire away. You don't need to jump off at Jarrow on my account, me tubes are tied anyway. Fuck, it's so good." and she rocked harder and faster to bring him off while still masturbating. He groaned at his first big spasm of release.

"Oh, I can feel it. It's so hot." Babs slowed to watch his body jerk as he completed his climax. She leaned forward and put her hands on his chest, squeezing her pelvic muscles to try to keep him inside her.

"Pass the box of tissues, Pet. I think you've made a bit of a mess!" As he calmed, he reached over while still being pinned to the bed and handed the tissue box to her. She pulled out a handful, and as she lifted herself up, she caught some of the sloppy discharge.

"Wow, that was just…lovely. A shame we don't have more time."

There was another knock at the door.

"Ma'am, are you coming?"

Babs and Matt both giggled at the timely double entendre, and Babs responded, "Shortly! Give me a few minutes."

She lay on her back and, grabbing Matt's right hand, placed it on her soaking gash.

"C'mon, Pet, do some magic with those fingers. I am so close it won't take long."

Matt flattened three fingers and massaged the area on and around her clit, using her juices and some excess semen as lubrication. Babs was right, almost as soon as he started, she was on the road to her 'heaven' and the nearer she got, the louder she moaned until she climaxed with a sort of growl through gritted teeth. His fingers were awash with her own juicy release. As soon as she did, she grabbed his hand and whimpered for him to stop - it was much too sensitive for him to persist.

He held her to him as her breathing slowed.

"Fuck, that was intense," she whispered.

"I'd better go before your daughter catches us," Matt said. Barbara clung to him. "Not yet, bonny lad, just a couple of minutes more, this is so lovely. Then I'll get dressed and keep her in the kitchen while you go back to your room. Breakfast is served from 7.30 but I guess there won't be too many of your lads there just yet?"

"Doubtful and I'll grab another hour's sleep." He hugged her to him and said, "Mmm, that was fab, Barbara from Scarborough."

"There's more if you want to later. I'll be finished by 11.00 pm tonight, and my other daughter does the late bar from then. I would so like to have more time with you in my bed and find out what you're really capable of," she chuckled. "Perhaps I should check out your technique to see if you're ready to get spliced!"

"I'd like that too, give me your mobile number and I'll let you know what's happening later," Matt said, trying to sound enthusiastic so as not to disappoint her but leaving the option open to duck out if he had second thoughts. She grabbed her phone from the bedside cabinet, and they exchanged numbers.

"You'd better just put some random name on the caller ID. It might be a bit obvious if the name Babs pops up on there," she said before padding off to the en-suite bathroom. He watched her get dressed and admired all of her wobbly bits.

"Don't look, I must be a proper sight first thing," she said, trying to cover up as quickly as possible.

"You look lovely," he said and meant it. Stick insects did nothing for him and he thought about saying as much before realising it might be a bit of a back-handed compliment.

She bent over and kissed him on the forehead. "See you at breakfast," she said.

"And hopefully later," he offered. She smiled and nodded. "Hope so. Now give me five minutes and then you can scarper, bonny lad. Enjoy your day." Then she took a peep out of her bedroom door and disappeared.

He got back to his room to find Dan snoring his head off. Matt quickly undressed and got into bed for an extra hour - he needed it. Dan woke him up when he got up to go to the toilet.

"What the fuck happened to you last night?" Dan asked. "Did you get your leg over?"

He told Dan about the drink with Rachel, his brush with the law and his entertaining mistake visiting a gay pub before making a vague excuse about getting lost. "I must have got the beer scooter back here, and you were already asleep."

Dan looked at him quizzically. "What time was that?"

"Not a scooby. I was well and truly bolloxed and just went to bed." Matt lied but although Dan felt his mate was being economically factual, he couldn't disprove it because he slept from the moment he got in bed until waking up a few minutes ago.

 Matt and Dan were first down to breakfast and Barbara's daughter had taken their orders for the full English with extra toast and a special request from Matt of making sure the fried eggs weren't snotty! They were already tucking in as some of the others appeared. Cliff sarcastically said to Dan, "Who's your mate?"

Matt just ignored him but then copped a fair bit of abuse for disappearing with the "Care Bear" and a couple of times was asked whether he had "*sorted her out.*"

He tried to turn the tables on Cliff and the others that were there and asked how they got on with the Chorley posse. The consensus was that they had a good laugh. Essentially, they just wanted guys to buy them drinks for the evening in payment for a few dances and– if you were really blessed – a snog. Rudy then said, "That dark-haired one, Debs – all she talked about was you, Matt!"

Matt was surprised, if not a little flattered. He tried not to sound too keen when asking Rudy what she had said.

"She couldn't work out why you went off to swap spit with her munchkin friend. Her words, not mine, but I think you missed a trick there because she was definitely up for it," Rudy told him.

"Rudy, my old mate, I'm getting married, so I most definitely would not be '*up for it*' as you put it!"

Rudy smiled cynically. "Yeah, sure!"

"Hang on a minute," Dan chipped in to the conversation. "There's still a steward's enquiry as to where you were in the early hours of the morning?"

Matt was saved by the bell as a few of the stragglers appeared with stories of drunkenness in a club and Gump nearly getting into a fight. Steve explained that they were standing near the gents' toilet when a guy wandered out who had obviously been powdering his nose. Everyone knew what Steve meant, and he continued, "And Gumpy boy here asked the guy why he had icing sugar all over his hooter," Everyone laughed.

"It looked like icing sugar to me," Gump said innocently.

"Oh, mate, have a fucking day off, will ya? Try and join the land of the adults, please," Cliff said to him. Gump just shrugged. "Well, I didn't know he was snorting stuff, did I?" Steve just shook his head and continued,

"Anyway, the guy got up close and personal, asking our mate here if he was taking the piss. I pushed him away and told him to fuck off, whereby he starts swinging the old haymakers. The thing was, he was so out of it he couldn't hit the back of a barn door from two paces, and the bouncers were on him in a flash. They dragged him off to the room at the back and then the rozzers arrived about ten minutes later. Turns out he was a dealer sampling too much of his own merchandise. Of course, as soon as Blackpool's Best arrived, the clientele disappeared, so we came back here."

Just as Steve finished his story, GG and Ollie turned up. GG slumped into his chair and held his head in his hands.

"Christ GG, you look as rough as a badger's arse!" Dan exclaimed.

"Hmm, that's maybe 'cos I feel as rough as a badger's arse," GG confirmed, trying to lubricate his tongue with orange juice.

"He had his own grab-a-granny competition and lost!" Ollie said. They all looked a bit confused.

"He tried to pick up some old dear who must have been seventy if she was a day," Ollie continued.

"Don't fucking exaggerate," GG said, still holding his head. "She was only sixty-two."

"You didn't shag her, did ya?" asked Cliff incredulously. "I mean, you're virtually engaged!"

Ollie shook his head. "He would have done especially when she said she had acute angina but that was to put him off, not encourage him!" They all just dissolved in mirth.

As they sat finishing breakfast and drinking coffee, they decided what they were going to do for the day. Most of them thought they would just go for a drink and play some pool somewhere. It was a pretty fluid itinerary (literally but Cliff ordered that the evening would begin in the bar at 6.30 pm. A quick beer, then out for dinner somewhere - a fish and chip restaurant was the consensus and then the Tower Ballroom again, plastic glasses and all.

The group reconvened at the pre-ordained time for drinks in the lounge. As they settled down, GG said to a few of them.

"Hey, have any of you been to a massage parlour?"

"No," was the general response. He went on to say that he had gone for a wander along the seafront and saw a neon sign for one down a narrow alleyway. A few more of the guys listened in.

"I thought nobody knows me here. I'll give it a go. I paid my money and was shown to a cubicle to get undressed. I'm told that I only need the towel and when I'm ready, I should go down the corridor to the massage room. I was met by this stunning young lady dressed in a short white medical tunic with buttons only done up halfway and showing a fair bit of her assets. She had dark hair, brown eyes and a great smile." Everyone was listening to him now.

"She asked me to lie face down on the massage table and got to work using scented oil to massage my neck, shoulders and back. Then she worked up from the ankles, calf muscles and thighs. I'm telling you, we should all have one of them after a match. Ian, you'll have to get that sorted."

"Didn't she offer any other services?" asked Cliff.

"I'm coming to that, calm yourself!" GG said. "So, she got to the top of my thighs and then pulled the towel up a bit so that she could massage my arse cheeks. It was seriously sexy," he said, and the enthralled gathering nodded, anticipating a lot more.

"And?" Cliff said impatiently.

"She asked me to turn over and I'm thinking she's going to see I've got a bloody great stiffy," he said to a few scornful remarks.

"I was a bit hesitant, but she said it was nothing to worry about. It was quite natural and anyway, she'd seen more cocks than a poultry farmer."

"So I did as she asked, trying to keep the towel covering it up. But she said, 'Oh dear, that clearly needs some attention. Would you like some relief?" The throng was now hanging on every word.

"I thought to myself, *why not* and told her I would. 'Okay,' she said, and she ran her fingers down my body from my chin to my chest and my stomach to just inside the top of the towel. She smiled and then leaned over to give me a quick kiss on the cheek."

Ollie interrupted with, "All four of them?"

"No, just this cheek, and then she said I'll be back soon and left." GG paused and took another sip of his beer.

"And?" Cliff was getting even more impatient.

"Ten minutes later, she came back and smiled at me again before saying, '*Have you finished?*'" He delivered the punchline like a professional, and the guys all collapsed with laughter. Even Babs smiled whilst giving a knowing glance to Matt.

They filed out of the B&B and shuffled off into small groups to find somewhere to eat. A few of them returned to the Tower Ballroom at the duly appointed time but Matt told Dan that he preferred a few more drinks in a quiet pub before going into battle.

"You're worried that they've got some dastardly plan, aren't you?" Dan said.

"Too bloody right I am, which is why I disappeared last night, but apart from that, I'm still knackered. I must have walked for miles all over Blackpool last night. I must be getting old!"

"Matty, we all are but you should have paced yourself. Tell you what, I'll have another with you here and then I'll go and join them and tell them I can't find you. They'll soon lose interest with all the talent that's on show."

"Cheers buddy." Matt knew Dan had his back.

They walked down a few back streets before finding an old people's pub, as Dan called it. Sitting at the bar in The Rose and Crown, Matt ordered a couple of pints of Guinness. They had a chat about the forthcoming wedding and also about how Dan was getting on with Sarah now that she had moved in.

"Mate, she's still plugged into the mains and there must be some occasions when she causes a spike in the National Grid. She's an orgasm junkie. It's sex every day without fail."

Matt just called him a spawny git but didn't believe him. No one does it that many times in a week after living with someone, even for a few months. If it's always on tap, what's the urgency? Quality, not quantity and suggested as much to Dan.

"Ha! She wants quality and quantity, and she isn't backwards in coming forward when she wants it."

Matt still thought about how fortunate his mate was, remembering how gorgeous she looked when he bumped into her at the flat.

"So, what's your plan? Are you coming with me or going to stick around with the coffin dodgers here?" Dan asked.

"I'm just warming up and think I will trot along there later but try and put them off any stupid stunts 'cos I really can't be arsed with having to thump the living daylights out of each and every one of them," Matt said with much bravado.

"Just one thing, though, I want to thank you for arranging all of this. I really do appreciate it."

"It was no bother, buddy," Dan shrugged. Then he laughed and added that he would do his best to distract the boys and he finished his pint. They both stood up and hugged. They were reluctant to let go and Dan whispered, "I'm not being soppy, but I love you, mate." Matt gave his pal an extra squeeze in response and replied, "Me too, bucko, we'll always look out for each other," and then Dan was gone.

Matt asked for another drink and reached for his phone. He'd already spoken to Kirstie before he went out, so wasn't expecting any new messages, although there was one from FAF – his code name for Babs, sent about twenty minutes ago.

"Want to play ??x"

He responded: *"Hey, Barbara from Scarborough, are you still available to check out my play-time techniques? I would value any input you might have. Matt xx"*

A minute later, he received another message.

"Yes, I can book a consultancy appointment for you at 11.00pm xx"

"Thank you madam, should I come in the back door? xx" and he pressed send before realising how ambiguous that was. There was a bit of delay as he sipped at his drink. His phone pinged after about ten minutes.

"There's an offer, back door? YES - I haven't done that in a while. lol xx"

His phone pinged again with a photo taken as a reflection in a mirror, with Babs bending over wearing high heels and a black fishnet body stocking. The caption underneath just said,

Your appointment is booked for 11.00pm — same consulting room as last night. You will need to be fully undressed and will have to stay overnight…don't be late! xx

He had an hour and a half to kill and decided to go for a walk, as the evening was much calmer than the previous night. His phone pinged again, and he hoped it was yet another teasing pose from Babs. Cliff's contact picture grinned back at him as he opened the message:

"Where the fuck are you? The place is overrun with skirt and we can't fight them off any longer. We need reinforcements!!"

Keeping to a military theme, he texted back – *"Sorry, been ambushed good luck."*

"AWOL? YOU ARSE!" was Cliff's immediate, irritated response.

As he walked, he knew he would have to come up with a good excuse as to why he wasn't in the trenches with his buddies. That would have to wait until the morning, *'A shag in the hand is worth two in the bush'* came to mind, with a wry smile.

Matt felt thoroughly refreshed just walking and taking in the sea air. He thought of Babs and her sexy underwear and those delightful mature curves. He got the "twinge" as he recalled how wet she was when they fucked this morning. He turned the corner into a very familiar road and there halfway down was "Churchill's." He didn't realise how near it was to the B&B.

Turning the corner again onto the main drag, he found another pub advertising the delights of the same George Michael tribute act that he'd seen last night. He thought of Rachel and Debs and then his mind returned to the very sexy Babs. He got his bearings now and it was just one big block to walk around.

Matt checked his watch again, slipped back into The Rose and Crown for one quick drink and then headed back to the B&B. It was

10.40 pm and as he neared his bed and bedmate for the night, he was getting excited. He texted Babs.

"I know I'm a bit early but is it Ok to slip in now?" He knew the innuendo would be well received. The reply arrived in less than a couple of minutes.

"You don't know what effect that has just had on me! The kitchen door is unlocked I'll be there in about fifteen minutes… don't start without me xx."

He made sure the coast was clear but doubted if any of the guys would be back yet anyway. All was quiet as he opened the kitchen door and stepped into the warmth. A few seconds later, he was in her bedroom. Matt then stripped off and took the opportunity to have a quick shower before using some mouthwash to kill the beer breath. He wrapped the big pink fluffy towel around himself and tucked one corner into the top to keep it in place. He left the en-suite, drying his hair with the smaller matching hand towel to see Babs standing by the bed in her heels and body stocking with her hands on her hips and licking her lips. Her desire was palpable.

"Hmm, pink is not your colour, Pet, but you still look cute anyway." She moved to meet him halfway and took the small towel from him, dabbing at areas of wet skin before he wrapped his arms around her to kiss her. She could feel his stiffy poking at her through the big towel, and she reached down to undo the tuck and let it fall free. He kissed her again as she took his length in both of her hands and stroked it.

"Lie down on the bed, and I'll dry you properly," Babs said, picking up the bath towel and putting it on the bed before Matt lay on it.

She pulled a pillow down for his head and continued to dab at his body, paying particular attention to his genital area before asking him to turn over onto his front. She gently wiped the towel over him and then asked him to spread his legs. Babs then dribbled some spit onto his anus and massaged it firmly before applying more saliva and fingering him with her index finger. He gasped as she penetrated him and then she got him to turn on his back again so that she could take his penis into her mouth.

She was nothing like Kirstie, who always seemed to be in a bit of a rush to stop and get on with sex. Babs took her time and was enjoying her "work." She showed no signs of letting up, putting her full oral and manual stimulation skills to good use before he suggested that he could and should return the compliment. They got off the bed together and he kissed her before caressing her boobs over the body stocking. Then he let her lie down on her back to get comfortable on the towel.

Matt knelt between her legs and returned to massaging her gorgeous, fleshy breasts, tweaking her nipples through the fishnet material as he did so. She closed her eyes with the pleasure of it as he now lay his head on her thigh to undo the poppers with one hand, exposing her sex.

"That's a useful trick," she laughed. He licked the second finger of his right hand and then slowly slid it into her rectum.

"Oh, that's good…mmm," she whispered.

He nipped her inner thighs before sticking his tongue out and sampling her natural musky juice from her welcoming slit. He focused on her clit, flattening his tongue against it, then pushed two fingers from his left hand into her vagina. Now his digits worked in time together massaging both her arsehole and pussy. These were all the techniques he used on Kirstie - if it worked with her, surely it could work for most females.

Babs was slow to come to the boil but when she did, she jerked violently, more so than she had that morning. As she climaxed, he stopped and was about to withdraw his digits when she said no and begged him to do it again. This was unquestionably different from his fiancée, who could only bear one orgasm before it all got too much. It was both a blessing and a curse sometimes. A blessing in that she was easily satisfied, a curse when he wanted to give her more pleasure than she could endure. Babs climaxed again and a third time before she stopped him.

"Fuck, that was so good, but I need your cock now!" she demanded.

They kissed ardently before he got into position. She reached down to hold his dick, which was now only semi-erect, but a quick double-handed wank from Babs, and he was up to the task. She clamped her arms and legs around him as he entered her to build up a nice, steady rhythm. Babs clung on for the ride and Matt was relentless. He'd had enough to drink to de-sensitise most of the feeling, remaining rock hard as they swapped positions several times.

They had a short break in between for a drink, chat and kissing and caressing. She lost count of the number of Os she had, and they changed positions yet again for him to fuck her doggie style in the forlorn hope of making him climax. She had already reached for the baby oil several times to stop herself (and him) from getting sore. They even indulged in a short episode of anal sex, and she climaxed again.

Matt couldn't remember a better fuck than this. Ever! Eventually, she couldn't take any more and asked him to stop. They cuddled up together and she whispered that she would finish him by hand, but they were now so tired that they just fell asleep.

Just before dawn, Babs woke first and draped herself over him. Matt woke a few minutes later and manoeuvred himself to cuddle her tighter. They enjoyed the warmth of each other's bodies in the cool of the morning.

"Are you okay?" he asked, recalling their marathon session and hoping for some positive reaction, if not a little praise for his performance.

"I am fine, thank you," she said, knowing what he was really after.

He breathed deeply. "That's good."

"Are *you* okay?" she asked, smiling to herself.

"Yes, a bit tired, but very okay, thanks," he said, dropping a hint. She started to laugh.

"What's funny?" he asked, feeling a bit confused.

"You guys. You can't help yourselves."

"Oh?"

"Whether a guy is good, bad or indifferent, he will always want to know the age-old question, *how was it for you?*" she chuckled.

"Ah, yeah, I think you're right. Sorry, I guess it's a confidence issue," he said, which Babs thought was quite mature of him.

"I'm sorry, I'm teasing you," Babs said, kissing him on the neck again and staring at his face in the moonlit room. Matt said nothing.

"But if you really want to know," she paused, "You were magnificent!"

"Really?" He was quite chuffed. Yes, he had sort of fished for a compliment but what he got far exceeded what he had hoped for.

"You will recall that we had to stop because I just couldn't take any more," she said, stroking his chest.

"I thought that was because you were tired," he said, believing that to be the case.

"Well, not so much tired, but most definitely well and truly fucked," she said with a huge smile.

"Babs, I'm not sorry that we called a halt, my legs are like jelly." She laughed again, adding, "Same as me then."

She then moved more onto him. "There was only one downside," she said, reaching down to play with his surprisingly flaccid penis.

"Oh?" he said, responding to her manual attention. She properly moved on top of him to lick his lips and penetrate his willing mouth with her tongue. She then moved to his neck, chest and nipples and spoke in between kisses as she worked her way down his body.

"The only issue… was that… you didn't… cum…but…that…is going to be…remedied… right…now."

She got down between his legs and, holding his balls and his shaft with her hands, took his cock onto her tongue to slaver over it. Matt loved how her hair softly caressed his tummy and her boobs swung against his thighs. He groaned with the pleasure of her mouth closing on the head of his prick with her tongue swirling around the glans while simultaneously being jerked off… The 'issue' was remedied in very quick time.

She sat up and licked her lips like the cat that literally got the cream, then wiped the excess juice from her mouth and chin. She lay down fully on top of him, and he again enjoyed the heat from her body. Matt then pulled the duvet up and over them both. She didn't care that he could smell the salty aroma of himself on her as she leaned forward to kiss him passionately.

"What a shame I have to let you go. I could stay in bed with you all day. Hmm, I have some handcuffs, and I might just use them on you." He embraced her but as much as he had enjoyed the physical pleasure of his escapades with Barbara, he was looking for his escape route.

"Barbara from Scarborough, you are so fucking sexy. I wish I could stay here as well but duty calls. I'd better get going before Danny wakes up and starts asking questions."

He kissed her on the forehead. She hugged him tightly to her but the realisation of the liaison of convenience hit home as each one had in the past. For some reason, Bob Seger's lyrics from his Night Moves classic succinctly hit the nail on the head but this time she would have liked a few more entanglements with young Matthew.

"Before you go, there's a ten-pound note on the side here for you."

Matt looked very confused. "Is that for services rendered?" he smiled.

Babs laughed, "You're worth a lot more than a tenner, bonny lad." She went on to explain that the cab driver on Friday night didn't want to take his money, but she had forgotten to give it to him yesterday.

"He said that you hadn't been any trouble. Now go on, bonny lad. It's all quiet, away with you and never darken my doorstep, bed, or muff again!" She laughed, although inwardly, she was quite sad. She watched him get up and dress and thought of things she would love to do with him. She was disappointed that he seemed to be in haste to get away but weren't they all like that, she asked herself?

At least he had the decency to bend down and kiss her properly before he went. He gave her a lovely smile as he turned and left quietly. Barbara had guests in her bed before and was under no illusion that it was nothing more than an opportunistic situation of friends who fuck. She went back to sleep until her daughter tapped on the door an hour later. She picked up her phone - there was a message from Matt.

"Hey Babs, thank you so much for a lovely weekend looking after my friends and being especially attentive towards me. We all meet lots of people in our lives and most of them are soon forgotten…I won't forget you EVER xxx"

"Smooth-talking bastard," she thought to herself, but she was elated. She texted back:

"Thank you, kind sir, looking after your pals was a pleasure and looking after you (and vice versa) was pleasure in the extreme. If you're ever this way again, I do hope you would pop in to see me and maybe have breakfast in bed? xx"

At breakfast, the lads who turned up were fairly quiet. There was some chat about who got off with whom and a rumour that big Cliff was seen down a back alley shagging some woman from Rochdale. The big man wasn't there to confirm or deny it. Rudy piped up,

"Tell you what, though," then he started whispering, "I think Babs got off with someone 'cos she was screaming blue murder just after midnight. Someone was really sorting her life out!"

"Perhaps it was Cliff?" Ian ventured before turning to Steve.

"Did you hear back from your missus?"

"Yes," was the pithy reply.

"And?"

"Twenty-two missed calls and twelve texts. It appears she's not overly enamoured with my absence," Steve replied.

"How odd!" Dwayne said sarcastically.

"I'd better get my steel helmet and flak jacket ready for when I get back," Steve added.

"Have you thought about turning your lounge into a one-bed studio flat?" added Ian. "It might be a cheaper option than a B&B!"

Breakfast was served and done. Babs stayed in the kitchen and knuckled down to work. At 10.30 am, Dan was at the desk to pay the bill, which Barbara dealt with as quickly as possible.

"I hope you've all enjoyed yourselves," she said to Dan as she completed the receipt.

"Brilliant, we've all had a great time. Thank you, we'll put a reference on TripAdvisor. We loved it all."

"Thank you. What have you done with the bridegroom-to-be? You haven't put him on a train to John O'Groats or tied him to a bus shelter, have you?"

"Er, no. He went missing again but he's turned up and he'll be down shortly." Dan then left to load his bag on the bus.

As soon as the door closed, Matt called Babs from the first-floor landing for her to come upstairs. Her heartbeat accelerated as she quickly moved up the staircase. He pulled her into his room and, holding her close, kissed her cheek before eagerly kissing her properly.

"Thank you, you gorgeous woman," Matt said before kissing her again and he was off. As the door closed behind him, she took a few deep breaths and then sat on the bed, wondering how a young man twenty-five years her junior could cause such palpitations. She was delighted and sad all in one go and tried to make sense of it when really there was no sense except to describe it as infatuation. Five minutes later, she received a response to her earlier message saying, *Bank on it. Love, M xxx."*

She got up, went to the kitchen and made herself a cup of tea…it had been a very good weekend.

The trip home for all of them, not least the driver, seemed interminable. The only real highlight came after their comfort break at the services just north of Birmingham. As they set off full of fast food, ABBA's *Take a Chance on Me* came on the radio. Ollie, the real hard man midfielder, started singing along to it. GG and Gump joined in with the backing, which was rather impromptu and almost in tune.

"Fucking ABBA, bollocks," Cliff said disdainfully.

"Oh, come on, Cliff, everyone likes ABBA." Billy said, "What's your favourite track?" he asked the big man. Cliff shook his head and didn't answer, so Billy asked the rest of the group.

"Stevie, you start. Favourite track?"

Hesitantly, Steve looked around at the interested faces.

"*Winner Takes it All,*" he chuckled, first at the irony of the song given his situation with his wife and then at the notion of admitting he liked the Swedish super-group.

"This one – *Take a Chance on Me,*" Ollie said proudly before continuing to sing along.

"What about you, Chris?" Billy asked.

"*Super Trouper,*" he responded. Dwayne agreed.

"*Rivers Of Babylon,*" Gump added to a few smirks and groans from the ensemble.

"*Chiquitita,*" Ian piped up.

"*Fernando*" was GG's offering

"*I have a Dream,*" Danny said quietly.

"This one's a bit obscure, but *The Day before You Came,*" Matt said to a few quizzical looks. "It was their last UK single, I think."

"*Mama Mia*" was Rudy's choice.

"*Dancing Queen*," said Paul enthusiastically.

"Come on, Cliff. Give it up. You know you want to," Billy said, almost accusing the top dog.

Cliff looked around at everyone staring at him, including a few furtive glances from Chris in the rear-view mirror.

"Fucking ABBA? Are you lot having a laugh?" he said again, shaking his head as if the whole subject was absurd and yet they all still stared, almost shaming him into an answer.

Cliff looked at the expectant throng and then glanced out of the window before quietly saying, "*Winner Takes it All. It should be our team song!*"

Most of the guys laughed, not at his choice but because he had caved in to peer pressure. Cliff smiled but said "Cunts" under his breath before turning to Billy and saying, "Come on then, what's your favourite?" Billy took a deep breath before responding.

"*Chiquitita*"

"You soppy Irish sod!" Cliff said.

The bus was silent apart from a few chuckles and then Cliff repeated his earlier assertion.

"Fucking ABBA bollocks!"

Sunday was always a shit day for motorway driving but Chris relied on God's will, autopilot, sensible drivers, and a fair wind...

22

Girls Just Want to Have Fun

April 2013

A couple of weeks after the boys had run amok in Blackpool, Kirstie was off on a quiet two-night stay at an expensive Health and Spa Country Club near Birmingham for her hens' weekend. It was intended to be an altogether more staid affair for the gang of four, plus her mum, Julia. Kirstie was not into those wild escapades where young women have printed slogans on matching T-shirts while the bride-to-be is singled out wearing something equally naff or even more obvious, such as having to wear a veil in public. She thought it was all childishly undignified, totally embarrassing and utterly cringe-worthy. It just wasn't for her.

The weekend was for pampering - manicures, pedicures, massages, saunas, swimming pool, restaurant, bar and, if they preferred, the bright lights of the city for shopping and any other entertainment or nightlife. Party animal Sarah agreed with Kirstie that it would be nice to have Julia along as one of the girls for something a bit more civilised. Although true to form, she never stopped going on about the male staff in their tight white T-shirts and shorts.

Julia drove them all to the destination and the afternoon was spent having a long lunch, then a sauna and a massage, followed by a manicure/pedicure. They reconvened at the restaurant in the evening. Julia went off to bed at 10.30 pm to leave the girls to their *shenanigans,* and they duly got a taxi into town to sample some of the noisier entertainment before returning just after 1.30 am.

Saturday, over breakfast, they decided to go to the Bullring to shop. Julia said she was going to stay behind for some more treatments. She would only ever shop by herself at her own pace. Four young women would be like herding kittens.

At the salon, while sitting waiting for stage two of a full-body mud mask, a couple of chatty, middle-aged sisters started a conversation with Julia. They did most of the talking and after they all exchanged the basic pleasantries, one of them said that she was a hotelier in Lancashire and the other worked part-time in a town roughly a half-hour drive from her sister's hotel.

"And how is business outside of the summer season?" asked Julia.

"There's a few lively resorts even in winter," said the older one of the two.

"It's usually busy all year round. Families in the summer and lots of visitors for the spectacular scenery in the North West. Party crowds most of the year and of course, there's the ever-popular seafront illuminations season from September 'til November. It's really to keep small businesses going and get the Saga louts in."

"Saga Louts?" Julia asked.

"Over-fifties SAGA club – they're lager louts but more mature… in age anyway. Plus, there are the Christmas lights and the unofficial ballroom season inspired by Strictly Come Dancing from September to early January. There are no fools like old fools and some of these old dears feel like they have to show that they're the life and soul of a party when, in reality, it all looks so false that it just makes you wince. Forced fun at its worst but hey, I guess waiting for God can make you do odd things.

I could tell you stories about SAGA louts that would make your pubes curl even more than they do already. How about a threesome, all in their seventies, two men and a woman? And a party of eight guys that I thought was a golf society. Ha, all jobby jabbers! Trust me, it were damn difficult to get rid of the smell of buggery!" she laughed a raspy, cough-ridden smoker's laugh, even if she had given up the habit ten years ago. Julia surmised that a *jobby jabber* was a gay person.

"It must be difficult with the party crowds?" Julia said, trying to sound interested.

"It can be, hen parties are the worst. Lasses just can't handle their drink. Sure, the lads are loud and boisterous but their bark's worse than their bite. Normally, with stag parties, I give them all a free drink when they arrive and lay down the law. The threat of amputating their bollocks with a blunt penknife and serving them up for breakfast if they misbehave gets their attention. Get them onside early and they don't usually cause trouble."

"Do you run it with your husband or a partner?" Julia asked with the stag party comment, causing a little more interest.

"No, for the last five years I've run the business with my daughters, and the police are never far away should it ever turn ugly, which, thankfully, it hasn't. It usually depends on where the group comes from. We had a right shower of shite from Lincoln a couple of months ago that caused all sorts of trouble away from the hotel. I only found out about it when the party of ten suddenly became a party of two. The others had been arrested and spent the rest of the weekend at her majesty's pleasure. The two guys who were left needed us to open all the other rooms to pack their stuff and take it with them on Sunday when they were due to leave.

We found out that they were football hooligans ready to mix it with the home team's supporters at the match that weekend. I mean, for heaven's sake, just enjoy the football and the night out afterwards. What a bunch of twats. Then, by comparison, we had an amateur football team on a stag weekend up from the south a few weeks back. Your neck of the woods, I think, Herts or Hants, something like that, south of Brummie, is a mystery to me, Pet. Nice lads, some of them a bit earthy like but so well mannered. Aye, most of them were drunk of an evening but were very respectful and kept the noise down."

Julia's ears really pricked up. "Don't you worry that they might take advantage of yourself or your daughters?" Julia asked.

"Ha! It's not them taking advantage of us," she snorted. "It's us taking advantage of them, poor little lambs. Anyway, my two girls are built like Turkish wrestlers, so no worries there. I work on the principle if they might fancy me, then they'll behave so I try to keep myself in some shape and never get larger than a size fourteen. Although Christmas is a challenge, of course, and we all know what Christmas is like, eh, girls? Rhinos on the rampage!" she laughed loudly at her own joke. Julia thought the woman was rather stretching the credulity of the size fourteen comment but was still intrigued.

"So, when you say you take advantage?"

"Oh, not with everyone. It's not a shag a slag fest but just occasionally there'll be a young cocker that makes me flood the basement, if you know what I mean. If they like more mature women, then why not?" she laughed. "I suppose in modern parlance I'd be a MILF or Cougar. You know, a lot of younger blokes find older women sexy and they think we're gagging for it. We are, after all, supposedly mature and we know what we want, which isn't that unbelievable when you get down to it, eh Jules?" She was quite sure her opinion was shared.

"Yes, that's spot on," the younger one said. "Even I got off with one guy a few weeks back. They were from down south as well. There's a lot of staggers come to Blackpool from the south and all over really, including Scotland and Wales."

Her elder sister responded with, "Yeah, I think the southerners like to see how the other half live." Then she suddenly realised what her sister had said.

"Wait, *you* got off with one? You kept that quiet, you little minx!"

"Well, just snogging and I'm sure we would have got down to it but like the Nativity, there was no room at the inn. Least of all yours, I'll bet!" the younger one replied.

"Ooh, you dirty cow, you were going to use my establishment like a knocking shop?"

Her little sister laughed. "Trust me, he was worth the hassle of trying to get home in the morning - he was as sexy as fuck. Don't forget, I haven't had a shag in so long I'm re-virginising!"

"He sounds a bit desperate to me, and how would I know what you get up to in the bright lights of Chorley Sis? For all I know, there's a pineapple in everyone's front window!" They both laughed at the *swingers'* connotation. Julia didn't understand but let it go.

"What happened to your husband?" Julia asked, wanting to say how much the name "Jules" grated with her, more because of the accent than the name itself.

"He had a really bad accident working at the meat factory," the younger sister started to laugh and said, "Oh, not that old chestnut again."

And then both sisters said in unison, "He got the sack for sticking his dick in the bacon slicer."

Julia was horrified before the punchline was delivered again from the two of them.

"And she got the sack as well, *boom, boom!*" they chuckled together.

"Ah," Julia said with a false laugh, "Very good, yes, very funny."

"The truth is my ex is a long-distance lorry driver, and I'd always wanted to run a hotel. So, when we had the money, we bought a going concern from an elderly couple, even though the kids were little. Then, as the business took off and I was working longer hours, so did the distances he was driving, supposedly," she said with lots of emphasis on *supposedly*. "Of course, he was avoiding helping me when he could sit on his fat arse all day in his cab."

"But I got suspicious about a second phone he kept in his truck, which, stupidly on his part, didn't have a password or passcode. Maybe he was hoping I'd find out anyway. I also found some paperwork relating to an address in Salford. It appears that he'd set up home with one of the women who worked for the haulage company he drove for. God, did she get a shock when I turned up on the doorstep with a couple of suitcases full of his stuff. It was a classic double life. Sadly, he wasn't around much for the girls' upbringing - they rarely see him now."

"And you only married him cos he had Ford Sierra and a big cock," said the younger sister and they both laughed.

"Yeah, and you only married Tony 'cos he had a big cock and played rough!" There was no laughter from the younger one this time.

"That's a low blow, Sis!" was the response.

"Yeah, okay, sorry," her older sister knew she had overstepped the mark.

"Sorry, ladies, remind me of your names. I don't think I heard you at the beginning."

"I'm Barbara and this is my younger sister, Rachel," Julia made a mental note.

Rachel went off to the toilet and Julia steered the conversation back to stag weekends, making a joke of it.

"I guess the good thing is that you can enjoy these guys when you fancy one, and there's no commitment."

"Aye, exactly," said Barbara. "But don't think I'm some northern slapper with a vag like the Mersey tunnel Pet. They have to have something more about them than just be pretty boys and I always remember their names. I mean, we're into April now and I've only had three since Christmas. Jacko from Leeds, Tim from Middlesborough and Matty two weeks ago. He was a lovely lad."

Julia was shocked and, with her heart thumping with what revelation might come next, kept the conversation going for more detail.

"Yes, selective indeed! I'm intrigued how do you choose because there's a lot of guys go through your…establishment," *and through you, if truth be known,* Julia thought to herself.

"As I said, it's not just down to looks, although a handsome face will always loosen the elastic. No, there has to be a bit of class and manners about them. Oh, and discretion. The last thing you want is to be serving breakfast to a herd of them and one being like a bloody town crier telling everyone about me in bed. But the fact is, I'm divorced and can shag who I like. If they're attached, that's a matter for them to come to terms with."

"Quite." Julia showed some empathy to keep her onside.

"Take this lad the other week," Barbara said.

"Matty," Julia added helpfully.

"Yes, something in computers. It was his stag weekend, and I saw it as a last throw of the dice for him before he settled down. He was well-mannered, funny, one of the boys and just a really lovely guy. And pretty good in bed too, given a bit of direction."

This was more than just circumstantial evidence, for it not to be the same "Matty" that was shortly going to be her son-in-law. AND this was the young man she had lusted after since her daughter first brought him home. Yet this northern slut had got her hands on him first! Julia was annoyed at Barbara for taking the opportunity with Matthew and she was even more annoyed at herself for not doing so sooner. Rachel returned.

"So, this lad you nearly got to grips with, what did he look like, some baboon from Chester Zoo, I guess. Oh, wait, he was a southerner. London Zoo, maybe?" said Barbara dismissively.

"No, tall, dark and handsome, well, fair-haired really, but two out of three ain't bad," Rachel said, a bit miffed that her sister was being so derogatory.

"Really? How did you pull that off then? You're normally left with the untouchables?"

"We were in the Tower Ballroom. I'd had a couple of drinks, a slow one came on…I just asked him to dance before anyone else got to him and he said yes. You should have seen Deb's face because she was after him first."

"Dazzling Debbie. Miss Chorley 1990, the one who always gets what she wants, or rather, *who* she wants?"

"Aye, she was fizzing when I got back on the coach," Rachel said smugly.

"I just said you snooze, you lose, and she did see the funny side, but she ended up groping with one of this lad's pals. So, as far as I'm concerned, she had to settle for second best."

"Oh, and you didn't?"

"No, this lad, Matthew, we were on the way back to the coach park and saw a couple down a side street shagging. You know, a knee trembler and he just said, '*God, some people have got no class!*' I had to agree but he could have had me anywhere he bloody-well liked Babs. I was ready to have his babies if he wanted!"

Barbara laughed, Julia smiled and thought that would have been the last straw.

"Wait, what was his name? Matthew?" Barbara questioned. "What did he look like again?"

"Here, I took a selfie with him," Rachel said, thumbing through the photos on her phone.

"*Oh, my Lord*, that's him. MY MATTY!" exclaimed Barbara, surprised at the coincidence.

No, *my* Matthew, thought Julia as she looked at the photo on Rachel's phone.

"So, you went to bed with him?" asked Rachel.

"Well, it was an accident really," Barbara said rather coyly.

"An *accident?*" Julia said in a sort of laughing, contemptuous manner, trying to contain her irritation.

Looking at Rachel for a moment, Babs said, "I think after he left you, he got lost, being a bit worse for wear. Two bizzies brought him back because he could only remember my name as the owner and one of them knew me from when our kids were at school together. He was very fortunate because they would have had to arrest him for his own safety if they didn't know where he was staying."

"Bizzies?" Queried Julia.

"Aye, Bobbies, coppers, Blackpool's finest. These two were women police constables. One of them is a friend of mine. They thought he was too charming to lock up, but this was their only chance to avoid it," she continued.

"The laugh of it was one of them said if you don't want him, I might just take him home with me, just to save all of that paperwork, of course!" Barbara was undoubtedly amused by it all.

"Anyway, I took him into my little apartment because he didn't want the other lads doing some stupid stag stunt of stripping him off somewhere in public. I made him a coffee to sober him up while I went back to the bar to serve any stragglers who might fancy a nightcap. It can be quite a profitable time if lads fancy a few more beers. I went back an hour later after closing the bar and thought he'd buggered off back to his room." She paused to take a sip of water.

"I went to my bedroom, stripped off buffo cos that's how I prefer to sleep and as I got into bed, he was there. He must have been so out of it that he thought he was in his own room."

"So, you jumped on him?" Rachel said. No, was the response from Barbara.

"Well, not that night and in my defence, I did try to wake him to get him to leave but he was dead to the world, so I just had a nice nudie cuddle with him."

"Not that night?" Julia quizzed, but expecting the worst.

"No but we had a quickie in the morning. He also managed to get away from his pals later on that evening and, you know, two consenting adults and all that," Babs laughed and seemed quite smug with herself.

"I'll bet he was good 'cos by heck he could kiss," Rachel said.

"Aye, Pet, he was outstanding. He'd had just enough to drink to stay rock solid but couldn't or wouldn't…you know…"

"Play Mister Squirty?" said Rachel obligingly.

"Yes, I had to stop him in the end so we could sleep," she laughed again.

"And what about you, Sis?" Rachel asked jealously.

"Did I? Hell, I lost count. Best nookie I'd had since 1989!" Both the sisters laughed loudly.

Julia did not see the funny side.

"Jammy cow!" said Rachel. "If we had found somewhere, you wouldn't have got your claws into him, you child molester," Rachel laughed.

"Gosh, you ladies have had a fine old time. I really should get a life!" Julia said, managing to contain her anger and frustration. From then on, she was determined she was going to have Matthew. He was evidently susceptible to seduction and playtime with mature women and although he didn't know it, Julia was going to be his next. There was absolutely no thought of telling Kirstie of his nefarious activities. As far as Julia was aware, Matthew and her daughter were blissfully happy, so why throw a huge spanner in the works just because of his stag weekend carry-ons?

The female attendant then arrived and completed each of the ladies' treatments before Julia went off to the swimming pool to "cool down."

Late Saturday afternoon, Kirstie and Sarah had returned from shopping and were sitting at the bar for a couple of cocktails before getting ready for the evening. Sarah gave Kirstie a gift-wrapped present, a box lengthwise about half as much again as that of a mobile phone. Kirstie was quite surprised and hugged her to say thank you. She then said it really wasn't necessary.

"Ha, it might be one day!" Sarah laughed her dirty little laugh and Kirstie was deeply suspicious, so much so she started to undo the wrapper.

"Not here. I'd die of shame!" Sarah said, physically stopping Kirstie from going any further.

"Saz, whatever you die of any time ever, it will not be of 'shame.' You have to be the only person I know who is ultimately shameless," Kirstie said with a smile.

"Just open it when you're by yourself, okay?" Sarah smiled back as she squeezed Kirstie's hand.

"I hope it isn't what I think it is," Kirstie added, sort of hoping that it was exactly what she was thinking it was, as she would never buy an item like that for herself. She would be totally embarrassed just filling out an online form on one of those websites. She smiled again at Sarah and said she would open it upstairs.

One drink in, Kirstie decided to tackle her best friend about Jenny and asked her for everything she knew about her. She had now worked with the very tactile and over-friendly Jenny Marinello for a few weeks, and whilst she did like her and her way of working, there was something about her that didn't sit well.

"If you know her from way back, then I think you should forewarn me in case it impacts my job. You know I never judge you because you're a free spirit and I love you as a friend but I'm worried that my boss might have some ulterior motives."

Sarah always opened up to Kirstie. She was her soul mate and confidante, and several months ago, she told her about a number of things that had gone on before she went to Ireland. Sarah was a tad coy to start with by saying that she knew Jenny from parties in the social circles that they moved in. She said that Jenny might seem over-friendly and tactile but that was exactly what she was like. She was not putting it on. Sarah went on to say that Jenny told her that if you knew how to play the game with men, they would be putty in your hands, and you can get anything you want.

"I've always taken that on board. She is an expert at that game! But let me tell you, I know you think I was a bit of a slapper before I met Dan–"

"No, not at all. Popular with guys, perhaps, but not a slapper," Kirstie interrupted.

"Okay, popular/slapper, what's in a name? But my point is that I am not in the same league as Jenny Marinello. I am Accrington Stanley to her Real Milan."

"Madrid," Kirstie corrected her.

"Madrid? Oh yes, Real Madrid. Anyway, you get the analogy."

"But Jenny is gay, isn't she?" Kirstie pointed out.

"No, Jenny is not gay, Jenny is bisexual. In fact, I'd go so far as to say she's omnisexual, excluding children and animals." Sarah thought for a minute. "Although there was a story about her and a large male Old English Sheepdog belonging to one of the lecturers at Uni but that was never confirmed," Sarah threw in as a bit of a curveball.

Kirstie laughed, "A dog? Don't tell me he was called Roger?"

Sarah wasn't laughing but raised her eyebrows. "Apparently, his name was Ben, but she was very upset afterwards."

"Why?" asked Kirstie, rather concerned.

"He never wrote, he never phoned…" Now Sarah laughed after delivering the punchline. Kirstie nearly spat out the sip of drink she'd just had.

"Okay, whatever she is, bisexual or gay. She's with Mia now, so she's in a committed relationship, isn't she?" Kirstie said, as a matter of fact.

"Is she fuck!" Sarah said with some disdain. "I don't know if Mia is aware or not, but Jenny sees who she wants whenever she wants. You can trust me on that."

"Oh? And what do you know to back that up?" Kirstie said, almost disbelieving her long-time buddy. Sarah looked at her, then pulled her phone out of her bag. She scrolled down a number of messages to one from Jenny M.

"I got this the day after we all went round to Mia's that night."

It read: *"Great to see you last night, totally unexpected but I enjoyed our kiss. Mmm, I'm thinking of that session with you tied to my bed! If you fancy getting together for old time's sake, you know where to find me. I still have the furry cuffs and the DED lol. C'mon Let's Play. J xxx"*

Kirstie's jaw dropped. "So you *have* slept with her then? Wow, you know that I'm not that way inclined but watching you two kiss that night was *so* sexy. And what's a DED?"

"Don't ask but it's making me damp just thinking about it. Kay, her kisses are something else. I mean, I've kissed a lot of people but hers are like heroin, they are just so addictive. Believe me, I was on the verge of an O when she kissed me that night," Sarah said, thinking back on Jenny's dextrous fingers.

"That and the fact that you also let her digits do the walking as well, of course," Kirstie added.

"God, yes, she has a super, sensual touch," Sarah shivered. "It's making me feel frisky now," she laughed.

"You're always frisky! So, how did you meet Jenny? What is she like in bed and what's that about being tied up?" Kirstie asked, knowing that Sarah wasn't going to hold anything back now and she was also getting horny at the thought of some juicy titbits.

"We often met and chatted at some of the parties I told you about and I recall one time I was in the kitchen, and she came up behind me, put her hands on my hips and started kissing my neck. God, I just melted into her arms. She was just so sensual. Then she lifted my skirt slightly and put both her hands down my knickers and brought me off with her fingers there and then."

"Wow."

"Yes, she is that good. I had to hold on to the worktop to stop myself from falling down like a sack of spuds. As unsteady as I was, she turned me around and kissed me long and hard and I climaxed again. I kid you not, it was indescribable," Sarah stared wistfully at her cocktail.

Kirstie was incredulous.

"She whispered that we should both go upstairs and she would make me forget men forever!" Sarah said. They both laughed.

"You know me, that was never going to happen but for that next hour and a half, she was bang on. Not that it was all one way. She was very demanding as well, but you know what it's like when you lose yourself in passion. It's no chore to pleasure the person you're with in any way they desire. Sometimes you're just so delirious with the ecstasy of it all that it's just a blur," Sarah said thoughtfully.

"As for being tied. We used to meet occasionally, maybe once every couple of months, for a drink and a chat first before…" Sarah raised her eyebrows and then poked her tongue out and waggled it, simulating cunnilingus. "And this one time, she had me handcuffed to the bed and blindfolded with a number of toys at her disposal, including the DED, a double-ended dildo! And that's all you need to know," Sarah said, chuckling and reminding herself of how euphoric it all was.

Kirstie nodded and as good as making love with Matt was, she didn't ever recall being so lost in the moment that she would indulge without realising what she was doing…was she missing out, she wondered. They were quiet for a few minutes, and Kirstie stared pensively at her drink before speaking.

"I know you've, well, as Matt would put it, batted for the other side occasionally because you've told me as much, but you've never made a pass at me?" Kirstie questioned.

"I know and that's deliberate," Sarah said emphatically. "You're my best mate and have been since school. I would gladly snog your lovely face off but if I attempted that and it was rejected, it would make things so awkward that the dynamic of our friendship would be ruined, don't you think?" Sarah said, staring straight into Kirstie's eyes.

Kirstie hugged Sarah to her and whispered, "You're right, of course. But maybe just one kiss and nothing more?"

Sarah pulled back and looked at Kirstie and nodded, smiling, "Maybe later if the time is right and we can blame it on the alcohol?" They both laughed.

When Kirstie got back to the room, she quickly unwrapped the gift and sure enough, she was now in possession of a Glitterati Rechargeable Rabbit Vibrator. She smiled to herself and thought of checking out its capabilities after her shower. Unfortunately, she fell asleep in the bath and by the time she woke, she was too pushed for time to play. Rampant Rabbit would have to wait to be introduced to Betty Beaver, she thought, sniggering to herself for dredging up an adolescent name for her lady parts.

When she came back down to the bar, her mum and the others were already there. Kirstie looked at Sarah with slightly raised eyebrows and a big smile. Sarah stifled a chuckle.

Julia loved being accepted into the group. She could still remember when they were all pre-pubescent teenagers who would be scared to say boo to a goose. Now they were lovely young women, and she was grateful that Kirstie had some charming, reliable friends. She made a point of not overstaying her welcome when the meal had finished and wished everyone a "good night" when the time came. She was unaware of the admiring looks from a couple of the male staff as she sashayed through the bar towards the exit.

Kirstie loved the whole intimacy of the gang of four's friendship within the confines of the Health Complex. She saw no need to go gallivanting into town to listen to loud, irrelevant music surrounded by drunken know-nothing numpties out for a quick shag.

Later that evening, when they all went to bed, Sarah and Kirstie walked down the corridor to their adjoining rooms, having a chat and a laugh about the evening's events. When they got to Sarah's room, she unlocked the door and pushed it open before turning to give Kirstie a hug and then, remembering their earlier conversation, turned her face to Kirstie's and looked her straight in the eyes.

It was a meaningful look and Sarah moved nearer to tentatively kiss Kirstie on the lips before pulling back ever so slightly, seeking affirmation in Kirstie's eyes. Kirstie delicately licked her own lips as if to taste Sarah and then they kissed again. This time, Sarah did not move away but slowly pushed her tongue into Kirstie's mouth. Kirstie's heart was thumping in her chest with the thrill of being *properly* kissed by another woman for the very first time. It was tender, passionate and so, so horny.

Sarah pulled away again and still holding Kirstie, said, "Just one kiss?"

23
Wicked Game

May 2013

Just over a month or so since their return from the Stag Weekend, Matt and Dan reconvened for their periodical after-work pint and did a quick post-mortem of the Blackpool adventure. Matt thanked Dan again for arranging everything, but Dan was just happy that it all went off without any "*fatalities*!"

"I am a bit surprised that no one got a shag either!" Dan said.

Matt raised his eyebrows as if in shock. "Jeez, mate, least of all you!"

Dan waved it away as if it were a joke and continued,

"Apart from Cliff," Matt replied.

"Well, that was never confirmed, not even by the big man himself," Dan replied, shaking his head.

"You were pretty tame as well. It has to be said, given your reputation," Matt added, looking at the "stud" sat before him.

"Mate, me and Monty were glad of the rest, although Barbara from Scarborough looked as though she could be tempted!" Dan said, staring directly at Matt. Matt wondered if he knew something but decided to bluff it out.

"You should have given it go, Danny. I can't see how she could have resisted your charms."

Matt was still in awe of his buddy's revelation of how he lost his virginity to Mrs Malin and told him as much. Dan just smiled and replied.

"It's my animal magnetism, you know. God has blessed me with a decent body, a good sense of humour and a face that doesn't scare the bejaysus out of anyone, um…not often anyway, so from a female point of view, what's not to like?"

Matt just shook his head. "You are a jammy bastard, and you kept that quiet about Mrs Mmmm, didn't you?"

"I was sworn to secrecy and anyway, could you imagine if the local papers got hold of it, her career would be ruined and–"

"-You'd be a local celebrity stud-muffin!" laughed Matt.

"And I wouldn't be able to show my face anywhere," Dan said after the interruption. "It's the mature women thing, isn't it?" he added.

"Oedipus," Matt said.

"What?" Dan didn't understand.

"Oedipus complex," Matt repeated.

"What's that?" Dan asked, wiping his top lip after a mouthful of Guinness.

"It's a psychoanalytical term which specifically means the love of a son for his mother."

"Well, that's normal, isn't it?" asked Dan.

"Not when they want to shag the living daylights out of their mother!"

"Oh, that's a bit naughty," Dan looked quite horrified.

"Some bloke called Sigmund Freud came up with it but it's now sort of developed into younger men fancying more mature women and the other way around. You know, the cougar culture," Matt said.

"Right, okay, it probably works well for both camps. Young blokes think more mature women are hot because they aren't so inhibited and the more mature women like the exuberance of youth, as Mrs M told me."

"Lucky sod!" Matt said with envy, although he could now directly relate to what he spoke of after his dalliance with Barbara.

"So, enlighten me about your mum's friend being naughty with you then?" Matt said.

Dan smiled.

"It was at a party at our house for my dad's 50th birthday and the place was packed. Both the toilets were occupied with women queuing like they do and I needed a slash, so went outside and doused the dahlias. Anyway, about halfway through Christine, my mum's bestie, came outside for a ciggy and caught me irrigating the flower bed."

Matt was captivated.

"She said, '*My, you've grown. How old are you now, Danny?*' I told her I was seventeen and tried to turn away but just as I finished, she came over to me and said, '*so you're legal then!*' She didn't hang about and introduced herself to Monty, who was very pleased to see her. Oddly enough, I didn't stop her," Dan said, as though he surprised himself.

"Funny that!" Matt added, chuckling.

"It didn't take her long before I was spunking off and she seemed really pleased with her work before she kissed me and said it would be our little secret."

"Naughty lady!"

"Christine was a very naughty lady, I can tell you. Married three times, countless affairs and a bit of a black sheep, by all accounts. She was always a good laugh, though and everyone loves her."

"Especially you?" Matt asked. Dan smiled.

"I am still very fond of her, especially when she taught me to drive," he laughed.

Matt shook his head and resigned himself to hearing about the driving lessons.

"How did that come about?" he asked.

"My mum and dad couldn't afford driving lessons for me and Dad also didn't fancy teaching me in the family car, which you may remember was that bloody great Lada Riva estate. It was marginally less manoeuvrable than a combine harvester and a lot less pretty. It had the same fuel economy as well. Dad paid three thousand pounds for it brand new, and I reckon that was about two thousand nine hundred and fifty quid too much."

Matt laughed out loud.

"Anyway, Christine…naughty Christine," Matt added to make his pal feel a bit guilty.

"Yes, naughty Christine offered because she had taught some of my other cousins to drive and her old beat-up Fiesta would be perfect."

"So your mum and dad were to blame for handing you over to a sex pest!" Matt suggested.

"Yes, they were, and there isn't a day that goes by that I don't thank them for it," Dan laughed.

"So, the lessons started, and she also taught me how to drive!"

Matt shook his head with a smile and asked what had happened to her.

"It took four months to pass my test, although half of the time I was supposedly out for a driving lesson, Monty was getting taught a few lessons instead. When I did get my licence, our liaisons were scaled back somewhat, and then she met a guy that she's now shacked up and living in Cornwall. I still get the odd naughty message from her from time to time, usually on my birthday or at Christmas or when she's had a few drinks." Dan said fondly.

Dan continued reminiscing about older women. "Remember I was away at Dundee Uni?"

"God, yeah, you must have shagged your way through half the campus and the principal's wife," Matt said, hopeful of another juicy tale of erotica.

"I did alright, but I much preferred the mature ladies when I got the opportunity. The principal's wife had passed on, so I gave that a miss," Dan said with a straight face and then they both laughed.

"And did you get the opportunity with any mature ladies?" Matt asked.

Dan took another sip of his beer to heighten the drama.

"How long have you got?" He smiled. "Before my final year, I got a summer job with a small landscaping company. It was brilliant. The weather wasn't bad and on quite a few occasions, I had to put sun cream on.

"Wow, sunburn in Scotland!" Matt said, chuckling at how absurd that sounded.

"A lot more common than you think, mate. Don't forget, a lot of them are fair-skinned, so ten minutes of sun and they're burnt to buggery!" Dan continued, "Anyway, it was quite physical work and kept me fit and I'm sure the boss liked me tagging along as eye candy for bored housewives."

"Oh, yeah, here we go!" Matt said, shaking his head in recognition of yet another saucy little tale from the king of Cougar Town.

"It was very flattering when they hung about longer than was necessary, talking about a job or constantly making tea or coffee. Davey, the boss, was convinced there were a few follow-up jobs and the odd maintenance contract because the women liked to have a bit of a letch, not just at me but him as well. He was in his early forties but also had a great physique and he wasn't slow chatting up some of the ladies either."

"Was he married?" Matt asked.

"Yes, and his wife was a sexy little cow, too. If she was half as horny as she looked, then I don't know how he could spare the energy. There was a lot of flirting with customers, although most of the women would run a mile if you ever really responded but it was great fun."

"So, you never got any offers?" Matt asked, looking a bit disappointed that there didn't seem to be a story to tell.

"Oh well, you'd get a comment like maybe you could come and cut the grass when hubby's away."

"Or trim their bush," laughed Matt.

"Of course! But they probably didn't mean it. Although there was one…"

"Ah, thought so! Go on," Matt was all ears, ready for the nitty-gritty.

"Davey picked me up from my bedsit at around 7.30 am, the usual early start and explained it was just a bit of garden maintenance at this big house just outside of Dundee. Nothing too heavy, tidying the borders, cutting the grass, etcetera, all easy stuff. He added that I'd like the client because she was some posh totty from England. We got started and the lady of the house came out to the patio in just a sort of red and black silk dressing gown and asked if we'd like tea or coffee. She was about 5'5, early forties, properly curvaceous - all woman and she had really shapely legs. I half noticed she was fully made up with bright red lipstick and some pretty expensive jewellery. She was also wearing high heels and I thought it was a bit odd to wear heels at that time of the morning. I brushed it off, thinking that she might have been in the middle of getting dressed for work." Dan paused for another sip of beer.

"Davey said he had to get some fuel for the mower and was also going to the bank. He'd be about an hour and left me to it. Carol, the lady's name, retreated inside but left the patio doors open. She then just stood there watching me doing a bit of weeding on the large pots on the patio about ten yards away. We heard the truck pull away and she was still standing there watching me.

I looked up and she smiled, licked her lips and then slowly undid the tie holding her gown together. I was mesmerised as it fell open. She put her hands on her hips, exposing herself and underneath, she was wearing stockings and suspenders, red knickers and a red basque-type thing with a half-cut built-in bra."

Matt corrected him, "Half cut? You mean half cup, don't you? You know, as in bra cups?"

"Yeah, half cup, well, whatever it was, half cut or half cup, it should have been awarded the George Medal for services over and above the call of duty because the amount of flesh it was trying to hold back was something else, she had magnificent boobs. Honestly, her nips arrived a good ten seconds before any other part of her."

Dan sipped some more of his beer before continuing, "She made sure I got a complete eyeful as she started to take off the gown but before putting it to one side, she reached into the pocket and pulled out a big rubber dildo."

"Wow, what happened then?" Matt asked, utterly engrossed.

"She put this rubber cock into her mouth and licked it up and down quite sensuously, still looking at me. She stopped, put her hands back on her hips and said, *What do you think?*"

"What *did* you think?" asked Matt, hanging on to his every word.

"I was gobsmacked!" Dan said. "I remember thinking she was just so confident."

"More front than Harrods by the sound of it," Matt added.

"In more ways than one!" Dan laughed. "She could put the M in MILF and the F comes to that. She was as sexy as fuck and Monty responded in the time-honoured fashion,"

"So, what did you say?"

"I told her exactly that. I said you're as sexy as fuck!" Dan said, recalling the whole adventure from four years ago like it was just yesterday.

"She asked me what I was going to do about it. I just said whatever you bloody well want, Love."

"She told me to come closer, and we could see what develops. I then said that it was already pretty much developed, if that helped? *Definitely,*' she said, *'A real cock is so much better than a rubber one, especially when it's attached to a handsome young man,*' and she smiled. I just took my gloves and rigger boots off, left them on the patio and went into the house. She had her arms around me in no time, and we were snogging each other's faces off. What a kisser. She was like a hoover once our tongues met. I had my hands on her gorgeous bum when she stepped away and told me to stand where I was."

"She went over to the big settee, dropped her knickers to reveal her trimmed ginger minge and I really don't think my dick could have got any harder. She sat down, put the dildo to one side and slowly opened her legs. I could see her growler opening up and how wet she was. The juice was glistening in the sunlight."

"Dan, have you ever thought about going on an adult version of Jackanory?" Matt laughed.

"Honest, this is true." Dan was quite emphatic.

"Oh, I don't doubt you at all. I just love how descriptive you are," Matt added.

"Mate, I remember every bloody second of it." And he continued, "She then told me to strip while standing where I was because she wanted to take in what I had to offer and imagine what she was going to do with me."

Matt laughed. "Dan, you really do make me sick with envy."

"So I slowly peeled off my T-shirt first and she sort of purred," Dan said, laughing. "She was fingering herself and it was *so* erotic. She asked me to turn around and face the garden, and I heard her grunt a little as she triggered her little mushroom."

Matt nearly spat out the mouthful of beer he'd just taken, causing a bit of a dribble, which he mopped up with a bar towel.

"Little mushroom, I think the term is flicking the bean?" He said, still chuckling.

"Yeah, exactly, her clit, you know?" Dan said.

"Yes, I know what they are and where to find one. I've just never heard it called a mushroom before, but I suppose it could be a button mushroom!"

"Well, this was more like a mini prick!" They both laughed.

"Anyway, she said, and I quote, *'I'm going to be running my fingernails up and down that smooth skin of yours and I usually leave my mark,'* then she laughed a real growly sexy laugh and finished with, *'I'll leave you to explain it to your girlfriend.'* I didn't say anything.

She then told me to lose the socks and shorts, which I did, leaving me standing there in my pants."

"That must have turned her on even more 'cos you like the budgie smuggler type of skids, don't you?" Matt said.

"Yep, and I had a nice clean white pair on that day, showing Monty Python off to perfection. I heard a *'mmm'* and then she told me to turn around again, and I was hoping she might appreciate the obvious stiffy that was barely contained in them," Dan said proudly.

"What did she say?" Matt asked vicariously, trying to put himself in Dan's shoes…or pants.

"Her very words were, *'Oh my god, bring that thing here. I want to devour it NOW,'* Dan said.

"The thing is, in a first encounter, it's where the control is in question," Dan said as though he were an authority on the subject. "It's really about who has the most confidence because no one wants to be rebuffed or thought of as clumsy and inexperienced. She bloody well knew what she was about, and although I'd had a little bit of experience with a few girls, they were just that, girls who were experimenting themselves. The only limited education I'd had 'til then was from Mrs Mmm and naughty Christine. It is so much more enjoyable when one person directs operations if you know what I mean; otherwise, you're like we were at school and our late teens."

"Have you ever had an older woman? You know someone who took the lead?" Dan asked. Matt said no because he knew Dan would be like a dog with a bone for more detail but added that he was insanely jealous! "Mate, it is quite the thing. It takes away all the responsibility that blokes feel that they need to do the business."

"So go on then, you're in your budgies and she ain't gonna take no for an answer," Matt said, quickly deflecting the question.

"Yep, so Carol just has that real look of complete *'Come and Fuck Me'* lust in her eyes. You know they talk of body language and stuff, but until you see a mature woman smiling and drinking you in with her eyes and licking her lips with so much desire, you ain't lived!"

"I'll bet," said Matt, now trying not to think of Barbara and, of late, his future mother-in-law, who regularly gave him that look.

"I walked slowly over to her, and she just reached for the sides of my keks as I stood in front of her. She didn't pull them down straightaway, though. She just looked me in the eye again. I've realised, on looking back, it is all part of the build-up to show how much that person wants you. They don't have to say anything, they just speak with their minces. I know it sounds like I'm talking bollocks but if you've ever experienced it, you'd know what I mean."

"Go on," Matt said impatiently.

"She just twiddled her fingers in the sides of my pants, pulling the material more tightly across the bulge and then rubbed it against her cheek. She then looked up at me again and said when I let this beast loose, you're not going to disappoint me, are you? I mean, fuck, what are you supposed to say to that?" Dan said.

Matt shrugged his shoulders and replied, "You're a captive audience. I can't see you saying 'sorry, Love, I'm out of my depth. Best to let me get on with the weeding!" Dan laughed.

"Exactly, I just said there's only one way to find out!"

"She gradually pulled the material down and, of course, the biggest dribbling budgie in the world sprang out and nearly hit her in the face. She didn't hesitate and the helmet was in her mouth quicker than a wank in the Arctic. Mate, her mouth was so hot my legs nearly gave way, and I had to hold on to her shoulders as she got to work. She made a lot of noise doing it, which is always off-putting. You know when some girls do it to show you that they're enjoying it when they're probably not? But Carol was definitely enjoying it. She had her hands on my backside, stroking it and pulling me harder into her mouth. I'm in ecstasy when suddenly behind me someone says, *'Fuckin' hell, Carol, ya cood nae wait?'*" Dan said in his best Scottish accent.

"Was it some Spanish bloke?" Matt said.

"Ha, ha," said Dan. "She backed up and just held my cock in her hands and said, *'No, you were taking an age, and this young man is too fucking sexy to leave alone.'*"

"Wow - it was a set-up all along?" Matt said.

"I didn't know it, but Davey and her were having a fling and she said she wanted a threesome, but it had to be some sort of role play where the third party, *me*, was totally unaware and would be seduced by her."

"A Highland Fling then?" Matt said, giggling at his own joke. "But I guess it went okay?" Matt continued sarcastically.

"Fucking hell, you bet. There wasn't much garden maintenance going on, I can tell you." Dan said, picturing one particular act where she was on her knees with Davey in her mouth, gagging on his cock while he (Dan) was slowly fucking her from behind and pushing a small vibrator into her arsehole.

"Wow, she sounded like a bit of a pheasant. Weren't you worried you'd catch something?" Matt asked, as though he was concerned about Dan's health.

"Pheasant?" Dan queried.

"Yeah, a game bird!" Matt threw in a fake laugh to emphasise the comment. Dan ignored it.

"Right, we only visited a few times, and she always made us wear rubbers. But what a gorgeous house she had. Her old man was in the oil industry and away a lot."

"Oil industry, what, he owned the local chippy down the road?" Matt offered.

"Ha ha. No, something to do with geology. He was a bit of an expert in oil exploration."

Matt sat there looking at his friend and smiling, then shook his head.

"Some people have got it and most don't," Dan said smugly.

Matt finished his drink and waited for Dan to get another round, which wasn't immediately forthcoming. He made a big deal of tipping his glass over and saying, "Jeez, good job that was empty." No result. Donald, the landlord, was hovering and could see that Matt was subtly trying to get his buddy to order two more pints. Dan seemed quite distracted, so Matt had another go.

"Dan, how do you spell Guinness?"

Dan looked at him and spelled it correctly.

"You forgot the F," Matt said.

Dan looked confused and said, "There's no F in Guinness!"

"Correct!" Matt said, looking at his empty glass. Donald chuckled and said, "Same again, lads?"

They had another pint each and a couple of games of pool, then finished their drinks and, with a farewell til the next time, they went home.

But what Dan didn't tell Matt was that on his third encounter, Carol slipped him her mobile number and told him emphatically just to message her. It transpired that she wanted Dan alone and Davey would be consigned to history. They duly became regular fuck buddies and Dan was besotted with her. When her husband was away (which was an awful lot), Dan would visit, and they would play for hours. Her husband was minted, and she had a very nice lifestyle as a housewife but there were no kids, which she never felt the need to explain.

Over a four-month Uni break, he rarely went home and was just thrilled to get messages from her to come round. Some were sexually explicit, others were more subtle, but both added up to the same thing. She was in need of his "services". Dan didn't want Matt to know how he had fallen for this woman hook, line and sinker. He wasn't just infatuated; he had fallen wholeheartedly in love.

24

Heart on My Sleeve

May/September 2013

As Dan drove home from the pub, he reflected on his great fortune regarding the opposite sex but for all of the pleasure he derived from his liaisons, there was an awful lot of emotional pain that went with it. He adored Christine, who had provided a basic practical education in the pleasures of the flesh. He was extremely unhappy when she rightly called time. He reminded himself of how distraught he was when he heard of Monica Malin's tragic demise. And then there was Carol. He smiled to himself and sang the opening lines of Neil Sedaka's classic song.

Carol was on a whole new level of tutelage. She taught him the importance of erogenous zones, adding that lots of women are different. Even so, paradoxically, they are the same when, with the right man and with a deep cerebral attraction and lust, a woman becomes one big erogenous zone. Anything touched or kissed will be electric to a lover. She also schooled him in delaying techniques for the male orgasm, like squeezing the muscle behind his testicles or stopping at the point of ejaculation just to release some semen, like releasing a pressure valve.

She showed him how to masturbate and, at the right moment, slow almost to a stop and orgasm without ejaculating, which, she said, again reduces the excitement. Subsequently, when indulging in full-blown intimacy with a partner, maybe an hour or two later, it doesn't compromise the final unloading if that's something that turns a woman on.

Carol introduced him to the delights of giving and receiving prolonged oral sex and mutual anal play, including rimming and finger work. They tried anal sex a couple of times, but his cock was too big for her to enjoy full penetration. Another great reward she gave him was teaching the technique of 'grinding the corn'. This is a variation on the missionary position in which the man shifts upward just a bit, so his pubic bone stimulates her clitoris while his penis is still entering her vagina. The position provides maximum contact with both the clitoris and the G-spot (of vaginal intercourse). The first time they tried it, she squirted, much to her and Dan's surprise. She decided that the extremely intense orgasm and 'female ejaculation' should be kept for special occasions when she was really climbing the walls.

He learnt much from her on seduction, flirting and how to cerebrally steer a woman towards the bedroom because, as she put it, *"Stimulate our minds and our bodies will follow — make a woman laugh and you're halfway home and the fact that you're drop dead gorgeous should seal the deal."*

In early September, after a particular marathon session just before they went to sleep, Carol asked him what he was doing the following weekend.

"Davey will probably have some work lined up," he said, but was intrigued by her question; she rarely arranged anything with him more than a couple of days in advance. He knew, as she did, that whenever she called, he would always come running.

"Could you get out of it for a long weekend, Thursday to Monday?" she asked nonchalantly, but then surprised him by adding, "You could say you were going home, couldn't you?" It suddenly appeared to be quite important to her. She snuggled into him, and he loved how she enjoyed the afterglow of not wanting to break contact.

He pretended to think about it, trying not to sound too keen but the excitement got the better of him. "Yeah, I'm sure I could swing it. What did you have in mind?"

"Do you have a passport here with you?" Carol asked, stroking his muscly arm. Dan said nothing but then pulled the quilt away and started searching imaginary pockets around his naked body.

"Bugger! The only thing on me now is you, you sexy thang you. But yes, it's back at my digs."

"Ha ha ha," she said in mock amusement but squeezed into him harder and kissed the nearest part of his flesh that she could reach. She half rolled onto him and, looking into his eyes and stroking his hair, said, "I'd love to get away with you for a few days, is all. The thing is that the only time we ever meet is to play and as much fun as that is, I'd like to do what normal couples do, even if it's for a short break. Does that sound stupid?" she paused.

"I mean, I'm no spring chicken and I know if we go out to a restaurant, people are just going to point the finger at an old bat and her toy boy, but frankly, I don't care."

Dan thought about it for a few seconds and cuddled her to him before saying, "Carol, I'd love to, but I'm embarrassed to say if we're going abroad, I just can't afford it."

She turned slightly and propped herself up before moving towards his ear and nibbling it. She then whispered that it was her treat because it was near his birthday - it wouldn't cost him a penny. She left it at that, feeling that if she added anything, it would sound like she was desperate.

"How did you know it was near my birthday?" he asked.

"You left your wallet on the side a few days back and I checked your driving licence. Dan, I insist…just the two of us would be lovely, don't you think?" She stared at him, willing him to say yes.

The thought that this gorgeous woman wanted him was massively flattering and the fact that she wanted to treat him was thrilling in the extreme. Carol didn't wait for his answer.

"No buts. Please, I'm very fond of you and I just think we could have some fun together, an escape, you know? It's not been a great summer, and I need some sun. Hubby is working, so why shouldn't I take a friend?"

"But how could you get away with it? Do you have your own bank account?" he asked, and she was quite taken aback at how astute he was, worrying about the possible evidence of her adultery.

"Dan, I have my own personal account and anyway, I often go away by myself, especially when I need a change of scenery." She was very convincing.

He hugged her. "I'd love to, but I want to pay my way. Could I pay you in instalments?" Carol had a quick chuckle at how naïve he was.

"Do people often pay for their own birthday presents?" she said sarcastically but could see that he was genuine in his offer. "If it helps, then, okay, let's discuss terms when we get back, yes?"

"Okay, I would really like that. Thank you. Where are we going?" He asked as he kissed her on the lips.

"It's a surprise but I'll make all of the arrangements. Text me your passport details as soon as you can. Now, get off to sleep. I have a hair appointment at 8.00 am and other stuff to do in the morning, so I need to set the alarm for six o'clock."

"*Six?*" he was a bit shocked and confused at such an early start. "What do you have to do at that time before your hair appointment?" he asked.

"*You*, silly, now, switch the light off and kiss me good night." He did as he was told, and they both slept soundly after quite a boisterous playtime.

The following day, he texted his passport details and she promptly replied with a thumbs-up emoji and a kiss. He was very excited about their 'dirty' weekend and her 'toy boy' comment didn't bother him one bit. He was already in love with her.

Davey phoned on that Friday evening and told him he was needed from Monday for the next few days. It was a fortunate call, which gave Dan the opportunity to say that he was away from Thursday for a long weekend – family stuff and left it at that. Davey wasn't overly happy with it but accepted it without question. Dan assured him he was available for what was left of the summer, as he knew there was a lot of work coming up. As soon as Davey ended the call, Carol phoned.

"Hi, handsome, before we go away, I need you on Wednesday evening, please." Carol went on to explain that she was hosting an Ann Summers Party for some of her girlfriends.

"What's an Ann Summers Party?" he asked naively.

"Oh, Dan," Carol said, thinking he was being deliberately dim.

"No, really, what is it? I've never heard of Ann Summers," he said obliviously. Carol went on to explain it was like a Tupperware party, but much more fun.

"What's a Tupperware party?" Again, he genuinely didn't know.

She briefly explained but eventually said simply, "Be here at 7.00 pm. tight jeans and a tight tee-shirt, clean shaven and that nice after-shave you wear. All you have to do is pour drinks, flirt and make the girls happy. The happier they are, the more they drink. The more they drink, the more they'll buy. I don't need the money but it's nice to show hubby I try to contribute to the household and I'm not a complete freeloading slut."

"You're not a slut." He was mortified that she could demean herself like that.

"Oh, Dan, you are so sweet but so naïve. Never mind, it's nice that you think I'm not. Anyway, Wednesday, wear a tight white T-shirt and maybe not jeans. How about those dark grey clingy jogger shorts - commando?" she suggested.

"But without pants, they don't leave much to the imagination!" he was quite concerned but was then buoyed by her response of, "Exactly, Danny, you're the eye candy but I promise to protect you!" She laughed.

"From what?" he was openly perturbed.

"Half a dozen drunken, sex-starved women at a party selling all sorts of sex toys and stuff and you'll be the only guy? You work it out for yourself, but Kim is the one to look out for. She's newly divorced and hasn't had a decent shag in years," she paused. There was no response from Dan.

"Don't worry, you'll be safe in my hands," she added.

He laughed. "Yes, I already know that."

"I'm thinking that if you get your stuff ready for our weekend, I'll pick you up at 6.30 pm, and you can stay overnight before we head off in the morning. Don't forget your passport," and she was gone.

Fuelled by plenty of booze, the Ann Summers party was a raucous occasion. Dan was suitably attired, as Carol had requested and the guests were not slow to comment. He served plenty of drinks and, after having a few drinks of his own, he was persuaded to model some of the ridiculous undergarments and "role play" outfits – fireman, US Navy white uniform, James Bond, etc. As a final treat for the ladies, he came out just wearing a novelty thong, which was nothing more than a grey cock sock (supposedly an elephant's trunk, together with elephant ears and eyes, it brought the house down.) Comments like *does your cock go all the way in that trunk* and *I'll bet he cums in pints* were rife before Kim asked if it could pick up peanuts off the floor. She then led the chant of "*Take it off, take it off*".

He looked at Carol, who raised her eyebrows and, with a smile, said, "You had better oblige or you may not get out of here alive." With a few drinks inside him, he was never shy about stripping, and he did so to cheers and a lot of compliments. One really drunken soul mimicked the lines out of Jaws. "I'm gonna need a bigger pussy. It must be an eight-incher."

Her friend cottoned on and laughed before saying, "Nine and the girth to match."

"I'm gonna need a bigger pussy, right?"

Kim led the follow-up chant. "Make it hard, make it hard!"

Dan shrugged and looked at Carol, and just as he went to stroke himself, she stepped in and pulled him towards her, making sure his length was on full display. She firmly grabbed his buttocks and gave him a full-on tongue-dancing snog, knowing what effect it always had. In seconds, he was fully erect to more cheers from the adoring gaggle of women.

"We have lift-off!" one of them shouted.

"Carol, you are one lucky bitch. I'd love to see what comes out of it. Shall we have a raffle, and the winner goes upstairs with him for an hour?" Kim suggested. Dan looked horrified in case Carol agreed, and Kim won.

"Oh no, girls, he's all mine and in any case, an hour of his handiwork and you'll think you've died and gone to heaven!" Which was greeted with a lot of laughter and a few admiring looks. Carol whispered to him, "Best go and get dressed while I get rid of this pack of cougars." As he scuttled off to the kitchen, she turned to the throng and told them to drink up.

"I've spoilt you enough already. *Go home!*" she demanded.

Two of them were within walking distance of their homes. The others went with Audrey, their designated driver. Audrey had spent most of the evening shaking her head at the degradation of dignity brought about by too much wine and Prosecco. She was rather prim and proper, the oldest of the bunch and possibly in her mid to late fifties. She kissed Carol on the cheek and, smiling, said, "Next time you have one of these, dear, I'm going to get a taxi. I loved the entertainment."

When the guests had left, Carol kissed Dan passionately.

"You were brilliant," she said before kissing him again.

"Thanks, I really enjoyed it, although it did get a little bit scary near the end there," he said, returning her kiss. "Am I staying tonight, or shall I get a taxi?" He never took sleepovers for granted.

"You're with me – I want you." They tidied up and went to bed.

When Carol woke in the morning, she had a number of texts from the previous night's guests. As Dan stirred, she read silently through a few messages thanking her for the party and for the "cabaret".

"Good morning, Big Boy. You should see these texts. I should pimp you out, I could get hundreds of pounds a time for your services. So far, I've had four of the girls asking for your number."

Carol continued to thumb through the approving messages. Dan smiled before rolling over onto his back and staring at the ceiling.

"I also had three give me their numbers last night, including scary Kim. Did you know she cornered me in the kitchen?" he said, reliving the event like it was a trauma.

"Dirty Cow! What did she do?" Carol asked as she started to respond to her messages.

"She came in on the pretence of wanting a top-up and, as I was doing so, stood next to me and stroked my backside, saying that she could do with a top-up herself and would I be interested?"

"And what did you say?" Carol asked irritably.

"I told her I'd love to and then snogged her face off. In fact, if you hadn't called for more drinks in the front room, I would have given her one on the breakfast bar there and then." He nonchalantly picked up his phone and said, "Oh, look, she's messaged me!"

Carol stopped what she was doing. "What? You said what to her? Show me your phone." She grabbed it to see nothing at all, as he hadn't even switched it on.

She shoved him playfully. "I thought you were serious," she said, relieved at his little jest.

"Well, it's true that she did start stroking my backside and asked if I was interested but then you did actually call for more booze and I made my excuse and got away. Even so, she slipped a note into my back pocket while accosting me." He looked quite pleased with himself.

"What did it say?" she asked, quite perked up now.

He reached over for his shorts and pulled out three bits of paper. The first one was Kim's handiwork, and it read, *want to play? K x* together with her number.

Carol checked it on her contacts list and sure enough, it was Kim. The next note made Carol laugh out loud. *Garden Maintenance, Audrey McFadden,* with her number.

Dan looked at it and said, "Oh yes, while you were saying farewell to some of your posse, she came into the kitchen and very politely asked if it was true that I did landscape gardening work. I presumed you had told them all and I said I did. She then asked if I'd be interested in some regular maintenance work, as the garden was getting a bit much for her."

"Oh, did she?" Carol said cynically.

"It all seemed quite genuine to me," Dan said, wondering why Carol seemed a bit put out.

"She's a dark horse, that one, quite the brooding mare," Carol said, shaking her head.

"Why say that? She seemed quite out of place last night."

"Because, young Daniel, she lives in a second-floor flat with communal gardens maintained by the Council."

"Oh." The penny dropped.

"Show me the third one," Carol asked.

Dan handed the crumpled piece of paper over. It was a number written in lipstick with an imprint of someone's lips on it, followed by an 'X'.

"Hmm, who could this be?" Carol wondered out loud and again began to check through her contacts list. She was rather shocked and not a little dismayed that Lucy was the culprit, though she said nothing.

"Who gave me that one?" Dan asked, although he knew he probably wouldn't fit a face with a name when she told him. Carol said nothing but pretended to scroll through the numbers.

"Carol?" Dan seemed overly enthusiastic, adding to her irritation.

"The number's not here," she fibbed. "Perhaps it was just a wind-up. You could see most of them were shit-faced." Inside, she felt a little betrayed that her good friend Lucy had also gone behind her back, asking him to contact her.

"You wouldn't pimp me out, though, would you? I mean, I only want you," Dan asked, seeming to accept that the lipstick note was a joke.

"Don't get clingy, Daniel. You are mine but I am *not* yours, okay?"

"But you know I Lo—" Carol put a finger to his lips.

"You know the rules. We don't use the L word!" She was trying to be stern with him.

Dan looked a bit forlorn. "Okay, but you know I do," and he kissed her on the lips to emphasise the point. She stretched out and then pulled him close to her, feeling his flaccid penis starting to stir.

"Hmm, well, if she or any of the gang contact you separately, you're to tell me." Carol seemed to calm down a little.

"What about Audrey?" Dan asked tentatively, but was trying to make a joke out of it.

"Especially Audrey, fucking old witch!" Carol scowled.

"Do you know if I didn't know you better, I'd say you were a bit jealous!" Dan said, immediately wishing he hadn't.

"Jealous? *Jealous!* Why do I have any need to feel jealous? Ask yourself, whose bed are you in at the moment and who are you going to be fucking all over the weekend?" she said, massaging his stiffening cock.

"Mmm, a good point well-made, but we make love, we don't fuck," he said sarcastically, then he took a deep breath and stretched out, letting her play with his ever-swelling length.

She suddenly stopped and said, "Go and shower. I can still smell those treacherous cows on you, and we need to be out of here in an hour. I'll join you in a sec." She pushed him out of the bed. The penny dropped, Carol *was* jealous, and she didn't like it one bit.

25

Nothing Compares 2 U

In less than sixty minutes, they were on their way to Edinburgh airport in her eye-catching Mini Cooper with sporty British Racing Green livery. Despite his size, he swung into it quite easily. She looked stunning in a short white denim skirt and a low-cut, shocking pink T-shirt under a white denim waistcoat. He could see the outline of the typical half-cup bra she usually wore, and he got the resultant twinge. He studied her as she drove and when she noticed and smiled, he told her that she looked so sexy.

"I don't suppose we have time to stop anywhere for a quickie. I'd love to christen this beautiful car with you," he asked.

"I might have managed it twenty years ago, but I'd need to be a contortionist to play in this car. Let's wait until we get there and do it slowly. What do you think?" she said, concentrating on her driving.

"How about both?" he laughed. "So, just where are we going?" Dan asked, stroking her bare leg.

"It's a surprise. If I could get away with it, I'd blindfold you for the whole journey," she uttered, not realising the sexual connotation.

"Carol, you could blindfold me anytime you want," he said suggestively.

"Mmm, noted. What about handcuffs?" she replied, still concentrating on driving but enjoying the idea of incorporating restraints into their playtime.

"There's a thought. Have you brought some with you?" he asked excitedly.

"No, but you don't need cuffs to tie someone up, do you?" She recalled a couple of times Davey had her tied to the bed and she had quite enjoyed that, although to her chagrin, he wouldn't let her do the same to him. However, she now had a willing pupil and the idea quite excited her.

"Good point!" he said but then changed the subject, much to her disappointment.

"How long does it take to get there?" he asked.

"Where? Edinburgh? Usually about an hour," she said, smiling, knowing that wasn't where he meant.

"No, wherever our destination is," he said, a little irked that she had played dumb.

"If I told you that, you'd narrow it down," Carol said, still being coy.

"Doubtful, but I guess it's in Southern Europe. I can't imagine it will be a long haul just for a weekend."

"You'll have to wait and see," she teased.

Parked up near the terminal, they were at departures within minutes and with only hand luggage, they cleared security quite quickly and headed off to an eatery for breakfast.

"No clues then?" he probed as he tucked into a full Scottish breakfast.

"Nope. We'll test your knowledge of geography when we arrive for boarding," she said, finishing off a salmon croissant and a large latte coffee. Carol checked the departures board carefully for the gate numbers and caught him staring at her.

"Like what you see?" she smiled.

He smiled back. "Yes, but I'm not allowed to say what I really want to."

She held his hand on the table.

"Best not, my lovely man. Let's not complicate things. Hey, did you get any follow-ups from the party last night?" Carol asked.

"None of them know my phone number and anyway, I think I made a bit of a prat of myself, especially with that elephant thong." He looked a bit disappointed but doubted if he would have taken up any opportunities. Anyway, Carol was all that he wanted.

Carol was cynical. "Listen, my friend, those so-called ladies are a resourceful bunch. You were a big hit amongst the girls, *especially* with that elephant thong. I've had some follow-ups to my *sod-off* replies, which were quite amusing." She was throwing a few crumbs of comfort because she could see he needed some flattery.

"Kim, who also tackled you direct, said, '*You are one selfish bitch keeping a gorgeous young boy locked up in your bedroom, I've a good mind to report you to the appropriate authorities, or you could let me rescue him from your evil clutches… out of your frying pan and into MY FIRE! lol, by the way, Girl's Night Friday – up for it? Kx'* Evil clutches? That's rich." Carol moved on to the next message.

"Fiona just said, '*Lucky cow, if there's anything left of him when you're done, give me his number.*' She is out of luck because there won't be anything left of you when I'm done. Why would you want second best, anyway? Gillian sent an unsmiling emoji, and Audrey, whom I texted, querying why she needed a gardener when she lived in a flat, replied, '*I really don't know what came over me but I'm sure I could find something for him to do!!*' So, you see, you made a real positive impression."

Carol checked the departure board again and said they should make their way. She reached for her purse, but Dan said he would pay as a small gesture towards the cost. She was grateful for that but told him he really didn't need to; there were other ways to contribute to the weekend!

Dan paid with cash and then set off quite quickly, but she told him there was no rush, only queues beckoned. A queue to the dispatch desk, a queue to get airside and the irritating queue behind the people taking an age to get cases into overhead lockers, oblivious that they selfishly hold others up who need to get past.

"The art," she said, "was to get there with just a handful of people left and walk straight on the plane and sit down. Sure enough, there was only one couple in front of them at the boarding desk and two others behind. Dan noted the destination – Faro!

As they strolled down the final walkway to the aircraft, Dan piped up.

"Faro? Isn't that in Portugal?"

Carol nodded. "Geography is unmistakably a strong point but you're saying it like it's a third-world country!"

Dan laughed and said in a smaltzy American accent, "I don't care where it is as long as we're going there together."

"Oh, per-leese!" was Carol's answer and she shook her head before holding his hand.

The three-hour flight passed quietly between them. Carol read something on her Kindle for most of the flight while Dan listened to music on his phone and played FreeCell. They both had a coffee from the in-flight catering trolley and Carol couldn't help but notice how the two flight attendants looked at Dan. One of them was male! She also noted how the female attendant quizzically looked at her, trying to figure out the relationship. Dan, of course, was totally oblivious to the extra attention he seemed to be getting from them.

As the aircraft landed, Dan tried to glean some more information about their eventual destination. Was it a hotel or an apartment? Was it near Faro? Was there a beach nearby? Carol just gave him an enigmatic "wait and see" look and he knew he was wasting his time. Passport border control and customs were negotiated within minutes, then they were outside in the very hot early afternoon sunshine, heading for the taxi rank.

Carol spoke to the driver in Portuguese as though she were a native and they were on their way. Dan took in the dusty, dry scenery typical of the southern Iberian Peninsula and asked how long the trip would be.

"Twenty minutes," Carol said, slipping her right hand onto his upper left thigh and moving it so that her little finger was stroking his balls through his jeans. She then turned to him and whispered, "Twenty minutes, and I can't fucking wait!"

They turned off at the Almancil junction and almost imperceptibly, the landscape went from dusty dryness to an area of manicured lawns and palm trees. Shortly, they pulled into the Vale do Lobo Estate, littered with picturesque white villas and what appeared to be a very classy golf club.

Carol paid the driver in Euros and his very enthusiastic "Obrigado Senhora" indicated that she had added a handsome tip. Dan then grabbed both of their bags and followed Carol through the complex before arriving at a very palatial villa.

"This is it," Carol said, unlocking the door and as they stepped through the entrance, she dropped her handbag and turned to fling her arms around his neck and kiss him.

"Come on, I'll give you a little tour," and she grabbed one of his hands to lead him around the property.

He was amazed at how delightful it all was. Three bedrooms, tastefully decorated and furnished, a decent-sized contemporary kitchen, a lounge with two big, red leather settees, a huge TV and an upright piano in the corner. The large bi-fold doors at the rear led onto a small deck with loungers and, just beyond them, a very nice-sized pool, the backdrop to which were the green fairways of the golf course.

"This is fantastic, but it must cost a fortune to rent even for a weekend," Dan said, open-mouthed at how classy the place was and wondering how he was going to afford his share of the costs.

"Don't be silly, this is my holiday retreat, along with hubby, of course," she said nonchalantly. She went to her handbag and pulled out an envelope to give to him.

"Happy Birthday, Lover," she said with a kiss on his lips. He was quite surprised as she had said nothing all the time they were travelling. He opened the card that had an Amazon Voucher for fifty pounds.

"Oh, wow, thank you!" He was sincerely touched by her gift and then he read the card, which on the outside just said *Happy Birthday*. On the inside, it repeated the salutation and added, *To My Best Friend*, and it was signed off with, *Love you, Carol xxxx*. Then he noticed a neatly folded A4 sheet of paper in the envelope and when he opened it, there was a handwritten poem. He read it slowly, no one had ever written poetry to him before:

Dream Lover,
Silver tendrils of light grasping at my nakedness,
limbs entwined in cotton sheets,
Sleep evades me, entranced by the glow of the moon.
A tune fills my head, lilting blues carried on the sultry night air,
My eyes close as I absorb the music, lost in the moment.

I reach that heaven between sleep and waking,
The place where desires are realised and passions heightened.
Still, feeling each beat of my heart. Rhythm merging with blues.
Senses aching for fulfilment, open and willing.

In a breath, I feel him. A chill air dancing over my naked skin,
As his presence descends, each nerve grasps for his touch.
His fingertips trace a line over my body, circling my nipple.
That dances to his attention, taut and pink and alert.

Warmth as I feel his mouth caress my breast.
Lips I have felt a million dreams before, ecstasy.
Fingers that bury deep into my buttocks,
My sex pulled close to his face, transfixed as I feel his tongue.

The warmth of me merging with your breath,
Silky wetness under your lips as you explore the sex that awaits you.
Breathless, my fingers find your penis, unwrapped and evolving
To the primaeval animal, seeking its prey.

A length I have known yet, one I seek to explore, stands before me

The urge to caress, to taste, is overwhelming.
Eyes closed to savour the sensation. My lips meet you.
Warm, glistening, powerful, your cock lies against my tongue.

Buried deep inside my mouth, he is home, tension pushing
Climax growing. I cherish his taste, making love with my lips.
Raw animal drives us as he kneels behind me,
Back arched, sex presented, feeling the longing to be filled.

Grasping at my hips, he enters me and pulls our bodies close
Our bodies welded, as one, complete.
The tenderness of foreplay is transcended, passion now urgent
Thrusting, pounding, intense, unrefined, our bodies work together.

Orgasm marching resolute toward our intercourse, bodies tense
Plateau reached, we sit, sensation extreme on the precipice.
Eruption, we move together and savour the release of energy
Howling like the night beast, we are king.

As the intensity ebbs, I know his departure is near,
I cling to my dream, still wanting of his touch.
And he is gone, yet I know he will never leave,
I will know his body again, I will feel his touch, I will taste his lips.

For he is a dream lover, bound with the moon, the blues,
My wild lover, from whom the morning brings wilderness.

Carol stared at him intensely to see how her muse would affect him. He shook his head slightly and looked at her briefly before looking back at the card and then back at her.

"Wow, I don't know much about poetry but that is…" he struggled for the right words and mouthed nothing apart from. "…thank you so much." He was truly moved, and she was heartened to see how much it had affected him.

"You are so very welcome." Carol smiled.

"What do you think of the view?" she asked, trying to save him from welling up. He looked at her and was perceptibly quite emotional.

"Gorgeous!" he said and held her close to him.

"Thank you. but I mean outside," and she waved his view to the vista from the patio doors. He turned and was even more open-mouthed as he took in the whole panorama. Carol then stood behind him and, with both hands, started massaging his groin area before undoing his zip and slipping a hand inside to get him hard. She then stood back.

"Stand there, strip off and don't move," she ordered.

"But."

"No one can see you. It's totally private," she assured him.

As he stripped and was now almost fully erect, she came up behind him again and pressing herself to him. He could feel that she was also naked, with her erect nipples and ample breasts pushing into his back. He loved the eroticism of her desire for him. Her hands came around him again and she tied her thong around his balls and the base of his cock, with a scrap of material just covering his length as she massaged him with it.

"Can you feel how wet this is?" she asked, continuing her manipulation.

"Mmm," was all he could respond with as he closed his eyes with the pleasure of it all.

"You've done that to me, and I've been soaking ever since we got off of the plane."

"Sorry," he said, not meaning it one bit.

"Well, now you are going to make amends for causing me to make such a mess."

"Yes, ma'am," he said in his fake American accent. She walked around in front of him to take him over to one of the cushioned sun loungers by the "lead" she had tied around his genitals.

Carol sat down and, lying back legs wide apart, told him to sit on the lounger between her "spread" with his legs also on either side of the sunbed and slowly feed his cock into her.

"But what about a condom?" he pointed out.

"No need, I've only insisted previously because I didn't know where you've been sticking that lovely weapon but I trust you and I much prefer au naturel."

He sat down and they shuffled together to get fully intimate. She removed the thong from his genitals and they were ready. In their sort of L-shape, they found that he could rock backwards and forwards to fuck her. Long, slow strokes, short, quick ones and in this position, he could massage her breasts and stomach and, with his right thumb, rhythmically rub her clitoris in time with his thrusts.

He watched her writhe in pleasure over the next ten minutes or so and build towards her first climax. With cheeks flushed and pink blotches around her neck, she finally gave quite a loud shuddering groan, which Dan thought anyone within fifty yards couldn't have mistaken as anything other than a woman in the throes of orgasm. Not that he cared, except her climax usually triggered his own and he slowed almost to a stop to delay it. She was aware of his predicament.

"No, Baby, keep going. Fuck me and fill me up with it. I want to feel it shooting into me." She clawed at his stomach, barely able to reach him, but she enjoyed the sensations of his sensual pumping. Carol watched as his eyes closed, his mouth opened and he threw his head back at the moment of release. His body jerked and the hot spending swamped her insides in several spasms. She clenched her intimate muscles to milk as much as she could from him and sighed loudly when he flooded into her. As he slumped forward slightly, she pulled away and drew her knees up to her chest.

"Oh God, that was lovely. I can still feel it all," and she rocked slightly from side to side as if to try to get more feeling. Dan leant back, supporting himself with his arms behind him.

"Welcome to Portugal Lover," Carol said, staring at him and smiling. "Be a darling and grab a couple of beers from the fridge and let's enjoy the sunshine," she requested.

"Okay, but are you sure we can't be overlooked?" Dan said, looking around to see if there was any possibility of an audience.

"Who cares? If they can, let them witness the show."

Dan went to get the beers and just before he returned, she slipped on her thong to catch the aftermath. They spent the rest of the afternoon relaxing before showering together and then going to bed for a long, leisurely fuck. Their evening was spent at a local restaurant where they dined alfresco and drank and talked until the small hours.

When Dan awoke the following morning, Carol was already sitting up in bed. As he gradually came to, he asked her what the time was.

"Good morning, it's 7.00 am," she replied.

"That's early for a holiday morning."

"I don't like to waste the day and I'm getting up soon. Did you sleep well?"

"Like a log, you must have worn me out."

He then noticed that she had put on a T-shirt and mentioned it to her.

"You know I'm a bit self-conscious about my body, especially these things," she said, jiggling her boobs.

"But they are gorgeous, just as you are, so no need to cover them up," he said, and then saw that she was doing something in her puzzler magazine.

"Doing a crossword? Can I help?" he asked, quite keen to get involved.

"If I get help, I won't be doing it myself, will I? Tell you what, make yourself useful and make us a coffee each — white, no sugar for me, please," she asked as she briefly looked over the rim of her glasses at him. Dan stretched and sat up before kissing her on the cheek and, taking a quick glance at her crossword, she playfully pushed him away and covered it up.

"I'm sure I could help," he offered.

"Yes, you can, with a nice cup of coffee. Mmm, coffee and cock, aka breakfast in bed," she chuckled before he got up and walked over to the bathroom. She checked out his gorgeous manly frame, paying particular attention to his delectable arse. She made a growling noise before saying, "Don't be long. The bed feels empty without you!"

Carol returned to the puzzle in hand as Dan came back with two coffees. He had donned a pair of briefs which nicely showed off his growing bulge and joined her in bed, sitting up next to her.

"If you're stuck with one that could shift things along, I'm sure I might be of assistance," he half-jokingly persisted. Carol tutted but she loved how naturally funny he was.

"Okay, you're only going to be a pest until I let you," she was resigned to the fact that he would just keep badgering her.

"Four down, yoga position," she said, staring intently at the crossword grid. Dan thought for a couple of seconds.

"Sixty-nine."

She tutted again. "Six letters."

"You could write smaller if you need to cram it all in. Or just write in the numbers that would leave you four spare spaces," he said, trying to make her laugh.

She looked at him over her glasses and smiled, knowing he was being deliberately obtuse.

"You haven't quite grasped the concept, have you?" she said, shaking her head.

"How about cowgirl?" he said. "No, wait, that's seven letters." He thought for a few more seconds.

"Got it – Doggie, yes, has to be Doggie. That's got six letters." He pretended to be chuffed with himself at supposedly getting the right answer.

"Hmm, here's another one. Twelve across, incident beginning with O?" Carol asked.

"Orgasm," he said quickly.

"Ten letters!"

"Well, if I do it well enough, you could draw it out over a longer period that might fill up the space."

"You have been no help whatsoever. Last chance and there's an incentive," she said, resting her hand on the significant swelling between his legs. "If you get this right, I will give you a BJ to completion. If not, you will have to do me instead," and gave his bulge a little squeeze.

Dan laughed. "Excellent. Win, win because I adore kissing you there."

Carol felt a little twinge where it really mattered and smiled at him before returning to the clues. "Eight down, Spanish invaders of Central and South America in the sixteenth century, starts with a C and that's all the clues you're going to get," she said sternly. He thought for a moment.

"From what I remember reading about them, I'd say they were cruel, conquering …counts!" he said. Carol was a bit surprised at his deliberately corrected naughty word, but he continued, "I don't know whether to intentionally get this wrong or not, but I'm guessing umpteen letters?"

"Yes," Dan lifted his bum from the bed and slipped off his pants. His penis was already at half-mast, and he grabbed her left hand to place it on his length.

"So go on then, smart-arse!" she said, stroking the hardening appendage and fully expecting a silly answer.

"I was going to say cunnilinguists. But the real answer is conquistadors!" he said smugly.

Carol stopped stroking his stiffened weapon and filled in the blanks. He was correct.

"Well, I am impressed! But to be honest," she paused as she took off her glasses and put down the magazine and her pen.

"I am more impressed with this magnificent invader." Then she positioned herself between his legs so that her mouth was directly above his fully hardened tool.

"Just remember, I will be getting as much pleasure giving this as you will receiving it," she smiled and dipped her head downwards. In less than seven minutes, he gave in to his blissful climax. They then swapped positions, and he teased and tongued her to orgasm in fewer than ten.

They showered and went for breakfast in the little piazza near the golf club before strolling back to the villa. In the afternoon, they went outside, she asked him to strip naked and lie on a towel on the patio in the shade. She then poured a copious quantity of baby oil onto his back, which she smoothed over his muscles, bum and thighs, leaving him slippery to the touch. She was naked herself and then lay fully on him to just squirm about so that he could feel all of her body massaging his. He had never felt anything so sensual or erotic, and he loved her even more. After a good few minutes, she stopped and just whispered, "Go to sleep, Baby. Eu nunca posso ser seu, mas eu te amo muito".

"That sounds lovely. Should I ask what it means?"

Carol chuckled, "It means put the toilet seat down when you've been for a pee, please!" She then squeezed his hands and said, "Just go to sleep."

An hour or so later, he was awoken by the sound of a piano playing and someone singing. He thought he was dreaming at first but he realised that the sound was coming from inside the villa. He got up, pulled on a pair of shorts and went inside. Carol was sitting at the piano in her bikini bottoms and a thin cotton beach robe. She was softly singing *Will You Love Me Tomorrow*. She hadn't heard him come up behind her and when she got to the title of the song, he whispered, *yes and forever*. She smiled at him and continued to play out the song before stopping and turning to kiss him. He picked her up in his arms and took her to bed, where again he orally brought her to orgasm before making love to her. She climaxed again, moaning loudly, he did so very soon after. As they spooned afterwards, Dan asked her about her singing and piano playing.

"When I was single, I used to sing and play in a pub band at weekends all over Essex and around the Thames Estuary. It was decent money and inevitably led me to meet my future husband when we were playing at some posh club in the East End of London. After a whirlwind romance of six months, we married. Today was the first time I've sung properly in twenty-two years and that is because of you. The song, the poem, Daniel, you just seem to inspire me. Thank you," Carol said, holding his hand and slowly intertwining her fingers with his.

"I am flattered. I didn't know you were so talented," he said, hoping for her to elaborate. She chuckled.

"Daniel, my talents know no bounds. Not only do I give the best BJ in the Universe but I'm sure, given the opportunity, I could win X-Factor," she laughed at that ridiculous idea.

Dan agreed with both statements, but Carol laughed again and shook her head.

"Nah, I'm only joking about X-Factor anyway. There are thousands upon thousands of great singers in the UK. Ninety-nine per cent of them will never make it past the pub and club circuit because if you don't write your own stuff that appeals to the masses, then you're just another very good singer!" she said as a matter of fact. "But music is incredible, isn't it? Whether you can sing or not – it just stirs the mind, body and soul."

He didn't know what to say, so he just cuddled up behind her and gave her a hug.

The pair showered together again, dressed, and wandered down to the Club House for a leisurely, relaxing dinner at a quiet little table in the corner. Even so, Carol couldn't ignore some of the stares they were getting, not so much because of Dan's good looks but more, Carol suspected, through the age mismatch. She didn't care. She could happily shut out the rest of the world as they enjoyed their holiday romance.

Saturday and Sunday were spent much the same as Friday and they never felt the need to leave the complex other than to walk and talk around the pretty estate and occasionally onto the beach. Carol just loved the whole escape. It was idyllic and Dan was the perfect companion.

Sunday evening, they sauntered down to *their* restaurant and sat at *their* table to order some drinks and their evening meal. As she sat there trying to catch people staring at them, Dan suddenly blurted out.

"Can we do this forever?"

Carol turned and looked at him quizzically, then, thinking he was joking, said.

"Of course," and laughed. She looked him in the eyes then and saw that he was serious.

"I mean, let's run away together, live together—" Carol stopped him mid-speech and held her hand up to emphasise her next utterance.

"Daniel, this has been a wondrous few days. Let's enjoy the evening. Tell me about Hampshire. It's been years since I went there. As you know, I'm from Essex, the land of bimbos with white handbags and matching stilettos, whose only ambition is to marry some rich guy." She hoped this would distract him. Dan stared at her before she smiled at him and continued.

"Luckily, twenty-two years ago, I met and married a very well-off man who has kept me in a lifestyle I could only dream of. I came from a two-up two-down mid-terrace slum in Jaywick Sands. It sounds nice, doesn't it? But trust me, as seaside resorts go, I'm not sure it would trouble the top five hundred in the UK. In fact, it's more like a one-horse town without the horse."

"But you sound quite posh?" Dan said, totally side-tracked from his forlorn quest.

"Mate, I'm as common as muck with not a GCSE to my name and very questionable parentage to boot. But I knew that accent wasn't going to get me anywhere other than as a checkout girl at the local supermarket," she said in her best Cockney accent.

"You don't talk much about your husband," Dan whispered so as not to attract attention.

"Why should I discuss my personal life with my lover?" She sipped at her wine and continued, "You, my lovely man, are the exciting distraction, the escape from the normal routine of providing a house and home to my husband, who works damned hard to provide an affluent lifestyle for him and me. Just think of it that you get the absolute best of me. The suave, sexy nympho who is always in a good mood and you have no other responsibility other than to please me, which you do so well, so that should be enough." She looked him directly in the eyes.

"I want more," Dan said, reaching for her hand. She met his movement halfway and their fingers locked together.

"Let's just be happy with this and see, okay? We've only known each other a few months." She didn't want to spoil the weekend with complete negativity. Dan hesitated but then said, "Could I ask a personal question?" Carol was ahead of the interrogation and smiled.

"We don't have kids because we're too selfish. We did try a little while back, but it wasn't to be. The doctors suggested it's to do with poor quality egg production," she hesitated. "Anyway, too much detail but we, as a couple, just accepted it. As I said, the very comfortable lifestyle of nice houses at home and abroad, long-haul holidays and new cars every other year is pretty compelling. My husband is one of the top dogs in his field of expertise, which is drilling for oil and that's why we live not too far from Aberdeen. He's away a lot and Dundee is much nearer to the long-haul flights from Edinburgh and Glasgow airports than the Granite City, even if it is the oil capital of Europe."

She stared at their hands and continued, "He wouldn't thank me for saying this, but he's seventeen years older than me, and he's never been the best in bed. But…but I still love him and not just for his money. I can do what I want without question. It gives me a great deal of self-worth to work for a couple of charitable organisations, not just contributing financially but also my time." Dan looked crestfallen and had nothing to say.

"Enjoy what we have, Daniel. There's no need to think ahead." In her heart of hearts, she knew he was totally smitten and as much as she wanted to keep a lid on things, she, too, was almost lost in the bliss of it all.

"Come on, drink up, lover. I need you to take me to heaven once again because we won't have time in the morning," Carol said with a last squeeze of his hand.

She paid the bill and left a generous tip, as usual. As they left the restaurant, she smiled at anyone who was looking and even winked at an older couple who she felt had been staring and talking about them all night. Carol was taken aback when both of them responded with judgmental scowls, so much so that she let Dan walk ahead before going over to their table.

"Good evening, we've evidently been the subject of your conversation all night and no, he isn't my son, but I *am* old enough to be his mother. Anyway, as we're going now, I'll tell you that within about fifteen minutes, that handsome fellow, as a precursor to fucking my brains out, will be burying his tongue in my pussy with a couple of fingers up my arse to get me wet. I am rather moist already just thinking about it. In fact, he's been rogering me senseless all weekend as we've been working our way through the Kama Sutra, which is why I appear to be a bit shag-bandy. So, if you hear any screams when you're on your way back to your pad, it will probably be me in the throes of ecstasy. I'll let you conjure with that image while you sip at your Horlicks later!" Pointedly, she addressed the woman directly, "You should try a young man, Sweetheart. It will take years off you 'cos hubby here doesn't look as though he's got a decent shag left in him if indeed he ever did! Good night," and she walked off.

They went to bed and made the most tender, passionate love they had at any point in their relationship. Towards the end, Carol told him that she wanted his cock in her as deep as he could and lay on her back with her legs akimbo. He needed no further direction and, lying on her, lifted her ankles onto his shoulders. She advised him to be careful and made him laugh when she said that she didn't want her tonsils damaged.

"Long and slow, grind the corn and say my name when you cum," she whispered.

It was absolute ecstasy as he touched every part of her soaking sleeve and having squirted, she was almost delirious when she had a full body shaking climax. He ejaculated soon after and kissed her deeply as he did so. Her cunt was full of his cock and cum, and her mouth full of his tongue. She locked her ankles together and pulled his arse tight against her, digging her nails into his flesh to get the last few sensations as his hardness subsided.

Afterwards, he was asleep almost as soon as the light went off. Carol cuddled close to him and whispered, "Daniel, I love you so much." She was awake most of the night, wrestling with a potentially life-changing decision.

Early the following morning, she woke to find him massaging her pussy and she sighed with pleasure as she opened her eyes.

"Good morning, Gorgeous," Dan said. "Shower or shag?"

Carol looked at her watch. "We just have time to combine the two!" she said, cuddling into him. It was hot, short, sharp, wet, and ultimately very sticky. They kissed passionately as they dried each other off.

Within an hour, they were breezing through Faro airport security. They had time to kill, taken up with breakfast and coffee, which again Dan paid for. Carol appreciated that he made an effort financially but wouldn't hear of any of his suggestions to pay for anything else. She told him to give the money to charity because he had more than repaid her enough with the joy that he brought her and pointedly said, *not just the sex*.

"Love making," he corrected her.

"Yes, that too," she smiled. "Especially that."

They barely said a word on the flight or on the journey home as she dropped him back at his digs. Just before he got out of the car, she turned to him and took off her sunglasses.

"Kiss me, Daniel," Carol said, looking rather tearful.

They shared a passionate embrace, and she reached into her bag, pulled out a blue envelope with a card in it and gave it to him. He looked at her and went to open it before she said he should wait until he got back to his room.

"Now, off you go."

He kissed her on the lips but could see she was about to break down.

As he got out of the car, he said, "You'll call me, yes?" With a weak smile, she nodded before looking away. He shut the door and walked a little way down the road before crossing over. Carol hadn't driven off, but he could see she was dabbing her eyes with a tissue before putting her sunglasses on. He waved as she drove past. She didn't acknowledge him.

When Daniel got back, he picked up his mail and went to his room. His heart was pounding and he hoped this wasn't bad news. He opened the card, which just said LOVE and had hearts on the front. Inside was a handwritten letter and on the inner part of the card, she'd written Love you, God Bless, Carol xxx

He read the letter, he barely got past the opening, and he knew this wasn't going to be good:

My Dear Danny, this is the hardest letter I have ever had to write. Even as you're sleeping beside me, the right words won't come.

I cannot possibly explain how much you mean to me and how you have affected my life in the short time we have known each other in every way.

Our last few beautiful, wonderful days away made me think long and hard about my marriage and there were times when for two pins I would have agreed to go away with you when you asked me a few hours ago.

You are such a lovely, good-hearted young man and as sincere and genuine as your plans were, I am sure in your heart of hearts you know it wouldn't work. I love my husband. We have a long term, tried and tested relationship, but you and me could never have that same stability and security.

The Ann Summers evening last week highlighted insecurities that would eventually finish us. I felt threatened by all of my friends' attention and flirting with you and the longer it went on the more jealous I became and that is just not like me. It wasn't your fault but it hurt, I knew at that point I wouldn't be able to keep you and I had let things go too far. You were just supposed to be a friend with benefits and a project, starting as a bit player in role play in my short affair with Davey. I then felt I could teach you a lot about women and sex that would stand you in good stead in years to come. You learnt well and it was wonderful sexy fun as you became so skilled. However, you quickly became a lot more than that which I hadn't bargained for. You, you handsome sod, stole my heart and I need to take it back.

It is with a heavy heart and much sadness I cannot see you anymore.

Please do not contact me, my mind is made up and it will just make things so very difficult. I know you wouldn't want that for me or you. A clean break is best.

Take care, my gorgeous lover, I will never forget you or the love we have shared and I wish you all the very best for you and your future loves.

Eu nunca posso ser seu, mas eu te amo muito (I can never be yours, but I love you so much),

It was the classiest, most emotional letter he had ever received. The fact that he was dumped almost paled into insignificance, except that he *was* being dumped. As old as he was, he began to cry and more so when he started from the beginning and read it through again. In his mind and in his heart, he had found love, and she loved him. In the days to come, he tried to make sense of it while trying to overcome that awful feeling of emptiness. Even when he forgot about it for a few minutes, some tiny thing reminded him of her, and it just plain hurt emotionally and physically. He vowed never to love someone so intensely again.

Carol was not long through the door at home when her phone rang. It was her husband.

"Hey, Caz, how are you?" He sounded bright and happy with himself.

"Oh, hi, I'm good. Where are you?" She was shaking, and she didn't know why. Perhaps it was a feeling of guilt.

"I'm at Heathrow. I know I should have contacted you before, but you know how it is with work and stuff," he said and rattled on about the job he'd been on in Nigeria. Yes, she knew exactly what he was like with work and stuff. He would go days without a phone call or message, and she had become used to the lack of contact.

"Anyway, Sweetie, I know I said I'd be back on Wednesday, but I'll be home tonight, and we can either celebrate my birthday going out to dinner or stay in. Your call but I can't wait to see you. I've missed you so much as usual."

"Oh, that's…" She was surprised. It was rare that he wouldn't stick to dates of comings and goings, she was stumped.

"Yeah, yeah, sorry, look, if you've made other plans, we can postpone." He sounded his usual accommodating self, and she quickly regained composure.

"No, Vincent, that is good news and Happy Birthday to you. We'll stay in and have a nice romantic evening because I've missed you too," she lied.

"Brilliant, thank you." The voice at the other end of the phone sounded excited.

"Vince, there is something I need to tell you." She said quite firmly.

"Oh? That sounds ominous." The tone in Vince's voice changed significantly and he sounded worried.

"I know we've given it a go before, but I would like one last try over the next week while you're home. The timing couldn't be more perfect." She had gained the upper hand quite skilfully. There was a brief pause.

"Ah, that! Are you sure you wouldn't like a puppy instead?" he suggested, trying to make a joke of it. She didn't answer, and he knew she was serious.

"Yes, of course, Sweetheart, whatever you say, I'm with you a hundred per cent but you better be prepared 'cos I've rarely had any time for DIY over the last three weeks, so maybe quantity might do the trick," he laughed.

"Don't be vulgar," she laughed with him. "Are you coming to EDI or ABZ and what's your ETA?" she asked in a machine gun burst of acronyms.

"ABZ but I must go to the office first. Don't worry, I'll get a driver to bring me home. I should be there by five-ish?" he suggested.

"Okay, phone me when you're about ten minutes away and I'll get some fizz ready for us." She, too, sounded excited to see him.

"Do you know, the best part of going away is coming home to you. See you later. Love you."

"Laters, Darling, love you, too." They hung up simultaneously and she was actually quite happy for that moment, even if her heart ached for Dan. She had decided not to drag things out before she went away and was proud of herself that, despite the temptation, she had stuck to it even though she loved him. Her husband coming home a couple of days early couldn't be more fortuitous.

Nine months and three days later, Carol gave birth to a healthy nine-pound, five-ounce baby boy and the happy couple were overjoyed. They called him George Daniel - George after Vince's dad and Daniel after no one in particular, except that Carol said she had always liked that name.

26

Obsession

Since Julia's incredible but brief liaison with Michael in South Africa, she returned to the UK promising herself that she would indulge in "sexciting" short-term affairs. She created a profile for herself on a swinger's website and was surprised at the enthusiastic response from quite a number of men, couples and some women. However, having sorted the wheat from the chaff and the men from the boys, she was dismayed at the choices left to her.

Julia wanted intelligence, humour and a promise of passion with the utmost discretion - what she got was anything but. Responses came mostly from undateable morons who could barely string three words together. It's said that a picture paints a thousand words but on receiving dozens of penis photos every day, all she could think was, "What an arse." It was like looking for a golden needle in a haystack full of pricks!

She did meet three guys over a two-year period, but they never progressed further than a social rendezvous as they just didn't 'measure up' (in more ways than one). Julia gave up on the idea, resorting to watching porn and frequently masturbating, imagining herself as the female in the videos. That was until Matthew came into her life courtesy of her daughter.

She had lusted after Matthew, now her son-in-law, from the moment that she set eyes on him. When Kirstie brought him home for the first time, she felt that tingle of desire, and since then, even a hint of his aftershave brought back the joy of that initial contact. Julia had desperately resisted and suppressed other opportunities since her daughter married him almost a year ago, but her obsession would not be quelled any longer. This was the day, Julia knew it was now or never.

This was her birthday weekend. It was convenient that Kirstie and Matt had stayed overnight on Friday to help with arrangements for the big day's celebration, beginning late afternoon and going long into the evening. She would not get a better opportunity.

Julia had a plan in mind for the seduction of the object of her infatuation but was waiting for the right moment. She knew that Alan and her daughter were going into town mid-morning to get some last-minute provisions. There would never be enough alcohol or finger-picky bits, as a friend of hers always called them. Whatever reason they were out for, it would leave her alone in the house with Matthew for a couple of hours. The cougar sharpened her claws.

With Kirstie up and gone, Matt had a fifteen-minute snooze and then got up and stretched. He thought to himself that it was going to be a long day but was excited for the evening ahead. It wouldn't be a big affair, but it was lovely to meet up with friends and family, even though most of them were more from his in-laws' side. The house was quiet, and Matt padded off to the family bathroom in just a pair of snug boxer shorts. After completing his morning ablutions, he had a leisurely shower and was ready for the day. He dried himself off, slipped his shorts back on to go back to the bedroom and was rather taken aback when he met his mother-in-law on the landing, lying in wait for him. It was a premeditated ambush.

"Ah, I thought I heard you in the shower. Come with me. I need you for a few minutes," Julia said, turning and heading off to her room.

"I'll just get dressed," he protested.

"Oh, don't worry about that. You're decent enough. It'll just take a few seconds!" She wasn't taking no for an answer.

What the hell, he thought, it was a good opportunity to show off his physique to his sexy, tactile mother-in-law, who often liked to squeeze his backside. As he entered Julia's bedroom, he saw her standing in front of a full-length mirror, trying to zip up the back of her dress. It was the clichéd "little black number", sleeveless and a very tight fit, showing off her curves perfectly. It finished a few inches above the knee with a small split at the back.

She saw Matthew in the reflection of the mirror, and she desperately tried to control the nervous anticipation of how she hoped her plan would come to fruition. Her heart beat a little faster as she admired his athletic body. In his mid-twenties, he was at his peak and the desire in her was all too palpable. She breathed deeply and tried not to betray her nervy excitement.

"Be a love and get the zip on this for me. I'm thinking of wearing it to the party later," she asked nonchalantly. Matthew moved closer to her but could feel an involuntary "awakening" below. Julia again glanced at him in the mirror as he fumbled for the small zipper. She knew that as the zip went quite low, he would get a glimpse of the black suspender belt and the thin scrap of material of her thong that she was wearing underneath. He would also realise she was not wearing a bra.

"I think it's the kind of dress that shouldn't show too many lines under it, don't you agree?" Julia asked. "A bra would be too obvious, and my boobs haven't gone south for the winter just yet," she laughed, a nervous sort of chuckle. Matt didn't know what to say but pulled the zipper up slowly so as not to catch it and also to allow him to take in the delicious sight of her bare skin. Her plan A was a hope that this would be enough to make him take the initiative and grab her from behind. No such luck, as she knew he was far too restrained, even if he might be thinking it.

She moved immediately to Plan B.

"I think black is quite sexy," she added. Again, he said nothing except for "Mmm." This was crunch time.

"Black lingerie is your favourite, isn't it?" Julia stared at him in the mirror. She desperately tried to control her breathing. Matt stared back with a look that said, *How did you know?*

"Oh, I'm just teasing. Kirstie mentioned that you bought her some for her birthday."

"Er, yes," he started to feel a little awkward and as much as he just wanted to take her in his arms and kiss her, he thought he'd better leave before he couldn't control himself any longer.

"Anyway, I'd better go and get myself sorted."

Julia turned around. "Just a couple of more minutes. I want the male perspective on the whole outfit. Could you get my shoes over there by the bed, please, the black ones with the heels?"

He turned quickly as he now knew his inappropriate arousal would be quite obvious. She watched him as he picked them up, and when he turned back towards her, she was hugely encouraged and delighted to see that he was 'showing'. He handed them to her, keeping them directly in front of his nether region, desperately hoping his stiffy would subside – no chance, his heat-seeking missile was primed and ready.

She took the shoes from him and took the opportunity to make sure he was suitably excited. Julia then made the excuse of holding his arm to keep her balance as she donned one shoe and then the other. As she bent down to use her finger as a shoehorn, she could see Matt's horn snaking in his shorts. She smiled at him and then turned back to the mirror to smooth the dress down, first at the front and then the back, lingering over the curves of her luscious backside.

"What do you think?" she asked him pointedly.

He tried to sound ambivalent, but the crack in his voice and the dryness in his mouth gave him away.

"Very nice," he said, awkwardly keeping his hands in front of himself.

Now fully aware of how uncomfortable Matt was, she was enjoying the effect she was having and as she took control, she became less nervous.

"Now for some bling to complete the ensemble," she said, crossing the room to the bedside unit. From a drawer, Julia took some spangle bracelets and a pearl necklace. She put the bracelets on each wrist and then turned to Matt.

"Sorry. Another fiddly catch. Could you do this for me, please?" She held the necklace in front of her. He was mortified! He knew she was bound to see how even more aroused he was. He tried to conceal it as he moved quickly towards her. She smiled and stared at him before turning around and holding the necklace up to her neck. He stood behind her and took the two clasps in his fingers. He could hardly manage to clip it together as his hands were shaking so much. It didn't help that Julia moved slightly backwards, making sure they "accidentally" touched. She felt a slight prod of his cock before he moved away, having completed his task. She turned again and took his hands. He tentatively held hers.

"What are you thinking?" Julia said, smiling.

He said nothing but took a deep breath. Julia held his hands a bit tighter and, looking directly at the obvious bulge in his shorts, said with a smile.

"I can see my outfit has had the desired effect."

Matt knew he'd been caught, so he gave up hiding the straining appendage.

"I... I think I'd better go and get dressed," he stammered with his heart pounding. He didn't pull away though and his fate was sealed. Continuing to smile at him, Julia asked him if he really wanted to leave. He said nothing but looked at her before closing his eyes like one of the three wise monkeys.

"Matthew, you know as well as I do that there is a simmering tension between us that has been obvious for quite some time. Yes, it's difficult for me being a married woman but even more testing for you because you're married to my daughter. Just know that I am discretion personified. If we give in to this animal desire, as I think we should, I will never speak of it to another living soul," she continued to stare at him.

"But…it's wrong Julia." He couldn't think of anything else to say.

"Yes, it is, but isn't that what makes it so exciting?" She almost dared him to look her in the eyes. Eventually, he did.

"We mustn't. I wouldn't do anything to hurt Kirstie," he proffered.

"Really?" She knew she held the ace card.

"Yes really, please Julia, you are so sexy and you're making this very difficult!"

"Was Rachel from Chorley so sexy, or because circumstances were against you with her, maybe Barbara from Blackpool, your hotel landlady, was even sexier that you couldn't say no then?" She still smiled, knowing that he was completely ensnared in her trap.

Matt's jaw dropped. How could his mother-in-law possibly know? He just looked at her and was so confused.

"It's all right. Your secret is safe as long as you keep me satisfied. It really wouldn't be such a chore to do that, would it? And be honest, don't you think I'm much sexier than Babs?"

Matt knew he was hooked and there was no option but to give in to Julia's desire. She could see that he'd given up the feeble protest and kissed him passionately – they both loved it.

"Sit on the bed." He did as she asked.

She bent forward and put her hands on his upper thighs within fingertip reach of his encased member.

"The thing is…I want you and I won't be denied." She paused. She was so close to him that he could smell her intoxicating perfume. His heart was thumping now, his cock jerked and seemed desperate to make friends with her adjacent hands.

"I want your penis in my mouth." It jerked again in response. "I want your beautiful cock in my pussy. I am so ready for you," she said, almost growling. "I want your hot, hard dick to fill me up," she sucked on his earlobe before kissing his neck and her hands moved ever closer to her target. His eyes closed with the delightful sensation and delicious anticipation.

She then knelt in front of her son-in-law and gently parted his knees. She released the aching staff by pulling down the front of his shorts. Easing back the foreskin, she revealed the purple, glistening head of his stiffened cock. Julia looked directly into his eyes, daring him to stop her before she lowered her head, parted her lips and enveloped his prick in the warm, silky wetness of her mouth. Holding his manhood in both hands, she slowly began to suck and roll her tongue around its bulbous head. Matthew gave in to it all because it was just complete bliss. He lay back on his elbows, watching his mother-in-law bring him to climax.

Julia was giddy with the power of taking so much control. Breathing only through her nose, she never once allowed him to slip from her mouth. She enjoyed the time it took and eventually, she could feel it twitch quite violently as Matthew neared his orgasm. She fondled his heavy balls as he tried to hold back but Canute did a better job of turning the tide. He succumbed to the inevitable and felt himself erupt into her mouth and collapsed backwards on the bed. She didn't miss a beat. She sucked harder, swallowing once, twice, and finally a third time. Matt's hips lifted from the bed in an attempt to fuck Julia's mouth but eventually, fully spent, Julia finally released his cock in one long, loving suck to collect the remainder.

As he recovered, Matt sat up and, leaning forward, cupped Julia's face in his hands, kissing her fervently, their tongues entwined. He could taste his own salty jizz as they embraced. Julia then stood up and deftly unzipped her dress, where it became all too apparent that at no point was he ever required to 'help' her with it. She let it fall and bent forward to pick it up before laying it on the nearby chair.

"Gorgeous," was all he could say.

Julia stood before her son-in-law, displaying her beautifully rounded breasts and erect nipples. He realised that his wife and his mother-in-law were like two peas in a pod. He drank in the sight of her simple yet elegant suspender belt, smooth black stockings and tiny thong. The high-heeled shoes and jangling jewellery completed the delightful, decadent spectacle. He sat open-mouthed and waited for direction.

"Take my thong off," she demanded.

He leaned forward and reached out towards her.

"Oh no, you delightful man. With your teeth, if you please!" she giggled.

Matt smiled and moved onto his knees. He tenderly held her hips and kissed her stomach. His hands stroked the bare cheeks of her arse. She was relieved that he knew what he was doing, and she closed her eyes in anticipation of his intimate attention. He kissed and nibbled his way down to the silky black thong and pulled it away from her with his mouth. As he did so, he could now smell her 'perfume'. Then there was that delicious moment when a little shimmy from her caused the scanty garment to fall to her ankles and she stepped out, leaving it on the floor. Julia smiled.

"I shaved especially for you." She paused.

"I hope you like what you see and what you taste," she said, stroking his hair in encouragement. She parted her legs and could smell her own musky aroma drifting up from her engorged cunt. She desperately wanted to run her own fingers between her swollen lips but resisted.

"Gorgeous," repeated Matt.

"Now," said Julia in a stern voice, "I think you owe me a favour!"

"I think I do," agreed Matt.

Julia stood directly in front of her son-in-law, her smooth, hairless mound level with his head. Matthew reached behind her and ran his open palms up the back of Julia's stockinged thighs until they again rested on the firm, bare flesh of her backside. Julia closed her eyes as Matthew pulled her ever-moistening slit towards him and kissed it as if he were kissing her mouth.

"Oh, God," Julia let out with a long sigh.

Matt ran his tongue between her wet pussy lips until he found her swollen pleasure button. He began to lick and suck her to orgasm.

"Oh yes," she gasped. "That feels so good," she sighed loudly, with joy at his attention.

He was rhythmically persistent. Julia could feel her climax building. A small knot in the pit of her stomach grew more intense. She opened her eyes and behind the chair hanging on the wall was a mirror. Julia looked at herself, her neck flushed pink with arousal, her nipples hard with lust, watching herself caress her own breasts while her daughter's husband continued to eat her. She took her nipples between the thumb and forefinger of each hand, squeezing until the pleasure was almost painful. Looking behind her reflection, Julia could see the full-length mirror on the other side of the room. In this, she could see herself from behind with Matthew's strong hands cupping her buttocks. The blackness of her stockings and suspenders contrasting with her milky white skin, her spike-heeled shoes making her legs look impossibly long.

Julia continued to gaze at herself from this unique angle, caressing her boobs, pinching her nipples, her climax rising. It was like an out-of-body experience as she gave in to Matt's relentless oral attention. Her whole sex was craving release. So close now he could hear her moaning. He felt a small shiver from her, she let go of her nipples and pulled Matt's head and mouth hard against her ravenous sex. If, at that moment, her husband and daughter had walked into the room, Julia could not have stopped herself. The need for sexual gratification was irresistible and with quite loud moans, her orgasm erupted deep inside, a shock wave of pure pleasure engulfing her jerking body. Matt felt Julia's legs begin to fold and steadied her as she collapsed into his arms. He held her trembling body and kissed her head. She was quivering more through emotion than physical reaction and he held her tightly.

Minutes later, as they both calmed, Julia whispered, "That was wonderful. It's been such a long time since…" She was unsure of how to describe it and left it at that. She lifted her head towards his and pulled him towards her to kiss. When he pulled away just to cuddle her, he could see she was quite misty-eyed.

"Are you sure you're okay?" He was hugely concerned.

She held him tightly to her and whispered, "Yes, that was fabulous." Julia smiled back. "Just fabulous."

"In that case, I'd better quit while I'm ahead and before the others return," he said.

Julia, now almost fully recovered, said, "Oh, I'm not done with you yet, Matthew and we still have time." Essentially, she was so invested in this incredible sexual episode that she could not have cared less if they were caught en-flagrante.

"I want you inside me, stretching my insides and taking me to heaven. Come onto the bed and fuck me from behind." She crawled onto the quilt, urging him to hurry up. Matt stood and then also knelt on the bed behind her. He stroked her bum cheeks as his admirable recovery period saw his stiffening member gently probe at her gaping maw. He then stroked her pussy lips to lubricate his fingers, which he then transferred to his penis. He probed a couple of more times, but she was not going to leave it to chance as to whether his dick chose the right path. Julia reached between her legs to hold his rod and position it before telling him to push slowly. He obeyed and was amazed that he was up to his pubes in one prolonged go. She groaned with the pleasure of his penetration and tickled his scrotum before putting her arm back on the bed to ready herself for their first-ever fuck. He slowly withdrew, almost to the point of slipping out to push in again, hearing her groan once again.

"Oh...yes." She relaxed and readied herself for whatever he was about to impart.

He then started a steady piston-like action for a few minutes before pushing hard into her again, just to hear her grunt with the different lengths of penetration. More piston work and then another full hit. She lifted herself up so that as her boobs swung backwards and forwards with every thrust, her nipples lightly brushed against the material of the duvet cover. Such exquisite caresses.

"Oh, fuck. Fuck me, Matthew…please fuck me," she mumbled in between gasps of joy. Matt then pushed his slippery thumb into her anus. He knew this had a huge effect on his wife and, indeed, on Barbara. Then why not this wanton woman begging to be taken? He was not wrong. She jerked backwards onto him and sighed loudly.

"Pull my hair hard," she gasped. He did so.

He kept up his action with occasional pauses to try to keep control of himself. Thankfully, her orgasm hit her like a steam train, so much so that she collapsed flat on the bed, taking him with her. They were both breathing so hard that they needed to compose themselves for the final onslaught. He held her from behind while she recovered her senses, with her still fully penetrated. She laughed and said.

"This scene must look so ridiculous, but God, what a fantastic fuck!" She paused and, between deep breaths, said, "I need your seed in me properly now. I want to ride you until you give it all to me." Then she directed him onto his back.

He withdrew and lay on the bed beside her while she sat astride him. She was so wet and gaping that this time, it was no surprise that he was balls deep in one go. They were again fully intimate in the way nature intended for a husband and wife, albeit an incongruous dynamic. If Julia's husband and Matthew's wife could see them now, she wondered if she could ever live down the shame. But she leaned forward to kiss him passionately as his arms encircled her and stroked her back before his fingers entwined in her suspender straps. Fuck the shame, she thought. She just didn't care as she whispered in his ear.

"Shoot every last drop into me, I want it running out of me all afternoon so that every time I move in my wet knickers full of your cum, it will remind me of our wicked playtime today."

Then she sat upright and slowly fucked him, steadying herself with her hands on his stomach while his hands were all over her breasts, nipples, arse and thighs.

Julia was steady and methodical as she moved up and down on his erection, literally as though she were riding a horse at trot. She was in control as she slowly came up to the point where he might slip out of her, only to plunge back down where their pubic bones met.

She spoke to him as she rode, giving a cerebral stimulus to the sensual intercourse.

"Matthew, I've imagined this since the day I met you."

Gasps of pleasure interrupted her monologue.

"Visions of us fucking have occupied my thoughts both day and night. I've dreamt about you and lusted after you but know this is all so very wrong. But fucking hell, you feel so good inside me." Her pace quickened.

"Oh God, I'm going to cum again," and she did with some muted grunts as she dug her nails into his chest. It wasn't as intense as their doggie-style fuck but blissful, nonetheless. Composing herself again, she asked, "Are you close?"

"Fuck yes, I can't hold it any longer," was the response.

Julia leant forward and he held her tightly as they kissed. He pumped hard and fast from beneath her. As he felt his own climax rising, her breathing had become a series of more grunts, animal lust driving her into another climax. Matt briefly stopped the kiss as he sighed loudly and gave his mother-in-law his semen. She could feel the hot ejaculate flood into her guts.

For several minutes, they lay there fully entwined in the afterglow, exhausted and satisfied, before Matt asked her how she knew about Blackpool. Julia smiled.

"Fate conspired against you and I'll tell you one day but I don't want to ruin your marriage to my daughter by letting slip what dalliances you had on your stag weekend." Julia kissed him on the cheek and said, "But I'm sure she will never find out and if we can also keep this to ourselves, then I would like us to indulge from time to time. Discretion is key." She didn't wait for a response before adding, "You'd better go and take another shower, they will be back soon."

Matt kissed Julia one last time, and he made his way back to the bathroom for his second shower of the day. She watched his toned body and peachy arse leave the room and thought of handcuffs and silk scarves for the next time. As he left, his mind was in overdrive. Not just because of the enormous sin of fucking his wife's mother but of how she came to unearth secrets that no one else knew of. The liaison with Rachel was virtually innocent compared to the multiple intimate indiscretions with Barbara but then neither of those two knew about each other and that was a secret he alone could confine to memory. Matt was dumbfounded that his "carelessness" was being used against him and now he had become his mother-in-law's plaything.

The truth was he really didn't mind one bit! Round two was a week away.

"Kirstie, you know Alan is useless with mechanical things, and anyway, he's away on a golfing weekend with some of his friends in Norfolk. I'll only need Matthew for two or three hours this afternoon." Julia was careful to be brief in her conversation with her daughter. She implied that she needed her son-in-law to fix her tumble dryer. The "need" was true enough and her compliant, naïve daughter was about to send her lamb to the slaughter.

Julia had a couple of hours to prepare herself, a leisurely scented bath and dress appropriately for their second rendezvous. Since she had skilfully seduced her son-in-law, the anticipation, lust, and longing were back at fever pitch. The thoughts of his body, hands, lips, tongue, and that rock-hard cock and tight balls were uppermost in her licentious mind. Last week was just a taster. This week, she mused, the boy won't know what's about to hit him.

White silk stockings, a suspender belt, white lacy knickers and braless under a tight white crop top, together with a short black leather skirt and some matching stilettos, would greet him when he finally arrived early afternoon. A note was pinned to the back door that just said, *Come In… (ME!) xxx.*

Julia was waiting for him when he arrived. She looked stunning, and he told her so. They kissed passionately and his hands were all over her body, paying particular attention to her unfettered breasts and nipples. *God, I could just let him fuck me here on the kitchen table,* she thought but then rapidly regaining control of herself, said, "Stop…this is all very nice, but I have plans for you."

"Don't tell me the tumble dryer is really fucked?" he laughed.

"Matthew, the only things that are going to be fucked this afternoon is us!"

Julia was not wrong. She felt much more comfortable about taking control, knowing that Matthew was a willing accomplice and now they had a few hours of complete privacy.

It was a full-on session of three hours or so, with a few mini breaks for a drink and a chat before going at it again. Julia felt like she was making up for so much lost time all in one afternoon. In the final stages, before they called time, the phone rang.

"Hi, yes, he's still beavering away," she smiled at Matt, who grinned back. "Well, he's a bit tied up at the moment, but he's been doing a great job. Hopefully, he'll be finished with me shortly, and then you can have him back." She paused to hear what her daughter had to say and finished with, "Okay, I'll tell him. Have a lovely evening, bye."

"Tell me what?" Matthew asked.

"You're to pick up a bottle of wine on the way home as you're celebrating your first wedding anniversary tonight rather than tomorrow. Oh God, how I remember that day watching you get married to my daughter and thinking how much I'd love you to consummate the marriage…but with me!"

"Oh, fuck, I forgot about that. She'll want to play afterwards as well, and I'm knackered. Julia laughed and then cradled his face in her hands before whispering, "Care to join me in the shower? I'll make sure you're spotless before you go and fuck my daughter."

"You're a wicked woman, Julia," he said. "If I go in that shower with you, you'll have to pour what's left of me through our letterbox afterwards!"

"A good point," she said. "But sometime soon, let's try to make a whole day of playtime…yes?" And then she really played with his mind when adding, "When you make love with my daughter tonight, you must not think of me, okay? I insist that you don't think of me!"

27

Insatiable

Dan and Matt missed a few weeks of their regular get-togethers at the local pub. The football season had yet to start, and opportunities for a swift pint were few and far between. Matt had ordered the drinks when Dan sauntered in. He looked absolutely shattered.

"Blimey mate, are you well? You look knackered," Matt asked

"Yeah, yeah, I'm fine," then, after a pause, he said, "Just tired."

"Busy week at work?" Matt asked again, staring at how drained his friend looked.

"Work's fine. I go to work to get a rest," Dan said, taking a good swig of his pint.

Matt looked at him quizzically.

"It's not work, it's Sarah."

"Sarah? Nothing wrong, I hope. Is she well?"

"You remember me saying that first time when I brought her to the flat, that when she was in bed, it was like she was plugged into the mains?"

"Yes," Matt remembered only too well how vocal she was with Dan and how fortunate he was to bump into her outside of the bathroom that morning.

"Almost everything about her is perfect. We hit it off immediately, as you know. She's intelligent, runs her own business, she's funny–"

"- Gorgeous," interrupted Matt.

"Yeah, gorgeous. I mean, she just turns heads wherever she goes and…"

"And?" Matt asked.

"Mate, she is sex on legs."

Matt smiled. "Yes, there's something about the way she looks at people. I mean, she's a really confident girl."

"It's not just that what she doesn't know about sex ain't worth knowing. I thought I was pretty good in bed, but she wrote the manual, I'm sure of it," although he knew that Carol was the real oracle.

"Lucky boy!" Matt said with a hint of envy.

"You'd think so, wouldn't you? As most men would," Dan added.

"As you know, we moved in together some months back and got engaged soon afterwards."

"Yes, of course, and the hen weekend is coming up, but you still haven't said what you want me to organise for a Stag do?" Matt said, and then suggested that it was an opportunity to get away again.

"Yeah, there's been a development on that score, but I'll come to that. Anyway, everything at home was great. She can cook as well, you know!" Dan said with some pride.

"Lucky boy again, winner winner, chicken dinner!" Matt said again with an ironic chuckle.

"But lately…" Dan hesitated, taking a drink.

"Arguments, bickering?" Matt suggested.

"No, nothing like that. I really don't know. Just lately, she's turned into a raving, fucking nympho. These last couple of weeks, she just…" Dan didn't finish the sentence and started shaking his head. Matt said nothing.

"Right from the start, it used to be every time we met. Then, when she first moved in, it would be every night and then twice a day at weekends."

"A good way to start the day, but sorry to say, it has affected your football!" Matt said, laughing.

"Hardly surprising," Dan added.

"Then, one Monday, she wanted it before I went to work. She works from home 'cos she's set up a little office in the spare bedroom, so it didn't affect her, but I was late for work. So she then set the alarm earlier so that we could knock one out before I did the daily commute."

"Still a nice way to start the day, though," Matt added helpfully, but stifled a smirk.

"Occasionally, yes, and the thing is, because she is such a turn-on, I can't help but respond. Once Monty opens up his eager eye, it's very difficult to say no," Dan said in a resigned fashion.

"I'm sure."

"She knows how to get me going and won't take no for an answer. Take Sunday afternoon, for instance, I was watching the Man United match, and she walked in wearing one of her sexy, revealing teddies, and thigh-high boots and stood in front of the TV saying, *What do you think?*"

"What did you think?" Matt asked.

"I just said you make a better door than you do a window," Dan said straight-faced. Matt laughed.

"She was very unimpressed, but we compromised. We fucked with her sitting on my lap and me watching the footie over her shoulder."

"Very inventive, lucky boy!" Matt added yet again with a chuckle and a little nod of the head.

"Hmm, you wouldn't say that if you were treated like a performing stud mate. The only respite I get is when she has to work away sometimes for some of these events that she's organised. But when she comes back, she's twice as horny." Dan paused to take another sip of his beer.

"Don't get me wrong, it's great that she wants me, but she is obsessed with sex. It's literally a fucking nightmare," he hung his head and stared at his beer before taking another good draft.

"But you're so devoted to one another from what I've seen of the pair of you, and Kirstie's so looking forward to the hen weekend and the wedding," Matt enthused.

"That's good, but Sarah never seems satisfied in bed," Dan added.

"She doesn't climax?" Matt asked, which he found incredulous, given Dan's experience with ladies.

"No, it's not that. She cums like there's no tomorrow, but she's hooked on it, and although it's good to hear a female moan for all the right reasons, we do it at least two or three times a day. Most guys would think it's paradise, but…Mate, we do very little else lately."

"Does she want a baby?" Matt asked, thinking how this would probably raise its head at home in the very near future.

"She says no, she just adores and craves sex."

Matt could see it was really troubling his friend. "You could get something from the doctors, couldn't you?"

"I sort of mentioned it, but that was greeted like an away goal at Old Trafford, and she accuses me of not loving her and asking why I want to stop having sex. You can't discuss it with her." He paused again to take a drink.

"It seemed to start at your wedding," Dan said.

"Oh?"

"You know, when they were doing the photos after the service, we were hanging around for our turn as Best Man and Maid of Honour. She started stroking my bum and then whispered that she fancied a quickie. I told her not to be so ridiculous and thought she was joking, but she grabbed my hand, and we went behind the church. There was a large outhouse at the back where they stored the ground machinery, tools and stuff. She dragged me over to the ride-on mower, bent over the seat and demanded that I fuck her!"

"On a ride-on mower, how apt and how romantic." Matt smiled, picturing the scene.

"Hmm, well, she looked an absolute sight bent over with her outstanding arse framed by the suspender straps and her soaking gash ready for me. She told me to hurry up 'cos she wanted me to, quote, *'fill her up with my big, fat cock'* 'cos she can get a bit graphic sometimes."

"Clearly," Matt said, waiting for more.

"So, I dropped the trousers and keks. She reached between her legs to grab Monty and guide him into her. She was so wet. I told her I wasn't going to last very long with her in that position and while I was banging away, she frigged herself to climax and I was a millisecond behind her!"

"Behind her?" Matt laughed. "Oh, the irony! Anyway, isn't it the best man's prerogative to shag the Maid of Honour?"

"Yes, but there's a time and a place. Anyway, we were done in less than ten minutes and quickly got ourselves reassembled. As we got out of there, I asked her what that was all about and she said that she just had this sudden urge to fuck in the sanctity of the Church grounds. It was just so damn naughty. Then she said that I wanted it as much as she did and complained that she was now going to have my jizz dribbling out of her all afternoon. Just as we turned the corner, they were calling for her, so I let her go on by herself so that I could check for any leakage. There's nothing worse than a wet patch on light grey trousers when people think you're post-piss and not shaken it properly!" They both laughed.

"The thing is, when we're at home, she pads about the place with a miniskirt or just a thong or skimpy knickers and see-through mesh tops or tight T-shirts, and she knows exactly what she's doing. She's become more of an exhibitionist as well. We went to Spain for a week just after your wedding, and all she wore during the day was a thong, no top. Evenings, a short skirt, low-cut tops showing off her cleavage as much as possible and no bra. It's a double-edged sword. Yes, she's so fucking sexy, but all these guys are leering over her, and she loves that. Of course, I'm proud of her, but I just know what these wolves are thinking. Like you, that I'm a lucky bloke but they also still want to shag the arse off her and, frankly, I'm jealous."

"She's also wanted to get a bit more kinky, being tied up or tying me up and like the wedding. She also keeps on about going outside and doing it places where we might get caught and stuff like that. Oh, and do you remember when she came to pick us up from footie after she bought her new car?"

"Yeah, the black Freelander with the high-end spec, a lovely motor," Matt said with a bit of envy.

"Do you recall what she was wearing?" Dan asked.

"Er…Yeah, she had a big coat on, which seemed a bit odd because it wasn't a particularly cold day, but she also had a black pair of stilettos. Christ, she could have used one of them to kill by looking at those heels."

"Hmm, well, when you went off for a Jimmy Riddle, we were waiting outside. She opened up her coat and gave me a flash of what she was really wearing."

"Oh, wow, don't tell me – just hold ups, cos she had something on her legs," Matt said, trying to imagine it.

"Better than that. Stockings *and* suspenders and a thong, nothing else, and she told me as soon as we dropped you off, we were going somewhere to christen the car!"

"I thought there was a bit of tension on the drive home. I thought you'd had a barney or something," Matt said, recollecting the occasion.

"No, but she made a right fucking row when we did it in Ducks Road Disco," Dan said. "The change of environment made her more excited and vocal than normal!"

"Jeez, I don't know what to say, mate. She is a little minx, isn't she?" Matt said, more as a rhetorical question.

"I love her, but I can barely keep up with her. It's doing my head in." He took another good swig of his Guinness.

Matt was speechless, but he really felt for his troubled buddy.

"It was heaven at first," Dan said, still staring at his beer, "But I'm struggling and I'm knackered. It's great that she's away on Friday for her hen weekend. At least I'll get some rest, but then I'm thinking what is she going to get up to?"

Matt tried to console him.

"Mate, she loves you. She's not going to put it about just before the wedding, is she?"

"Isn't she? Oh, and the latest development is that she's now mentioned that we should postpone the wedding for a little while, supposedly to give her more time to arrange something special!" Dan looked shattered emotionally and physically.

"Really?" Matt was surprised. "But anyway, no, she isn't going to put it about. Kirstie is pretty sensible. She'll keep her right. They'll just tease a bit and get drunk. You know what women are like when they're in groups. They're all trap and no flap," Matt offered.

There was silence for a number of seconds before Dan shook his head and asked quizzically.

"All trap and no flap. What the fuck does that mean?" Dan stared at him with a furrowed brow, but with almost a glimmer of a smile on his face.

"Not a fucking clue, sorry. Thought it sounded good, though." And they both laughed. Matt defined it as prick teasing when they stopped sniggering.

They were quiet for the next ten minutes, then Matt suggested a game of pool. Dan declined, saying that he had to get home. He'd just had a text from Sarah wondering where he was. He didn't show Matt the picture of her smiling and holding a pair of handcuffs in front of her beautiful, braless breasts.

They parted with a hand grasp and shoulder bump. When Matt got home, he swore Kirstie to secrecy. He never shared "boy chat" with her normally, but after explaining his earlier conversation with Dan, he asked her to keep an eye on Sarah during their weekend away. He also told her of the postponement, to which Kirstie said that she already knew. She had a look on her face that told him she was keeping something from him. Matt got right to it.

"What is it? What are you not telling me about her?" He knew she was holding something back. Kirstie was quiet for a few moments.

"I'd hoped that as she got a bit more mature, she would calm down," but knew in herself that was wishful thinking.

"Oh?" Matt queried as he made them both a cup of coffee.

"She is…how can I put this tactfully," Kirstie said, pausing for a few seconds.

"She is?" Matt was keen to hear what his wife had to say.

"Not to put too finer a point on it. Sex mad, I mean really sex mad and has been since she reached puberty. I think the medical term is hyper-sexuality."

"Wow." Matt was impressed with her medical knowledge and told her so. "Do you have a nurse's outfit to go with it?" he asked suggestively with raised eyebrows and a beaming smile.

Kirstie smiled her *really?* Sort of smile, knowing the sexual connotation.

"This must not go any further than these four walls," Kirstie was emphatic in her assertion.

"Of course," Matt was all ears as he sat at the breakfast bar.

"She lost her virginity at fifteen with a sixth former who was her boyfriend for a while. She then had a break from school for a week, and the rumour was that she had an abortion. I don't know if it's true because she never told me and I never asked. Her mother put her on the pill as soon as she returned," Kirstie continued.

"Even when she came back, she was always hanging about with older boys and, as you know, we've been good friends since we first went to secondary school. Sarah was always candid about her relationships, which were always full-on sex and, this might shock you further, she was also very popular with two teachers who were giving her extra curricula tuition."

"Wow, how did she get away with keeping that secret from each of them, let alone the school?" Matt asked, still dumbfounded about Sarah's activities.

"Because she was having them together!" Kirstie said. Matt's jaw fell open.

"Even when she was studying for her pre-university exams, she moved in with a guy in his late twenties when she was just seventeen. He was a sleaze-ball, nothing more than a pimp really. He took advantage of her sexual desire and let a few of his friends indulge their fantasies with her and made a few quid."

"Poor cow," Matt said.

"You say that, but she loved it. She told me that she learnt so much from some of these guys and really enjoyed role play and more than one partner at the same time. That relationship lasted for a couple of years until the guy ended up in prison for drug dealing. Thankfully, it's not something she ever got hooked on." Kirstie took a sip of coffee.

"Sarah is a very clever girl, and as you can see, she is so attractive that doors just open for her. She got a job at a law firm, just as an office junior to start with and studied events management in her own time with the Open University. She breezed through that and got her degree and an admin promotion in the law firm. She wanted to make some money to start her own company. She had a steady boyfriend that she had met in that sort of legal circle and moved in quite quickly with him. However, rumours and accusations started flying about regarding an affair with a senior partner at the firm who was married. Sarah and the legal eagle were eventually caught by a couple of cleaners early one evening when, as she told me, he was having her doggy fashion over the committee room table."

"En flagrante," Matt added in his worst Latin.

"Quite! She told me that they may well have got away with it, except that the arrogant lawyer told the cleaners to fuck off. Couldn't they see he was busy!" Kirstie said and laughed; Matt laughed as well before asking what happened after that.

"The hypocrisy was that she was asked to leave!" Kirstie said.

"Really?" Matt was incredulous.

"She was expendable, but nearly as bad some jealous bitch in her office sent an anonymous letter to her boyfriend telling him what she'd been up to."

"Wow, that was twisting the knife," Matt observed.

"And some. So not only had she lost her job, but her boyfriend too, and he threw her out of the flat."

"Poor girl," Matt added.

"Well, before you get the violins out, the rich guy she was shagging in the law firm set her up in a small apartment and found her another job with an Estate Agent friend of his," Kirstie said, finishing her coffee, Matt shook his head and smiled. "Get us both some fizz, and I'll meet you in the bath. There's more. A lot more!" Kirstie said.

"Fucking hell, really?"

"Yes, really!"

Ten minutes later, Matt was naked and stepping into the bath with a couple of glasses of Cava.

"Time was when you'd get in the bath and have that missile pointing at me," Kirstie said, reaching for the glass.

"Hmm, time was when you'd reach for the missile first before the fizz. I guess we're just an old married couple, and the alcohol is more important," Matt said.

"I suppose playtime is out of the question, then?" she laughed.

"Depends how good the continuing saga of Sarah's sex life is!" Matt said, taking a sip.

"Matty-boy, we are just scraping the surface, and none of this goes any further, okay?" she said, reminding him and wagging her finger as some sort of warning. Matt nodded before going for a recap of Sarah's story.

"Okay, so Sarah has been set up with a job and a flat by the Senior Partner. How old was he anyway?"

"At the time, he was sixty and extremely good in bed, especially with his tongue!"

"Wow, that's nearly forty years older than her," Matt seemed incredulous.

"She said quite recently that he was the best lover she ever had. According to her, too many guys would just have sex with her because she was easy. They were more interested in her for themselves and their own gratification." Kirstie said.

"Where does that put Dan?" Matt was now more concerned for his best mate.

"Oh, she adores him. He is the only guy that has ever got close to her old boy as far as shagging is concerned, and she literally can't get enough of him. Although I didn't realise it was as much physical as anything," Kirstie said with a chuckle. "Anyway, I digress," she added. "The thing is, she can't resist any sort of attention. So, she was set up nicely and embarking on a career as an Estate Agent, short-term, to build up capital for her new business. She then started an affair with the owner of the Agency, in his forties but also married," Kirstie said.

Matt raised his eyebrows as if to suggest that the married thing wouldn't mean any sort of taboo. It was something that never bothered a lot of people.

"Yes, but him and his wife were swingers and introduced her to their private parties! This would involve quite a few influential people, men *and* women, mostly middle-aged, who would pay a membership fee. Sarah was given a gratuity to be a type of hostess," Kirstie said, sipping at her drink.

Matt's jaw dropped. "What like a…"

"Yes, like a… There would be up to sixteen people, she'd serve drinks and nibbles and stuff dressed up like a real tart, sexy maid's outfit and all, just to break the ice before it all kicked off."

"And she would join in?" Matt asked naively.

"No, she'd sit in the kitchen and read cookery books, particularly by Mary Berry," Kirstie laughed.

"Well, you never know," Matt said and then smiled at how dim he sounded.

"Of course, she would join in because she was really hired as the catalyst to get everyone going."

"And she was happy about that?" Matt asked, but before Kirstie could answer, he added, "I guess if she was being paid, then why not?"

"Matty-boy, she said she would have done it for nothing. She adored being the centre of attention and the sex was fantastic with the men *and* the women," she said as Matt raised his eyebrows again.

"Yes, and the *women*. And she said that not only did she get the gratuity, as she put it, but she often received tips from most of the couples. She would regularly make three to four hundred pounds at one of these events, which happened every few weeks. There was one event where it was just six guys; she made over six hundred pounds."

"So, she was little more than a brass then?" Matt said.

"She never thought of it that way. She just loved the lifestyle, the money was incidental. It was damn good money, though, considering she had a job and lived rent-free. But as an old uncle of mine once said when he was a bit tiddly, '*You girls, you're sitting on a fortune!*'" Kirstie smiled, recalling how funny that was.

Matt laughed as well but then puffed his cheeks and shook his head. "I wonder what Dan would say if he knew?"

"The only way he is ever going to know is if she tells him, because if you blab to him, I will cut your balls off slowly with our front door key," she said, glaring at him.

"Wouldn't that be cutting your nose off to spite your face, in a manner of speaking?" he said, shifting back into the bath just out of her reach. She just stared at him with a look that almost meant his testicles were dispensable.

"What happened because she's with Dan now?" Matt asked.

Kirstie continued, "It came to a head after a couple of years. Now, what you must bear in mind was that the 'philanthropic' lawyer was not only enjoying Sarah but unknown to the estate agent, he was also having an affair with the estate agent's wife, although he wasn't a member of the swinging set!"

Matt's jaw dropped again.

"So, the scenario was that the estate agent knew the lawyer had Sarah, but the lawyer didn't know that Sarah was enjoying all the swinging set with the estate agent and his wife. The estate agent *didn't* know about the lawyer shagging his own wife and the estate agent's wife didn't know about the lawyer shagging Sarah!" Kirstie looked at Matt and said, "Questions?"

Matt looked confused, looked at his glass and mumbling to himself, said, "The lawyer was shagging his own wife, the estate agent's wife and Sarah…the estate agent was shagging *his* own wife and Sarah and a number of other women."

"And men!" Kirstie added, eyebrows raised.

"And men? Wow, and Sarah was being shagged by anything that moved. Was the lawyer's wife shagging the estate agent behind her husband's back as well?"

"I don't think the lawyer's wife knew anything about anyone, so her lasciviousness is unknown," Kirstie said, laughing. "But let's not confuse the scenario any further."

"I guess it finally came to a head when they all turned up at the Clap Clinic together?" Matt asked with a comical, quizzical look on his face.

"Nothing so farcical, but it would make for a good story over dinner," said Kirstie, pondering the scene in the clinic's waiting room.

"No, the lawyer took Sarah out to dinner one evening, nice fancy restaurant, she told me she was dressed very provocatively– high heels, short skirt, low-cut top, boobs barely contained, you know the sort of thing." Kirstie was painting a very vivid picture. Matt knew exactly the sort of thing. She continued, "Needless to say, it caused some stirring with her lover, and her flirty conversation wound him up even more. Sarah told me that she was so horny she would have had him on the restaurant table, and she always said that great sex starts with the brain and the anticipation."

Matt was quiet, but he could feel a rousing in his loins and slid back towards Kirstie, hoping that she might take the hint.

"So, they got to the car and were just about to get in when Sarah said that she had something for him."

"I'll bet!" said Matt.

"She then told him to hold out his hand and close his eyes, which he did, whereupon she hung a damp pair of skimpy knickers over his fingers and said they were a souvenir, and he should now fuck her brains out as a repayment."

Matt was now almost fully hard, and his dick was peeping through the bubbles.

"Ah, my little story seems to be having an effect," Kirstie said as the pink periscope popped up.

"I was just picturing the scene. Anyway, carry on while I top up the hot water."

"Ok, they got in the car, and although Sarah wouldn't have cared if they performed in front of a packed house at the Royal Albert Hall, the lawyer had his reputation to think of, but, like her, can't wait. Sarah suggested the estate agent's offices, which were only five minutes away, and the thought of having sex in the work environment was a delicious piece of irony - she wanted to be fucked on the EA's desk by someone other than the EA."

"She is a naughty little scamp, isn't she?" Matt said, understating Sarah's behaviour.

"Anyway, Sarah had a set of keys, and they arrived at the premises PDQ. She pulled him into the Manager's office, and well, you can guess the rest," Kirstie said, finishing her glass of fizz.

"Oh, I thought you were going to be more specific," Matt said rather disappointedly.

"Wouldn't that assume that Sarah went into specific detail with me?"

"Shame," Matt said, sliding a bit nearer. Kirstie took the hint and slid her fingers up and down his stiff member, using the soapy water as lubrication.

"Mmm, well, as it happens, you're in luck," Kirstie said, giving his balls a little squeeze with her other hand, which prompted a grunt from Matt.

"They got down to it straightaway and losing her top she pulled her skirt up and he first had her bent over the desk before pulling her over to the couch for her to straddle him which in his excited state didn't take long for him to produce the goods," Kirstie's handwork sped up as she was becoming rather agitated herself.

"Now, as Dan probably told you, she loves to climax and normally doesn't take long herself, but he'd beaten her to it this time, in fact, he usually did but always had time for seconds, even if the recovery period seemed to take a bit longer than younger men. So on this evening, she was quite demanding and pushing his head back on the cushion of the sofa, got up and planted herself on his face!" Kirstie seemed to blush a little but still found it funny, as did Matt.

"Good for her. I'm all for equality," he said, breathing a little heavily. "But how does all of this relate to how it all finished?" Matt asked.

"When they went into the offices, she disabled the alarm, but such was their desperation, she forgot about the CCTV."

"Oh, fuck," Matt groaned.

"Oh, fuck, indeed!" Kirstie said, thinking he was up to speed, then it became clear what his exclamation was about as he his seed erupted over her hand and into the bubbles. "Hmm, let's hope your recovery period is much less than that of a senior lawyer," Kirstie said, washing her hands in the water. As Matt recovered, he wanted to know more.

"So, the CCTV?"

"Yes, the CCTV. When she got into work the following morning, she was immediately called into the manager's office where Mr Estate Agent and his wife were waiting for her. She was asked to sit down and then shown the footage of the previous evening. The couple were not enamoured, and Mrs Estate Agent was particularly nasty, which in hindsight was understandable."

"Yeah, that's for sure."

"She was dismissed on the spot. Although you know Sarah, she was cheeky enough to ask for a copy of the film," Kirstie smiled, and Matt laughed out loud.

"The repercussions were that Mrs Estate Agent was overly vengeful and had her lawyer lover evict Sarah on the pain of dobbing him into his wife!" Kirstie said with a lot of sympathy for her mate.

"Her sexual circle was kaput. And her job and her flat all in the space of a few hours?" Matt said, stating the obvious.

"Yes, and she went back to live with her mum for a while. We went for a drink shortly after, and she was very upset, although she hid it well."

"Bloody unfair, really," said Matt. "I mean, apart from using the office for a shag, she hadn't done anything wrong."

"It was Mrs Estate Agent, she was monumentally pissed off that *her* secret lover had a secret lover of his own, and she wanted her pound of flesh."

"Hell has no fury like an adulterer adulterated against," Matt said.

"A case of the biter bit!" she suggested profoundly.

"Are we going to play and then have dinner, and then I'll get on to part three!"

"Part *three?*" Matt stared back as Kirstie got up and stepped from the bath. Matt thought she looked so sexy (and slippery!) with the glistening soapy water dripping from her as she reached for the large towel.

"You do want to know how she came back from that setback, don't you?" Kirstie asked.

"Yeah, but first things first," and he also stepped out of the bath and pulled her towards him to kiss her, pulling apart her towel to slide his slick, wet body against hers.

"How would you like to sit on *my* face while I complete my recovery? I have this ability to breathe through my eyelids," he whispered, standing behind her and cupping her breasts, causing her nipples to stiffen and his own erectile tissue to re-awaken. She reached behind her to hold the aroused member.

"Seems like your recovery period is top drawer?" she said, massaging it further just to make sure.

"Maybe so, but I'd still like you to nestle down on my mouth and lips and let me tease you with my tongue."

Kirstie turned around to kiss him again, still holding his cock.

"Okay, take me to bed and do with me what you will."

They moved to the bed and first spread the towels. He lay down, ready for her to straddle his head and position herself on his mouth. She held on to the headboard and leant forward slightly to allow "wiggle" room and she laughed to herself, which abruptly changed as soon as his tongue parted her pussy lips. Kirstie closed her eyes as the pleasure swept through her and her hips moved to make sure his tongue and lips hit the spot. They had never done this before, and for once, she felt empowered to take what she wanted and how she wanted it.

Matt was also enjoying it, but several times had to stop to swallow her natural sap; he also had to make sure that she didn't push down too hard and deprive himself of oxygen. He'd done this once with a rather sturdy girl at Uni and nearly blacked out when she enjoyed herself too much. He could sense Kirstie was nearing orgasm and reached up to fondle her breasts and nipples, which was the final impetus to get her over the line.

As she calmed down, she moved onto her back and, breathing deeply, told Matt that they should do that again sometime. Matt turned over to rest an arm across her.

"Mmm, yes, I'm glad you liked it. Was there anything that Sarah's done that you'd like to try?"

Kirstie pondered that for a moment and said, "I'm sure there is, but it might take a couple of lifetimes to get through what she's tried." She laughed and then, acknowledging the urgent prodding from lower down, said, "Anyway, there's something far more pressing to deal with."

"Pizza?" he asked.

"No - cock!" they both sniggered, but to her surprise, he rolled onto his stomach and said it was a lovely thought, but right now he was starving.

"Will you go and get the pizzas or shall I?" he asked.

"I'll toss you for it," Kirstie said unwittingly. Matt laughed and immediately replied with, "Tell you what, give me a blow job instead of a wank, and I'll go and get them." And she dissolved into a fit of laughter. "Fizz, jizz, and pizza - the perfect combination. Although not necessarily in that order!"

The oral 'deal' duly completed, he dressed and returned forty minutes later with two medium-sized pizzas and a side of potato skins. They had dinner on their laps and shared a bottle of white wine as Kirstie continued with Sarah's escapades.

"You can imagine Sarah might have been a bit down, no job, no flat and her social circle, or at least her sexual circle, was gone, but you know, Sarah is always bubbly, always upbeat."

"What did she do? Where did she go?" Matt asked, finishing the last segment of his meat feast.

"As I said, she packed up her stuff and moved back with her mum. We went for a drink that evening, and typically she was laughing about the CCTV finishing with, '*I never got a copy of that film, but what I saw of it, I did look damn good lodged on his face, especially from the front 'cos it looked like I was giving birth!*'" Kirstie and Matt laughed, but deep down, they both admired Sarah's resilience.

"I was able to get her some temporary work with my mum at the betting office, where she was a hit at the counter and the clientele doubled in less than a fortnight."

"That's not surprising, especially if she got her tits out!" Matt said, laughing.

"Don't be vulgar," Kirstie said, also sharing the joke.

"Anyway, her mum, who is Irish, was as intuitive as she always was. She contacted a cousin of hers in Ireland, um…not far from Dublin, I think. He owned a very nice hotel and restaurant, and if he could give her a job, it would kill two birds with one stone. It would provide an escape to a different environment *and* provide an income. He was only too pleased to help. He's a lovely man, according to Sarah, and she learnt a great deal about the hotel industry."

"So, why did she come back?" Matt asked.

"Her mum became quite poorly, and she wanted to come back to look after her. Remember, I told you that Sarah had got a degree in Events Management, or at least something to do with that? So, in between looking after her mum, she set up her own company to do that sort of thing. It was mainly weddings, but she did okay. Then she got in with some guy who had a big company doing the same thing, and from what she told me, she got a lot of regular customers from that."

"When you say Sarah got in with the guy, do you mean?" Matt asked as if he already knew the answer. Kirstie laughed.

"What do you think?" she said sarcastically. "And yes, he was married, but it ended after about six months or so." Matt just nodded.

"Did her mum get better?" Matt asked.

"Sadly, no, she had heart disease, which she hid from Sarah for a long time before she became really bad. They did have a couple of weeks together, to which Sarah said she was grateful. Her mum insisted that whatever was going to happen would happen, so why burden her daughter with the pain that goes with watching a loved one suffer for so long?

Sarah is very much like her mum. Problems are yours and yours alone. Don't heap your issues onto someone else. I've tried to talk to her about it, and she can see my point about sharing - you know, a problem shared is a problem halved, etcetera, and she just laughed when telling me her favourite saying was, '*A friend in need is a pain in the arse!*'"

"Dan never said anything about it," Matt said, visibly shocked.

"He met Sarah not long after she lost her mum, but she never went into detail about it to anyone, really." Kirstie continued, "It was all very sad. Her dad was from Sri Lanka and died when she was only a few months old. Her mum, being Irish, never remarried, sticking to her Catholic beliefs of once you're married, that's it," Kirstie said.

"I thought that it was a *death do us part* mantra. It was divorce that wasn't allowed," Matt was pretty sure about it.

"Maybe yes, but I think she was so heartbroken she never got over it." Kirstie looked a bit sad.

"I don't want to go all psychoanalysis, but maybe that's why Sarah likes men so much?" Matt offered.

"And women!" Kirstie laughed. "But yes, I'm sure of it. Would you marry again if anything happened to me?" she asked.

"In a heartbeat," he said, laughing, "Just as you would!" She pulled a face as if shocked by his reaction.

"Oh, come on, Kay, you would have blokes queuing down the street at the mere whisper of my demise!" he said. "Since we're on that subject, ask me if I would let her drive your car," Matt said, staring at her with a soppy grin.

Kirstie looked confused but then asked, "Would you?"

"Of course, now ask me if I'd let her sleep in our bed," he was still smiling. Kirstie shrugged but played along and again said, "Would you let her sleep in our bed?"

He nodded. "I'd need someone to keep me warm at night. Now ask me if I'd let her use your golf clubs."

"But I don't play golf!"

"Go on, humour me," he still grinned.

"Would you let her use my golf clubs?" she said in a staccato manner, tipping her head from side to side on each word just for the sake of saying it.

He burst out laughing and then, when he composed himself, he said, "No, of course not, anyway no point, she's left-handed!" and he laughed again.

Kirstie shook her head and didn't get it. Then the penny finally dropped. "Oh. Ha ha!" and slapped him on the shoulder.

"So that's Sarah's history then. Wow, she's a horny little soul and no mistake. It's still a bit odd about postponing the wedding, though, but if it's just for a few weeks, then that's fair enough," Matt said, trying to convince himself that it wasn't unusual.

"A few weeks? Whatever gave you that idea?" Kirstie asked.

"That's what Dan said."

"She didn't specify any time span to me," Kirstie added, "I think she's getting cold feet."

"So why go ahead with the hen's weekend?" he asked.

"Because she's only recently decided to postpone the wedding, and the weekend is all paid for, so we'd never get our money back," Kirstie said as a matter of fact.

"Well, as Dan said to me, at least he'll get a rest for the weekend," Matt said.

"Poor Dan, I feel a bit sorry for him. I love Sarah to bits, but men have treated her very badly, and I think she's just very unsure of things at the moment," Kirstie said, genuinely sympathetic to her hubby's best mate, mostly because of what she knew was an indefinite postponement of the wedding ceremony.

28
Guilty

September 2014

After Julia and Matt's second excursion into the dark side of extra-marital playtime, Matt decided he must try to cool it a bit. Remembering back a couple of months or so ago to that Saturday, his first wedding anniversary. He'd gone home to Kirstie totally drained, physically and emotionally.

Matt and Kirstie enjoyed their anniversary dinner at home - it was loving and relaxing just to eat, drink, and chat with his gorgeous wife. However, he then had to muddle through a session of love-making instigated by her to celebrate, which he just about managed, even if Kirstie was a little miffed that her mother had tired him out on the 'supposed' repair of a tumble dryer.

As the young couple kissed goodnight, she was asleep in seconds. Matt thought he would be too, but lay on his back, staring at the ceiling in the dark, trying to take in all of the machinations of the day - and night. Two women in one day, and even more wicked, a mother and daughter scenario. He knew one thing for certain, his cock was sore. And he felt as guilty as fuck!

As he lay there, he wondered how, in the space of *that* week, his happy, if comfortable, existence had been turned upside down by a wanton middle-aged woman whom he was related to, albeit by law. But he knew from the first day that he met Julia, something about her said *sex*. Not least of her attributes was the gorgeously curvy figure that only a woman of that age can have, and that she could flirt for Britain. He initially thought it was just a tease, but didn't she confirm that she had "*wanted*" him from the first day that they met? Of course, he was flattered, and by God, the two escapades so far were magnificent, yet he started to question his part in this. Had he encouraged her in some way because he knew in his heart of hearts, he also wanted her?

She had sometimes filled his early morning fantasies when he would wake with the usual morning glory, imagining it was her (and not his wife's) fingers running up and down the length of his cock before straddling him and easing it into her slippery warmth.

Sometimes, at a family gathering, it would be a day of increasing sexual tension between the two of them. He would later masturbate, believing it was Julia's hand wrapped around his demanding penis. He had become infatuated with Julia, but had he communicated this somehow, which triggered her desire? Could he really claim to be an innocent victim?

So, this *'foreplay'* went on for weeks and months and then the opportunity was manufactured by his delicious, sexy mother-in-law. Lust and passion were at their fingertips, regardless of the obvious family relationship between them. Where there's a will, there's a way, she said. Her "will" and her "way" won the day.

Recalling the initial seduction and how his heart pounded as she skilfully contrived to get him alone and semi-naked. His mind strayed to that afternoon seven days later, where his cock was hard again, given her dress, her perfume, the heels, and not least the seductive lingerie. Even more, the kisses, the nakedness, her hands, mouth, her scent, her taste, the fucking, her orgasms and, inevitably, the awful guilt. As he lay next to his wife, the guilt overcame him, but like anyone who has an addiction, addiction wins. He wanted more.

Matt had successfully avoided Julia for a number of weeks, more so through work commitments. Sunday would be a bit of a test as he and Kirstie were going to her parents for lunch. He was hoping Julia would behave and not flirt like she usually did. Then again, if she didn't, would Kirstie think it a bit suspicious and start to wonder if Matt and Julia had fallen out over something? Better that than the truth, he thought.

For her part, Julia was a bit disappointed that Matthew hadn't made some sort of contact. Likewise, for him, despite his thoughts of cooling it, he too was a little put out that she hadn't sent a little message affirming her desire. He didn't like the notion of just being used, then he considered the irony of the times he had done exactly the same to girls in his younger days.

Sunday came, all seemed to have settled down to the normal family status quo. Kirstie and Matthew arrived on time and received the usual greetings of pecks, handshakes and usual small talk. Matt was more than happy to see her wearing her sexy white crop top and tight blue jeans, and how tenderly she kissed his cheek. Alan poured drinks and then asked Matt, "Matthew, you're good at DIY stuff. Can you have a look at the radiator in the study, please? It won't heat up for some reason. No rush whenever you get a moment." He was quite blasé about it.

Matthew was always eager to please, as his mother-in-law would testify firsthand.

"No problem, I'll have a quick look now," Matt replied.

"Love, do the honours, could you, while I get some more drinks," Alan said to Julia as he went to the kitchen. His wife was only too keen to oblige. The illicit lovers went to the study in silence. Ever the gentleman, Matt ushered his mother-in-law into the study. As soon as he entered, she turned, pushed the door shut, then, pulling his hand to her mouth, took one then two of his fingers between her lips in an obvious simulation of fellatio.

She looked straight into his eyes and said, "You've played it cool, Matthew, which, for appearance's sake, is the correct way to go, but do you regret our playtime?"

"Honestly?" he questioned.

"Yes, we must be honest with each other." She continued to suckle his fingers.

"Yes and no," was his truthful response. She waited for more.

"Yes, I regret being deceitful to Kirstie, but no, because you are the most exciting woman I have ever known."

"Okay." She seemed to take the compliment as a given and then quickly followed with, "I wore this top especially for you, and the big question is, will you play with me again, soon?"

He withdrew his fingers and put his hands on either side of her face to pull her close for a very intense French kiss.

"Does that answer your question?" He asked. She was quick to reply.

"God, if we had time, I'd bend over that desk and you could fuck me senseless, but…"

He finished her sentence, "It wouldn't look so good if we go back in fifteen minutes with my jizz dribbling down your leg!"

She laughed. "Quite! By the way, I'm sure it's just the radiator valve that's stuck, having done a bit of research online."

"No problem. And how are your valves?" he asked.

"Fit to explode if you don't do something to relieve the pressure very soon," she replied, stroking his semi-hard cock through his jeans.

They made their way back, pinching his backside, before she went off to the kitchen. Over the meal, the conversation turned towards Kirstie's best friend, Sarah, who was supposedly getting married soon. There was no need to elaborate on the current postponement. Kirstie reminded Matt that she was off to Dublin for the hens' weekend in a couple of weeks' time. Julia and Matt shot a fleeting, but knowing, glance at one another. Matthew's cock jerked in anticipation of a perfect opportunity to fuck his mother-in-law yet again, even for just a few hours. The rest of the day went off without incident, but both protagonists felt the heightened anticipation of what was to come.

The days passed slowly, and the impending third bout of unbridled lust with Julia was front and foremost in Matthew's mind. There was very little contact between them, apart from one text from her, just saying that a number of valves required attention very soon. He was virtually climbing the walls by the Thursday evening of Kirstie's weekend away. Kirstie cuddled up to him while watching TV and whispered, "You know I'm away in the morning, so are you going to make love to me tonight? We haven't played for a whole week, Mama needs *lurve*."

"A week? That long? But who's counting, eh? I'm not sure I remember how," he replied sarcastically.

"Well," she said, "I'm going to run us a bath and maybe you can recall what to do while we have a soak."

They bathed together, drank some wine and chatted about nothing in particular, all the time though his mother-in-law was on his mind. They adjourned to the bedroom and made love. They assumed their usual positions for him to orally pleasure her to climax, and she pushed him away immediately after as her clitoris became far too sensitive to prolong the touch.

"Mmm, now where do you want me?" she asked after a few minutes' respite.

Moving up her body, he said, "Right where you are." They kissed, and she spread her legs wide for him. He slid in easily. She hooked her legs onto the back of his strong thighs, and they fucked. She wanted tender, passionate lovemaking to feel that he would be the only man she would ever give herself to. Something within her mind told her he was not honest in his desire for her. Kirstie couldn't read his thoughts, but he seemed to be going through the motions. It happened often of late, and for Matt, when he was in the throes of fucking his wife, it was Julia who occupied his mind. When he finished, the guilt quickly followed.

Friday morning brought such anticipation and excitement, yet he had to show his wife that he was sad to be without her for the whole weekend. Kirstie was buzzing herself and, in almost equal measure, tried to rein in her eagerness at getting away with the girls. They both deserved awards for their acting as Matt dropped her off at the airport.

As he stepped through his front door after dropping Kirstie off, his mobile phone rang. He knew immediately who it was, even before looking at the screen. Picking it up, he said, "Hello." The voice at the other end said, "Alan's gone to Sheffield on an urgent job for a few days. So, your place or mine?"

Guilt would need to take a back seat for a while yet.

29

(I've Had)
The Time of My Life

September 2014

Kirstie sat alone at the hotel bar in Dublin. This was the first night of Sarah's hen party, and it wasn't how she imagined.

At the eleventh hour, the Gang of Four became a gang of two. Unfortunately, Mia and Samantha had dropped out - Mia through ill health, and Sam due to a late call-up by the England hockey team.

Sarah was as belligerent as ever. "Fuck it – if it's just us, Kay, then so be it. I'm not wasting good money to sit at home!"

Hubby Matt had dropped the pair of them at Heathrow that morning, and they moved through the busy security to the departures lounge. They cared less that it was only 10 am - the hen party started here!

"So, Kayzee, did you get a farewell shag last night?" Sarah asked with a smile and eyebrows raised inquisitively.

"I'm an old married lady!" Kirstie said as though she was disgusted by the suggestion. She left it a few seconds before saying, "Absolutely, and very nice it was too!" She paused. "What about yourself?"

In feigned horror, Sarah responded, "I'm an unmarried Catholic woman and as pure as the driven snow, I am a virgin!"

Kirstie countered, "Yeah, right. Virgin on the ridiculous, so?"

"Well, if you promise not to tell the Pope, I may well have played the game of hide the sausage, culminating in him giving me a show at my request!"

"A show? What, dancing and singing around the bedroom?" Kirstie asked, trying to imagine the scene of Dan cavorting around their bed. Sarah laughed, "No, not that sort of show. I like to watch him cum. I just love his gentleman juice, especially when he squirts it all over me!"

"No, too much detail!" Kirstie was a bit taken aback.

"If he does me when he's on top, I sometimes get him to sit back on his haunches and pull out on the vinegar stroke, but then press against me so that his dick is pointing upwards when he fires off a volley or two. Or three. Or four!" Sarah laughed. Kirstie grimaced at the finer portrayal of her friend's intimacy.

"Last night was a bit disappointing, though, because while I was expecting Vesuvius, all I got was a piping bag emission which puddled onto my landing strip." She sniggered as Kirstie nearly spat out her sip of wine.

"Damn tasty though, and it was my fault as I'd already had one load from him earlier."

Kirstie smiled and shook her head, trying not to imagine the scene.

"Ok, if you're a Catholic, don't you suffer from '*Catholic Guilt*' and go to church occasionally to confess your sins?" she asked.

"You *are* joking, of course?" Sarah replied. "The only thing I'm guilty of is having no guilt about enjoying myself. Anyway, I'd be there for days, and the poor priest would die of a heart attack or at least a rush of blood to his nether regions!" she sniggered.

Kirstie was dubious. "I'm not so sure, given recent scandals in the Roman Catholic Church."

"Good point," Sarah said. "He'd probably find normal carnal behaviour quite disgusting. I'd be exiled to a convent to live with nuns for the rest of my life. Oh, how I could rock their world!" she laughed loudly. "Do you think a nun's habit would suit me?"

"Only if it was a dirty habit and you were allowed to wear your saucy undies underneath it," Kirstie replied.

"Dirty habit?" Sarah giggled. "I see what you did there!"

The short flight to Dublin went without hassle. They were in a taxi on their way to their hotel in no time at all. The old taxi driver gave them some blarney about the history of various pubs on the way into town and pointed out some places of interest. Sarah was about to try her luck to blag another free fare, but Kirstie told her to behave. By mid-afternoon, they were checked in and back downstairs to the lounge bar for hen party drinks.

Kirstie and Sarah enjoyed a couple of cocktails and toasted absent friends. After just over an hour, they decided to adjourn for a few hours to recuperate, then get ready for the evening - meeting back in the restaurant at 7.30 pm.

It was bliss to take a long soak in the bath and relax. Kirstie really unwound and let her mind drift back to last night's lovemaking with Matt. Lately, it had all become so… comfortable, bordering on vanilla. Matt used to be quite enthusiastic, but lately, she began to feel something wasn't right and it caused some real soul-searching. Kirstie wondered how she could broach the subject with her husband, but her immediate thought now was that she needed to hear his voice. She phoned her lovely hubby to no avail. She left it for a while and phoned again with the same result. Oh well, he was probably at work or commuting, and although peeved that he was unavailable, she now needed to get ready.

Out of the bath, Kirstie dried herself and sat in the fluffy hotel towelling robe. She applied her make-up then dressed for her evening out. She had bought some new underwear and felt quite sexy as she put on the matching lacy black bra and knickers and sheer black hold-up stockings with some decent-sized heels. It wasn't too outrageous, after all, she was that "old married woman". Kirstie then donned her new black faux leather miniskirt together with a blue and black long-sleeved patterned blouse which had a short, round, upright collar. It buttoned all the way down the front, and she undid one button more than necessary to show off her delectable cleavage.

Arriving at the restaurant, she at the table, ordered a glass of white wine and waited for Sarah. Ten minutes passed – it was unlike her best friend to be late for anything…except for her period when she was fifteen, she thought, then berated herself for thinking something so nasty.

Kirstie texted her bestie.

"Hey Saz – are you coming or just breathing heavy?"

The reply was not immediate, but eventually, Sarah texted back.

"So sorry Kay, I've been as sick as a dog and worse!!! Will have to cry off. Sorry, sorry sorry. xxx"

Kirstie texted back straightaway, asking if she needed company or anything. The reply came back in five minutes. *"No, K, the room is not fit for human habitation after what I've done to the wc. Thanks, babe. I'll sleep it off, and I'll be great in the morning. Go and paint the Emerald City red – it's a very friendly place. (SORRY)!! Love S xxxx"*

She responded with a *'get well soon, Love Kxxx'* and resigned herself to an early night. She had another glass of wine with dinner, then returned to her room – it was 8.45 pm. She tried to get hold of Matthew, yet again, with no luck. Kirstie texted Sarah to ask if she needed anything. Sarah responded fairly quickly to say that she was *"done in"* and was going to have an early night.

"Damn," Kirstie said to herself, I'll go down to the bar and do some people-watching. That'll kill a couple of hours.

She planted herself on a high-backed stool at the far end of the bar, where she had a good view of the comings and goings. As she sat, she realised her skirt was a bit shorter than she had initially appreciated, and she pulled it down a little to cover the stocking tops. The young bartman approached her.

"Hello, my name is Tim. What can I get you this evening?" he asked in his sing-song Irish accent.

"Hello Tim, I'd like a gin and tonic, please," Kirstie replied, still checking the hem of her skirt.

She surveyed the room, which was fairly busy with the usual type of people you would expect in a hotel bar, couples mainly and three guys in suits having a "swift half" after work, as Matthew would put it. As Tim placed her drink in front of her, a strikingly handsome man entered the bar area and went over to the three 'suits'. He was a mature guy, maybe in his late fifties or early sixties, with neatly cut grey hair, tall and well built, wearing a perfectly tailored dark grey suit, white shirt with the top two or three buttons undone and shiny black shoes. *'Always judge a man by how he dresses,'* her mother told her, *'especially how clean his shoes are!'* He was the sort of guy who would hold court with his peers, a man's man, successful in business, life, and love. One of those guys who could charm his way through life. Peter Perfect, she thought.

She watched them as she sipped her drink before the three 'suits' shook hands with Mr Perfect and said their goodbyes. With that, Mr Perfect came to the bar and beckoned Tim over to him. He spoke to the barman within earshot of Kirstie.

"Timothy, do you think the gorgeous young lady to my right here is probably the most beautiful woman to frequent these premises in a long while?"

Tim responded, "I would truly say so, sir." Tim looked at Kirstie and smiled. Kirstie half-smiled back and then raised her eyebrows as if to say, 'Isn't that the corniest line you've heard in these premises for a long while?' The man continued, "Do you think she would accept if I offered to buy the young lady a drink?"

"I've come to the conclusion, sir, that to take opportunities in life, you just have to go for it," Tim replied, switching his gaze between Kirstie and Peter Perfect. Kirstie turned to the man, who was now looking admiringly at her. He had piercing blue eyes and was even more attractive close up.

"Ach, Timothy, you have such a wise head on such young shoulders," he turned to speak directly to her now.

"I would be most honoured if you would allow me to buy you a drink, Madam," he smiled a very disarming smile, and she thought about it briefly, the choices were an early night or engage in conversation with this mature but intriguing, handsome man. Hobson's choice.

She turned to Tim. "I would like a gin and tonic, please," and turning to the man, said, "Thank you."

The man replied, "You are most welcome. Same for me, please, Tim," and he moved nearer to Kirstie. Still standing, he held out his hand and said, "My name is Patrick, not Pat or Paddy - Patrick, but you can call me sir." He smiled.

"Yes, sir!" Kirstie said cheekily. She shook his hand and told him her name. She could now smell his aftershave, it was delightfully mesmerising.

"Good, you learn fast, young lady." It was an odd reply, she thought. He was obviously Irish but very well-spoken, with no discernible regional accent. For a small country, Ireland seemed to have more than its fair share of strong regional accents.

He sat on the stool next to her. "Your face seems awfully familiar. Have we met before?" he asked, staring at her. She thought it was another corny line, but replied that this was her first visit to Ireland.

"No, it was somewhere more exotic." He shook his head and seemed puzzled, as though he was genuine with his question.

"I never forget a beautiful face, and you look so familiar. Never mind, it'll come to me. So, Kirstie, I was going to ask you the usual '*get to know you*' questions, but I wonder if I might play a little game with you and let me tell you about yourself to see how accurate, or not, I am?" He smiled again. She delayed a few seconds before saying, "Okay, that might be interesting."

"Could I ask you to hold out your hands, please?" he asked, sitting square onto her. She did so, and he held them with a firm but gentle grip. He first looked at her palms and then at the backs of her delicate hands. She could see that he had a very expensive watch and also wore cufflinks. This guy exuded class.

"Okay, you're English, which is why you have that unwitting air of arrogance and, from your accent, you probably reside in the south of England, Home Counties maybe, erring on the south of London. You're in your mid-twenties, as you have the confidence to sit in a bar alone. Obviously, you take great care of your appearance; you're clearly married, but not here with your husband. I'd say a girls' weekend. I'm struggling as to why you're in the bar alone, but maybe you're waiting for someone who is inexcusably late.

Kirstie said, "Okay," and was about to continue when he said firmly, "Please, wait until I finish."

Suitably admonished, she sat there quietly.

"You come from an upper-middle-class background with good parents who have brought you up well. You went to university, studied hard, and no doubt got a suitable vocational degree in law, banking or business management, and that's where you're building your career. You live in a nice semi-detached house and drive a modest saloon car, probably Japanese. So far, children and pets are not yet on the agenda. You've drifted into the classic family cliché too young without realising it. You are wasting your full potential, but maybe that's how you want it?" He smiled and let go of her hands.

Kirstie was a little affronted by his analysis but countered, "I'm not sure how you picked all of that up just by looking at me and my hands, but your generalisations are not too far from reality." She explained why she was there on her own, but then went on to ask why he thought she was wasting her potential. He smiled.

"Because a greater percentage of young women in their mid-twenties want the husband, the house, the car, the career and, a little way down the line, the kids. Many have the brains, body and potential to do so much more, and yet they let it slip away for some long-term mediocrity. More especially, wasting their sexual potential."

"They settle for a couple of intimate episodes a week, mainly to keep their husbands happy. They never really let go with regard to physical pleasure until they're in their forties or fifties, by which time their perfect bodies, their weapons of mass seduction if you like, may have lost their edge somewhat and yet are still hugely desirable."

Kirstie was determined to stand her ground. "I enjoy making love with my husband!"

"I'm sure you do, but if you haven't been married too long, then you're still literally in the honeymoon period. Another few years… it'll be a drudge, a chore to get over with for both of you. That's where the relationship comes under serious threat."

"I don't agree, my husband and I are very good together," Kirstie said and was immediately embarrassed at how naïve that sounded. The alcohol was clearly to blame. Patrick smiled but continued in his calm manner.

"How many men did you sleep with before you married your husband? Four, maybe five, add a few short-term Uni relationships with boys straight out of school, just wanting to get their ends away. Maybe a one-night stand because you were drunk, and a holiday romance in Benidorm. Not really setting the world alight on a sexual résumé, is it?" He was quite sarcastic but very accurate. She just looked at him.

"Men get bored when they realise that their forever partner is only going through the motions and is reluctant to spice things up or take the initiative. If they did, sex or lovemaking or just plain old fucking would be something to look forward to, something that gives a tingle in the anticipation, something to be adored and desired." He paused.

"Tell me, when was the last time *you* initiated intimacy when he wasn't feeling up for it?" She made no reply.

"Have you ever tied each other up, giving complete control to the other person? When was the last time either of you was so spontaneous that wherever you were at that moment, you just had to find a secluded spot and get down to it?" Still no response, but Patrick could tell by her body language that his not-so-subtle assault on her personal life was working.

"Do you get turned on knowing how much a man wants to bed you?" He stared at her intensely with those piercing blue eyes.

"Yes, with my husband." She was quite emphatic, but she knew he had all the answers.

"He doesn't count. I'm talking about a complete stranger like me, you can surely see it in my eyes how much I want to pleasure you. You know in your heart of hearts that I'm fully equipped to be able to do so," he didn't let her answer, but continued.

"Have you ever wanted a threesome with two men, or have you ever made love with another woman?"

"No," was Kirstie's immediate reply. She hid the fact that she'd had ridiculous fantasies about being taken by two men and was definitely curious about girl-on-girl play. She was surprised when Patrick blatantly called her out.

"Hmm, I'll bet you've thought about those scenarios, though. Don't forget if you're a fully committed heterosexual, you're denying yourself fifty per cent of potential play-friends." He stared at her and shook his head.

"My case rests, wasted potential and yet so easily cured." He finished his drink and called Tim over again for another round. Kirstie thought about his very personal questions and wanted to leave it, but the curiosity got the better of her.

"How is it easily cured?" She asked, finishing her G&T and saying thank you for the next one. Patrick pretended he hadn't heard the question and seemed fairly distracted as he signed the chit presented by the barman.

"Sorry, I didn't quite catch what you said."

Kirstie was pretty sure that he had heard and, although a little irritated, asked the question again.

"How is it easily cured?" She studied his face, awaiting a reply.

"I can use a thousand words, which still wouldn't get the message across. Or I can show you." Patrick was so matter-of-fact that she nearly succumbed. She then smiled at the realisation of his seduction technique.

"Oh, I get it. You're just after a quickie in the hotel with a lone female. You must think I'm still wet behind the ears," she said cynically.

"Madam, I guarantee you will be wet because you will never have experienced anything like this before. Look at me. Do you think I am a man who indulges in quickies?" He let her think about it. Even though she'd had a few drinks, she was still compos mentis enough to present a reasonable defence, or so she thought. However, the alcohol also made her horny. This distinguished, experienced man was unquestionably attractive and talking a very good game.

"Well, if I were single, I might consider your proposal, but hey, I'm married and devoted to my husband. We'll learn everything we need over our lifetime together." Kirstie claimed the moral high ground. He nodded, blinked slowly and smiled the sort of smile that meant, "Yeah, sure."

"Devoted? For now, maybe, but it won't last. No details because it would ruin the anticipation and the excitement of what might come next. You see, if you want to come with me on this path to sexual appreciation and knowledge, you must do everything I say without question." He held her hands again, "I promise there will be no pain involved, and nothing will happen against your wishes. You would have a safe word to use where everything would stop. You would just have to trust me." He smiled that disarming smile again.

She was shocked at his blatant suggestion of taking her to bed to have sex with her, but before she could put forward any resistance, Patrick could see she was weakening. He pressed home his advantage while she was on the back foot.

"I'm a great believer in fate. Let me spin a coin, and if it comes down as heads, then you're mine for the evening. If tails, I will thank you for your company and leave," he waited for her decision. He seemed a little impatient.

Kirstie stared at him and said, "But I'm married." It was her last effort to combat his seduction. Still holding her hands, he took her engagement and wedding rings off and asked her to put them somewhere safe.

"If they're not on your finger, you are free to do what you want until you put them back on," he said, still staring intently at her.

She looked at them in his hand and hesitated. Heart pounding, she took them from his hand and slowly put them in her bag. She looked at him, paused and then, with a deep breath, said, "Spin the coin."

Patrick called Tim over.

"Timothy, we're having a little bet here that requires the toss of a coin, as you have no vested interest in the outcome. Would you do the honours, please?" He handed the coin to Tim.

"Of course, sir."

It seemed like slow motion as it spun. Tim caught it and flattened it against the bar. Patrick looked at her, staring at Tim's hand.

"Thank you, Timothy, just cover it with that beer mat, please and leave us to see," then he turned towards Kirstie as Tim went off to serve another customer.

"Last chance, you can say no, and we'll finish our drinks and part company," he said, confident that she was already hooked. She tilted her head towards the coin as if giving him permission to show her what the fates had decided.

The alcohol, the charming Irishman, and the coin had sealed her immediate future. It was heads.

Kirstie gently bit her lip and took a deep breath.

"You understood all that I said, didn't you?" Patrick asked.

"Yes," she hesitated. "What happens now?"

"What contraception do you use?" he asked.

"The pill." He nodded in approval.

"First, to demonstrate to me that you are willing to do as I say, you will go to the restroom and remove your bra. When you come back, you will give it to me, and then you will sit on the stool and allow your skirt to ride up a little to show your stocking tops. I couldn't help getting a glimpse of them when you moved occasionally. Very sexy. I think you have enormous potential."

She took a sip of her drink and went off to the Ladies. She looked at herself in the mirror as she performed the magical trick of bra removal without undoing her blouse and said to herself.

"Fuck it, Matt's not here, and he can't even be bothered to answer my calls. I'm away from home; no one will know, and I'm downright fucking horny!"

He watched her unfettered breasts wobble as she made her way back. She sat down and sure enough, her stocking tops and bare thighs were subtly visible to anyone who cared to look. She started to understand how Sarah got a kick out of exhibitionism. Kirstie gave him the folded-up bra. In turn, he gave her a room key card with instructions to take the lift to the top floor. She was to be there in ten minutes' time.

"Your safe word is *shamrock*. If you say that at any time, then everything stops, and you can get dressed and leave." Patrick got up and thanked Tim, surreptitiously slipping him a ten Euro note for a tip. He kissed Kirstie's hand and was gone.

Kirstie continued to wrestle with her conscience, but looking at where her wedding ring should be, she thought how could anyone find out, so what did she really have to lose if she could stop at any time. She looked at her watch. It was time. Heart pounding, butterflies trembling, she gathered her bag, smiled at Tim, said thank you and good night. Kirstie took the lift as instructed and pressed the button for the top floor. There was only one door on that level.

She was shaking as she stood outside Patrick's door and tried the key card, but it didn't work correctly. She tried again, the door mechanism bleeped, and the green light flashed on. Kirstie took a deep breath and pushed the door open to see Patrick waiting for her. He had removed his jacket and unbuttoned his shirt. God, he was fit!

He gave her no chance to say anything before embracing her and then going for a full-tongued French kiss. Not only was he fit, but he could kiss. She felt a tingle all the way down to her inner thighs and, dropping her bag, held him tightly around the neck. He turned her around to face the door and said nothing as he unbuttoned her blouse from behind to slip it from her shoulders. He let it fall to the floor. He then did the same to her skirt. Patrick then ran a finger down her spine to the top of her knickers before putting his arms around her, drawing her close to him and fondling her boobs and erect nipples while gently biting her neck and shoulders. It was thrilling, and Kirstie could feel his stiffened appendage through his trousers, pressing against her bum as she tried to respond to his attentions by reaching behind her.

"No," was the firm command. "All in good time," he said.

He turned her to face him and stepped away from her to really appreciate her delectable form. "You are a very beautiful young woman." She was flattered by his admiration.

He took her hand and led her into the room; it wasn't just a bedroom, it was a whole suite. She was extremely surprised to see a young African man sitting on the edge of an enormous bed wearing the briefest of white slips. Patrick introduced him.

"Kirstie, this is Michael, a very, very good friend of mine. I had planned an evening with him, but three is not a crowd where you are concerned. We are going to introduce you to a world of lust, passion, desire, dominance, subjugation and ultimate sexual satisfaction."

Michael stood up, revealing a huge bulge in his briefs, which had barely enough material to contain his manhood. Kirstie said nothing but just stared, heart thumping and totally dumbfounded. He was about six feet tall, with a toned, hairless torso and a lovely smile. Without any prompting, he pulled down his pants, allowing his flaccid cock and heavy balls to show in all their glory. She could not help but be drawn to his beautiful, circumcised penis. Even in its limp state, he was easily a couple of inches longer than her husband's cock when he was hard.

Patrick spoke again, "Michael is yours to do with what you will. Whatever fantasy you've ever had about a man, whether it's what you want him to do to you or you want to do with him, can be realised tonight. He is literally a sex machine. As you can see, he's hung like a horse and has a tongue like a lizard. His fingers and hands know everything that there is to know about a woman's body and, if truth be told, about a man's as well and with some direction from myself, you will know the true meaning of sexual bliss!"

Kirstie was still speechless, and it all seemed so surreal so quickly. Patrick spoke again,

"Michael is going to lie on the bed, and you are going to kiss him before indulging in a 69 with him. Do you understand?

She was trying to take the whole situation in but hesitantly said, "Yes." Patrick was abrupt in his response. "When you respond to me, you say *Sir*!"

Kirstie was a little shocked at his rebuke but replied, "Yes, Sir."

Michael was ordered to lie on the bed, and Kirstie went to him to kiss him. As she bent over, he held her face and invaded her mouth, squashing her tongue. He was passionate and forceful, and she had never been kissed like that before. She let him do what he wanted - it was exhilarating. He eventually broke off the kiss, and she removed her knickers to allow him to guide her into the position that Patrick required.

Kirstie was still mesmerised by her whole situation that she had allowed herself to be so controlled. She was lightheaded, not just through gin, but the whole experience so far. She straddled his face and reached out to grasp his ever-hardening length, wondering how she was going to accommodate the monster dick before her.

Michael pulled her sex towards his waiting tongue and, without hesitation, lapped greedily as her pussy opened up to him. She couldn't believe how much of her he could pleasure all at once. His tongue seemed to be everywhere – it was absolute heaven. In turn, she closed her eyes and did what she could to the bulbous head of his cock while her fingers stroked up and down his length and cradled his balls.

"Yes, that is so erotic – two beautiful people of contrasting skin pleasuring one another, sensational!" Patrick said as he moved towards them.

Michael's hands were stroking her back and buttocks, but now she felt a third hand also massaging her bum. Patrick had lubricated his hand and fingers and was now massaging her anal entrance. She gasped as he pushed a finger in, and she could barely concentrate on Michael. Patrick pushed a second finger in – it was tight, but she was lost in the whole tongue and finger invasion. Before she knew it, her orgasm swept through her, and she went limp, but they did not stop. Normally, one climax would be enough, but Michael and Patrick overcame her "sensitivity" barrier with their persistence.

She was flushed with embarrassment and self-consciousness, but let them continue the ecstasy. Half-heartedly, she wanked Michael's cock, but couldn't concentrate as another orgasm built inside her. The men slowed, but while Michael tried to poke his tongue into her vagina, Patrick was now pushing something else into her anal passage.

"This is a butt plug, my dear. Have you had one of these before?"

"No, sir."

"It's a little reward for your progress so far. You will feel some pleasant sensations when you move." He expected a response.

"What do you say?" he said in a sarcastic tone as if he was talking to a five-year-old.

"Thank you, sir," she said, and then she felt it get a bit bigger.

"It's inflatable, so we'll stretch you in stages. It will prove most useful later."

She said thank you again, but was now concerned about what was going to come later.

"Isn't he a fine specimen of a man, Kirstie?" Patrick said.

"Yes, sir." She could not argue with that statement.

"He is a male model now, you know. I met him when I was on holiday in South Africa. He was working at a holiday village where I stayed. First time I saw him, I knew he had enormous potential and his… *reputation* went before him, according to his workmates."

Kirstie thought it was well justified.

"Look at his penis and testicles," Patrick said. She was unquestionably studying them carefully.

"What a work of art!" Patrick came round and stood at the end of the bed and asked Kirstie what she thought.

"Beautiful," she said, and meant it.

She now took the opportunity to look at the elder man's body and was even more turned on. He was extremely fit, and as he took off his trousers, she could see the outline of a large penis in his tight boxer shorts.

"I want you to ride him now while facing me," Patrick ordered.

Kirstie hesitated, wondering if she could actually accommodate such a freakish weapon.

"Now!"

"Yes, sir," and she moved down Michael's body. She was both excited and apprehensive in equal measure. She held his staff and pointed it at her vulva. Michael then grabbed her hips and carefully pulled her down onto him. The feeling of being stretched by this weapon was exquisite, but she decided to try to restrict his penetration in case he caused some damage. She moved slowly on him.

Patrick was now completely naked, and Kirstie knew he wanted his cock in her mouth. She licked her lips as some sort of acceptance and then reached for it to pull it toward its target. Then she got into a steady rhythm, working on both cocks at the same time. Every movement upward off of Michael was a movement that took Patrick's dick into her mouth and vice versa. The men were not idle either. Patrick massaged her breasts and nipples whilst Michael toyed with her clitoris. It was not long before she reached her crescendo again, and they kept her on that plane.

Her orgasms fused into one long state of euphoria, and she just gave in to the complete bliss of pleasuring and being pleasured. They were all so in sync it almost became effortless, but Patrick hadn't finished with her yet. Kirstie was ordered to face Michael cowgirl style, and although she felt empty when getting up and turning to face him, she soon felt the exhilaration of being filled again. Patrick knelt behind her and fondled her boobs and stomach while she squirmed about on Michael.

The Irishman then told her to kiss Michael, and as she did so, he deflated the butt plug and removed it. She was empty again, but not for long, as he slowly but relentlessly pushed his well-lubricated, hot, white cock into her anus. Swearing at first, she then just gave a low moan and a grunt. She was pawed, kissed, nibbled, stroked and clawed while they were like pistons fucking and buggering her until she was again in one long orgasmic stupor.

Eventually, Patrick called a halt and said, "Michael and I need to give you our seed."

She lay on Michael, totally breathless but almost grateful for the respite.

"Stand up if you can," Patrick asked. She couldn't help but find it highly amusing that her legs were so unstable that they couldn't hold her up. Michael carried her to the bathroom, and she was made to kneel in the shower enclosure, where both men stood on either side of her.

"We are going to give you our liquid now. I will unload in your mouth, and you will hold it there until I tell you to swallow. Michael will put his all over you." It wasn't a request, but she welcomed it anyway. If they were in any doubt, she added, "Give me all of it. I want every last drop, sir!"

The men got to work slowly, masturbating and making her watch. She was particularly intent on how Michael brought himself to climax. Patrick held the top of her head and turned her face towards his erect member. "Open," was his one-word command, and he positioned himself with the underside of his cock resting on her bottom lip so that he could watch spurt after spurt flood into her eager mouth. She did as she was told and held it in there.

"Show me," he demanded.

Kirstie opened her mouth wider to show him the pool of semen nestling on her tongue and at the front of her mouth, some of which spilled out and down her chin.

"Swallow." Swallowing was her least favourite sexual act with Matthew, but in a night full of least favourite acts, this too was now one to be savoured. Patrick ordered Michael to "shoot his load," and he wanked his cock hard and fast, so fast his hand was almost a blur. Kirstie turned to him and, running her hands up his strong, muscular thighs, said, "Come on, you gorgeous man, give me all of that hot, sticky spunk!" She squeezed his balls with one hand and stroked between his buttocks with the other, and it was the final assistance required for him to erupt and erupt he did.

He climaxed with a loud growl and a huge skein of thick cum hit her in the face and hair, another one in her half-open mouth and on her chin, yet another in her face, and another over her breasts. It was so thick that some of it looked like opaque albumen. His body shuddered as he squeezed out the last few drops. Kirstie leant forward and took his spent cock into her mouth, putting her hands on his butt cheeks to pull him into her. Shortly, he stepped away, and Patrick told him he could go. "Thank you, sir, thank you, madam," was his only reply, and he left the bathroom to get dressed.

Kirstie looked at Patrick as if to say, "Where has he gone?" He told her that Michael had his own room one floor down.

"More importantly, how are you?" Patrick asked, sounding genuinely concerned.

She looked at him and said, "I hope I have lived up to some of my potential, sir."

Patrick laughed and said, "We can resume an equal footing, young lady." But added, "You have made excellent progress. Do you want to stay with me tonight or go back to your own room? It's your call, but if you stay, as I would like you to, room service is an added bonus."

She thought about it for a number of seconds.

"I'd like to stay, please and as lovely as all of this cum juice is, I'd like to have a shower first, if I may?" she asked, wiping some of Michael's jizz from her chin and massaging much more of it into her breasts.

"Of course, my dear, join me in bed when you're ready. I have some champagne as a nightcap."

Kirstie duly showered and borrowed one of the fluffy towelling robes hanging up on the door. Patrick had already poured a couple of glasses of bubbly and patted the bed next to him. She joined him there and asked him how he seemed to know so much about her when talking to her in the bar.

"Ah," he said with a big smile, "women do not drink alone if they're with their husbands or partners. It's not in a man's nature to let their better halves go to a bar by themselves. So, it would have had to be a girls' weekend. You're young and very attractive, but have that more mature attitude that being married brings. I think I have a sixth sense about levels of intelligence, etcetera, but–"

"But how could you have known where I come from?" she interjected.

"Well, I also have a sixth sense about that, too. It helped massively that I was in reception when you and your friend checked in. You may have probably guessed that this apartment isn't a run-of-the-mill hotel suite."

"Yes, I did wonder," she chuckled.

"I own the hotel, and I was hugely attracted to you when I saw you at the desk, so I had to check out your details when you'd gone to your room. Then, when I saw you in the bar later, I just couldn't miss the opportunity to talk to you," he said.

"But what did you learn from holding my hands at the bar?" she wondered.

Patrick laughed out loud. "Absolutely nothing. I just thought the physical connection would add emphasis to my assessment. Also, it was a good excuse to touch you. You are a very special young woman," he said in all sincerity.

"I don't think there's anything special about me. I think you came to chat because I was the only girl alone there."

He smiled and then, looking directly at her with his piercing blue eyes, said, "No false modesty, Kirstie, you are stunningly attractive. You remember the three guys I talked to when I came in?"

"Yes."

"They were about to have a game of rock, paper, scissors to see which one would come and chat you up first until I told them you were with me."

"Rather arrogant of you," Kirstie said, although she was secretly flattered.

"It was more to save you from their crude chit-chat," he replied. Kirstie looked rather relieved.

"Who booked this hotel for you?" Patrick asked.

"Sarah, she's supposed to be getting married soon, and this was a little hen party."

"Hmm, I wonder."

"What do you wonder?" Kirstie asked. She was intrigued now.

"Would you say Sarah is sexually aware and worldly wise with regard to certain lifestyles?" he asked.

"Lifestyles? I'm not sure what you mean."

"Hedonism, my dear." Patrick could see she was still a bit confused. "Is she a swinger?" he added.

"Oh," then she laughed. "Sarah is no stranger to enjoying sex for the sake of it." But then she decided not to elaborate. "Why do you ask?"

Patrick laughed, "My hotel is a renowned swinger's venue. Our whole basement area is divided into areas for pleasure seekers. We have a dungeon, sauna, private rooms, and areas for those who have more exhibitionist tendencies."

"*Wow!*" Kirstie was quite shocked. Patrick went on to say that most of the couples who were in the bar earlier were just having pre-playtime drinks. He also explained that Sarah must have known when she made the booking because, by law, he had to add a disclaimer to the confirmation receipt regarding the consequences of any sexual activity carried out on the premises.

"Oh, I see. That reminds me, I must check on my friend, as she hasn't been well." Kirstie sent a short text to Sarah.

"Hey you, how are you doing? Is there anything I can get you – even if it's just some company?" A reply pinged back five minutes later. *"Fucking rough, I literally don't know which way to turn when I get in the bathroom. I'm thoroughly pissed off, pretty sure it's food poisoning…God paying me back for my blasphemous comments about the Catholic Church LOL. I'm going to try to sleep it off but hopefully better in the morning. Love xx"*

Kirstie replied with an *"OK, see you tomorrow and hope you're better. Love Kx."*

She mentioned it to Patrick.

"Food poisoning?" He looked very concerned.

"Airport food." She could see he was a touch rattled that Sarah might have got it from his hotel.

"If she's still bad in the morning, let me know and I'll get a doctor to visit."

Kirstie then explained that there should have been four of them, but two of their other buddies had to drop out, and the whole trip had turned sour, really, except for…

"Yes?" he queried.

"Except for being shown some delights of a hedonistic lifestyle!" she added with a smile.

"My dear, we've only scratched the surface, but for now, I think it's time to recharge the batteries."

Kirstie could only agree. It was a marathon session for her, and she needed rest. She stood up and took off the robe, prompting Patrick's response of, "Yes, you are stunningly attractive. Now slip into bed and let me tell you a bedtime story."

"Ooh, I can hardly wait," she giggled.

"I'm still puzzled as to where I've seen you before, you know?" he said.

"Perhaps you just dreamt it?" she offered.

As the lights went off, Patrick pulled her in close to him and kissed her. The same groin-tingling kiss as the first one on entering the room. He then whispered in her ear, to which she replied,

"Really?" Cue a very dirty laugh, and they spooned and fell asleep.

30
Infatuation

September 2014

"Your place or mine?"

"I'm open to suggestions," Matt's cock was already starting to stiffen, listening to Julia's welcome revelation about Alan.

"Yes, I'll bet you are," Julia giggled. "This might sound very selfish, but now Alan's away, how about you stay here with me all weekend? If nothing else, we might just get this 'want' and lust out of our systems. What do you think?" Julia had her fingers crossed that he would be as excited about the suggestion as she was.

Matt took a few seconds.

"Er, yes, why not? Although I am going out with the lads tonight," he replied, wondering if he hadn't been a bit hasty.

"That's fine. Why not come over here after work? You can have dinner, and I'll run you into town after. Then you can get a cab back later." She made it all sound so innocent.

The day dragged for both of them, but after work he popped home for a quick shower, grabbed some clothes and duly arrived at Julia's at around six o'clock. The back door was on the latch, so he let himself in, heart beating fast and penis hardening with anticipation.

"I'm upstairs!" Julia had seen his car arrive and was equally excited. Matt got to the top of the stairs and said what he hoped was a joke, "Am I in the spare room?"

"Only if I am as well," was the curt reply. He walked into the master bedroom and saw her.

"Wow!"

She was leaning back on the dressing table by the window, legs crossed and hands on the edge of the unit, supporting herself. He drank in the vision of ecstasy that he would very shortly be swamped by. Her hair was as perfectly coiffured as always, her eyes betraying the look of desire, more importantly, desire for him.

She licked her ruby-red lips as his gaze slowly trailed lower. A white silk scarf hung loosely around her neck and trailed between the cleavage of her braless breasts, which themselves were barely covered by a matching tight white silk wrap-over top, done up in a bow at the side. Her protruding nipples told him all he needed to know about her 'want'. The top was a few inches shorter than the skirt, showing off her belly button, and the skirt itself was a ridiculous but so sexy tartan miniskirt that was too short even to hide a glimpse of white knickers. Protruding from it were white suspender straps holding up sheer white stockings which encased her very shapely legs, mounted on new killer red heels.

"I'm guessing this meets with your approval?" She already knew the answer - she could see the growing bulge in his jogger bottoms.

"For fuck's sake, Julia, what are you doing to me?" he said, still gawping at her.

"Well, I rather hope that I am turning you on. I am a complete and utter cum slut for you. This weekend, I am all yours!"

Alone, with no possible chance of getting caught, they let every lustful thought, deed, and word go. Hot, open-mouthed kisses, tongues battling to get into each other's mouths, hands pawing at each other's straining bodies, urgently undoing buttons, zips, and clasps. The days and hours of built-up tension released in those frantic moments. They came up for air and still standing, she pulled off his T-shirt, then nibbled, licked and bit his flesh as her hands went into his track bottoms and boxers and her fingers were now stroking his fully engorged prick. She wasted no time in pushing his clothing down to fully undress him and then pulled him back towards her. They stumbled to the bed and, pulling the gusset of her pants to one side, they were intimate immediately. It was wild, exciting, sweaty and gloriously short and sweet and messily complete.

With a short kiss and cuddle to finish as they calmed themselves, they dressed – Matthew in jeans and tee shirt, Julia likewise. After dinner, they were on their way into town. There was no awkwardness in the silence as she drove, but out of the blue, Matthew said, "Do you mind if I ask you a personal question?"

"Matthew, you have seen all of me. You've fucked me senseless on three occasions, and you've known me for some time. Do you think I would be concerned about personal questions? Anyway, I could always lie or make it up," she replied with a little chuckle.

"Alan…"

"Alan?" she questioned.

"Yes, Alan, you might know him. The guy that you're married to, Kirstie's step-dad, and my father-in-law - that Alan."

"Matthew, I'm married to you this weekend. I have you on loan!"

He smiled but continued, "Do you indulge in some of the naughtiness we've enjoyed?"

"Oh, Matthew, you're a lovely lad but so naïve." She was a tad dismissive but went on, "No is the answer, which is why I'm satisfying myself now before I'm too old and infirm to enjoy it. I married him when I was at a very low point. He is a lovely husband, dedicated to home and family, and he's been a very good father to Kirstie. Our relationship is very enjoyable, we are extremely comfortable with each other, and that's all you really need to know."

"Oh, okay, I think I understand," he said, understanding very well that her relationship was, bluntly, platonic. He was shocked but kept his thoughts to himself.

"As I say, he has been a marvellous father to Kirstie, and I would love him forever just for that."

"Right," he replied, still aghast at what she had said. He really didn't want to hear Kirstie's name, as that stoked his guilt.

"In any event, if we're careful, no one will know how thrilling we are for each other at the moment."

"At the moment?" he questioned.

"Yes, who knows what will happen, but let's enjoy it while we can because it is so damn exciting!" she said with a little laugh.

They spoke no more, she dropped him off in town, down a side street, so that they wouldn't be spotted. She leant across and they had a quick snog. Her hand drifted between his legs, and she gave him a squeeze.

Julia gave him a key to let himself in, just in case he was late. As he went to get out of the car, she held his hand and said, "I am *so* looking forward to sleeping with you tonight."

"Me too," was Matt's genuine reply, then she gave him a quick peck, and he was off.

His five-minute walk to the pub had him thinking about Alan. He wondered why a guy living with such a sexy woman would not *fill his boots*? The only logical conclusion was that he preferred the company of his own gender, but then never, ever gave a hint of that. He let that go and thought about how he could surprise Julia tomorrow with something that maybe she hadn't tried yet. He then recalled a video on a porn website and had a eureka moment.

Matt stumbled in just after midnight but took care to check all the doors and windows were locked before coming to bed. Julia was awake and propped up in bed. Her bedside lamp was on, and she put down the book that she was reading.

"Did you enjoy the evening?" she asked.

"Yep, fan-bloody-tastic," he replied, slightly slurring and then pausing as he started to strip off. He said, "And seeing the boys tonight wasn't bad either!"

She smiled. "Good Answer!" Which was followed by, "Mmm," as he pulled off his jeans. "Come to bed, Matthew. I just need to cuddle up and go to sleep."

He went off to the bathroom for a leak and then to clean his teeth. He also took the opportunity for a swig of mouthwash. He didn't want to be breathing stale beer fumes over her all night.

"Where do you want me?" he asked innocently.

"Hmm," she pondered. "I want you any way that you can slip that gorgeous weapon in me and give me pleasure." She smiled. "But for sleeping, you can have the right side of the bed." She pulled his side of the quilt open, and he got in. They embraced and kissed before she turned over.

"G'night, Matthew, hold me please," she said. He kissed her shoulder, cuddled her to him in a spooning position and also said good night. She was so warm and cuddly, and his prick was nestled into her bum cheek. Inevitably, it started to twitch.

"He can go to sleep as well," she said dismissively.

Matt slept well, Julia not so much, but she just enjoyed being in bed with him. Julia eventually drifted off to sleep, wondering how all of this magical lust was going to end. Would her heart and mind come out of it unscathed?

At 9.15 am, they were rudely awakened by the landline phone ringing on the bedside unit on *his* side of the bed. Out of habit, Matt reached for the receiver. Before he could say anything, Julia, scrambling over him, grabbed it and hung up.

"That was close!" she said, breathing heavily, more through nervousness than exertion. Matt was still half asleep, and the reality of what might have been started to dawn on him. Julia was now sitting astride his lower stomach, just touching his morning stiffy. He forgot about the phone.

"What a vision to wake up to." And he started to stroke the outside of her smooth legs as his cock jerked against her backside. Within seconds, the phone rang again, and she put a finger to his lips.

"Hello? Oh, hi, Kirstie. All okay? Yes, sorry, I just woke up and pressed the wrong button." He could then hear his name being mentioned.

"Matthew? Well, I spoke to him last night to find out what time he was coming here. Yes, he's going to fix that radiator valve and a couple of other things. I have plans for him!" She chuckled at the fact that she wasn't lying. "I think he was just on his way out, meeting some of his friends in town."

He could hear a bit of a rant on the other end of the phone, and Julia looked at him, drew a finger across her throat and gave him a look, silently mouthing, "Bad boy!" She carried on talking to her daughter.

"Well, I don't know why…Oh Kirstie, cut him some slack, you're away, so why not let him have a beer with his buddies?" Matt silently mouthed back a thank you and waited for his wife's response. The voice on the other end of the phone started to calm down, and they talked about Dublin, shopping, plans for the day. Why use ten words when you can use a thousand? He thought.

He was still pinned to the bed, and he took advantage of the fact. He worked his way from the outsides of Julia's thighs to the insides, knowing how it turned her on. She grabbed one of his hands and admonished him with a little smack. He persisted, and she got off him to continue the chat while standing up.

The chat continued for a short time, ending when Kirstie asked her mum to get Matt to call her at around 6.00 pm, as she would be out shopping for the rest of the day. She said her goodbyes and hung up.

"You're in the doghouse. She says she phoned you a number of times last night and sent half a dozen texts." He already knew that and said as much. He got up and cuddled her with his stiffy squashed between them. "The thing is, I was in the pub and…well, you know what she's like. It would be the Spanish Inquisition with lots of dos and don'ts and, as you well know, she could talk for England."

He stroked Julia's back and bum and knew she was weakening to his side of the story. "Selfishly, I just wanted to think of you. Okay?" She gave him a squeeze and said, "Okay, just make sure you phone her tonight at six."

"Of course, anyway, how do you know she hasn't been playing away herself?" He laughed at the absurd notion of it.

"Are you accusing my daughter of having the morals of an alley cat on heat?" Julia said, as though she also thought it was ridiculous.

"Like mother, like daughter, perhaps?" He laughed again before Julia said she was off to do breakfast.

"Whoa," Matt said. "I'd like to give you a little morning prezzie." He smiled.

"Oh, would you now? What would that be, I wonder?" she mocked, reaching down and stroking his ever-hardening member and cupping his balls.

"Well, maybe you should turn around and bend over," was his suggestion.

Conscious of his possible hangover breath, he was determined not to lose the moment to have a quickie before he set his plans in motion later for the next sensual, sexual assault on her gorgeous body. She complied, also aware that morning breath can be a passion-killer and steadied herself on the edge of the bed. Matthew pulled down her thong and reached for the baby oil on the dresser. He deftly lubricated his cock and generously applied some to her sex.

Julia sighed her approval, and he positioned himself ready for penetration. There was no teasing, no subtlety, but he was careful not to force himself into her.

"Oh, that's good. Yes, nice and slow," she groaned. He pushed the head in and withdrew slightly before pushing in again, a little deeper this time, giving her natural lubrication time to work. She also backed up to him to help with the penetration, and eventually, he was balls deep. She squeezed her vaginal muscles to hold him there before saying, "Go on, fuck me, Matthew." He needed no further encouragement, and he reached around to randomly slide his oily fingers up and down her slit while shagging her with short, sharp strokes. Julia reached back between her legs and tickled his scrotum. Morning sex for him never lasted long, and within minutes, with one long, hard stab, he climaxed, pulling her back onto his pulsating dick as his cum jetted into her.

"Mmm, a nice little wake-up call. I can feel all of that lovely stuff shooting into me. Don't pull out. Stay in me as long as possible."

He was getting used to this little quirk of hers to prolong the intimacy to the very last second and she held on to his testicles to make sure he didn't pull away.

Eventually, he slipped out of her and, like a cork out of the bottle, a good portion of his 'gift' came with it and onto the carpet. He quickly got a towel from the bathroom and held it against her weeping pussy. Julia then took over the mopping-up operation while he went to brush his teeth.

Julia joined him and pulled him into the shower with her. They kissed under the deluge of hot water, and when finally breaking away, she said, "I've been dying for that kiss since I woke up."

They soaped and washed each other, delighting in the slipperiness of their hands and fingers all over their bodies, and they kissed again. As they held each other closely, his cock, yet again, was waking up.

"Gosh, he's frisky today. I can't think what has made him like this!" She tried to sound like an innocent schoolgirl and failed miserably. She was about to step away when Matt looked her in the eyes and said, "I have plans for you today!" He kissed her cheek.

"Oh?" She smiled, but did seem a little flustered. As she pulled away, she gave his "semi" a little tug, smacked his backside and then, regaining her composure, said, "I'll get the breakfast on, and after that, you can do those little jobs if you don't mind. Bacon and eggs okay?"

"Yes, please, but can you make sure the eggs aren't snotty? I cannot abide snotty eggs!"

Julia laughed. "You've just squirted a large amount of your snotty stuff in me, and you're moaning about snotty eggs!" Then she quickly dried herself and put on a towelling robe before disappearing downstairs.

After a while, Matt could smell the bacon cooking and quickly dressed. He'd go commando and slip on a tee-shirt and a fairly tight-fitting pair of soft cotton sweat shorts. The bulge was obvious, and he hoped it would keep Julia's "fire" burning until they were ready to play again.

A very filling breakfast and coffee finished, Julia undid her robe, fully exposing herself. She sat astride Matthew's lap and kissed him while he slipped his hands inside her garment and around her back.

"So, what do you have in mind?" she asked, stroking the obvious mounting excitement in his shorts.

"You're just going to have to wait and see," he teased. "Now let me get on with those jobs and we'll reconvene playtime when I'm done."

"Hmm," was her response, and standing up, she let the robe fall to the floor. She was naked. Leaning down and placing her hands on his thighs whispered, "You're sure I can't tempt you into postponing those jobs?"

She kissed his neck and shoulder, and, like Pavlov's dog, his penis responded, the outline of which was clearly visible.

"Are you like this with every workman that comes here, madam?" pretending to be a stranger. She played along.

"Only the ones I want to take upstairs and get them to fuck the living daylights out of me."

"Well, as interesting as the offer is, work must come first!" He tried to seem ambivalent to her advances.

"All work and no play makes Matthew a naughty tease." She nibbled his ear.

"You gorgeous, sexy woman, let me get the jobs out of the way and then I'm all yours. Or rather, you will be all mine!"

She tutted and stood up, reluctantly conceding that stuff had to be done.

"Okay then, you win, but just know that I'll be ready to pounce if I'm within a few yards of you. Tools are in the garage," and she picked up her robe and flounced off upstairs. He called after her,

"We'll need your scarves and cuffs!"

Julia turned, raised her eyebrows and smiled.

It was just after midday when he finished, and, after putting away the tools, he went off to find Julia. He heard her voice coming from her bedroom and quietly crept in. She was sitting on the edge of the bed, still in her towelling robe, evidently talking to Alan.

"Yes, of course, you have to see the job through. I just didn't think it would take so long. Let me know when you have a better idea of when you're coming home." Matt took off his T-shirt. "Yes, all okay here, Matthew's doing those jobs that need sorting," she said, trying to sound as normal as possible, even though Matthew was undoing the laces on his shorts and deliberately, slowly, dragging them down to stand directly in front of her, *buffo*, except for a smile and an ever-growing prick. She continued to talk to her husband, trying to sound as though she wasn't distracted by the stiffy waving about in front of her, demanding her attention.

"Um, this afternoon, not sure. I might give Karen a call and go shopping. What about you? Have you managed any downtime, or is it all work?" She was mesmerised by Matt stroking himself.

Alan trotted out some banal chat about the job and staying in at night for room service. In reality, he had attended an all-male session at a local sauna last night, and even while he was talking to Julia, he recalled how thrilling it was to be seduced and serviced by like-minded gay men covering his arse and face in cum.

All the time Alan was talking, Julia was looking at her son-in-law. Matt smiled and silently mouthed the words, "Fancy a fuck?" He got on the bed behind her and put his hands on her shoulders to slip her robe off. His hands then went to her exposed breasts, and he cupped and fondled them, bringing an audible gasp from Julia, which Alan evidently queried.

"Sorry, hiccups! Sorry, gotta go, yes, you too, bye." She ended the call, and as Matt continued to caress her boobs and nibble her shoulders, Julia said, "That was very naughty."

He asked her to come further onto the bed and lie back. She did so, lying between his thighs. Matt lowered himself to let her feed his penis into her mouth while she tickled his balls and anus with her fingers. Even these little variations made such a difference to playtime compared to the regimented positions with Kirstie.

"Mmm," she was ahead of the game at this moment. "A sixty-nine would be lovely, but let me go on top, please, and then I can control how much of your delicious cock goes in my mouth."

He did as instructed and, with his head towards the end of the bed, he waited for her to position herself on top. The next ten minutes were spent orally pleasuring one another with their hands and fingers caressing and fingering anything they could reach.

Eventually, Matthew stopped and said, "Right, it's time for your just desserts," and he smacked her backside gently to make her move.

"Oh, I was enjoying that," she said, giving his dick a final kiss before getting off him.

"Trust me, what I have in store for you will be even more enjoyable!" he added.

Matt instructed her to stand up and close her eyes. She did so without question. She could hear him fiddling about, and then she felt one of her soft scarves being tied over her eyes.

"This making me very horny!"

"Bloody hell, Julia, you are permanently horny. In fact, you only have two settings on the horny scale, on and off, and it's only off when you're asleep!" he said, picking up the handcuffs from the dresser and placing them on her wrists in front of her.

"Ah, but you don't know what I'm dreaming about, do you?" she replied.

Matt agreed, stepped away to get something from his bag, then carefully led her into the bathroom and further into the large walk-in shower enclosure.

She could then feel something being tied around the chain of the handcuffs before he asked her to hold her hands up above her head. He manoeuvred her towards the shower head, and then tied the soft chord around the shower head clamp that was screwed to the wall.

"There, you are at my mercy!" He threw in a mock maniacal laugh for good measure.

"I'll probably be back by six. Don't go away, will you?" She heard him leave the shower and head into the bedroom. On his return, he embraced and kissed her before turning her to face the shower wall and standing directly behind her. Suddenly, a jet of liquid hit her between her shoulder blades. She gasped in surprise at the coldness of it, but knew immediately by the smell that it was baby oil. Matt squirted more up and down her spine and then proceeded to use both hands to slowly massage it into her skin. Another squirt hit the small of her back and more on each cheek of her shapely buttocks. It was more than enough for massaging and was now just a lubricant for his hands and fingers to slip and slide all over her. Starting at her shoulders, he used both hands to smear the liquid over every inch. He gradually and sensuously worked his way lower to increase her anticipation of where he might dwell. Of course, she knew where he was going, and her breathing increased as he got closer.

Julia opened her legs to assist his access and sighed as fingers of both hands massaged and caressed her more intimately, concentrating on her anus and eventually the real target - her wanton pussy. She moved her lower body in sync with his manual stimulation and gasped, "Oh, that's so good."

Matt's hands were in sensual perpetual motion and didn't concentrate on just one part of her nether region. It was full-on stimulus all over her sex and arse. Gradually, his hands moved away on a reverse path from how they got there. Her whole cunt was tingling, and her juices mixed with the sexy oil. Matt reached around her now and squirted a lot more oil over her boobs and tummy, so much that it was dripping from her. He pressed against her to feel the slipperiness of her body rubbing erotically against his, and then, while his left hand worked its magic over her breasts and nipples, his right hand caressed her stomach and slowly moved lower to allow all of his fingers again to manipulate, fondle and stroke every part of her sex, this time from the front.

Matthew was persistent and all-encompassing with his attention to her genital area. His fingers easily slid into both orifices, and she knew she was totally unable to prevent his full access, not that she wanted to. Her sighs, whimpers and whispered expletives were telltale enough of her mounting ecstasy. He deliberately avoided her clitoris for the most part, just occasionally letting a finger or two stray across it to keep her at a peak without pulling the trigger.

He had seen the way women masturbate and, pushing three fingers together, he employed his digits in a steady circular motion specifically targeting her clit. With all the previous erotic provocation, her orgasm was swift and inevitable. She was leaning hard against the tiled wall, breathing heavily, and he just carried on. Still squirming and sliding against him, she climaxed again with loud gasps and incoherent mumbling. The only word he could make out was, "Fuck." He slowed his manual stimulation for a few seconds and then went for it again, frigging her button. Her moans were really loud now, and when she came for the third time, she actually squirted. He slowed and then held her in position. "More?" he softly enquired. "No, no, no. Stop, too much, stop," was her breathy response.

"I think you want more." He nibbled the back and side of her neck. Her breathing calmed, but she didn't reply.

Slowly, so very slowly, Matt's fingers went to work again. The brief interlude was enough to blunt the sensitivity but not bring her completely down from a blissful plateau.

"Oh fuck yes, yes, yes," Julia cried as yet another orgasmic wave swept over her and another vaginal ejaculation. If she hadn't been tethered to the shower clamp, she would have doubled up. Such was the intensity of it. He slowed his ministrations each time she came before speeding up again to give her more pleasure. It was like an orgasmic blur, and eventually it was all too much.

"*Stop*, Matthew, please stop, *stop*." He could tell in her voice that she was crying. He quickly untied her, removed the blindfold, and released the cuffs. He took her in his arms and held her firmly, as it seemed as though her legs were about to give way. She was crying, and he was unmistakably quite surprised and concerned.

"Oh God, Julia, I am so sorry. Are you okay? I wouldn't do anything to hurt you."

"Matthew, it was incredible, I don't know why I'm crying." And even though the tears were streaming down her face, she laughed. "It was beautiful. I have never cum so hard and so long before and as for…"

"Squirting?" he added.

"Yes." She couldn't bring herself to say it. "As for that, well, never before".

She put her arms around his neck, and they kissed passionately.

"Let's shower and go to bed. I just need you to hold me," she said.

As they washed, Julia insisted on bathing her own important little places, saying that she wasn't certain Matthew wouldn't start her off again. She paid particular attention to him, though and *his* important little places. She did not bring him off even though he was still aroused by her play, but he didn't press the matter. Within minutes, they were drying each other off and then curling up in bed, kissing and embracing and just enjoying being naked together.

Matthew looked intently at her. "I need to ask you something," he hesitated.

"Then go for it, Matthew." She was back to normal; her vulnerability that was plainly exposed in the shower was under control.

"Simply," he said, "Why me? You're a very sexy and attractive woman and could have anyone you want, so why choose me?" He was genuinely after the truth.

"Ah, I wondered if that would rear its ugly head. Why you? Well, apart from the fact that you're drop-dead gorgeous and have a lovely personality. Apart from the fact that we know each other and can avoid the awkwardness with strangers. Apart from the fact that I know you will be discrete because you have just as much to lose should we be discovered!" She paused. "So apart from all of that, I don't have a clue," adding one of her infectious giggles.

"Okay," was his response, and he was content that he wasn't just a cold-blooded shag to her.

"Let me turn the question on you, then," she was just as intrigued.

"Easy, you're the hottest, sexiest, funniest woman I have ever known. You know what you want, and you go and get it, even if you did blackmail me!" He kissed her.

"I didn't blackmail you; you are as guilty as I am for making this happen. It takes two to tangle, you know. I'll bet you're still wondering how I found out about your little seaside shenanigans?" Julia said, staring at him and smiling.

"Yes, I am." Matt still couldn't fathom it.

"I might tell you one day, now, cuddle me and let's have a little nap. My body and especially my womanly parts are still tingling. I need to calm down. I will deal with you and 'him' in due course," she said, giving his balls and todger a quick squeeze.

It was late afternoon when Julia woke a few seconds before he did. He pulled her towards him and kissed her as she reached and held his manhood to ready it for her attention.

"Now I think I owe you after your exertions in the shower," she said, slowly stroking him.

"Lover, you don't owe me anything. I adore giving you pleasure," he replied. "And I, you," was her response. "Did you use all of the baby oil?" she asked.

"No, there's still some left, but I brought an extra bottle just in case."

"Okay, my lad, turn over and get yourself on all fours," she commanded.

"Yes, Miss." He was intrigued as to what she had planned now.

She got up and went to the shower to pick up the bottle with the remainder of the oil. She brought back a bath towel and asked Matthew to spread it out on the bed under him. In an afternoon of mutual sexual exploration, he was thrilled when Julia actually rimmed him before massaging his prostate to induce an elongated shuddering climax. They were both now utterly drained.

"Fuck, that was incredible..." He was amazed at how blissful it was.

They kissed, and she held him to her.

"Thank you. If you liked that, we can do it again sometime. It's been a memorable day. Let's order a takeaway, have a few drinks and enjoy a cuddle on the sofa, listening to some music. Now you need to phone my daughter!"

The Chinese meal was delivered by 7.30 pm and eaten at the dining table, romantically lit with candles. Beer for him, wine for her and a great sense of calm, with some lovely slushy music in the background.

"So, what did Kirstie have to say?" she asked.

"Bad news," he said solemnly. "The pair of them are coming home tomorrow afternoon. Sarah has had food poisoning since yesterday, and they're calling the trip off early." He was extremely disappointed.

"Is Kirstie okay?" Julia was understandably concerned.

"She said she was, but she did sound a bit distracted."

"Maybe she's just disappointed," Julia ventured.

"Well, oddly, she sounded more excited and in a bit of a rush." He looked quite confused.

Julia stared at him, "Perhaps she can't wait to get home to you and all of your ecstatic lovemaking!" she smiled. He actually blushed, probably more through guilt.

"I know I shouldn't pry, but have you ever done the shower scenario with her?"

"No, she's still a bit coy about playtime outside of the bedroom, and kinky stuff is not for her, unfortunately," he said. If he only knew half of what was happening in Dublin.

"So, this is our last night?" Julia said, looking a bit down. "Hmm, a shame. I had a master plan for tomorrow," she chuckled.

"Oh?" he perked up. She asked him to come and cuddle on the sofa, "It can wait. I'm actually quite tired and need you in my bed to sleep."

They both slept soundly. In the morning, he pulled her towards him, dragged the quilt over them, and they embraced but didn't advance to full intercourse. They were both quiet over breakfast, and as he got up to get his stuff together, she met him halfway across the floor and hugged him.

"We've been very naughty, and I really don't know what might happen in the future, but I just want to say thank you for…well, making me feel alive again!"

Matthew kissed her and desperately wanted to tell her that he had fallen in love with her, but at the last moment, bottled it. It had been such an exciting weekend, and if his affection wasn't shared or, worse, rejected, it would be a humiliating disappointment for him. Unbeknownst to him, Julia felt exactly the same and, looking into his eyes, knew what he was thinking.

"Whatever your thoughts, just know that I have loved every minute we have been together." He gave her another squeeze, kissed her quickly on the lips, then grabbed his stuff and left.

Julia made herself a coffee and reflected on how exciting it had all been. She felt like a teenager discovering sex all those years ago, but with her maturity, she now understood how to really let go and enjoy it. She felt guilty about it being her daughter's hubby, but on the highway of remorse, there was no turning back.

31

Erotica

September 2014

Kirstie woke early with thoughts of the night before, soberly, she felt massively guilty about her behaviour. How had the man sleeping next to her so skilfully seduced her into what she considered to be complete and utter debauchery, and the total betrayal of her marriage vows. She was shocked at herself and then also recalled how the two men made her feel, which could only be determined as sexual self-esteem. She would not be a shrinking violet in the bedroom again.

She then thought about Matthew - why hadn't he responded to her calls and messages. Perhaps if he had, she wouldn't have been so vulnerable to seduction. Of course, Kirstie knew she was kidding herself. She was hugely flattered by their desire for her, and she indulged herself like an unattended child in a sweet shop. Kirstie looked at Patrick and, reaching over to stroke his back, snuggled close to him before dozing off again.

Just after nine, she woke with a start. She sat up in bed and, fumbling with her phone, checked to see if there were any calls or messages. There was one at around midnight from Matthew saying, *"G'night LY xx"*, and that was it. She was annoyed at his apparent ambivalence to her absence, but rather than have a row with him while her lover was within touching distance, she texted him again. No response, this infuriated her even more. She phoned her mum on her mobile, no luck as it was switched off. She tried her mother's landline. After a few rings, it was answered and then suddenly hung up. This was all a bit weird. She phoned again.

In the leafy glades of a Hampshire suburb, her mother answered the phone.

"Hello? Oh, hi, Kirstie. All okay? Yes, sorry, I just woke up and pressed the wrong button."

Her mother's own lover (Matthew) could hear his name being mentioned.

"Matthew? Well, I spoke to him last night to find out what time he was coming here. Yes, he's going to fix that radiator valve and a couple of other things. I have plans for him!"

Kirstie asked about his whereabouts. Her mother responded that he had mentioned he was going out with his mates.

"I've phoned him a number of times and texted him, but got nothing. It's like I'm out of sight, out of mind as far as he's concerned," Kirstie added.

"Well, I don't know why…Oh Kirstie, cut him some slack, you're away, so why not let him have a beer with his buddies?" Julia offered in support for her son-in-law.

"Well, I'm not happy with him," Kirstie said, and her mother skilfully steered the conversation around to Dublin and how she was enjoying herself.

Guiltily, Kirstie kept the dialogue brief or as brief as she thought it was and yet, to most men, any conversation that lasted more than a minute was at least forty seconds too long. Thank heaven for 'WhatsApp' or just a plain old text. The chat continued for a short time, and then Kirstie asked her mum to get Matt to call her at around 6.00 pm, as she would be out shopping for the rest of the day. She said her goodbyes and hung up.

Patrick had now woken up, and so had his penis.

"Everything tickety-boo in the family nest?" he asked as he stretched and sat up slightly.

Kirstie explained that she hadn't been able to contact her husband at all since he dropped her off at Heathrow and responded with, "The sod was out with his mates last night."

Patrick replied, "Don't be too hard on him, my dear. You're away, letting off steam, and so should he. Now, you will observe that I also need to let off steam." And with that, he put his hand around the back of Kirstie's head and gently but firmly pushed it down towards his erection. She didn't resist or hesitate to hold it and direct it into her mouth.

"Mmm, yes, suck on my manhood, you little English slut, and I just might reward you with a huge mouthful of my semen."

Kirstie was growing into and enjoying the role of being subordinate to this mature Celtic Dom. While she was attending to Patrick's cock, unbeknownst to her, hundreds of miles away, her very own husband was penetrating the very birth canal that she came from. Eventually, Kirstie expertly triggered the Irishman to squirt a copious amount of spunk into her mouth, so much so that she nearly gagged on it, and she loved it!

"I think next time I should decorate your womb with it and send you home with an Irish baby!" Patrick laughed, Kirstie joined in the scenario.

"I may just about get away with that, but if it was Michael's, it may take a bit of explaining."

"I'll say!" They laughed again, but Kirstie then had more pangs of guilt. Coincidentally, at that very moment, her husband wasn't having any such misgivings as he unloaded his fertile baby paste into her mother.

There was a knock on the door, followed by a call of "room service" from the maid.

Hunger got the better of them, and a full Irish breakfast from the hot plates trolley stirred them into action. They both donned towelling robes and set about the enticing repast. It was leisurely, if a little awkward. The evening's conversation under the influence of alcohol was so much easier. In any case, Patrick explained that he had some business to attend to during the rest of the day but would love to take her to dinner later. He understood if she had other plans. Kirstie was

thoroughly intrigued by him and said, "Actually, I'd love to, but…"
She hesitated. "I think it really depends on how Sarah is." She felt quite
guilty that she had hugely neglected her friend.

"Of course, well, the offer is there. Here's my card. Just text me."

She smiled, then made her excuses and went off to the bathroom
to don her rather crumpled black dress and heels. Her underwear went
in the bin, and she was too embarrassed to ask for her bra back. She
then kissed his cheek, squeezed his hand and, with a "Thank you," she
gathered her handbag and departed.

Getting back to her room, she checked her phone again. One
missed call and a text, both from Sarah.

The text read: "*Hey Kay, not sure where you are, but hope you had a good
evening. Had a rough night and thoroughly drained now. Sorry to be a cow, but I
really need to go home and have changed the flights. Earliest I could get for us is
tomorrow at three, taxi picks us up at midday. I won't be out tonight. Sorry I'm
just washed out xx*"

Kirstie texted back, "*Really sorry to hear that…*" and, remembering
Patrick's offer, continued with, "*Can I get you a doctor?*" There was no
immediate reply, and she took the opportunity to have a long, hot bath
and a power nap. When she finished, she donned the complimentary
bathrobe and checked her phone. There was a reply from Sarah.
"*Thanks Kay, but I just need to rest. How was your evening? Xx*"

Kirstie's response was to say that she had a quiet night in the bar
and then bed, which, in a court of law, would probably be held up as
true. She amused herself by thinking she could add – *and I was fucked
senseless by two donkey-dicked guys, swallowed a gallon of sperm and I have turned
into a raving nymphomaniac!!*

There was a knock at the door. Kirstie got up and answered it. She
was handed a gift-wrapped box, and the young man said, "Hello, my
name is Liam, this is from Mr Malone, with his compliments."

"Malone?" she questioned before realising it was Patrick. She thanked the young man, and he left. On the box was a note from Patrick.

"Hi Kirstie, what an incredible evening. I can categorically state that you are well on the path to true hedonism. I hope that this small gift will go some way to replace some items of clothing that may not be fit for purpose after last night's revelries. The offer of dinner still holds if you're available – 7.30pm in The Nook Restaurant adjacent to the bar. Yours in lust, Patrick xx"

She brought the box into the room, and on opening it, she found some very expensive lingerie. There was a silk bustier with attached suspenders, knickers similar to the ones that were casualties of her evening, and nylon stockings, all in black. She laughed at herself for being totally charmed by this attractive Irishman and thought about refusing the gift. However, as she was minus last night's underwear, effectively through his actions, she should accept them. Not only were they beautiful, but they were very, very sexy. She texted him:

"Hi Patrick, thank you for the beautiful gift and although it wasn't at all necessary, it is very much appreciated. It would appear that due to circumstances beyond my control I will be leaving with my friend tomorrow, but I am free this evening and would very much like to accept your offer of dinner. Thanks again Kxxx"

The response was immediate, *"Excellent news, see you later Px"*

Kirstie spent the afternoon wandering around shops near the hotel and bought a few items, mainly clothing, she always avoided the souvenir tat shops. She had a coffee and people watched and thought about her incredible Friday evening. Something in her just clicked when Patrick spoke of wasted potential, and she pondered on his assessment of the accepted 'drudge' of life, love and monogamy. Nevertheless, could she really lead a double life?

The short-term answer was yes, and her thoughts then turned to the evening ahead. What revelations lie in store? Maybe a visit to the licentious basement area? She resolved to let Patrick decide on the next stage of her "education". After all, he was the experienced master of all of this.

She got back to her room at about 5.30 pm and had another soak in the bath. Matthew phoned her at 6.00 pm, so he had plainly got the message from her mother. He explained about his lack of availability, and Kirstie replied that it was ok, but didn't expand on that. She felt guilty that she was enjoying all sorts of lascivious activities with two complete strangers while he was just out with his mates, having an innocent beer or two. She explained that she would be home early tomorrow afternoon because of Sarah's illness, and could he pick her and Sarah up from the airport.

Oddly, he sounded a little disappointed and when she queried that with him, he just said he was disappointed for her, especially as the weekend had been a bit dull. Kirstie felt both guilt and elation at her anything but dull weekend. They finished the call with a mutual "*Love You*", and she stared at her wedding finger, which was still ringless. Kirstie told herself that her safe married life was still hundreds of miles away in Hampshire, and she hadn't realised how much she needed this escape to feel free again.

She got out of the bath, dried herself off and looked at herself in the full-length mirror, maybe Patrick was right and not just spinning a line, she could almost accept that she was gorgeous, but would need to make sure she stayed in shape. Kirstie tried on the new lingerie and again stood in front of the mirror. It all fitted perfectly. She really began to understand how important the visual aspect was to men and resolved to buy more naughty underwear to maintain Matthew's interest. She actually got quite a buzz herself, and if she turned men on, then she would be the beneficiary of their heightened excitement.

Kirstie was getting pushed for time, but all she needed was to choose a dress. She had a simple, elegant red number, sleeveless, short and with a loose black belt which accentuated her hips and made the skirt look shorter. Her black high heels were the order of the evening. Time was moving on now, and she quickly got her bag and room key.

As the lift descended, she noticed there was no basement level on the panel – very curious. Ground floor doors opened, and she let the others go first before taking a deep breath to try to calm her nerves.

The Maître D' was very welcoming and asked if she had a reservation. She explained that she was dining with Mr Malone.

"Of course, madam, please come this way," he said. Hmm, Patrick seems to make me cum anyway he likes, she thought. Kirstie was led to a discreet corner of the restaurant, where Patrick was already seated. He stood, took her hand and kissed her on the cheek before saying how beautiful she looked. He made a point of rubbing her wedding finger and smiling the smile that said, "You're still mine." She thought how handsome he was, a man easily old enough to be her father but with the poise of someone much younger and a body to match. He was dressed in an expensive blue suit and a stylish white shirt, undone at the neck, revealing a delicate gold chain which she hadn't noticed last night.

"Welcome to my nook within the Nook," he said.

"I just want to say thank you again for the lovely gift," she added.

"Think nothing of it, my dear, but I do hope to be given a fashion show later, just to make sure it all fits, of course." He smiled that smile again, and she was entranced by his blue eyes.

He asked her about her personal relationship with Matthew and was not surprised to hear that it was "love's young dream" as they were only fourteen months into their marriage. She was intrigued to hear about some of his (Patrick) early relationships when he was a younger man and got to understand how he was devoted to this lifestyle of pleasure-seeking. He never went into too much detail, but apparently, a chance meeting with a slightly older couple, coincidentally from "her neck of the woods", set him on his chosen path. He first came to Dublin from Limerick as a very young man in the late sixties and, meeting them, developed his appetite for sexual activity with both men and women as well as all manner of kinky fun. He was quick to add that none of it involved children, animals or bodily functions to do with "unwanted excess material", as he put it.

Kirstie thought he was a little patronising when he said that he could see why a lot of people settle for the daily routine of marriage because it's just a comfort zone. She tried to defend the sense of responsibility that marriage brings, especially when kids come along, as a rewarding achievement, even if it was difficult on occasions. He agreed but countered with, "How many people in marriages would gladly have an escape on a regular basis? To go away and fuck their brains out with someone different, with no strings attached and no chance of any consequences?"

He had a point. After all, in the relatively short time that she had been together with Matthew, she had already taken the first opportunity to come her way. Patrick went on to explain that his experiences with that couple and others made him realise that there were many people who would pay very good money to visit a safe environment where like-minded pleasure seekers could congregate and indulge their various sexual fantasies. Thus, the hotel and its basement were the perfect venue. She had to agree again and asked if she would be allowed to go there tonight.

He looked her in the eyes and firmly said no.

"My dear, you have come a very long way in such a short space of time, and I have no doubt that you will reach your full swinging potential, but at this moment, you're not ready for the shameless debauchery of the bullring." He was quite forceful in his refusal.

Kirstie was very disappointed but trusted his judgement. Patrick could see that she was rather crestfallen.

"My lovely Kirstie, I think we should continue this elsewhere, don't you? I will enlighten you about the basement later, but first I need to kiss you 'til my lips fray at the edges." He smiled.

"Yes, sir," she smiled as well. "Will anyone be joining us tonight, sir?"

"No, it's just us tonight," and then Patrick called the Maître D' to the table.

"I'll sign this off in the morning, Gerry, but compliments to the guys and girls in the kitchen, it was all excellent," Patrick said to Gerald's obvious delight.

"I shall convey your compliments, sir. Thank you," Gerald said in quite a subservient manner.

"Yes, thank you," Kirstie added.

"Shall we, my dear?" Patrick said, standing up and holding her hand to assist as she also stood. He guided her through a different exit and led her to a locked door.

"I think we'll be very comfortable in here," he said, unlocking it. She was both excited and nervous as the door opened to a darkened room. He flicked one of the switches on the wall, and a number of wall lights dimly lit the space. He closed and locked the door.

"This is my private dungeon," he said with a certain amount of pride. "Don't worry, though, there's never been one drop of blood spilt in here. All the equipment is purely for pleasure, whether the recipient likes it or not!" Then he laughed.

She looked around the room, which was the size of a very large hotel bedroom. It was tastefully decorated and furnished, unlike any dungeon you would imagine, apart from the large X-frame with requisite manacles on the left-hand wall. There were various mirrors on the walls and the ceiling, and a super king-sized double bed, which also had some scarves tied to the headboard. On the far wall was a leather sofa, and near that, in one corner, there was a sling suspended from the ceiling. Opposite to that, on the floor, sat a saddle-like contraption with a penis-shaped pink dildo protruding from the middle and on a small table next to it, other dildos of various sizes. Patrick saw her looking at it and explained that it was called a Sybian, and she would be welcome to partake of the ecstasy that it could impart later, if she chose.

He suggested another glass of champagne from the bottle he had just opened, while she surveyed the room, and if she needed the toilet, there was an en-suite bathroom through a door on the left of the bed.

"Take your dress off," he commanded. She did so, and he took it from her and hung it over a chair.

"You look amazing, I'm glad it all fits, is it comfortable?" Patrick said, admiring her new lingerie.

"Yes, sir, and it makes me feel very sexy," she said, smoothing out the bustier and checking the suspenders. Patrick stood behind her and ran his hands up and down her body while kissing the back of her neck. He pulled down the top of the garment to let her beautiful breasts spill into his hands, her nipples were already erect, and she just adored his touch.

Patrick then moved away to sit down, he removed his shoes and socks and then stood up to strip off completely. He then gently pushed her to her knees, where she was expected to take over.

"You may take it in your mouth and make it hard," he ordered.

She hesitated but said nothing.

"Madam," his tone was quite insistent, expecting subservience."

"Patrick," she said as she stood up to look him in the eyes. Then, holding his cock firmly in her right hand told him that sometimes women do need to take the initiative. She paused and squeezed his hardening shaft and balls to emphasise the point. At that instant, she recalled her boss Jenny saying, *"when you have them by the balls, their hearts and minds will quickly follow!"*

She continued, "You asked the question last night, have I ever taken the initiative? Half-heartedly, I have with my husband, but tonight, I'm in charge and if that doesn't suit you, then fine. I'm sure there would be plenty of takers in your basement. Your call!" she added while stroking his fully erect cock and squeezing his balls quite hard. He groaned a little and said, "You appear to have the upper hand. What do you have in mind?"

"Last night was fantastic. It was the best sex I ever had. It was so good that in parts, I'm sure I was having an out-of-body experience." She continued to stroke his cock. "Your seduction technique worked like a dream, and it helps, of course, that you are a very attractive man. I questioned myself on how I succumbed so easily, and although I understand your hedonistic ideals, I've also had time to reflect on my attitude towards my relationship with my husband." The stroking became a little more urgent.

"Have… you… reached a conclusion?" He asked, trying to concentrate on two things at once and finding it very difficult.

"Yes, but I want your undivided attention, so I think we'll see *your* conclusion first." She wanked him harder and faster while tickling his balls. She had seen how he and Michael brought themselves to orgasm last night by doing it fast, and sure enough, the telling signs of quickened breathing and tensing muscles signalled his impending climax. Kirstie watched his face as his eyes closed. He held his breath, and his lips tightened. She lifted his member so that it was pointing upwards, and as his body jerked, the first few spurts of cum hit her exposed breasts. Another couple just flew into the air, and a few more dribbled over her fingers.

She laughed, "You boys, you're such mucky pups!" She let go and made a big show of licking her fingers and scooping up the excess from her boobs and taking that in her mouth as well.

His breathing calmed a little, and then she added, "Now, you promised to decorate my womb and pussy, so I'm going to hold you to that."

Patrick held her in his arms and kissed her. *Fuck*, she thought, *how can he have such an effect just by kissing?* And she asked him the exact question.

"I read somewhere that kissing is the main catalyst to sex. The better the kiss, the better the sex. I just appear to be quite good at it," he said with no false modesty and then went on to say, "Anyway, you've seen to my conclusion with quite a knowledgeable dexterity, so you have undoubtedly been paying attention. What conclusion did you reach with regard to hedonism versus the matrimonial drudge?"

"Let's go to bed. I want to be naked and cuddled up with you in those nice silk sheets while I give you my version of the meaning of life"

Patrick slid into bed with her and, in a tangled embrace of arms and legs, kissed her passionately, bringing that same pussy tingle.

"So, in your mid-twenties, you have pondered the meaning of life and come to what conclusion?" he asked, kissing her again, knowing how distracting it was for her.

"I can only tell you how the two aspects of sex and love affect me and my attitude going forward," she said in a mature, matter-of-fact sort of way.

"But I have a question for you first," she asked.

"Oh?"

"Have you ever really fallen in love with someone, not just for sex?"

"Yes," was his slightly hesitant answer.

"How many times?" She asked.

"Two, and they ended very badly for reasons I don't want to share, but the answer is that yes, I know what all-encompassing love is." He seemed rather melancholy.

"Okay, my dilemma is that I love my husband very much, and part of me does want the comfort zone secure marriage - good job, lovely house, nice car, loyal hubby, and eventually 2.4 children, a dog named Rex, a cat called Tiddles, and nice holidays in the sun. But now that you've shown me the dark side of carnal pleasure. I want to be able to take the rings off my finger and the one through my nose and just enjoy fucking and being fucked by men and keep those two avenues of life separate." She paused but looked slightly perplexed.

"Go on," he said, waiting for her verdict on life.

"I have come to the conclusion that if I am very careful…"

"Yes?"

"I can have *both*. I have recently got a new job, which, after a few months of training, I will be required to travel to some of our offices around the UK and here to Ireland." Patrick went to speak, but she put a finger to his lips while she continued, "Travelling will afford me the opportunity to live a double life because…it was so damned exciting. I know now that I cannot live just to go to bed with one man for the rest of my life, and I honestly believe that no two people can ever stay monogamous without getting bored to tears." Kirstie felt quite shocked at her own revelation. Patrick thought for a while and then responded.

"I have always thought that youth is wasted on the young, but then age is a high price to pay for experience. You, my dear, seem to have the capacity to compartmentalise areas of your life…at least in theory. How that works in practice will take much micro-management, but I'm sure you are very capable. Welcome to the dark side," Patrick said, trying not to sound patronising. He kissed her, and she could feel something prodding her leg.

"It would appear that you have worked your magic again," Patrick said, lifting up the covers in pretend surprise at his stiffening member.

"Mmm, yes, and may the force be with you."

"And now I want you to make love to me, I mean, really make love to me, Patrick," and she stared into his eyes before indulging in that rare mutual physical and cerebral connection.

Their intercourse was passionate and tender, with much kissing, caressing and penetration in several different positions. It was a world away from home. The one which tipped her over the edge to climax was doggie-style with long, deep thrusts and a small vibrating butt plug in her anus. For *his* finish, they relied on the trusty missionary position with her legs clamped around his backside, and at the point of his ejaculation, he firmly grabbed the cheeks of her buttocks and groaned loudly. Breathing heavily, they held each other for a long time before he spoke.

"There, I've kept my promise to decorate–" then Kirstie cut him short with, "Don't spoil a beautiful moment!" And they both chuckled.

"I've got something to show you," he said as he rolled over and sat up.

"I think I've seen all of it," Kirstie said, also sitting up. "But you could tell me about that tattoo on your arm. I never really paid it any mind last night."

"What, this?" he said, turning his left arm outwards to display a picture of a sprig of shamrock with some Gaelic words underneath.

"What does it say?" she asked as she stared at the words. He spoke it out loud in Gaelic perfectly without reading it.

Kirstie smiled and said, "Sorry, I have no idea what that means!"

He laughed and re-told his well-rehearsed translation and explanation.

"Basically, it's about standing up to you, nasty British people invading our homeland." He laughed again. "Walter and Oliver should have stayed home!" he added.

"Who are they?" she asked blankly. He tutted and grinned. "Nasty, bullying, puritanical Proddys! You must have heard of Walter Raleigh and Oliver Cromwell?" He seemed surprised that she wasn't so well informed about prominent figures in British history.

"Oh, them, did they upset the Irish, then?" she asked naively. Patrick smiled and shook his head.

"How long have you got?" he chuckled. "They were very bad men," he said, putting it rather succinctly.

Kirstie smiled back and said, "Perhaps I've gone some way to furthering English/Irish relations then?"

Patrick nodded before saying, "Perhaps." Then went on to explain the requirement for two national anthems.

"I see." Kirstie felt sufficiently informed, along with her own understanding of a difficult period of Irish history.

"Dad reckoned that the Catholics in the North might…er, procreate their way to a united Ireland if there was a referendum at some point," she ventured. Patrick smiled and agreed that it was quite plausible.

"Shag to Unite!" he said. "Certainly, better than bombs and bullets. I am not a political animal, but Irish history would have been better served had the British stayed away. We have benefited from a development point of view, but at what cost? When a nation is controlled by a foreign power that allows a million people to die through a famine and slaughters hundreds more because they resist foreign rule, you'll understand the hostility."

He allowed a short period of silence before adding, "Both countries have moved on, and that's how it should be, but the British Government at the time should have done much, much more. If they had, this innate vilification of the Brits would not be so profound.

Kirstie thought about it and made a mental note to research some significant periods in Ireland's past. Patrick was unemotional, given the presentation of what every Irish person was taught in schools and yet was conveniently ignored in the United Kingdom's education system. There was a pregnant pause before Patrick gave her a hug.

"Now, I was going to show you this," he smiled, and grabbed a TV remote by the bed. He pressed a button, and the large mirror on the wall in front of them suddenly sprang into life as a TV.

"Oh, that's impressive," she said, enthralled by the technology.

He flicked through a few menus until he got to one that said CCTV. Up popped a list of areas in the hotel, such as corridors, reception, lifts, restaurants, bars, lobbies and… the basement. He selected that final option, and Kirstie was fascinated as the whole screen showed each of the areas of play within that underground floor. Patrick gave her the remote and explained that if she selected a room and then pressed the okay button, it would zoom in to the full screen. Each screen was titled so that the viewer would know which area they were looking at. Kirstie was immediately intrigued by the "Men Only" room, which she selected for closer perusal. Patrick poured some more champagne for them both.

"You evidently like cocks!" Patrick laughed as the screen became a window to a number of men engaged in various homosexual activities, from mutual masturbation to oral to full-on sodomy. Patrick went on to explain that there was always a plentiful supply of lube and condoms in every room, clients could please themselves whether they used them or not. Kirstie asked why everyone had wristbands with different colours.

"It's to identify a person's sexual orientation. So, if they're a gay man or woman, they would have a pink wristband, strictly straight - blue, and bisexual - yellow. It doesn't restrict them from anywhere but helps to prevent any unwanted attention."

He pointed out the zoom function on the remote while she watched one man standing over another who was kneeling, wearing a black mask with an opening only for his mouth. She zoomed in just in time to see him receive a few squirts of spunk over the mask and on his body.

"Mucky pups!" Kirstie said again, to Patrick's amusement. She exited that room and had a brief excursion to the sauna to see a number of people just relaxing in the whirlpool hot tub, conversing, drinking, kissing and fondling.

"The sauna and hot tub room is where a lot of foreplay starts," Patrick said, and she moved on to the dungeon where a guy, who was blindfolded, was manacled to a large wooden X-frame similar to the one in this bedroom. There were two big, beautiful women dressed in leather Basques and knee-length black leather boots, both holding small whips that looked like cat-o'-nine-tails. The guy was helpless as they randomly flogged his torso, legs and genitals. Patrick said that she could use the volume control to hear what was being said. She was quite perplexed watching the physical and verbal abuse.

Kirstie just shook her head and said, "Weird!"

"Not weird," Patrick corrected her. "It's just his particular kink - each to their own." Then he laughed.

More rooms, more people and more action. Scantily clad men and women wandering about, she was amused to see one woman wearing a mask with cat ears and also what appeared to be a furry tail sticking out from her backside. There were two glory hole rooms where guys could stick their dicks through a hole according to their gender choice for oral satisfaction. There were smaller, private rooms for couples, threesomes or moresomes.

Kirstie then selected the Viewing Gallery, where, from one camera angle outside of a room, showed people watching through a one-way mirror. Inside the room, six guys were standing around a shapely, dusky young woman with short dark hair. She was sitting cowgirl style, riding a man who was fondling her tits. She was wanking two others and taking another in her mouth while others waited their turn. All very interesting, and selected it for a better look. Her heart began to beat a little faster.

It couldn't be…could it? Kirstie zoomed in, but because of the guys circling the young woman, it was difficult to see her face. At one point, she caught a glimpse of the girl's pierced nipples, but Kirstie couldn't recall Sarah ever telling her about having her nipples pierced, and anyway, her friend surely wouldn't be fit enough to participate in this energetic debauchery. One thing that was clear was that Michael was the guy being ridden by this greedy girl.

"Bukkake!" Patrick said.

"Sorry… what?" Kirstie was still engrossed in the scene and wasn't really listening.

"Bukkake, it's a Japanese word meaning 'to splash', that's what all those guys are doing. They are going to cover her with a deluge of jizz," he explained.

"Well, I like cum, but I'm not sure I'd want to be smothered in it," she said, still engrossed as two men climaxed in quick succession, aiming at the girl's face, still partially obscured by other bodies tossing themselves off.

Patrick laughed. "It's an acquired taste, if you'll pardon the pun, and yes, that is Michael on the floor. He's always a popular guy with both men and women. I have to say that girl seems awfully familiar. She reminds me of someone that used to visit here occasionally, not so long back."

"It would appear that they're all coming to the boil," she said as another couple of guys behind the girl shot their juice over her back and hair.

"She's going to be like a bar of soap when they're finished," Kirstie said, chuckling.

She convinced herself that while the girl on the screen was getting plastered with jizz, it couldn't be Sarah. Sarah had long, dark hair. This girl's was fashionably short and spiky, and Sarah didn't have pierced nipples. Anyway, as liberated as Sarah was, even she wouldn't indulge in this sexual humiliation. Kirstie had seen enough and switched it off.

"That is some den of iniquity!" She was quite taken aback.

"It certainly is and participants have to be totally uninhibited with all guns blazing, really," Patrick said, moving over to her to kiss her and then continuing, "Maybe next time you're here?"

"Maybe," she welcomed his kiss and embrace and then said, "Patrick, I've enjoyed every minute I have spent with you and as much as I'd like to sleep with you again, I really must go to my own bed - it's a fairly early start tomorrow."

He could see that her mind was made up.

"Of course, I too, have thoroughly enjoyed your company. Have a safe journey home, and please keep in touch, especially if you're returning to the Emerald Isle," he smiled his entrancing smile. She gathered her clothes and handbag and went to the bathroom to dress. She could still feel his semen seeping from her as she dabbed herself to mop up the excess. She blew him a kiss when she got to the bedroom door, and he called out, "Follow the signs to reception and don't forget to put your rings back on!"

The following morning, she rose early, showered, and dressed. She packed and went to meet Sarah for breakfast.

"Wow," Kirstie said, "I love the new hairstyle!" And pennies dropped like a fruit machine jackpot. Sarah explained that on Friday and Saturday morning, she just felt awful, but after a long sleep and a hot bath, she began to recover in the afternoon. She went for a walk to get some fresh air and happened across a hairdressing salon. Fortunately, and on the spur of the moment, they had some availability. She then said that she'd been thinking about changing her hair for a while and just went for the more fashionable, shorter style.

"What did you do last night? Saz, if you were feeling better, we could have gone out together." Kirstie asked.

"I still felt tired, and I thought you would have already made plans, so I had a bar supper and a drink, and that was it for me." Sarah was not entirely convincing.

The girls enjoyed a leisurely coffee to finish breakfast, and Kirstie nonchalantly asked Sarah when she'd had her nipples pierced.

Off guard, Sarah squeezed her own boobs. "A couple of weeks ago, it was my recognition of the last days of freedom before I had a rethink," she laughed, referring to the postponement and then realised what she'd said.

"But how do you know? Only Dan, me and Vlad the Impaler, who did the deed, know about it."

Kirstie smiled as if to say, "Gotcha", and just tapped her nose. She finished her coffee quickly to let Sarah stew on it and left, saying, "See you in reception."

As she walked away, she could picture Sarah being drizzled in lots of sticky semen and thought, "She's a mucky pup as well!"

Kirstie arrived at reception and asked to settle her bill. The receptionist checked her room number and just handed her an envelope, saying that it had all been settled, and she thanked Kirstie before wishing her a safe trip home. Kirstie was extremely surprised and managed to say, "But…" before the receptionist interrupted with a lovely smile and just said, "Everything is settled. I believe the explanation is in the letter there." She smiled again and then excused herself as another customer came to the desk. Walking away to wait in the lounge, she opened the envelope. The letter read:

Dear Kirstie,

I hope you don't mind that I've settled your account with us as a small gesture of friendship and as partners in hedonistic "crime". Regrettably, I can't be there to say goodbye. I don't do them very well and I wouldn't want to be the cause of awkward questions should your friend be there.

Thank you again for our sexy time together. I hope you had as much fun as I did. I also hope that should you ever return alone to Dublin, stay here and we can revisit our bedroom skirmishing. You never did try the Sybian!

With much affection,

Patrick

PS - I've enclosed the coin that set you on your new chosen path…always choose heads xx

Kirstie tipped the envelope downwards and caught the double-headed coin in her hand.

PART 3

THE ROAD TO HELL

32

I Would Give Everything
I Own

October 2014

Two days after the Dublin Hen Weekend, Kirstie arrived home from work at the usual time. She was still on a high from the sexually liberating weekend away, although she was sure to keep it low-key whenever the subject was mentioned in any subsequent conversation. What goes on tour stays on tour is the time-honoured mantra, and maybe telling Matt that, with Sarah being ill, it all ended up being a bit of a chore. Truthfully, she initially welcomed the distraction and re-engagement of the single life just for a few days. *"We all need a little break from the humdrum haul,"* she told herself. The humdrum haul was nice, secure and comfortable. It was the perfect description, *but* the opportunity arose for something more risqué. She gambled and hit the jackpot in sexual awakening.

Matt was already home, which was not normal, but she then thought this might be an opportunity to play. The thoughts of the hen weekend had made her a little frisky, and with her newfound confidence, she could enliven the physical aspect of their marriage. He had a difficult project at work, which caused a few late nights and inevitable tiredness more through stress than physical exertion. Whatever the reason, the result was, apart from their lovemaking last Thursday, intimacy, in the last couple of months, wasn't what she would have expected in their first year of marriage.

Matt was sitting on a stool by the breakfast bar in the kitchen, going through the mail.

"Hey, Matty boy, you're home early, you okay?" she asked casually as she walked in and grabbed a glass to get herself some cold filtered water from the fridge's water dispenser.

"Hey, Kay," he said as he instinctively raised his head to welcome her peck on the lips. Kirstie immediately sensed something was wrong. Nothing he said or did told her, but she knew.

As she pulled away, she came straight out with it.

"Tell me," Kirstie was so attuned that her question was instantaneous. Matt looked at the letter he had just pulled out of the envelope, but she could see he was looking straight through it. She sat next to him, and she could see that he was shaking. It was almost imperceptible, but he was shaking. He was gritting his teeth and swallowed hard to try to keep control, fearing his face would give the game away, and it was clear he was about to break down. She took the letter from him and held his hands.

"Tell me." She repeated her request, but now worried that somehow he may have found out about her infidelity. He was desperately looking upwards to try to stem the obvious welling in his eyes.

"Matt?" She clasped his hands to elicit a response. From her point of view, it was a natural demonstration of empathy, but from his side, it was sympathy bordering on pity. Whichever way you want to describe it, it was the last straw that demolished his crumbling emotional fortress.

"It's Mum," he said slowly as a tear fell, followed quickly by another. He hesitated, trying to gather himself.

"She had biopsy a little while back that she never told me about." Another tear fell, and then another, and then it was a steady stream. He was tight-lipped and swallowed hard again, trying to regain some sort of control to tell his wife more. He closed his eyes, hoping to stem the flow of tears without much success. Kirstie also started to well up.

Rarely had she ever seen her super-bubbly husband in such distress. She said nothing but embraced him, hopefully to give him support.

"Cancer," he managed to say into her shoulder. She could feel him really shake with emotion as he couldn't control himself any longer - it broke her heart.

"But they do great stuff now and—" Matt cut her attempted positivity short.

"No, it's beyond that," Matt said, sitting back and taking deep breaths to try to compose himself. He continued to stare at the table.

"She had the results and went to see the doctor today. She wanted me to pick her up."

He started to break down again, with a heavy sigh, he held his head in his hands.

"It's terminal," and that word, the worst word in the world, was enough. She held him as he gave in entirely. Fully ten minutes passed before he could gather himself to pull away from her.

"She didn't go into details," he stuttered. "Just that it's…" He took more deep breaths. "Breast cancer already spread everywhere." He broke down again.

"Weeks," he managed to say. "Fucking weeks!" He openly sobbed. "She never said anything."

Kirstie was distraught as well now.

"Oh, Matt, she was just protecting you. She would have thought that she would have worried you if it was a false alarm, you know what she's like. She never bothers anyone with her problems." She held him closer, kissed his forehead, and then kissed him on the lips, tasting the salty tears. He gathered himself again and kissed her back before getting up.

"Kay, it's not fucking fair!" he said, staring out of the kitchen window.

"What life has she had?" He was angry now.

 "She lost her elder brother in the Falklands War, and she lost Dad in Northern Ireland. They were only married for three years, and all she's done is mother me and work at the Council, and now she's got a death sentence," he said before breaking down again.

Kirstie stood up and held him close to her again. He was trembling.

"Babe, nothing in this life is fair, is it?" She squeezed him. "Sit down. I'll get us a drink. Tell me how she's feeling about it all?"

"Beer," he mumbled, forgetting his usual impeccable manners. She nodded and got herself a glass of wine in the process. Matt took the bottle from her with a curt "thanks" and then went on to answer her question.

"She's just her usual self," he shrugged, knowing his wife would understand how her mother-in-law would react to the situation that faced her. Matt continued.

"She takes it in her stride and says she feels fine."

He stared out of the window and took a good swig of his beer. Kirstie stared at her broken man and tried to encourage him. She understood that he was feeling desperately sorry for his mum, but like everyone in this situation, he was also feeling dreadfully sorry for himself.

"Matt, you have to do the same, keep everything normal, because that is what she wants. We go to hers for dinner on Sundays as usual, and when it's more difficult for her, then she comes to us. In between times, we help with getting her to her treatment and all of that. We can share the 24/7 on-call help when she needs it. Okay?" She held him to her again and spoke softly.

"I was so very close to my great-uncle and watched him die of cancer a long while back. Nothing is more difficult for that person than people treating them with pity. Keep it normal, he told my grandparents." Kirstie tried to give him a weak smile, but he wasn't looking. Even so, she really did understand what was coming, having watched her great uncle die over a number of months and how he went from the size of a bear to the shape and weight of a pipe cleaner. The daily deterioration was demonstrable, and yet, on her evening visits, the old man told her that he had come to terms with everything and she shouldn't worry. She recalled his last few days and how he would drift in and out of consciousness. Kirstie always remembered his strained last words. He was a comic to the last.

"Love… I can… see what the attraction of drugs is…I should've done some… years ago." She remembered the last weak squeeze of his hand, and his whispered, "Goodbye, my lovely, lovely girl." Her mum had taken his hand and told him who it was that had grasped his frail fingers. There was a flicker of a smile, and his eyes half opened, breathing shallowly between each word said.

"Jules… don't fret…don't cry…I…am…so tired," he took as deep a breath as he could. "It's my time…and I'm ready."

Kirstie could now picture her mum kissing the old man and whispering that she loved him so much. She bent over and kissed him again on the forehead before moving away to let his wife have the final kiss. Kirstie's great auntie seemed as philosophical as her husband.

"Hey, you old goat, I know I've moaned about your snoring, but this is not the answer, you know?" she said softly, and she kissed the man she had lived (and loved) a lifetime with.

There was a hint of a smile from the failing old man before it slowly faded to be replaced by a couple of tears. She then leant in and kissed him fully on the lips before whispering in his ear, hoping the others wouldn't hear.

"I love you so much, and I will love you forever. Thank you for everything," she paused. "I'll be with you very soon."

The old man nodded slightly before drifting off to sleep. A nurse came in a few minutes later and briefly checked the machine readings. She smiled weakly at the family and, brushing the old man's grey fringe to one side, said to no one in particular, "Not long now, no more pain. God Bless," and left quickly as if to avoid any questions.

But there would be no questions. There could only be one result, and within five minutes, there was a last reflex gasp, and that was it. The machines flatlined, and the nurse was quickly on the scene to switch them off. She efficiently carried out the vital signs check before saying to the assembled family.

"I'm so sorry, but I believe he has gone. I've called for a doctor to confirm the pronouncement," she then quickly blessed herself as if she shouldn't be indulging in any self-religious ceremony. But in the brief time that she had spent with the old man, he had charmed her as he did with almost every woman he ever met. As a professional, she hoped the family wouldn't see the moisture in her eyes.

Kirstie vividly recalled that everyone present was inconsolable as he passed. The memory from a decade ago was as clear and intense as if it were yesterday, and she couldn't contain the tears. Her great-auntie died three weeks later. The official cause was a heart attack, but the family knew it wasn't an "attack". Her heart was truly broken.

Kirstie and Matt went to bed early and spoke of nothing save for a "good night" and "love you." She spooned up behind him, and while she just about managed to keep her tears back, she could feel him again shaking with emotion, and she felt so helpless. In her sadness, she couldn't help but think it was a "Divine" retribution on her and Matt for her weekend "fall from grace" but couldn't reconcile why Matt would also be punished.

More was to come a week later when he received a visit from the police. His mother had taken her own life and been found by a neighbour. The note that she left explained that she was not going to suffer any more pain or put up with the indignity of decline, and this was the one last bit of control that she had. She also left a large envelope marked private and confidential containing a folder for Matt with a number of relevant legal documents and, more especially, a handwritten note explaining that she had had enough and she knew that he would understand.

It would be easier on him not seeing her waste away. The funeral was paid for, and she ended the note telling him how proud she was of him and that he should look after all the things he treasured in life because, all too soon, they might disappear. He knew that it was a thinly veiled reference to how heartbroken she was at losing his father in a tragic, brutal civil war. He completely broke down when reading her last words to him.

"Matthew, I love you so much and I am so proud of you. You are the best thing that ever happened to me." It was signed off as, *"Mum xxx."* At the very bottom was a PS. *"Don't forget to make sure Alfie is looked after, I know he's a bit of a cuss sometimes but he does like cuddles under his own terms. He gets on well with Mavis next door and she adores him so that could be an option."*

Through his tears, he had to smile at the last bit, practical to the last and worrying about her cat. Mavis was more than happy to adopt Alfie, and Matt was content thinking it was best for the animal to stay in his own territory with a familiar human. He remembered how his mum cradled the cute twin kittens when she first got Alfie and his sister Lexie from Cat's Protection. Matt had briefly stopped crying, but then started again as he recalled that Lexie had been hit by a car and died shortly after. It was one of the very few times he ever saw his mum so upset.

Kirstie told him what he already knew that his mother's suicide was a merciful release. Matt said that he wasn't surprised that she would do that. She was a very practical woman.

The funeral took place three weeks later, and during the build-up to it and for a good month afterwards, Matt was in a state of depression. As much as Kirstie tried, she could not seem to bring him out of it. Of course, she understood his grief, but it did not seem natural to her to at least show signs of acceptance. He soldiered on at work, and although his colleagues thought he was justifiably rather morose, his work never suffered, yet the stress of the project must have also been a contributory factor to his demeanour.

A month later, Julia suggested a surprise week away for Kirstie and Matt and herself and Alan, somewhere hot and sunny and away from the same old routine, accompanied by the same old dreary early autumn weather. She rented a small villa in Estepona on the Costa del Sol and bought the airline tickets. She asked Kirstie to contact Matt's boss at work to give him the time off, and they presented Matt with a fait accompli. He didn't protest and actually welcomed the break.

The weather was beautiful, comfortably warm, not oppressively hot, and Matthew started to come around in a very short space of time. He had what was now his closest family around him, giving him support, and he began to realise that life has to go on. On the third evening, after a delicious meal at a local restaurant, the four of them returned to the villa for a nightcap. Kirstie went to bed, telling Matt not to be long, and Alan did the same. It was a glorious chance for Julia to talk to Matt, and she did not waste the opportunity.

"I've missed you, Matthew, but I know you've had a tough time of it, so just know that I am here for you in every way possible, given that I am not only family but…" She came over to him to sit next to him, resting her hand on his. "Also, your confidante and lover. I would understand if you didn't want to continue our…escapes, but I have genuinely missed you and the Matthew we all love. Except, of course, our affection is just…more personal and intimate." Matt nodded and smiled weakly at her.

"I am sorry–" he started, but she hugged him and told him not to be silly because she knew all too well the pain and grief of bereavement and then added, "It's been good to see you come back to us, though. You loved your mum, but she wouldn't want you to dwell too long on what is inevitable for all of us at some time or another." He nodded and hugged her back, Julia could see that he was sad at recalling the recent events, but she kissed him first on the cheek and then on the mouth before slightly pulling away and telling him how much people loved him and needed him.

"Especially me," she whispered and kissed him again, but this time pushing her tongue into his mouth. For a split second, he seemed surprised, but then fully engaged in their passionate kiss and embrace. She pulled away and, holding his hands, said, "I'll wait for you. Whenever you're ready, I'll be waiting." She pecked him on the forehead and squeezed his hands before getting up and bidding him goodnight.

Come the fifth day, he was more like his old self. Julia and Alan had gone to their room late afternoon for a short siesta before getting ready for the evening. From the rooftop veranda, Julia could see that Matt and Kirstie had pulled their sunbeds around to the end of the pool near the side of the building to catch the late sun where they thought they couldn't be seen. Not only did Julia have a perfect view from above from a side balcony, she could hear every word they said. The outlook was strategic enough that while she could see everything where they were, they were not afforded the same in reverse.

Alan was in the shower, and she grabbed a glass of wine and sat out enjoying the sun. She heard her daughter tell Matt to grab his lounger and move it to the little sun trap under Julia's balcony.

"Kay, what are you doing?" Matt asked

"I rarely get sun all over, so this last hour will be perfect." Julia watched her lose her bikini top and bottoms, to her mother's surprise.

"C'mon, now you!" Kirstie said.

"But…"

"But nothing, get those trunks off, get some sun on your bum!" Kirstie demanded. Julia's heart sped up, and she watched carefully as Matt looked around, checking that he couldn't be seen.

"Do come on. It's quite safe," Kirstie said encouragingly.

"What if your mum or Alan come out?" Matt said, still hesitating.

"We'll hear them long before they turn the corner, and we've got the towels to cover ourselves."

Julia watched as Matt slipped the tight trunks down. His gorgeous butt came into view as he had his back to her. Kirstie was already laying on her front but turned to reach out for him. Julia couldn't see, but Kirstie had apparently got hold of his cock by his immediate sigh of pleasure. Julia held her breath, hoping that he would turn and show himself in all his glory, but frustratingly for her, he lay down on his front. She was sufficiently turned on, though, and her nether region was tingling.

"Isn't this nice, proper sun on bits that literally don't see the light of day," Kirstie said. "It's quite liberating!"

"Just make sure we don't get sunburnt. Neither of us will be able to sit down for a week!" Matt said, pouring cold water on her exhibitionism.

"We won't be out here long enough, and a little while each day will chase the white bits away! I think we should go on a nudist holiday!" she chuckled, but Matt wondered if she was being serious.

"Turn over," she said to Matt. "I want to make sure your delicious, comfy cock gets some sun," Kirstie said almost demandingly. Julia's heart skipped a beat with excitement and anticipation.

"Comfy cock ?"

"Yes, it's the perfect size!" Kirstie laughed, Julia silently concurred

"I don't want to get that sunburnt," Matt said. "That could put a real dampener on the holiday."

Kirstie thought better of saying that lately he was only using it to go to the toilet, but opted for telling him that it would be nice to play again soon. He didn't respond. Kirstie sat up, her breasts swinging nicely as she did so.

"I have sun cream here," and gave his backside a playful smack before she squirted some on her hands.

"Let my fingers massage some oil into you, big boy," she said and Julia leaned forward to get an even better view. She could feel herself getting quite damp, and her dream was fulfilled as he turned onto his back, sporting a semi-hard erection that she would have loved to deal with herself. It had been some time since they indulged.

She echoed her daughter's sentiment of, "Mmm, looks like he's very interested in what I have for him here," and the slippery fingers of her right hand curled around his stiffening shaft. Julia watched Matt's eyes close with the pleasure of her daughter's handiwork, and she wished she could swap places with Kirstie right at that moment. It felt like she was watching a porn film rather than encroaching on the couple's perfectly legitimate fun. She was mesmerised by how Kirstie edged him slowly, bringing him to full attention.

"Fancy a fuck, lover-boy? It's been a while, and I miss your kisses," Kirstie said to him. Julia could echo that sentiment.

"I think I could be persuaded."

"Good," she said, taking her hand away and lying back down, "we'll have a quickie before we go out tonight," and she laughed. "Bloody bitch," Matt said jokingly. "Look what you've done to me." If Kirstie couldn't care less, her mother unquestionably could, but she could only witness her daughter's teasing. As his erection was unhanded, it stood to attention all by itself, almost waving at her to come and get it.

Matt turned back onto his stomach and mumbled something about revenge very shortly. Julia would make sure she would be in the vicinity of their bedroom before they went out that evening. How she wished she could take Kirstie's place in that bed. She consoled herself that he was back to the land of the living, which included the element of fornication and all the delights that accompanied it.

33
Roar

November 2014

"I'm not putting up with this weak-willy nonsense any longer, okay? Time to get your engine running!" Kirstie said. It was just after 8.00 am on the first Sunday, a week after they had returned from Estepona, where Matt had outwardly got his appetite for life and "love" back. Yet, on his return to familiar surroundings, he suffered some sort of relapse into sexual indifference and depression.

Kirstie was sitting up in bed, and Matt's hands were already tied to the headboard with one of her scarves, wondering what the fuck had got into her and said as much as he gradually woke up.

"Matt, you haven't touched me since we got back. Yes, I know you're still grieving for your mum, and I know you say the job is stressing you out, but I don't think you're being totally straightforward with me. You know I love you, but I think we need to address the situation before it becomes a slippery slope to…" She thought about how to diplomatically tell him before saying, "…Apathy. You were getting back to yourself last week, and now, a week on, we're loveless again." She sounded very unimpressed with the situation. Matt was still waking but knew he had to respond.

"Kay, I love you too, and you know that. It's just been a difficult few weeks."

Kirstie interrupted him with a "Shush. You don't need to explain. Yes, we do love each other, but intimacy is all part of that." She stopped short of accusing him of a lack of desire for her, although that's exactly how she felt.

As he fully came to, he sensed that there was a newfound confidence about her. Rarely did she take the initiative, let alone talk about making love, but here she was, totally in command. It concerned and excited him in equal measure. She pulled back the quilt, revealing his body as he always slept naked. It always turned her on, and she gently caressed his torso and stomach, keeping her eyes on his cock, hoping to see signs of life.

"Time was when I only had to be within about a mile of you, and *he* would be standing to attention better than the Grenadier Guards at the Trooping of the Colour, and yet here I am now naked, horny, and *he* literally couldn't give a fuck." She flipped his limp dick to demonstrate her point.

"Sorry, Love," was all he could manage. "I am below par, I know, it's not you, but I just seem to be a bit down," he said rather pathetically.

"Down? Below par? Dead people are more exciting!" She grabbed his flaccid penis and started to massage it slowly.

"So we're going to stay here this morning until you get hard and fuck me like you used to, okay? Or at least fuck me, even if it's not like we used to."

"You're not serious?" he said, shuffling about as much as he could. "It's just a temporary blip. I'm sure I'll be back to match fitness soon," he said, trying to make a joke of it.

"Yes, I'm sure too, and today's the day you're up for selection for the first team," she said, continuing to wank him, but to no effect.

"But…you're just adding to the stress to try to…you know, get things going." He sounded even more pathetic. She thought about her response.

"Okay, answer me truthfully. Do you still think I'm sexy?"

"Yes, of course."

"You don't think I've got old and fat due to our contented married life?"

"No, of course not."

"Does our lovemaking still excite you?"

"Yes, of course."

"Liar!" Kirstie said harshly, pulling the skin back on his member, causing a grunt.

"I'll be honest and say that after a couple of years, I do think we were both guilty of going through the motions. To the point where I believe you're thinking it's become a chore," she said.

"No, Kay, it's not like that," he tried to protest, but inwardly he knew she was right.

"So I'm going to run a few suggestions past you, but I don't want you to say anything, not a fucking word, okay? This once handsome beast will do all the talking that I need to hear," she said, leaning down to lick his exposed glans. He said nothing.

"You've always liked me dressing up, and I'll admit I haven't done that in a while. I haven't taken the initiative very much either, and that's going to change. But I'm wondering now if you would enjoy me dominating you occasionally or vice versa, to the point of properly being tied and used? Like now." Suddenly, there was an almost imperceptible twitch. Kirstie was a bit surprised but decided to build on it.

"Hmm, I wonder which scenario…You tying me up–" She hesitated to see if there was a reaction. "Or me taking full control?" Still some slight signs of life, but not enough to convince her.

"Maybe you want something a bit kinkier? Go outside, maybe like George Michael suggests, go to a field and fuck in broad daylight. I'll wear a short skirt and no knickers, and we'll do a bit of exhibitionism in a pub first before we go somewhere and fuck– whoa, that caused a reaction!" she said, watching his staff stiffen a bit.

"Close your eyes and imagine I've tied you to a tree in a wood near a footpath. You're blindfolded, so you don't know how near the path is, and I'm on my knees giving you a blowie." This was working. She took his hardening shaft into her mouth, then took it out again and continued to jerk it firmly.

"Maybe you'd like someone else to come past and join in?" His cock really jerked now. "Oh, wow. You want a threesome?" she questioned.

"No," he said, but she reminded him to be quiet and continued working his dick.

"So I could step away, and this other person would take over, and you wouldn't know until I stood up and kissed you properly on the mouth while she gave you a blow job?" He was fully erect now, and she took her hand away to watch it stand all by itself.

"So you fancy a threesome – got anyone in mind?" His cock still jerked in appreciation. She wanted to test him further. "You do? Who, Sarah perhaps ?"

Her mother, smothered in baby oil, came to mind as did the vision of the initial seduction by Julia, and he was as stiff as ever.

"Oh wow, you fancy Sarah?"

"No, Kay, don't make things up, your handiwork has done the trick as well thoughts of a quickie outside." He pleaded.

Kirstie wasn't convinced but took a good few seconds to wonder about her own intentions towards a double life.

"Things are going to change, Matthew, okay?" Kirstie sounded quite determined.

"How?" he asked, looking very concerned.

She thought for a minute and then said, "We'll have some variation in which of us initiates our playtime. Also, a change of venue with some surprise date nights to begin with. Maybe some dirty weekends away?"

Matthew nodded and said okay.

"Right, well, while I have you as a captive audience, I'm going to have this fine fellow in me because I need him… and you!" With which she straddled him and guided his probe into her. Morning dog breath be damned. She knelt forward and kissed him as her nether region worked itself backwards and forwards a few times, and then she reached behind to caress his balls. To her surprise and much disappointment, he climaxed.

"Fuck, that was quick!" she said, still trying to work his failing appendage.

"Are you really surprised?" he said, trying to defend himself. "It's morning. We haven't done it in more than a week, and I wasn't in any position to try to delay it."

"We'll revisit this later, but now I'm hungry, and I think we'll have a proper breakfast for a change." She untied the scarf and kissed him again before saying, "I so wanted you, thank you for at least listening to me!" He just smiled and a wave of guilt and embarrassment swept over him as he embraced her and kissed her cheek.

"I am sorry, Kay, truly, we'll get through this, I promise." he was genuine in his remorse.

Over a fried breakfast, he asked her about her newfound confidence in the bedroom, pointing out that only rarely did she take the lead, and that was occasionally after a few drinks.

"Does Sarah have anything to do with this after your Dublin adventure? I hope you haven't been discussing our love life with the biggest gob in the United Kingdom?" Matt asked.

"Certainly not, and anyway, the biggest gob belongs to Dan when it comes to carnal creations after last week's revelations, don't you think?" she replied.

"True," he said, finishing off his last piece of bacon.

"I didn't really have time to discuss her view of sex, especially to delve a bit deeper into Dan's accusation that she's become rather…"

"Demanding," he added obligingly.

"Yes, demanding," she said. "I wanted her take on it but obviously she was unwell for most of the weekend but I've known her for a long time and as I've said before, she just adores sex."

"Right," he said, but hoped for something a bit more compelling from his wife.

"Let's discuss it later. I have plans for a romantic dinner tonight, okay?" Kirstie said. "So you can go about your business." And she laughed before asking, "Where are you playing today?"

"We're at home against that nasty bunch of arseholes from Eltham, but I should be back by seven…ish," he was glad she was changing the subject.

"How much of an *ish* is that if I said dinner will be on the table by eight?" she queried, trying to gauge how much leeway she had time-wise for cooking dinner.

"Kay, I promise I'll be home already showered and will change for dinner and horses' derves by 7.30 pm, okay?" he crossed his heart and blew her a kiss as some sort of assurance.

"Yes, and I know you'll probably think it silly, but can you change into your smart navy blue suit and white shirt, please? No tie, just an open shirt. You really turned me on when you wore that the first time, and you look *so* sexy when you're smart. Well, you're always sexy, but it gives you that extra edge, you know?" She looked at him quite wantonly. The message was loud and clear. He gave a little knowing smile, "Sure, Kayzee," and he looked directly at her and nodded. It was all they needed to understand.

He was away by midday, autumn/winter kick-offs to matches were dictated by daylight hours, but as promised, he was home early enough to dump his gear and get changed. He was already in a good mood as the team won 5-3 win against an opposition that were their nearest challengers for the Divisional Championship.

When he came downstairs, the dinner table was set perfectly with two candles and their best crockery, usually used only for the Royal Family or his in-laws, whoever visited first. Lionel Ritchie was setting the scene with his first album on the iPod, and scented candles set the scene. They both loved Mr Ritchie.

Kirstie fussed about in the kitchen, but without looking at him, told him to sit in the dining room when he came downstairs. She wore a pale yellow, sleeveless, roll neck cashmere top with a short black skirt and also wore her black fishnet stockings accompanied with her black heeled ankle boots. Matt could see that when she moved, she was braless. She looked stunning, and he said as much. Kirstie smiled as she then brought a glass of wine and, looking at him for the first time, put the glass in front of him and slowly licked her lips.

"Oh, you are one sexy sod! Seeing you like this, I know exactly why I wanted to marry you," she said before she hurried back to the kitchen to start serving. She eventually sat down and raised her glass in a toast.

"Here's to us, Matthew. May we be lovers forever!" she smiled her sexy smile.

For the first time this evening, he noticed how beautifully made up she was. Kirstie was never one to overdo it, but the overall "package" with make-up, clothing and jewellery was so damned sexy, and he started to get the old twinge back.

"Yes, here's to us forever," and chinked glasses with her before picking up his knife and fork and enjoying the efforts of her day. They made some small talk, mostly about the game. Kirstie was genuinely interested in football and wanted to know how they had overcome their fiercest rivals. It sounded like a thrilling affair as they had gone 2-0 down within twenty minutes of the game, but fought back to win.

"Kayzee, it was a game to bring the crowds flooding back!" And they both laughed. If more than twenty people and a stray dog ever turned up to watch, it would be a major achievement.

"Did you score?" she asked, knowing that he hadn't because, on the rare occasions that he ever did find the back of the net, it would have been the first thing he would have announced when he came through the door.

"Don't be daft. You know, I get a nosebleed if I ever get over the halfway line. I'm happy in defence, and I just watch all the others take the glory. I'm just bloody grateful I get in the team at all," and he finished the last remnants of his dinner.

"Hey, all teams need a good defence. Otherwise, it turns into the football equivalent of basketball," she said knowledgeably.

He nodded. "You're right, and if they keep picking me, then I must be doing something right. But three goals against doesn't look good."

"Matt, the opposition are second in the league. They're no mugs. You won, enjoy it!" she said and raised her glass again.

"To winning the championship!" He chinked her glass again as she then finished her dinner. They said nothing through the next few minutes.

They then turned the discussion to organising a New Year's break with Dan and Sarah and another couple.

"Maybe Mia and Jenny?" he said with a smile. Kirstie picked up on it immediately.

"Ah, yes, we need to explore your thoughts on girl power from this morning, don't we?" she said very directly. He tried to laugh it off.

"Oh, it's every guy's fantasy to see two women play. Don't tell me you haven't thought about it?" Matt said. Kirstie said nothing and then tried to turn it on to him.

"What if I wanted to see you play with another guy? How would you feel about that?" she asked.

"That's not going to happen!" he said indignantly. "But then maybe you're thinking of having some rumpy pumpy with a different man?" he asked, hoping she would deny it.

"Hang on, don't switch the heat on me. You're the one this morning thinking about threesomes!" Kirstie was getting indignant now.

"Only 'cos you mentioned it and was working your magic on me at the time," he laughed.

"Hmm," was all she replied. "Anyway, we'll look at a third couple for the New Year break when I've had a chat with Sarah. Don't forget I work with Jenny. I'm not sure I want to spend too much leisure time with her as well."

She started to collect the plates and got up to take them to the kitchen.

"Oh, by the way, Mum has invited us over for Christmas, so we could go there first for a few days, and then we could tie up with Dan and Saz over in the West Country until New Year. What do you think?"

"Brilliant idea." And he got another twinge, thinking of the horny Julia waiting to get her hands on him.

Lionel then sprung forth with: *You Mean More to Me* and within the opening bars. Kirstie came back and bent down from behind to put her arms around him. He put his right hand on her arm and leant his head backwards to her shoulder, took a deep breath of her perfume and closed his eyes. Then, she sang along perfectly with every word that Lionel put forth.

When it finished, she kissed his neck and then leant further forward to kiss him properly and very tenderly.

"We could sit and listen to more music. Or…" Kirstie said, knowing quite well what her pregnant pause would suggest.

"The music is great. But 'or' sounds…very exciting," said Matt, taking her hand and intertwining his fingers with hers.

"We could do both, of course," she pointed out, which was exactly what they did. Saying nothing else, they headed upstairs.

It was memorable. The iPod Nano provided the entertainment to beautiful lovemaking between a couple that felt that they knew virtually everything about each other and were now lost in one of those magical love-making episodes that emotionally touched each other's souls, even to the point of tears. At that moment in time, they could not have been more in tune in mind and body. As they held each other closely before sleep, Kirstie whispered, "This will be all in good time, my darling, but when we make a baby, it has to be exactly like that."

He squeezed her into his body. "Yes, perfect." And as he drifted off to sleep, he questioned his ability to be a father, but the wine, good food, and emotional lovemaking got the better of him. He was asleep within seconds.

Kirstie felt quite empowered that she had successfully taken control this morning. Matt obviously enjoyed it, and the shackles were off. In the height of desire, she not so innocently ran a brief hint of perversions outside of the marital bed, and he seemed to be on board with that. Matt, for now, was back to his attentive best, and she loved him for it.

34

Your Cheating Heart

In the run-in to Christmas, Kirstie felt that they had overcome their playtime issues and were more in love than ever. Matt was more relaxed, and although not as rampant as he was when they first got married, he was a lot more enthusiastic than he had been in recent months. One thing was for certain, they were both looking forward to the Festive Season.

For Kirstie, it was a break from work and time for her family and friends. It was the same for Matt, but with the added anticipation of a possible stolen moment or two of sexual impropriety.

They both finished work during the early afternoon of Christmas Eve and arrived home within minutes of each other. The couple shared a relaxing bath, heading off to Julia and Alan's for their Christmas break away in the country. Their only real chore was to pack enough clothes for a week, as they were then due to spend time with Sarah, Dan, Mia and Jennifer in a rented house in a village in Gloucestershire and celebrate the New Year in a function held at a local hotel. Sam and Olivia were, unfortunately, double-booked.

Early evening, they arrived at Julia and Alan's. Alan, the perfect host, had thrust drinks into their hands almost as soon as they stepped through the front door. They lived less than forty minutes away, but it took the whole drinking and driving complexity out of the equation for the Christmas break. Matt and Kirstie could just sit back and relax for the next few nights, like it was their second home.

There was never any pressure to do anything as a foursome, but usually, they would go for walks in the countryside or maybe to the pub or just chill out. Matt also wondered if Julia would be manoeuvring situations so that they could get their hands on one another. Their intimate interludes had cooled over the last few months, not least because of how Matt's recent bereavement had affected his libido, but also due to Alan being moved onto a project nearer to home. Matt was fairly sure that Julia still had the hots for him when he received the odd naughty text message from her – sometimes with a picture. It was dangerously exciting, but they diligently stuck to the rules of engagement and knew that messages had to be deleted immediately after receipt.

Dinner that evening was a simple Indian takeaway, all very relaxed with plenty of alcohol.

Kirstie and Matt sat opposite their hosts with Julia, making sure she was facing her target to at least play footsie with him, running her foot up and down his leg while conducting a conversation.

"So, are you guys back at work on Monday?" she asked, lingering her foot on the side of his calf.

"No, we're off now until the New Year," Kirstie said.

"If it's okay by you, we'll stay until Monday morning, and then we're heading straight off to Gloucester, where we're meeting Sarah and Dan and another couple. We're staying in a rented house until New Year's Day," Kirstie said.

"Oh, that sounds good, but you've only come here in your little Fiat. I thought you would have taken the Beamer?" Alan asked.

"The BMW needed fuel, and we just wanted to get going. We couldn't wait to get here to enjoy the hospitality and relax," Matt said, laughing, stealing a furtive glance at his mother-in-law.

Alan raised his glass. "Here's to a Merry Christmas to us!" They all clinked glasses, and Matt got an extra leg rub from his own personal predator.

"Why don't we adjourn to the expensive seats, and I'll light the fire," Alan said, getting up to lead the way without requiring discussion or approval. Kirstie was next, and as soon as her back was turned, Julia squeezed Matt's hand as he smiled at her. She silently mouthed, "I want you to fuck me!" He squeezed her hand back but let go quickly in case they were caught. As they followed the other two, Matt stepped aside to let Julia go first through the doorway, and she casually rubbed his cock over his trousers with the back of her hand before saying, "Mmm." He goosed her in return.

They relaxed in the front room with its seven-foot Christmas tree, other miscellaneous decorations, and a roaring open fire. Idle chit-chat ensued, listening to a Christmas compilation CD and wallowing in the Christmas spirit - specifically, more alcohol.

As if there hadn't been enough to eat, the compulsory tubs of Quality Street and Roses hit the table and, of course, the pitiful handful of the best ones in each box were gone in seconds.

At 11.30 pm, Alan decided it was time to call it a night, as "There was a lot to do in the morning, and anyway, Santa won't come if we're still up after midnight," he laughed.

Matt chimed in with, "Many hands make light work," as an offer of help with dinner prep tomorrow.

"You go up, Darling," Julia said to Alan and, picking up some of the glasses, added, "I'll sort this stuff and be with you shortly."

Kirstie was halfway out of the door before Matt casually said, "I'm a qualified dishwasher loader, so I could do the dinner plates to get them out of the way. It'll be one less task tomorrow." His mother-in-law agreed that it would be helpful when Kirstie said, "Yes, good point, I'll clear the table. You load the machine."

Matt glanced at Julia, who realised their little off-the-cuff plan to be alone together for a few minutes was now well and truly scuppered. Too many cooks spoil the broth... and the stirring.

Chores done, they all headed off to bed, two of them feeling a tad frustrated that their impromptu subterfuge had been thwarted. Their frustration would have to continue. "Santa's not the only one not coming at the moment!" thought Julia.

It had been a tiring day, and a kiss and "Love You" was Matt and Kirstie's final action of the night before turning out the light.

Hours later, Matt suddenly woke in the darkness to find Kirstie kneeling beside him, stroking his very hard penis. It took him a few seconds to come round and mumble, "Wha…what?"

"I woke up rather tipsy and downright frisky, and I want sex!" Kirstie said as she straddled him and pointed the head of his dick into herself. He looked at his watch – it was 3.25 am. He thought he was dreaming, but the pleasure was real enough.

"Ooh, that is so nice, and I don't know about Santa, but you can empty your sac in me, please!" Kirstie said with a sigh.

They had an audience! - Julia, in the room next door, where the headboards were only separated by the thickness of the plasterboard partition. Alan was asleep, but she could hear Matt and Kirstie's headboard rhythmically nudging against the wall, and she could faintly hear Kirstie's sighs and gasps of pleasure. She could not resist masturbating as she imagined Matt's cock working its magic. She desperately wanted that magic to be with her and cursed the lack of opportunity to get her hands on it and on the man it belonged to. After ten or eleven minutes, the man it belonged to couldn't control it any longer, and it spewed forth its sticky, hot lava. Kirstie didn't climax, but she enjoyed taking control for the short time that they fucked. The couple's frustrated listener bit her lip as she quietly brought herself off, picturing what had happened in such close proximity. She needed him spunking off inside her before they left.

It had snowed lightly overnight, which set the tone for the perfect Christmas Day. It was a lazy start for each of them except Julia, who was up at 8.00 am to start the prep. It was her hope (against hope) that Matthew might fulfil his promise of many hands, make light work and show up by himself so they could at least have a squeeze and a snog. As she peeled carrots, parsnips and spuds, she relieved the boredom by trying to manufacture a situation where they could spend half an hour together for a short, sharp shag. Her frustration wasn't helped by the fact that the kitchen was directly below the creaky-floored guest bedroom, and the occupants were again noisily exchanging some physical gifts. She put the TV on to listen to Christmas Carols from King's College, Cambridge and turned the volume up, possibly in an effort to let the fun-seekers know that their exertions hadn't gone unnoticed.

The young guests lasted longer this morning, but as they had already indulged only four or five hours before, it wasn't surprising. As Julia attacked another potato, she thought that *the next time I get my hands on him, I'm going to fuck him raw.* Just at that moment, Alan arrived, gave her a cuddle, a kiss on the cheek, wished her a Merry Christmas and offered to make her a coffee. He, too, was not oblivious to the steady rhythmical creaking of floorboards and, looking up towards the source of the beat, said, "And a Merry Christmas to both of you, too. I suspect it's the cheapest present each of them will give each other," he laughed.

"Hmm, quite possibly." Julia tried not to show that she was as jealous as fuck!

All the prep was done by the time Kirstie emerged, and Julia and Alan were sitting watching some TV before getting things together for breakfast.

"Is Matt coming down shortly? Because I'll start breakfast," Julia said.

"He's just having a quick shower, and he said not to wait for him as he'll do himself some toast," Kirstie said.

"Ah, okay," Alan said. "We wondered if he was right behind you," to which he got a slap on the arm and a slight grin from Julia. Kirstie pretended not to hear.

"I'm not sure I changed the towels in the bathroom yesterday," Julia said, and she was about to get up when Alan reminded her that he had done it under her instructions…foiled again.

"I'm going up to have a shower, anyway," she said and put her coffee cup in the sink. "Alan, can I leave you to sort out breakfasts? There are cereals, toast or eggs and bacon if anyone wants them."

"Of course, Love," he dutifully replied.

From the kitchen, she could hear movements in the bedroom above and quickly made her way to the stairs. Halfway up, Matt came out of the bedroom, and her heart skipped a few beats.

"Morning, and a Merry Christmas to you," he said, leaning towards her to give her a kiss on the cheek in case someone was in the vicinity.

Julia looked downstairs to check no one was following and then grabbed his hands and pulled him into the spare bedroom.

"Merry Christmas? This has been purgatory having you here and not able to have you in my bed!" She held his head in her hands and pulled him towards her for a full-on tongue-dancing snog, she sighed with joy as he held her in his arms.

"Hearing you two during the night and then again this morning was just like rubbing salt in the wound!" she said, placing his hand between her legs, encouraging him to rub her mound over her leggings. She responded with a sharp gasp. Pointedly, he asked, "And just how is your wound?"

"It's going to heal up if you don't do something about it very, very soon. You've been neglecting me lately." He switched to moving his hands inside her knickers and clawed at her slit quite firmly. Her hands were not idle as one cupped and fondled his balls while the other grabbed at his hardening stem.

"Oh, wow. That's *so*..." She suddenly held his wrist as they could hear someone coming down the hall and making their way up the stairs.

Julia pushed him away and pointed to a place just behind the door. Quickly, she opened one of the wardrobe doors and tidied herself up as Alan stopped by the doorway.

"I thought you were going to have a shower?"

"Yes, I am, but I suddenly thought we'll need the Christmas napkins and candles for the table." She hoped that would satisfy the erstwhile inquisition.

"Okay, but you know we keep them in this first cupboard, not that one," and he stepped into the room with no more than three feet apart from him and Matt. He opened the wardrobe door and pulled down the box with the required items.

"Ah, well done," she said. "Could you take them downstairs for me, and I'll have my shower."

"Of course," and with a smile, he turned on his heel and was gone, oblivious to the deception that was so close to detection. As soon as Alan was downstairs, Julia signalled to Matt to go. She stroked his bulge as he went past and mimed a kiss at him.

Breakfast out of the way, they all exchanged gifts, though nothing too elaborate. They settled down and had a glass of Bucks Fizz each before taking a leisurely scenic walk to the local pub to kill some time before it opened at midday.

Julia and Kirstie left the bar a bit earlier than the guys to make a start on the dinner. It gave the boys a chance to talk sport and football in the main. Both Pompey supporters they delighted in their seven-year stay in the Premiership before financial mismanagement and a succession of penniless shysters brought the club to the brink of extinction. They toasted to the Phoenix of the South Coast with their one for the road.

The rest of the day was spent bingeing on food and drink with a short interruption for the Queen's Speech. An afternoon snooze at separate times for them all gave Matt and Julia another chance for a quick snog and fondle. Matt did give her a crumb of opportunity when he told her that Kirstie had to be away for work later in January, which would give them ample time to arrange something.

"It can't come soon enough, Matthew. I'm climbing the walls wanting to get at you, you have to know that I absolutely loved our weekend love fest," she said.

"Yes, it was fantastic," he said, trying to sound as enthusiastic as her, but whilst the sex and the sleeping together was great, he was worried that she was overstepping the "battle" lines. He continued with a cautionary note, "We must be careful, though, it's been so hot so far, but we both have a lot to lose."

She knew she had trodden in the minefield and needed to backtrack.

"Yes, sorry, it's just that I need all the sensual, sexy things you do to me, but of course, it is just sex, after all." He could see she was put out by his assessment of their affair.

"Julia, it isn't just sex, and you know that. We have a real passion and affection for one another, but we mustn't let it get out of hand, okay?" He hoped that would keep her onside.

"You're right. Anyway, I've stuff to do, and we mustn't get caught here." She pulled away and gave him a quick squeeze before going off to the kitchen. She knew he was right, but wiped a tear away, anyway.

Julia resolved to try to be a bit more ambivalent, but her mind strayed back to their "fuck fest" weekend, and she just wanted more. Once a month, maybe, but when she went to bed that night, she wondered if she shouldn't break it off altogether.

Boxing Day was another day spent relaxing, but nothing like the overindulgence of the big day itself. Julia was now clear in her mind about how she would play the situation. Matthew would have to make the first move, and then she would see how committed (or otherwise) he was to their affair. She would make no attempt to get him alone and would consciously avoid physical contact to prove to herself that she could resist him.

The long, relaxing, bingeing weekend continued, and on Saturday, they drove into Bournemouth to meander around the shops and have a long lunch. In the evening, the foursome dined out at the local pub. They revelled in the leisurely family dynamic. Sunday, Kirstie had a bit of a lie-in, but Matt got up. Alan had arisen early and had popped out to the local supermarket to get some 'essential supplies' that Julia had requested. As Matt entered the kitchen, she was at the sink, washing up. He was horny and wasted no time in cuddling her from behind and kissing her neck as his hands reached for her breasts.

Remembering the deal she had made with herself, Julia tried to resist saying that Alan would be back any second, but Matt could see that the car was gone and persisted with the intimate fondling and then moved one hand down the front of her leggings. The resistance crumbled, and with an elongated sigh, she just let him stoke the fire.

"Kiss me, Matthew," and she turned her head to accept his tongue into her mouth. It was awkward but very effective. She reached behind her to feel his bulge and manoeuvred her hand into his joggers' bottoms to grab and fondle his prick. He was about to take this a step further when he heard a car and saw Alan's motor reversing into the drive.

"Fuck!" Matt said in annoyance, and he swiftly moved off to the front room to watch TV as if he was waiting for breakfast.

Alan came into the kitchen carrying the shopping.

"The supermarket was busy this morning. You'd think the shops had been closed for a month, but I've got everything, I think." He looked at Julia and commented, "You look a bit flushed, Love, are you ok?"

"Yes, it just came on all of a sudden. Must be the start of my change!" She gave a false laugh. Alan suggested that she might have just been overdoing the Harvey's Bristol Cream, and he chuckled before asking if she wanted him to do the breakfasts. Julia said it was all under control. She considered that had he arrived minutes later, he would have witnessed someone doing *his* job. If nothing else, Matthew had more than proved his desire for her.

The rest of Sunday passed without incident or opportunity. It was Kirstie's and Matt's last full day before they were to set off to Gloucestershire in the morning for part two of their festive break.

Kirstie woke on Monday morning with the familiar prodding around her bum and an arm draped over her.

"Are you awake?" Matt said, knowing full well that if she wasn't, she soon would be.

Without moving, she opened one eye to see on the bedside clock that it was 8.10 am.

"No. Fuck off." She wanted to have another hour. It had been a fairly heavy night drinking and playing cards.

"I think you *are* awake," Matt persisted. "I think you're awake, and if I ask nicely, I think you wouldn't mind playing hide the sausage." He prodded her again before adding, "I think you're awake, and for your information, I think you know I have a very nice 'comfy' sausage to hide, and I also think you know where I can hide it. What do you think?" he said as he stroked her arm.

She didn't answer, so he prodded her again, and his hand moved to stroke whatever part of her upper body he could reach.

"Do you really want to know what I think?" she said again, without moving or responding to his persistent attention.

"Yes." He started nuzzling her neck.

"As nice as your 'comfy' sausage is, I think you can take your sausage and hide it somewhere else. I want to sleep." She never moved except to take his hand and put it back over to his side. There was a "tut" of disappointment from him, but he knew she could sleep for England, so playtime would have to wait. He lay back, and while stroking his erection, he said jokingly, "Do you know in some countries, a wife would be a man's chattel, and as a chattel, she would have to do whatever he wanted." It sounded like a lecture, but she knew it was his humorous way of dealing with the lack of sausage hiding.

"Which countries?" she asked after about thirty seconds.

"So you are awake?" he said as though he'd caught her out.

"No, I'm not awake, but if I were, I would ask which countries?" She still didn't move.

He tutted again, "Well, all of the obvious ones, of course." As though she was supposed to know. Another thirty seconds went by.

"Such as?"

Silence as he tried to think of one. "The usual ones that have laws about chattels," he said quite authoritatively, still failing to give an example. There was another pause.

"Name one."

There was silence again before he piped up with, "Chattel-Arabiastan, there see, thought I didn't know, didn't you? So how about it?" he asked, knowing what the ultimate answer would be.

"Chattel-Arabiastan. Where is that, then?" She still didn't move, and although still quite sleepy, she enjoyed his persistence. Yet more silence, and then he said, "Head south towards North Africa and turn left at Libya, going towards, somewhere left of Libya, it's somewhere near Dubai. If you've got as far as Iraq, you've gone too far."

"Oh, right."

"So?" he asked hopefully as he put his arm across her again.

"Fuck off!"

He turned back to his side as his morning glory wilted and mumbled something about grounds for divorce, which made her smile, but she knew another hour's sleep would be perfect.

"What time do you want to head off?" he asked her.

She thought about it for a few seconds, "Dunno, I'll have another hour here, shower, then breakfast, maybe leave just before lunch. We can get something to eat on the way. How does that sound?"

"Yep, okay, but we could have a little tickle before brekkie, perhaps?" It was his last throw of the dice.

"Fuck off." And she pulled the covers over her head to signify closure.

"Right, well, I can see you're a tad undecided, but just remember, you are breaching the human rights of males in Chatel-Arabiastan if not Hampshire. Also, it wasn't so long back that you were a tad miffed at my apparent apathy, and now I'm hot, hard, and horny, and you want to sleep. Just saying."

"Well, you're clearly cured, so you can fuck off!"

"I shall go downstairs and have breakfast. I think Alan is already up anyway because he's back to work today, so me and my sausage are going to leave you in peace. So there," he stood for a few seconds and then added, "Or I might just go and see if your mum's interested." He thought it was highly amusing, like some sort of double bluff.

"Good idea. Fill your boots, or hers. Mwah," was her innocent response. He smiled and jokingly thought it was a licence to go and fuck her, and he started to stiffen again.

He slipped out of bed and went to the bathroom. He was still fairly piss proud, but that was easily solved. He was still horny, though, and it only took a few tugs before he was almost fully hard. Teeth brushed and wet fingers through his hair, he slipped on a clean white tee shirt and jogger bottoms, going commando.

There was still no movement in the bed, and he assumed Kirstie had drifted off to sleep. He went downstairs and could hear the noise of plates and cutlery being assembled, and thought Alan was tidying up before he did the workday commute.

He wandered in to find his mother-in-law all alone, who turned to see who had gotten up.

"Hey, morning. I thought Alan was sorting breakfast?" he said, drinking in what she was wearing. His mind strayed to picturing her gorgeous body, currently covered by her big, fluffy dressing gown.

"Morning to you too. No, Alan went to work early. He reckons he can get so much done in an empty office." She smiled at him, and they looked at each other knowingly. She continued to make eye-to-eye contact, and he took that as the green light to meet their needs. There would be no interruption today. Matt walked towards her as she backed up against the sink unit. He said nothing but took her in his arms and kissed her fervently. She put a hand on his chest as if to resist, yet again, her token gesture was futile, and they both knew it.

Julia gave in to her desire, wrapped her arms around him, and with lots of encouraging sighs, pursued the kiss with supine enthusiasm. When they broke off, she held him tightly to her and said, "You have no idea how much I've wanted to do that since you've been here, even since yesterday. Just having you here and yet so unable to have you fuck the life out of me has been so frustrating. I couldn't even get an hour to myself to indulge in 'my time' imagining you inside me." She clawed at him and held him tightly. He kissed her again, and she could feel him fully aroused under his joggers.

"You'll know exactly how it's been for me then," he said, undoing the tie of her bathrobe to expose her hot body underneath, clad only in a skimpy pair of pink knickers.

They kissed again, and his hands slipped into the robe to stroke her back and breasts.

She pulled away momentarily. "Is she asleep?" She used the pronoun as if it would make her daughter seem like someone she didn't know.

"Yes, and then she's going to have a shower. Turn round and bend over the table. We have unfinished business," She slipped off the robe and turned round to do as he asked. Matt dropped his joggers and, spreading her legs, pulled her panties to one side to finger her cunt, foreplay would be short and sweet today.

"Oh, God, that's good. Please get your cock in me. Now. No frills, just fuck me!" she begged.

He summoned up a mouthful of spit, which he dripped onto his fingers before lubricating the head of his dick. Shuffling forward, he poked at her entrance, whereupon she reached between her legs to steer him into her. It wasn't working.

"Wait," he said, and pulling away slightly, he ran his fingers over the margarine to scoop up some of it and use it as lube – needs must. He smeared his cock and then wiped the excess over her sex before attempting penetration again. She guided his shaft to where she wanted it, and very slowly, he pushed home.

"God, that's the best way to butter me up…" she chuckled before the pleasure of his invasion hit home.

"Fuck, that's so hot. Come on, Matt, make it quick, no time for fancy stuff, I need you," she said, tickling his balls. He grabbed her hair and fucked her hard. In less than ten minutes, he was spending inside her with one long thrust and a grunt. He held himself tight against her. As she lay on the kitchen table with eyes closed, she felt the hot seed squirt into her, although she hadn't climaxed. That feeling of being wanted and desired was enough to satisfy her and her exclamation of, "Fuck…yes. So good," told him as much.

As Julia calmed down, she opened her eyes to see the distorted reflection in the stainless-steel toaster of someone standing near the kitchen doorway. She turned her head to see Kirstie standing there with tears streaming down her face, holding herself in shock at what she had witnessed in those few minutes.

Matt was totally unaware as he also had his eyes closed in orgasmic bliss until he softened up, sighed and slipped out of her sleeve, dragging a glob of cum with it, which spilled on the floor. He pulled away, and Julia quickly pulled her knickers back in place to soak up the rest, telling him to cover himself up. He was confused until he heard his wife shout.

"You fucking cunts!" was all he heard before turning around to see Kirstie moving swiftly down the hall and running upstairs.

"Shit," he exclaimed, pulling up his joggers and leaving Julia to gather herself. She was also in shock. Her body and mind were trying to settle after some opportune smash-and-grab sex. Now she was trying to quickly evaluate what her daughter had just witnessed and how she could avoid the shit storm that was coming her way. She stood up and, although extremely flustered, she reached for some kitchen towel to stuff into her knickers to soak up his plentiful deposit. Julia then donned her bathrobe that had been hastily discarded on the floor in the act of pure lust. She moved to the sink and, putting her hands on the edge, looked into the garden and wondered how the fuck was she going to explain this?

Staring out at the pouring rain, other issues came to mind. What about Alan? And what would Kirstie do about Matt? Her heart sank thinking their affair was over and she would never see him again, and as a thousand scenarios ran through her head, the over-riding one was that through her pure lust for Matt, the whole family unit was…well and truly fucked. As she stared out of the window, she could hear raised voices upstairs. In reality, only one raised voice, and she wondered if she should intervene. Perhaps if she told her daughter that it was all her fault for seducing him, then at least the marriage might be saved, and maybe in time she would be forgiven. Kirstie's voice was even louder than before and then there was silence and a lot of stomping about, which moved across the floor directly above her and then down the stairs.

Julia went out of the kitchen into the hall as her daughter reached the bottom step. She looked at her mother with complete disdain as Julia begged, "Please, we can talk about this, don't go" but before she could finish her sentence, Kirstie stopped and shook her head, tears still streaming down her face. She cared nothing for her hypocrisy of obvious adultery before screaming at her mother.

"How could you do that? He's my husband. *Mine*. Not some fucking plaything of yours… Why?"

Her mum reached out towards her. "Kirstie, it's not how it looked." She knew it was the most ridiculous statement she could have ever made because it was exactly as it looked.

"Mum, don't." She batted her mother's hands away. "Don't say anything, because there's nothing you can say that can fix this. I caught you and him, fucking. And even now, with his cum in you, you're trying to say it's not how it looks." She shook her head, unable to speak any more and wiping away more tears. She opened the front door and walked out. Matthew was coming down the stairs without even looking at Julia and said nothing as he swiftly loaded up the boot of Kirstie's little car and got in. Kirstie drove off in an unthinking hurry, and he hadn't even managed to shut the car door as she pulled out of the drive.

Julia's whole morning had gone from last-ditch hopeful moments alone with him to intense, immediate anticipation, pure fucking lust and pleasure for the minimum amount of time to complete their union, and utter red-handed disaster, her wet knickers and semen on the floor an ongoing reminder of their guilt. She quietly shut the front door and walked back to the kitchen to put the kettle on.

Julia couldn't feel any more devastated than she did as she mopped up the excess spunk off the floor with some kitchen paper and then made herself a strong coffee, sat down, and cried. Another thousand thoughts went through her mind as to how she could explain or how it could be resolved, and then there was Matthew. Would Kirstie dump him? Would they work things out, but then have nothing to do with her? How would she explain all of this upheaval to Alan and her friends? Worst of all, though, was the loss of Matthew to her, which made her weep uncontrollably.

"Oh God, please, I never meant to cause such hurt. Please make her forgive me, please make all of this go away. Please, God, somehow make it all go away!" She closed her eyes and, as her shoulders slumped, she wept again.

As Kirstie drove off, Matt could see that she wasn't thinking straight by how aggressive her driving was.

"Look, Kay, please let me drive. I know you're upset, but let's get home and talk about it."

"Upset? FUCKING UPSET?" She thumped the steering wheel. "Why should I be upset? I mean, I come downstairs to have breakfast with my husband and find him sticking his fucking cock into my slut of a mother, who was obviously encouraging it. So why should I be upset? You CUNT!" She was almost screaming. "YOU ABSOLUTE FUCKING CUNT!"

"Kirstie, just slow down. You're driving like a lunatic," he was seriously worried.

"Yeah, I'm a lunatic. I'm also a fucking mug not to have seen what was going on. I should have known something was up with the way she was always touching and pawing you. Oh, wait, those trips to her house to fix things. They were always when Alan wasn't there, and I knew she didn't have a tumble dryer. You BASTARD!"

She thumped the wheel again with tears still streaming down her face.

"So how long have you two been fucking behind my back?" she shouted through gritted teeth.

"Kirstie, let's just get home and we'll talk about it. Please, let me drive," he begged.

"Fuck you!" was her angry response, and she hit him with her left hand.

They joined a slow-moving queue of traffic, and although she was looking ahead, she barely stopped in time behind the stationary lorry in front of her. The car was quiet. Matt just didn't know what to say before she glanced in the mirror and shrieked in horror.

Julia set about stripping the beds and doing some housework, all on autopilot. Over five hours later, there was a ring on the front doorbell. She hoped it was Kirstie, but through the patterned glass she could see that two large, uniformed people were standing there. On opening the door, two police officers stood grim-faced, and she knew before they even spoke that God had granted her wish in the worst way possible. They apologised for the delay in informing her, but they had to trace the registered keeper (her daughter) back to her previous address.

The first responders at the accident between two large HGVs didn't realise for a number of hours that between those two lorries was a completely destroyed Fiat 500, with its two occupants barely resembling corpses. The driver of the fully loaded articulated lorry that ploughed at speed into the back of Kirstie's car offered no reason for not seeing that the traffic had stopped. Crash investigators determined that although his brakes were working perfectly, he had made no attempt to apply them. The police arrested him and, under caution, charged him with causing death by dangerous driving. On further investigation, they found that he had been using his mobile phone to write, send and receive text messages. It was also found that he was already disqualified, had no insurance and had exceeded the limit for the effects of cannabis consumption. The only minimal consolation was that Kirstie and Matthew would have died instantly.

35

Time to Stay Goodbye

Julia woke to her 7.30 am alarm. She had slept fitfully during the night, and she recalled watching the clock meander from midnight until around 4.30 am. It was a day she was dreading, and although Alan had brought her a cup of coffee in bed as he usually did, she just didn't want to get up.

"Love, I will do everything I can to get us through this, but ultimately we must try to keep our focus for at least the time up to the event, okay?" Alan said as he set the coffee down on the bedside unit. Julia nodded, and she knew what had to be done.

They arrived at the crematorium at the time suggested by the undertaker to be present as the coffin arrived and was carried into the chapel. Julia and Alan were warmly met by Louise, the Civil Celebrant, who stood with them as the hearse entered the grounds. Julia cried as soon as she saw the vehicle and couldn't contain her grief as the coffin was taken out of the car and then into the chapel to be placed on the marble catafalque in front of the small, curtained frame. It was a beautiful coffin with a glossy white veneer and brass handles, but to her it was just a fancy box. A fancy box containing the remains of her daughter *and* her son-in-law and was, in a short space of time, going to be incinerated.

She sat and stared at it and vividly recalled how the oh-so-sympathetic undertaker had suggested a shared casket because he said, as delicately as possible, given the catastrophic damage caused by the accident, the two "loved ones" could share their eternity together. Julia had spent a lot of time contemplating what that really meant in the cold light of day. It was a wondrous sentiment, but the truth was so awful that she tried, rarely successfully, to chase it from her mind, not least the part she played leading up to that tragic event. Oh, if she had only said no.

However, that moment of snatched intimacy with someone that wasn't hers now led to her sitting looking at that fancy box containing what was left of her only child and her son-in-law. Even in this moment of complete sadness, she could still conjure visions of him pleasuring her. She silently begged God for forgiveness. Randomly, she considered the incongruous action of praying to God but employing a Civil Celebrant to conduct the service. It was her choice, but she had already asked too much of God.

At precisely 11.00 am, the crematorium staff opened the doors to the chapel to allow the large contingent of mourners to file in. "Time to Say Goodbye", sung by Andrea Bocelli, filled the room. So poignant, so emotional, and *so* clichéd. Five times a day, twenty-five times a week, the crematorium staff had it on repeat and were sick of it.

Dan and Sarah were last to arrive, having been detained somewhat by "domestic requirements", and as much as Dan would have liked to catch up with the boys from the footie team, they had already entered and were seated at the back. Dan and Sarah sat in the front row with Kirstie's immediate family, Julia, Alan and her grandparents, Rita and Dave. Mia, Jennifer, and Samantha sat behind them. Joey Porter and Cheryl from Julia's office were also there to give their support to her parents.

Louise introduced herself and explained what Civil Celebrants were about before starting the service with "All Things Bright And Beautiful".

To some, it might have seemed inappropriate, but Louise explained that it had always been Kirstie's favourite hymn, and she had even won a children's talent show at a holiday camp when she was five, singing that beautiful, cheerful song of praise. It brought many a smile throughout the congregation and was sung enthusiastically by all. Julia was too choked to utter a single word. It was followed by a eulogy for

Kirstie from Sarah, one from Dan for Matthew, and a final one from Alan for both Kirstie and Matthew.

The hymn "Abide with Me", well known for being played before every F.A. Cup Final, was Dan's choice for Matthew because of its football connotations. Louise then briefly spoke of how the couple would live forever in the hearts and minds of people they loved and who loved them. She then asked the audience to stand to pay their last respects before a violinist came near to the front, but standing well to the side began playing "Nearer My God to Thee". The coffin slowly and quietly slid through the closing curtains and out of sight. Alan held Julia tightly as he felt her almost give way.

At the back of the room, most of the group of big, strong lads were fighting back their emotions as their teammate and his wife disappeared.

As the music finished, Louise asked everyone to take their seats for a short period of quiet reflection, which essentially was to allow the immediate family to leave first. She went on to invite all guests to the church hall a little way down the road, where they would be welcomed by Julia and Alan and Julia's parents, who had gone a long way to making a lot of the arrangements with Alan.

Most people did show up at the hall to pay their respects before disappearing around the corner to the pub, which always did a roaring trade on "dispatch" days. Alan took Julia home as soon as respectability allowed, and Rita and Dave (Julia's parents), along with some willing helpers, cleared up the aftermath.

Julia went to bed early, somewhat heartened by words of support and consolation from everyone, but she wondered how she could ever get over the guilt she felt at being a major factor in this heartbreak. It was a guilt that she knew she would have to endure alone for the rest of her life.

When the lorry driver went to court some months later, he did not show any remorse for his actions, and after a severe reprimand from the judge, he was given a sentence of ten years' imprisonment for causing death by dangerous driving, plus a driving ban of five years when released from prison. He had barely served three months before he was found by wardens on his knees with his head down a 'soiled' toilet. Chicken wire was around his neck, securing him to the toilet seat. He was gagged, and his wrists were tied behind his back, also with chicken wire. He had been "kneecapped" probably with a lump hammer or something similar. Every part of both of his hands had been smashed with the same implement, and whoever did it had caused sufficient physical damage for him to be unable to ever drive again, let alone function normally. There was a scrawled sign around his neck saying, *"Live long and think on what you did, you are scum."* No one was caught for such a brutal, if fitting, act of retribution.

36

Lyin' Eyes

February 2015

It was a Friday morning. Dan woke and glanced at his bedside clock to confirm what he already knew. His own inner alarm went off at 6.00 am, but he had no need to get up. He was adjusting to the new norm of redundancy that seemed, in a blink, to already be six weeks old.

He lay on his back with his eyes closed, trying to take in the despondency of losing his job when the company went bust. He thought about the HR lady's call on that fateful Thursday evening, giving him the bad news, and how she could barely hold it together. It's a cliché to call some companies "family", but all eighty-four employees bought into the M.D's musketeer mantra that it really was, *all for one and one for all.* Sadly, all eighty-four were now unemployed. Unfortunately, a couple of bad business decisions coupled with a bear market in the IT industry found them struggling with cash flow. As a young company, the banks were not willing to take a punt on their ability to extricate themselves from their difficult financial predicament and with a lack of potential business, the plug was well and truly pulled. It was devastating news. The lack of personal income was a massive blow.

He sensed Sarah stir next to him and then felt her hand move across his stomach and rest there. He fully expected her hand to move lower to initiate their morning "muckiness" as she called it – but not today. Dan had grown accustomed to this routine as his morning wood testified, but oddly, she gave no indication that she was interested. Dan gave it no more thought, and they both went back to sleep, waking just before 8.30 am.

They filled their day as usual. She, being self-employed, went off to the study to work, although it was more to advertise her business than to engage in anything specific. He plonked himself in the lounge with his laptop and looked for jobs. It was soul-destroying.

Late afternoon, Sarah was in the kitchen and called out. She wasn't sure where he was.

"Dan, you haven't forgotten I'm out tonight, have you?"

"Again?" Dan appeared from the utility room and looked really down in the mouth. His depression over recent events with redundancy, Matt and Kirstie's fatal car accident, and not least, Sarah's surprise postponement of the wedding, was never out of mind for long.

"Yes, I told you a few weeks ago – the girls from the catering company I work with, Alison's birthday. I did tell you." She sounded rather miffed that he appeared to have forgotten. He frowned and then offered an apology. "Sorry, just had a lot on my mind lately."

"You'll be watching football anyway and won't even know I've gone. I won't be late unless they want to go clubbing," she said, as though it wasn't much of an issue.

He came up behind her and, cuddling her, kissed her shoulder.

"I think you'll find a quick twist of the neck is more efficient and less messy." He worked his way to her slender neck.

"Ha, ha, very good. Now stop that, as I've only got just over an hour to get ready and as nice–" she stopped mid-sentence, closed her eyes and leant her head back onto his shoulder as he hit the zone on her neck that made her horny. She gained control of herself and gently smacked his hand, which was steadfastly working its way to her left breast.

"Stop. We'll re-examine this position when I come home," she said, trying to let him down gently. She was pushed for time. Dan released her, and she gave him a quick kiss before grabbing his cock through his jeans. He was discernibly aroused. "Mmm, there's a good boy always ready to play," and she turned and went upstairs to shower. He stared out of the window, some alarm bells that had been faintly ringing in his head for quite a number of weeks now were there again. He told himself not to be stupid or jealous. Or both.

Sarah's career as an Events Consultant meant that she was often required to work some weekends and evenings, and to a great extent, she had curtailed a lot of anti-social hours when she moved in with Dan. It was well paid, and he told himself that he shouldn't be so churlish when she easily earned as much, if not more, than he did when he was working. Now, he was dependent on her, as she was the only wage earner until he found another job, yet something still nagged away at him.

He gave her time to herself and, when he heard the hair dryer in operation, thought he would pop upstairs on some flimsy excuse just to see what she was wearing. He casually stepped into the bedroom, where she was just putting the finishing touches to her hair. She had magnificent black shiny hair, now spiky and quite short at the sides since her hens' weekend. It exposed more of her beautiful face and neck, and she could not have been more attractive if she tried.

"Just going to change my jeans. I might pop down the pub." He knew it was a pathetic reason, as did she, but she didn't answer and continued to run her fingers through her hair to further spike it up as she looked at different angles in the mirror. Sarah was sat on her cushioned stool in front of the dresser, naked except for a simple white cotton thong with string sides. He approached and lifted the laundry basket lid before pulling down his old jeans and depositing them in the open basket. Sarah noticed then that he was sans underwear. She was immediately drawn to his semi-hard cock and then, turning to face him, reached out to hold it with her left hand as her right hand cupped his balls.

"Monty is very naughty, you know," she said, looking directly into Dan's eyes with a look that meant that he (Dan) was very naughty.

"I've only come up to change into my jeans, but do you blame him when you're so fucking sexy?" Dan offered in mitigation. Sarah smiled. She always loved compliments.

"I really don't have time for this, but I suppose a quick hand job might ease your discomfort." She dipped her left hand into the open jar of moisturiser on the side and smothered his full erection with the cool lubrication. He closed his eyes with the pleasure of her wrapping her fingers around his shaft and sliding them quickly back and forth over the slippery length. His hips moved slightly in rhythm with her manipulation, and, after a few minutes, his breathing became a little heavier and shorter. He put his hands on her bare shoulders to steady himself. She glanced at the bedside clock and quickened the pace. She still had to apply her makeup and needed to get this done.

"I can't decide if I want your tiddlers in my mouth, over my face, splashed on my boobs or…ok, my fingers and the carpet will have to do…" she giggled as she had to quickly grab a towel when the first volley of his juice hit the palm of her hand. Dan now held her shoulders firmly as the main flood emptied into the towel. She was always fascinated by how his face always seemed to contort with pain at the moment of ultimate pleasure. He sighed as the last emission left him, and on opening his eyes, watched her lick up the excess that had spilled onto her fingers. She added an accompanying, "Mmm, fuck, you always taste great," for good measure.

"Right, that's you sorted. Now bugger off and leave me in peace," Sarah said with a smile, but also in an almost dismissive manner and, turning back to the mirror, reached for some wet wipes to clean her hand properly.

"That was fab," Dan said and gave her a kiss on the cheek before wiping himself properly and placing the towel in the laundry basket. She continued with the task in hand and said with a smile, "You owe me one." In the mirror, she watched him turn towards her and said sternly, "Not Now!" He turned away, grabbed a pair of briefs from his drawer and put them on before delving into the wardrobe for a clean pair of jeans, which he also shimmied into. He took another quick look at his beautiful fiancée and then did as instructed.

The nagging doubt disappeared along with his discharged sap. He was then about to text Matt to see what he was doing. Sadly, the momentarily subdued ache of his best mate's death returned with a vengeance. He took a deep breath and turned on the TV. He was not surprised that the pre-match punditry was just the same old bollocks from masters of the blindingly obvious on over-inflated salaries.

When Sarah appeared, she looked stunning, as she usually did, but this time she was dressed to kill. She wore a black short-sleeved silk top, the plain square neckline was low enough to show some cleavage, and lengthwise, it barely covered her backside. Her lower half was encased in the tightest pair of white leggings you could imagine, which showed her legs and bum off to their full, stunning effect. The ensemble was completed with white stiletto ankle boots, and she wore enough bangles and bracelets to put an Asian market stall to shame.

"Fucking hell, Saz!" Dan said, gawping at her.

"You like?" Sarah said, admiring herself in the mirror, turning left and right and making sure she didn't show too much bum or gash as the leggings were so tight that the outline of her nether region left nothing to the imagination.

"Are you sure you're going out with the girls? That's a pretty full-on outfit for a girl's night out, don't you think?" The nagging doubts returned and multiplied.

"Oh, shut up," she said, trying to make a joke of it. "A girl has to look her best," and she bent over to kiss him. He noticed then that she wasn't wearing a bra as her breasts jiggled about as if they had a life of their own. The volume of those alarm bells went up quite a few decibels. Usually, those puppies were only unfettered when she was out with him just to attract attention.

Sarah's phone pinged, and she glanced at it quickly, "Taxi's outside, gotta rush, mwah." She grabbed her clutch bag and popped her mobile phone and keys into it before putting her coat over her arm and sashaying out the door. Her hips swayed as she walked, causing the top to ride up he gawped again as the leggings clearly showed each cheek of her backside and the parting in between. Those alarm bells now sounded like a wartime siren.

Dan had a few beers as he watched the football match. His depressed and worried demeanour was partly quelled by the alcohol and a convincing England win against what he thought was nothing more than a pub team. He smiled to himself and reckoned his own outfit could have seriously given that shower of shit a run for their money. It was just after 10.30 pm, and he decided to turn in for the night. There had been no messages from Sarah. He texted her to say that he was off to bed and hoped she was having a good time, signing off with "LY x".

In the ten minutes it took to get ready for bed, there was still no response, and he tried to suppress fears of what might be going on in her life. The poignant lyrics of that Doctor Hook song "When You're In Love With A Beautiful Woman" kept gnawing at him. He knew she loved him, but she was a very attractive young woman, and she knew it. After all, he told himself, it's no small part of what made her so successful. Of course, she worked bloody hard, but her beauty and, not least, her affable personality was that extra edge needed when securing work in such a competitive market.

He woke at 1.30 am and saw his phone flashing. It had to be Sarah. He gathered himself and checked, to his slight relief, it was from her. The message received was timed at 11.45 pm, and all it said was, *"Hey, we're going on to a club for a couple more and then I'll be home…g'night x"*

There was no LY! It's hurtful when terms of endearment are missing.

He slept fitfully for a few hours, and at 3.40 am, he woke and looked into the darkness. His insecurity was the first thing to rear its ugly, destructive face. He turned over, and at last, he wasn't alone. They had a super king-sized bed, so if he hadn't heard her, it was unlikely he would have felt much movement on the mattress. But at least, he could stop worrying about where she was. Now, he would concentrate his disquiet on what she had been up to.

Even though it was a Saturday, he was awake again at 6.00 am. Usually, he would just turn over and be grateful that he could go back to sleep. This day, he wondered how he was going to investigate his misgivings without her knowing. Dan hated himself for doubting that she had been anything but truthful about her reason for being out. If only those fucking alarm bells would stop. She was sound asleep when he quietly got up and grabbed a sweatshirt and a pair of shorts. As he left the bedroom, he surreptitiously dipped into the laundry basket to pick out her white leggings. He couldn't see the thong anywhere but considered that she may well still be wearing it.

He avoided the en-suite bathroom so as not to wake her and used the family bathroom instead. He employed his "can't miss piss" early morning technique of sitting on the WC and examined the leggings as he relieved himself. His stomach was in his mouth, and his heart was sinking. He was no Sherlock Holmes, but the evidence was damning, not just visually but by the smell. The still damp stain in the crotch of the leggings was obvious enough, and the salty smell of semen provided the guilty verdict. He felt physically sick that this substantial discharge had been deposited bareback into his beautiful fiancée by another man.

His mind was in turmoil now, and he desperately tried to find any extenuating circumstances. Perhaps she was raped, or maybe so drunk that she didn't know what she was doing. He dabbed his dick with a sheet of toilet paper, got up, pulled up his shorts and washed his hands. He then went downstairs to the kitchen and looked at the leggings again. They were so sexy on her. Why did he let her go out like that? It was bound to be asking for trouble. He then heard her phone in her clutch bag. It didn't ping, it just vibrated.

It then dawned on him that the phone would give him some reason to still believe in her. Heart thumping, he grabbed the bag and retrieved the device from its side panel, along with, to his disgust, her soaking wet thong reeking of that same salty odour that was on her leggings.

He slumped into the chair by the dining table and dared himself to look into the abyss. Tapping in her passcode, he told himself to be careful to open but then close the apps and pausing, with his heart ready to explode, he dreaded what he was going to find.

The latest message was from someone called Charles. All it said was, "All okay? x" so he didn't need to open it. He scrolled back through messages from yesterday, several from *Charles,* including one just before she left, saying that he was just down the road, out of sight. Historically, there were many more from him, and when Dan checked the calendar, they seemed to increase in frequency the further he scrolled back. Most of them gave her times and dates and the name of whom she was to meet. Wait, he thought to himself, were these business appointments to do with organising events? It was her career, after all.

He hoped he had found some excuse because he desperately wanted to. He went back to some other messages on her call list, and any shred of hope he had was shot down in the flames of overwhelming evidence. So many different names, the majority of which (but not all) were from men, and so many of them thanking her in one way or another for such a great time or words to that effect. He looked at the dates stretching back to long before they got together, up to when they first shacked up, and he recalled that was when she used to work many evenings and weekends.

Dan couldn't work out who Charles was or what part he had to play in this whole sordid business. He closed the messages window and looked through some of the apps on her phone. There were a couple of dating sites, one of which was for swingers, which he selected only to find, to his horror, that Sarah had set up a profile for herself as *Sarah Slut* with a picture of her face blurred, wearing her sexiest black lingerie. She was smiling and about to put a dildo into her mouth – the caption read, *"this could be your cock."*

He closed the app. It was all too much.

He heard some footsteps, and Sarah caught him red-handed. She stared at him for a few seconds, realising that the game was up.

"I do love you, you know that, don't you?" She said quietly.

He couldn't look at her and started to weep. He could barely speak apart from asking. "Why?"

She sat next to him, took her phone and, putting it to one side, held his hands in hers. She had known ever since she fell in love with him that the time of reckoning would happen one day. As upbeat and jovial as she always was, this was hard to endure, even though she knew she was the cause of his heartache.

She still spoke quietly but with purpose, she had to make sure he listened as calmly as he could.

"Don't torture yourself over all of this. I will explain everything. The one thing I ask you to focus on is that I love you. I adore you. You have brought so much sense and meaning to my life that I would be lost without you!" She leant toward him and hugged him tightly. She could feel him shake with emotion as her silk dressing gown mopped up his tears. "I'll make some coffee." She said, trying to bring the situation back to normality.

As she put a spoonful of instant coffee in each cup with a splash of milk, she took a few deep breaths and tried to compose herself. While the kettle boiled, she stashed the offending exhibits of soiled clothing into the washing machine. Sarah brought the coffee back to the table, gave him a kiss on the cheek and handed him a box of tissues.

"Dan, you've always known that I love sex. I have done ever since I reached puberty. I developed quite quickly after that and lost my virginity when I was fifteen. Since I was sixteen, I can't ever remember a time when I would go more than a few days without sexual intercourse. In my teens, I learnt a lot about men, their attitudes to women, their attitudes to sex, what pleased them in bed and what I could get them to do to please me. I was hooked on it and loved being a wild child. I know you think this insatiable desire can be calmed with tablets or something, but the thing is, I don't want to be calmed or cured. I get high on anticipation, lust and passion."

Dan sat there forlornly, wondering where this was going.

"When I left school, I had a number of different jobs, but I studied Business and Events Management in my own time and expense to get some business skills behind me, but you know all that. You also know I went to Ireland for a while, but came back to look after mum just before she died.

I worked hard to set up my own company, but it didn't matter how hard I worked. It is a real cut-throat business, and to get a foot in the door, you need contacts. I was at an Events Exhibition in Birmingham after my first year and met up with a guy called Charles Harding. You may have seen his name in my messages. He was a decent enough chap, and he invited me to dinner. It turned out that he is a top dog in the events business and also runs his own long-standing, successful company." She sipped at her coffee while Dan stared at his.

"I won't deny that we enjoyed each other's company that night, even though I knew he was married, and we had an affair for about six months. But all of this was before we met. He was clever, posh and good fun, but we both knew it had to end, especially as his wife was getting suspicious. Anyway, he was straightforward enough to say that my great ambition of being the world's greatest events consultant was a pipe dream. Sure, I could make a living, but I wouldn't be going further than small beer weddings and occasional corporate parties. Basically, I'd be fighting for scraps with the other one-man bands."

Dan had gathered himself a little and looked confused. "But what's that got to do with—"

Sarah interrupted and said, "I'm coming to that." She took a few deep breaths and continued.

"When we met for the last *nice* time, he said that he knew that I was struggling financially. He also said that he'd like to offer me a job, but that might prove quite awkward, given our liaison. He went on to say that he had a friend who had asked about me and whether I would like to spend an evening with him at some dinner and dance. Charles said that the guy didn't expect that I would do it for nothing and was quite prepared to give me a couple of hundred pounds for… well, to put it delicately, 'expenses.'

Charles said that the guy expected nothing more from me than to pretend I was his date for some Hooray Henry Army Regiment function. I was to be a paid escort, and do you know, I was so broke I thought, Why not? I could happily be polite for a few hours in the company of the upper crust, and getting paid for the fun of it would be the icing on the cake."

Dan, still sullen at the whole bombshell of the morning, just said, "And?"

"It was a lovely evening. The guy was quite charming, not overly handsome, but a thorough gentleman, and he offered me money to stay with him that night. I'll tell you now I would have stayed with him for nothing because I had got a bit tipsy and you know what I'm like when that happens."

Dan knew exactly what she meant, "How much did he pay you?"

"It doesn't matter," she said dismissively.

Dan insisted curtly, "It does to me!"

Sarah sighed.

"Okay, if you want to know – a grand. He paid me a thousand pounds to have sex with him and stay with him that night in the Savoy. Okay?" She said as a matter of fact.

"I was twenty-two years old and just been paid twelve hundred pounds to be wined and dined at a really posh 'do' in one of London's top hotels and also shag a guy that I would have done for nothing. Just for the fun of it." Sarah seemed irritated that she was being pressed to explain herself.

She had another sip of her coffee and mentioned that Dan's coffee was untouched.

"The following morning, I fucked him again. He was a virgin, and I enjoyed showing him what he'd been missing. I went home in a black cab, which was also paid for by him, I was elated – I loved it. I loved the whole lifestyle that these people lived on a day-to-day basis. I thought it was a one-off opportunity to make a substantial amount of money, but–" she hesitated. "He became a regular…client if you want to call him that, and the word spread. Charles vetted other possible clients, and I built up quite a fan base." She seemed quite proud of herself.

Dan interrupted, "So Charles is a pimp, and you're a fucking whore then!" He was moving from being distraught to angry.

"Dan, you can call me all the names under the sun if it makes you feel better. Whore, prostitute, slapper, slut, courtesan, harlot, but they all add up to the same thing, I get paid an awful lot of money to have fun, and that's all it means to me. It's just fun!"

"And what about that swinger's website? You don't charge the people you meet there, do you?" Dan said, taking the moral high ground.

"I work from home, and when there's not much work as is usual, I get bored. That website provides entertainment, even if most times it's just the amusement value of sarcastic banter with some of the idiots on there. On the plus side, I get a lot of compliments, which I absolutely adore. It excites me to think people are turned on looking at me."

"But you don't deny you've met up with people from there?" he questioned.

"No, I don't, couples mainly, and it's an education."

"But all these people… you have sex with them whether they pay you or not, you're giving them your body, which belongs to me," Dan offered as some sort of reason why she should not behave the way she was.

"Daniel, my body is my own. It belongs to no one except me. My heart, my mind and my soul belong to you, and that's the difference. How many times have you heard a married man who is caught having an affair bleat that it meant nothing, it was just sex or just a bit of fun? Well, that's exactly what it means to me."

"Right, so if I went off and fucked everything in sight, you wouldn't mind?" Dan snapped.

"As long as you did it discretely and always came back to me to be the same loving man that you are, then no, I wouldn't mind. I understand that sex and making love are not the same thing. And I'll tell you something else, having moved in some of those upper-crust circles, there are an awful lot of women, some quite beautiful, that want the same as these men. Not only that, but they are willing to pay well for the privilege of being escorted by a handsome man, especially one with intelligence, charm, wit and personality - like *you*. The fact that you are fabulous in bed would earn you a desirable reputation and the fortune to go with it." It sounded almost like a sales pitch to him.

Sarah finished her coffee, she held his hands again, "I know it's a lot to take in, and I'm really sorry that I've hurt you. I'm also sorry that I never had the guts to tell you, but I am so afraid of losing you. Please try to understand. We've both been through a lot of pain recently. We've lost our best friends with Matt and Kirstie gone in such tragic circumstances, and for you, it's worse because of your job and now this, but life is unfair, and we have each other." She kissed his forehead, and he began to cry again.

"Is all of this why you postponed the wedding?" He asked between his bouts of grief.

"I guess it is. I don't want any secrets between us, and I had to find a way of telling you before I committed myself to you and vice versa, heart, mind, soul…and yes, *my* body."

"I don't seem to have anything of you," Dan sobbed.

"Oh, my Love, you do. I've been yours since the very first day. Do you remember when we first met? When I saw you in that pub, I knew you were the one for me. I could barely breathe. No man had ever done that to me before or since, and I truly believe in love at first sight!"

Dan wiped some tears away and nodded. He forced a smile and said, "You got rid of the girl I was with that night. I thought you were drunk."

Sarah smiled

"Yes, dull Doris! But when we went back to your flat and made love, it was like nothing I'd ever experienced before with anyone. We just connected on every level. I fell in love with you at that moment. Later, when we really started talking, it was like I'd known you forever. It was surreal. Oh, and your kiss. I know people write poetry about the effect a kiss can have, but I swear to you, I went limp. But, of course, it literally had the opposite effect on you," she said with a little chuckle, stroking his arm.

"Perhaps we were lovers in another life?" He started to relax a bit.

"Maybe we were because that would explain an awful lot of why we are so good together."

Sarah squeezed his hands to emphasise the point.

"Do you remember how I cried that first time and still occasionally do?" she asked, hoping he would look at her. He nodded but kept his head down.

"Because it is all so wonderful. There's no other word I can think of to describe it. But I have always had one question I've wanted to ask you," she hesitated.

He nodded and said, "Go on, ask."

"Who taught you to make love like you do? No man, or woman, come to that, has ever made me feel so wanted and so wonderfully satisfied when we do what we do. I cannot explain how emotionally safe I feel being in your arms, which is the whole difference between making love and shagging for fun. A woman somewhere in your past must have been your mentor." He was about to speak when Sarah stopped him. "No, I don't want to know, but I would thank her because, in part, she has made you the wonderful man that you are." Sarah hoped the compliments would bring him around.

He started to weep again and thought about the devastation he felt when Carol ended their brief but explosive relationship. All those feelings came back to join with the sickening emptiness he felt now. Sarah needed to convince him more.

"I'll go and have a shower and then we'll go back to bed. I'll show you how much you mean to me. Even if we just cuddle, I need to know that you will, in time, forgive me for all of this heartache. I am and always will be yours," she was almost pleading with him now.

At last, he looked at her.

"Would you give it all up if I wanted you to?" He almost begged but stopped himself.

"Please don't ask me. It's not a decision I could make at the drop of a hat. I'd like us both to take some positives out of what seems to be a disaster when it isn't as bad as you think."

"Okay, so half the world is fucking my fiancée, some pay for it, others don't, and I'm supposed to find some positives?" Dan replied crossly, shaking his head.

"Please don't be angry, Dan. I know right now I'm a complete bitch in your eyes but think about what I've said, and we can move on from this." She leaned forward and kissed him full on his lips. They tasted salty from the tears.

"Come upstairs." And she kissed him again. Standing, Sarah held his hands as if to pull him up and lead him to their bedroom. He squeezed her hands and let go of them.

"Okay, just give me a few minutes." She smiled a weak sort of smile and left, telling him not to be long.

He stared out of the window, and the tears started again. He'd gone to the funeral of his best mate only a few weeks before, and, what with the redundancy, it all seemed to be an awful downward spiral. If that wasn't enough, he was now wracked with confusion and physical pain to find that the great love of his life, his rock, his confidante and lover, was not who he thought she was. He trawled through her words to find some justification for her being an absolute slut, *Sarah Slut*, and he could find none.

Sarah had her shower, after which she dried herself and waited. Fifteen minutes later, she called downstairs and got no reply. She called again…silence. She went down to find him - his car was gone. She phoned him but heard his familiar ringtone of Hall and Oates' *"Sara Smile"* playing upstairs, where he'd left his phone. Sarah panicked, he never went anywhere without his phone. She started to cry. What could she say, or do now, that would make him see how much he meant to her?

Sarah made up her mind that when he came back, she would promise to give it all up. She clenched her fists and, through a flood of tears, hoped he would return soon. She felt utterly helpless.

Twenty-four hours elapsed with no word from Dan, so she reported him missing to the police. Five days of purgatory later, a police car collected her from her home to take her to identify the body of a young man. The young man had ended his life by inhalation of carbon monoxide poisoning when he rigged up a tube from his car's exhaust into the inside of the vehicle and swallowed a handful of sleeping pills diluted with half a bottle of whisky. The coroner's court returned a verdict of suicide, and the coroner personally offered her condolences to the man's grieving fiancée.

A week later, that grieving fiancée drove to the same little dirt track leading to a small copse on the Hampshire/Dorset border where her forever lover had ended his destructive torment. She was suitably armed to join her soul mate by the same method he employed. Sarah knew she had nothing else to live for.

She was saved in the nick of time by an old couple walking their dog. They explained to the attending police and ambulance crews that they would never have found the car except that their dog went chasing down a narrow track. When they followed it, in the distance, they saw a young man in a sweatshirt and shorts frantically waving at them. As they got to the car, he was nowhere to be seen, and they considered he may well have been a jogger that didn't want to hang about.

37

Ain't No Sunshine

February 2015

Even on a Saturday, Alan had left early for work as usual and Julia decided that she must try to motivate herself despite her monumental grief. She got up early, showered and made a shopping list for groceries and foodstuffs. It wasn't exciting, but at least it was a distraction on a wet weekend morning.

She had often read how a traumatic loss of loved ones can take people to the depths of depression and despair, she was not going to let it happen to her. She blamed herself for the circumstances which led up to that fateful hour, but her remorse and guilt would not bring them back. She recalled the line from Shawshank Redemption: *"Get busy living or get busy dying."*

She had just sat down with a coffee when she heard a car pull into the drive. She immediately thought that Alan had forgotten something and got up to let him in. She went to the door and could see through the window two thick-set men alight from the vehicle. They looked like police officers. To her mind, nothing coppers could ever wear would disguise their occupation. Her heart began to beat faster, so much so she could barely breathe. Had something happened to Alan, not Alan, please, not Alan. This was that awful day six weeks ago, happening all over again. Her heart was in her mouth, and she couldn't think straight. She opened the door before they rang the bell.

They approached unsmiling and business-like as they reached into their pockets for their warrant cards. They were big men. One of them spoke, "Mrs McCann?" She nodded, too nervous to speak.

"I am Detective Sergeant Radcliff. This is Detective Sergeant Bone. May we come in, please?"

"Has something happened to Alan?" she asked shakily.

"Alan?"

"Alan, Alan McCann, my husband," she said nervously.

"No, madam, we're here on another matter. May we come in?" asked DS Radcliff.

Still nervous and now perplexed, she automatically stepped aside and, without saying anything, lifted a hand to usher them towards the living room. They made themselves comfortable on the sofa, unlike the other officers who wanted *her* to take a seat while they stood to impart the earth-shattering news. She started to slightly relax.

"Can I get you a tea or coffee?" she asked, not forgetting her manners.

They both requested coffee with milk. DS Bone asked for two sugars. She went off to the kitchen, thinking how uncouth he was. Did he expect her to sugar the coffee herself? Sugar would be in the bowl with a spoon, and his coffee would be in a cup on a saucer with its own spoon. As she made the coffee on autopilot, she wondered in her own mind, what the fuck did they want? Couldn't they see she was still grieving for her loss?

Julia returned to the front room, where the officers were sitting very upright.

"Please help yourself to sugar. I'm sorry, I don't have any biscuits. They are such a temptation, you know," trying to infer how fattening they were without being so obvious.

"Thank you, Mrs McCann, and that's very wise. DS Bone and myself have much difficulty with the temptation of biscuits," Radcliff answered with a hint of a smile.

"So, what can I help you with? I told a colleague of yours all I knew about my daughter's accident. I was told that they didn't require any further information. Is it to do with the court case or the inquest?" she asked, naively believing that was their reason for the visit. They asked what she was referring to and, on hearing the explanation, offered their condolences for her loss. No, they were here on another serious issue. DS Radcliff paused to let her take that on board for a minute. Julia was confused and stared back quizzically at both of the officers. In her mind, she was thinking, what could be more important than an accident causing two fatalities?

"I don't understand," and she was about to voice her thoughts when DS Bone said that they understood that she was married to someone called Gerald Irvine, also known as Gerry Irvine.

Her mind went to mush, and she shook for a few seconds, taking a rather deep swallow. The detectives seemed concerned at the reaction.

"Are you okay, Mrs McCann?" Radcliff asked.

"Yes, yes, sorry. I haven't heard that name for a very long time. I was married to him for a short while. It wasn't anything I happily recall apart from having my daughter by him." She paused, trying to compose herself. "The daughter I lost in the recent accident," she could barely contain the tears.

"I am so sorry to hear that. We were unaware of how recent that was," Radcliff said. Bone said nothing but just continued to stare at her before continuing with his statement, even sounding a little miffed that he had been interrupted. He then stirred two sugars into his coffee using the spoon from the sugar bowl and then put the wet spoon back in the sugar!

"So, you were married to this Gerald Irvine?" he asked coldly.

"Yes," she answered, dabbing her eyes.

"How long were you married to him?"

She thought for a number of seconds, "Just over a year."

"When did you last see him?" he seemed very intense to her.

She thought again and, after a short pause, "I'm not sure of the date, but summer 1990, I think."

"And?" Bone was quite cold and blunt.

"And what, officer?" Julia didn't understand what else he expected.

"What were the circumstances of the last time you saw him? Where did he go when he left?" he said in a rather curt manner. Julia took a deep breath and recalled the evening when she ended up in hospital. She looked Bone straight in the eyes and said that she saw him walking out of the apartment door moments after he had beaten her up.

"I couldn't say for certain where he went because I was lying on the floor at the time with a dislocated jaw and swollen eyes," she added, just to let him have some of the finer detail.

"Thankfully, he left enough in me to be able to phone for help." She said no more and watched Bone show Radcliff his notebook.

"You'll be able to check your records because he was arrested for assault," Julia was getting rather defiant now. "Sorry, alleged assault. To go with my alleged black eyes and alleged dislocated jaw."

Radcliff nodded, not so much to agree with her but more to take in how she was stirred by having to recall such a trauma. Bone made some notes and then asked if she knew what happened to him after that.

"No, I don't know, and I don't care. I hope he rots in hell for what he did to me and my daughter. He was a control freak and a bully," Julia said, and immediately cursed herself for sounding so pathetic as to not being able to stand up to him. The two officers exchanged an almost imperceptible glance at one another that, however fleeting, did not go unnoticed by Julia.

"Interesting that you suggest that he might be in hell, Mrs McCann," Bone said.

"Why?" she asked.

"Well, it would suggest that you assume he's dead," Bone said, stony-faced.

Julia looked aghast. "How would I know if he's dead?" she asked innocently, shrugging her shoulders.

"Well, you hoped he would be in hell, which would suggest to me that you know that he is deceased," Bone said, still staring. Julia was surprised at the inference. She took a few seconds before saying, almost through gritted teeth.

"Detective Sergeant Bone, it is a statement that is often employed when someone hates someone else with a passion and, trust me, I hated him with a passion."

Bone continued staring but said nothing. It was a stare that she felt was part of a detective's armoury. She remembered a TV documentary about police interview techniques, asking a question, letting the interviewee answer and then creating an awkward silence. It makes the interviewee want to fill that silence, and they eventually trip themselves up. Julia was not going to play ball.

"Hated him enough to kill him?" Bone eventually said emphatically.

She sat back, totally bemused by his accusation.

"Kill him?" she asked.

"Yes, you hated him. You wanted him to rot in hell, he'd have to be dead to get there, wouldn't he?" Bone said sarcastically.

"Do you seriously think I'd be I'd be capable after some of the beatings he gave me?" Julia was shocked at the suggestion.

"You clearly had the motive. You may have hit him from behind with something?" Radcliffe offered.

"And do what with the body? Do I look like I could lift a guy his size?"

"So, you had an accomplice?" Bone said.

"I didn't need one!" she said, leading them into a trap that they thought they had set for her.

"Ah, so you dealt with him by yourself?" Bone said, almost smugly.

"I didn't need an accomplice because I didn't do anything to him. So, tell me what's happened that you feel the need to visit and quiz me about that bastard?" She was quite annoyed now.

The two detectives stared at her for what felt like a very long five seconds.

"Well, Mrs McCann, human remains have been found not too far from where we are now, and although the body is somewhat decomposed, there is enough to be able to identify it through DNA and dental records to confirm that it is your ex-husband Gerald Irvine," Radcliffe said, watching for any sort of reaction.

Julia gasped, and she stared at them open-mouthed before saying, "DNA?"

"Yes, you were aware that he had a criminal record?" Bone asked and informed her of the legal requirement regarding the collection of DNA material from any suspect.

"I thought he might be up to some dodgy stuff, but I didn't know he had a criminal record." She answered honestly. Her mind was spinning, trying to piece it all together.

"There is no point in taking you to identify him for obvious reasons, but the senior pathologist is certain that the remains we have are of Gerald Irvine," Bone said bluntly. "We also have these items." And he produced a small see-through plastic bag with a watch and a ring in it. "Do you recognise these?" he asked, fully expecting her to confirm that they were Gerry's.

She looked at them intently for less than a minute, turning the bag over a few times before confirming that they were Gerry's.

"The ring is his wedding ring, and on the inside, it should say *Love You, Jx.*'"

The two detectives barely nodded at each other.

"I bought him the watch as a wedding present," Julia added.

"You're sure?" Radcliffe asked.

"Yes, you'll see on the back of the watch it says '*Eternally Yours, with all my love Julia x.*'"

Bone wrote some more notes.

"Where were the remains found?" she asked.

"We can't divulge that information at the moment," Radcliffe said.

"How did he die?" she asked, not really expecting an answer.

Bone looked at Radcliffe, who gave a slight nod as if to say you can tell her.

"It would appear that his skull was fractured by a heavy instrument. The pathologist thinks a bat of some sort, but the damage was probably too flat to be a baseball bat."

"He did play cricket," she offered helpfully, but thought she had better not say any more.

Bone made another note and nodded to Radcliffe.

"Well, Mrs McCann, we'll call a halt to proceedings for the time being. Thank you for your time. You have been very helpful," Radcliffe said.

Recalling the TV documentary again, the friendly approach also trapped guilty people into wanting to assist further. Again, she was having none of it.

"I haven't been helpful at all. You would have known all of this from the police interview about the assault. Why have you come here?" Julia was really annoyed now.

Radcliffe looked a bit surprised by her attitude, but gave it to her straight.

"Mrs McCann, this is a murder investigation, and as such, we are entitled to interview any and all witnesses, people with relevant information and, of course, possible suspects. I understand this is a lot to take in, so we'll leave it at that for now, but we will need to see you again. If you think of anything that might be helpful to us, you can call me on that number," Radcliff said, handing her his card.

"I'm a suspect, am I?" she said curtly. "You can put this in your stupid little notebooks. Towards the end of our marriage, I detested him. As I said, he was a control freak, a bully, and a cruel, hateful man. I can categorically state that if he had done anything to the detriment of my daughter, I would have gladly fractured his skull with anything I could have got hold of, and if it had been his beloved cricket bat, then I would have enjoyed the irony. If he's dead, then I wouldn't shed one tear for that cunt, do you understand?" and she stood up. They said nothing as they got up and allowed her to lead them out.

"If you want to chat to me again, please give me some notice so that I can have a solicitor with me," she said defiantly.

The two detectives just said, "Good Day," as they left, and she slammed the door behind them. Julia's mind was in overdrive. How dare they suggest that she was a suspect, and then she couldn't believe how bad the timing was for that awful name from the past to rear its ugly head. She fussed about the kitchen, putting the teacups in the dishwasher and then started to wonder what really happened on that day when Joey Porter made sure her ex-husband left the flat. She was glad that she didn't implicate him, but consoled herself that they never asked about him, anyway.

On the following Wednesday, DS Radcliffe phoned her to request an informal interview at the police station on Friday morning at 10.00 am. As it was informal, she was advised that she did not need to bring a solicitor, but it was certainly her right to do so. She said that she would be there, and she would be bringing someone with her. She was terrified!

Julia turned up at the Police Station on the dot at 10.00 am with Richard Reynolds, a solicitor friend that Joey knew and had often used in the past. She really didn't want Joey to know, but because she had to take time off from work, she needed to let him know why she wouldn't be there.

"You'll need a solicitor, and don't let the buggers bully you," Joey advised, "but whatever they ask about anything, tell them the facts because you have nothing to hide. They're looking for closure. It keeps their records up to date, so if they want to come and chat with me, they are very welcome to do so. Don't worry about anything."

Joey always had such a calm manner about dealing with a crisis, and this, for her, was a crisis dragging her demeanour to a very low ebb, if that was at all possible. It needed to be settled.

When she arrived at the police station, Radcliffe and Bone made her wait fifteen minutes. Another police tactic, she thought. They apologised, of course, but didn't mean a word of it. They sat down and informed her that although this was an informal interview, the conversation would be recorded. Julia looked at Richard, and he said that they were within their rights to do so. However, he also said that she didn't have to answer anything and could leave at any time.

DS Bone then went back over the same questions he had asked her at her home, and she gave exactly the same replies and cheekily, at one point, said that she seemed to be experiencing déjà vu.

Radcliffe asked her if she thought all of this was funny.

"No, I don't find any of it funny, but you've asked me all of these questions before, and it seems to me to be a complete waste of time."

"We'll be the judge of that," Bone said. "Now, for the tape, would you tell me again what you said you would do if your ex-husband ever hurt your daughter?"

"I said I'd gladly hit him with a cricket bat!" she replied.

"That's not what you said last time," Bone pointed out and was back to his intense staring game again.

"I don't recall exactly what I said," Julia replied, "but I'm sure that was the gist of it."

"That's okay, I have it here – you said – quote, *'You can put this in your stupid little notebooks. Towards the end of our marriage, I detested him, as I said he was a control freak, a bully and a cruel, hateful man and I can categorically state that if he had done anything to the detriment of my daughter, I would have gladly fractured his skull with anything I could have got hold of and if it had been his beloved cricket bat, then I would have enjoyed the irony.'* Does that sound accurate?" Bone was almost sneering at her.

"Spot on," she said. "You must have been a star pupil at The Pitman School of Shorthand," she said sarcastically. Reynolds looked down, but he could hardly contain his smile.

"So, earlier during our chat last time, you also said that you wouldn't have been capable of attacking him, and yet here you're saying you'd quite happily fracture his skull if he did anything to your daughter," Bone said.

"Any mother would find the strength to defend their little ones, and what you seem to have conveniently forgotten is that I also said that I wouldn't have been able to deal with the body of such a weight." She was irritated by the questions, but then calmed herself, knowing that was exactly what they were trying to do. Radcliffe and Bone both stared at her, and she just stared back.

After a minute or two, Reynolds said, "If that's all you have, gentlemen, I think my client would now like to leave." And he got up, inviting Julia to stand with him. Radcliffe held up his hand and said, "Just one last thing before I terminate the recording, would you voluntarily take a DNA test and allow us to take your fingerprints?"

Reynolds asked them for what reason, as she wasn't being charged with anything.

"Oh, come on, Mr Reynolds, it's a standard request to eliminate Mrs McCann from our enquiries," said Radcliffe.

"Oh yes, that old chestnut!" Reynolds replied before turning to Julia and shaking his head.

She thought about it for a moment and said that she would comply. Reynolds was horrified and told her that he would strongly advise against it.

"I've got nothing to hide. I'm happy for them to take whatever stuff they want!"

Radcliffe terminated the interview and asked Bone to get the necessary tests and prints done.

As Julia left with Reynolds, she told him that the interview seemed quite bizarre – it was short and not very sweet, just going over what they had already asked. Reynolds replied that they were only after her DNA and prints, and the "interview" was just the vehicle for making the request. Julia hoped that would be the end of it, although in her heart of hearts, she knew this was going to drag on and revive all the pain and suffering from twenty-five years ago.

A month later, Julia's mum called her and asked if she would like to come over one evening, but wouldn't say why on the phone. It was an odd request as they often got together informally for a coffee or dinner occasionally. Julia flipped it and said it would be better if they came to her for no other reason than it was her turn.

Her parents visited that very evening. Alan was late as usual, but Julia's mum said it was probably best that he wasn't there. Julia began to get worried as they took their seats around the kitchen table.

"What's this about Mum? You don't normally make a formal request to get together and visit." Julia asked. Her mum looked at her husband and said, "The police have been round…a couple of times over the last fortnight."

Julia shook her head and said scornfully, "That'll be Morecombe and Wise!"

"Radcliffe and Bone, I think their names were, anyway, they said it was to do with the disappearance of that scumbag ex-husband of yours. Apparently, they found his body and suspect foul play, which must have happened soon after he left you," her mum said with much discomfort.

"Yeah, and that was too good for him!" her dad said.

"Dave, shush, please," her mum was quick to admonish him.

"On the first visit, they wanted to know the whereabouts of your father at that time," her mum said, looking up at Dave.

"Oh, Dad, please say you didn't do it!" Julia said.

"Sweetheart, I'll be honest with you now and say I would gladly have done it and admitted it. What he did to you was obscene, and he deserved everything he got, although we didn't know it at the time," her dad said, almost snarling.

"Well, anyway, your father is a potential suspect because he can't produce an alibi," her mum said.

"How could anyone produce an alibi if nobody knows exactly when Gerry was murdered?" Julia asked again, resorting to her crime drama knowledge. Her dad agreed.

"They asked if we would supply DNA samples and fingerprints just to eliminate us from their enquiries, and, of course, we did. We went to the police station the following day," her mum then took a deep breath. "The thing is…" she started to shake. Her husband held her hand and told her it would be fine. Julia could see her mother was under a lot of duress.

"Go on, Mum."

"It appears that you did a DNA test for the police?" her mum said.

"Yes, I told them I had nothing to hide. Why, what's happened?"

Her mother started to well up.

"Mum, please."

"The police came again this morning to see us, not just about alibis, but to ask why your DNA result only shows me as a parent," her mum said and stared at Julia, who was trying to take in what her mother had just told her. She looked at her dad and then said to the pair of them that there must have been some mistake.

"It's no mistake, Sweetheart," her dad said whilst trying to comfort his wife, and then he came out with the hammer blow.

"It appears that I am not your biological father," he said quietly.

Julia was totally confused and began to cry.

"But you're my dad," she wept uncontrollably as he got up and knelt beside her to console her.

"In every aspect possible since the day you were born, I have been your dad, and I will always be your old papa. I just didn't start the process off." He chuckled, trying to make light of it to cheer the mood.

"Who the *fuck* is my biological father then, and what happened to him?" Julia was shocked.

Her mother sighed, and Julia could see the shame written on her face. Rita looked at Dave, virtually unable to speak.

"You know him," her dad said.

Julia was too flustered to think, "Who? Tell me *who?*" she asked impatiently.

"Joey Porter," her mum said.

"Joey? It can't be. Why are you telling me all of this? I didn't need to know," Julia said through a stream of tears.

"Because the police are bound to mention it if they interview you again, and I didn't want you to hear it from them."

"But why is *he* my biological father and not Dad?" Julia asked, trying to gather herself.

Rita looked at Dave again to explain.

"When we were a lot younger, we were very sexually liberated as a couple. We knew Joey as a friend, and anyway, one thing led to another, and we started a threesome relationship with him for about a year. Then your mum got pregnant, and we decided not to worry about who the father was because we loved each other, and you were wholeheartedly ours, and I was there at the conception. Until they discovered DNA, nobody really cared. We had a discussion with Joe about it at the time, and he magnanimously said that he was happy to go along with our conviction that I am your dad. Joe would not be a burden on our relationship by always being around us, even though there was a possibility that you were biologically his.

He maintained that whenever and wherever he could help you, he would, and he has been an absolute Trojan. He has always liaised with us about your welfare, and it hasn't been a problem."

"Until now!" Julia said. Her mum and dad nodded.

"And the problem is that Joey may have sailed close to the wind a few times, and the police may well have his DNA on their database, so it's just a matter of time before they include him as a suspect," her dad said.

"Close to the wind?" Julia asked.

"Joey is a lovely man, he is very community-minded, but if that is threatened by scumbags and other criminal arseholes, he won't put up with it, which has brought him into a bit of conflict with the police in the past, but he won't back down," her dad added.

Julia got the picture. She already loved him for the man he was and how protective he was of her, it seemed that the reason for that was all too clear, except that he was like that with all the people he cared about. This was a massive revelation to her.

"Jules, try to think of it as having an extra parent. We were both overjoyed when you were born, and we didn't even consider the extra... *input.* Just because one of his swimmers got there first made no difference to us. I know it's hard to understand, we've only struggled with it since this morning, but your dad and me are your parents and always will be. Joey is…well, over the years, your guardian angel," her mum said, reaching out to hold her hands.

"Did you tell them about Joey?" Julia asked.

"No, we just said we were a liberated couple. It could have been anyone, and we didn't even suspect that Dad wasn't the biological father."

"I don't think they believed us, but that's their problem!" her dad said.

"Does Joey know that they might be sniffing around?" Julia asked.

"Yes."

"Does he know that I know?"

"I told him we were going to tell you tonight. So, I think he might say something in the office tomorrow," Rita said.

Julia needed time to think and told her parents as much. As they left, she told them how much she loved them and wished them good night. They didn't seem fazed in the slightest about who her father was, so the only awkward thing she thought of was seeing Joey in the morning.

In reality, nothing was different. There was no relationship breakdown. Her parents were her rock and always would be. She was unsure how she felt about Joey Porter, but he was never anything other than kind and gentle, and she desperately hoped that he wasn't involved in anything so violent. They had only been gone about ten minutes when Joey was at the door. She invited him in, and he sat in the kitchen while she made him a cup of coffee.

"Your parents have told you about the DNA thing?" he asked. Julia nodded.

"None of us knew for certain that it was the case; of course, there was always a possibility, but it didn't really matter to them, and I was delighted for them; they're good people." Julia started to cry again.

"However you feel about the biological issue won't change how you've been brought up. Your mum and dad are still your mum and dad, and I have been…"

"Like a guardian angel, mum called you," she said, sniffling.

"Well, I wouldn't go that far, but I've kept an eye on you to try to make sure you didn't come to any harm. I am only sorry I didn't do a very good job as far as your ex-husband was concerned."

"You never told me what happened that day he left?" Julia looked at him quizzically.

Joey sighed and thought about not telling her, but he knew she wouldn't let it go.

"After we had our chat in the office that day, I needed to see him to point out the error of his ways. Wife-beaters are cowards, and I despise men that think they can control people with violence. Yet they regularly get away with it because the police seem to have difficulty proving it, even though the evidence is so blatantly obvious." He seemed resigned to the injustice of such behaviour.

"But isn't that what you've done in the past, control people with violence?" Julia wondered if the irony was lost on him.

"Violence is a last resort, and any skirmishes I may have had in the past were down to protecting my businesses and the people around me," he offered as an excuse. "To be frank, it's more of a defence and deterrent mechanism rather than control. If I make it clear that I won't be bullied by fighting fire with fire, I find that the problem goes away." Julia seemed to understand the difference.

"So, what happened?" she asked.

"He was at the flat and was already packing. I just wanted to call him out on his outrageous behaviour towards you." Julia was surprised that her ex-husband had already seen fit to leave just at that time.

"Why would he leave on that very day that you turned up?" She seemed to find it too much of a coincidence.

"I have no idea, perhaps he realised that he was just no good for you and decided to scuttle off somewhere else," Joey said as a matter of fact, although it still didn't ring true.

"So, what did he say when you spoke to him about what he did?" She wasn't going to let this go.

"He was his usual sarky self and denied that he had done anything to you. He said he'd already been interviewed by the police, who could find no evidence of assault."

"I just told him to carry on packing his things and get out of your life altogether or else," Joey said sternly.

"Or else what?"

"Or else he would have me to answer to, and so I stayed in the flat while he cleared all of his stuff. As you know, it's a fully furnished apartment, so it was just a matter of packing his clothes and any other sundry items that he could stuff into that shed of a car that he drove. He left, taking all the debts with him, and no one has seen him since. What's more, nobody bloody-well cares!" Least of all Joey Porter, she thought.

"And that's the truth?" Julia asked sceptically.

Joey moved over to her and cuddled her. She was reluctant at first, but then cuddled him back, sobbing into his arm.

"He had a lot of enemies, but I swear to you that the last time I saw him, he was driving out of the car park with all of his shit with him. Julia, it was the best thing that he went. He would have killed you and/or Kirstie in the end because guys like him never know when to stop."

She accepted his reasoning, and they sat drinking coffee without saying much else, although Joe did ask her how she met Alan again. She told him the story, and he commented that he thought they were a very good match. She nodded but didn't go into detail about their relationship. He asked to be remembered to him when he came home. Joey left soon after, asking her not to mention this at work. "There's enough nonsense gossip goes on anyway. This didn't need to be for public consumption," Julia was aghast.

"Joey, do you really think I want anyone to know my shame about this?" she said irritably.

Joey was calm.

"What shame? You bear no shame, and believe it or not, you were conceived during a loving act. I loved your mother then, and I still do. Dave is a very, very good friend. I like to think that all three of us are your parents and look after you as any loving parents would, so please don't ever think there's shame involved." He was quite insistent, and Julia sat there contemplating a revelation that her parents and her biological father seemed to accept it as 'just one of those things.' She was quite calm as Joey left, although she knew this disclosure would be with her for the rest of her life.

A few days later, Julia was called into the police station for another interview, which focused on the day that she returned to work. She was already aware that they had, by that time, interviewed Joey, although it seems he told them exactly what he told her, and she relayed those details to the police. As she was just about to leave, Radcliffe's parting shot was to mention the anomaly with her parents' DNA.

"I'm sorry that we had to break the bad news of the mismatch with your father's DNA, I'm sure nobody expected that," he said, almost sounding quite sincere with his apology. Julia said nothing.

"But the small consolation I can offer is that your biological father's DNA has not matched anything we have throughout the UK or Europe. Whoever he might be does not have a criminal record or been involved in any law enforcement enquiries." Julia looked at him, rather confused, but decided not to question him further for fear of opening another can of worms.

Two weeks later, in separate dawn raids, Julia McCann and Joseph Porter were arrested by the police. Both were charged with murder and conspiracy to murder and placed on temporary remand. Radcliffe and Bone were sure that the two suspects had the motive, the means, and the opportunity to murder Gerald Irvine so that he could indeed "rot in hell."

Richard Reynolds argued the case for bail in the next available court, and both were released with severe restrictions, including surrendering their passports and being electronically tagged.

Three months later, Joey Porter was interviewed by the police at his bedside in the hospice where he had been transferred to after a short spell in hospital. Those present were DS Radcliffe, DS Bone, Richard Reynolds, Father Stephen Kenny and Joey's common-law wife (of thirty years or so), Cheryl Pearce.

Six weeks earlier, he had been diagnosed with an aggressive form of pancreatic cancer, and he knew the time had come to make peace with God and, more importantly, himself.

"For the record – I am guilty of the dispatch of Gerry Irvine. I met him at the flat he was staying at with his wife, Kirstie, in 1990 or whenever it was, sorry, my mind is fuzzy with dates. It was a few weeks after he beat her up, and you wankers did nothing about it. I am in the brigade of *'an eye for an eye'* and he had already got away with it once before – not this time." He took a sip of water that Cheryl gave him, and she squeezed his hand as he drank.

"As I say, I met him at the flat and made it clear that he had to pack up and leave."

"Did he say anything or protest?" Bone asked, excited that they were getting a confession.

"He got lippy but a punch in the face normally quells argumentative aggression when they know they ain't gonna win," he added, "bullies are such stupid cunts!" and he chuckled to himself.

"Can I get you anything, Luv?" Cheryl asked, still holding his hand.

"Stop fussing!" he growled "you always fuss…" then he squeezed her hand weakly, "and I love you for it. Wait…coffee, you're not bad at that – white, no sugar." She shook her head and chuckled to herself.

Impatiently, Bone wanted more details, "Were you by yourself or did you have someone with you?"

"Of course, I was by myself. You're trying to suggest Julia was with me, aren't you? She was back at the office. You can check the dates and come on – what would she have contributed? Anyway, when Irvine realised he had to comply, he packed his stuff and loaded his car."

"Then what?"

"I took great satisfaction in making him drive to the spot where you found him. I made him get out of the car and literally knocked him out. I then took his cricket bat out of the boot of his car and finished him off. I cared nothing for him, and he deserved it because he would have continued doing the same thing to women for as long as he lived."

"How did you make him drive there?"

"I have a gun, or rather, I did have a gun – if you look very carefully, you'll find it in the Solent somewhere!" and Joey smiled to himself, knowing that it would be an impossible task to find the weapon in such a huge expanse of water – especially as the pistol never existed in the first place.

"What did you do with the car and his stuff?" Bone asked.

"Oh, for fuck's sake, use your imagination. I'm tired."

The two policemen made some notes and asked if he wanted to add anything.

"Nope, I am solely responsible for Gerry Irvine's justifiable demise. I watch out for people that I care about, and I have no worries about exacting appropriate revenge on people that deserve it. I know the real law actually has its hands tied behind its back."

He silently recalled that, with sibling assistance, Gerry Irvine, the Timmins brothers and the driver who killed Kirstie and Matt, plus a few others over the years, fell foul of Joseph Porter's acts of 'justice'. Then he wondered if this illness was God exacting some sort of revenge on him…Amen, he could accept that.

"Right, you rozzers can fuck off. I have more important business to conduct with this good lady here."

They left, with a signed confession, quite satisfied that the case was effectively closed but ultimately dismayed that the culprit would never see the inside of a prison cell again.

Joey turned to Cheryl and looked at her before looking down, taking a deep breath and then looking her in the eyes. He held both her hands and said, "Cheryl, I know I've never been what you really wanted, but you are the greatest love of my life, and I just wondered… will you marry me before it's too late?"

She squeezed his hands and cried, but smiling through the tears, nodded and said, "Yes, Joey, I love you so much." She felt quite liberated saying it out loud for all to hear after keeping the secret for so long.

"If nothing else, it'll tidy up all the legalities!" He surmised.

"You never quite got the romance thing, did you, Joe?" She had a wry smile on her face as she just accepted the man she loved forever.

They married two days later, with all of their close family and friends in attendance. The following day, the Catholic priest returned to administer the last rites, including communion, confession and forgiveness.

Joseph Porter left this world 48 hours later to face the 'supreme' judge and jury.

THE END

Acknowledgements

574

With acknowledgement to Sir Walter Scott and his epic poem Marmion.

I have listed details of all the musical references made in the book — the performing artists and the writers — what joy you bring to the world.

W.D. Jeffrey

Musical References

Great music by great singers, great musicians, great lyricists and great producers – thank you. There are a number of songs that were mentioned in earlier drafts of this muse but now do not appear in the completed manuscript. However, they are far too good to eradicate completely.

Title, Year, Artist and (composers)

Time to Say Goodbye 1995 - Andrea Bocelli and Sarah Brightman (Francesco Sartori) Lucio Quarantotto)

School's Out 1972 - Alice Cooper
(Alice Cooper, Michael Bruce, Glen Buxton, Dennis Dunaway, Neal Smith)

The Things We Do For Love 1976 10CC
(Eric Stewart, Graham Gouldman)

Let's Talk About Sex 1992 - Salt-N-Pepa
(Hurby Azor)

Love Is In the Air 1977 - John Paul Young
(Harry Vanda, George Young)

Amoureuse 1972 - Kiki Dee
(Véronique Sanson)

Smalltown Boy 1984 - Bronksi Beat
Steve Bronski. Jimmy Somerville, Larry Steinbachek

It's A Shame 1970 - The Spinners
Stevie Wonder, Syreeta Wright, Lee Garrett

What's Love Got to Do with It? 1984 - Tina Turner
<u>Graham Lyle, Terry Britten</u>

Love is a Battlefield 1983 - Pat Benatar
(<u>Mike Chapman</u>, <u>Holly Knight</u>)

I'm Still Standing 1983 - Elton John
(Elton John, Bernie Taupin)

I Want That Man 1989 - Debbie Harry
(<u>Alannah Currie</u>, <u>Tom Bailey</u>)

The First Time Ever I Saw Your Face 1972 - Roberta Flack
(<u>Ewan MacColl</u>)

The End of the Innocence 1989 - Don Henley
(<u>Don Henley, Bruce Hornsby</u>)

Jailbreak 1976 - Thin Lizzy
(<u>Phil Lynott</u>)

The Boys Are Back In Town 1976 - Thin Lizzy
(Phil Lynott)

I Kissed a Girl 2008 - Katy Perry
(<u>Lukasz Gottwald</u>, <u>Max Martin</u>, <u>Cathy Dennis</u>)

Girls Just Want To Have Fun 1983 - Cyndi Lauper
(<u>Robert Hazard</u>)

Nothing Compares 2 U 1990 - Sinead O'Connor
(Prince)

Obsession 1984 - Animotion
(<u>Holly Knight</u>, <u>Michael Des Barres</u>)

Everywhere 1987 - Fleetwood Mac
Christine McVie

Insatiable 2002 - Darren Hayes
(Darren Hayes, Walter Afanasieff)

Guilty 1990 - Barbara Streisand/Barry Gibb
(Barry Gibb, Robin Gibb, Maurice Gibb)

I've had the Time of My Life 1987 - Bill Medley/Jennifer Warnes
(John DeNicola, Donald Markowitz, Franke Previte)

Infatuation 2002 - Christina Aguilera
(Matt Morris, Scott Storch)

Erotica 1992
Madonna
(Madonna, Shep Pettibone, Anthony Shimkin)

I Would Give Everything I Own 1972 - David Gates & Bread
(David Gates)

Roar 2013 - Katy Perry
(Katy Perry, Lukasz Gottwald, Max Martin, Bonnie McKee, Henry Walter)

Your Cheating Heart 1953 - Hank Williams
(Hank Williams)

Lyin' Eyes 1975 - Eagles
(Don Henley, Glenn Frey)

Ain't No Sunshine 1971 - Bill Withers
(Bill Withers)

Scenes from an Italian Restaurant 1977 - Billy Joel
(Billy Joel)

Who's Sorry Now 1958 - Connie Francis
(Ted Snyder, Bert Kalmar, Harry Ruby 1923)

When you're in love with a beautiful Woman 1979 - Dr Hook
(Even Stevens)

Love and Affection 1976 - Joan Armatrading
(Joan Armatrading)

Weakness in Me 1981 - Joan Armatrading
(Joan Armatrading)

Home Thoughts from Abroad 1973 - Clifford T.Ward
(Clifford T.Ward)

Gaye 1973 - Clifford T.Ward
(Clifford T.Ward)

Memory 1981 - Elaine Paige
(Andrew Lloyd Webber, Trevor Nunn)

Danger Zone 1986 - Kenny Loggins
(Giorgio Moroder, Tom Whitlock)

Return to Sender 1962 - Elvis Presley
(Winfield Scott, Otis Blackwell)

In The Summertime 1970 - Mungo Jerry
(Ray Dorset)

Layla 1971 - Derek and the Dominoes
(Eric Clapton, Jim Gordon)

Help Me Make It through the Night 1972 **- Gladys Knight and the Pips**
(Kris Kristofferson)

No Woman, NoCry 1974 - Bob Marley and the Wailers
(Vincent Ford, Bob Marley)

Born To Run 1975 - Bruce Springsteen
(Bruce Springsteen)

Sultans of Swing 1978 - Dire Straits
(Mark Knopfler)

Hollywood Nights 1978 - Bob Seger and the Silver Bullet Band
(Bob Seger)

Night Moves 1976 - Bob Seger and the Silver Bullet Band
(Bob Seger)

Hi Ho Silver Lining 1967 - Jeff Beck
(Scott English, Larry Weiss)

Come Up and See Me 1975 - Cockney Rebel
(Steve Harley)

(I Can't Get No) Satisfaction 1965 - Rolling Stones
(Mick Jagger, Keith Richards)

Bohemian Rhapsody 1975 - Queen
(Freddy Mercury)

We are the Champions 1977 - Queen
(Freddie Mercury)

Another One Bites The Dust 1979 - Queen
(John Deacon)

Can't Explain 1965 - The Who
(Pete Townshend)

Queen Bitch 1971 - David Bowie
(David Bowie)

Sweet Caroline 1969 - Neil Diamond
(Neil Diamond)

Maneater 1982 - Hall and Oates
(Sara Allan, Daryl Hall, John Oates)

Sara Smile 1975 - Hall and Oates
(Daryl Hall, John Oates)

Will You Love Me Tomorrow 1960 - Carole King
(Gerry Goffin, Carole King)

Outside 1998 - George Michael
(George Michael)

You Mean More to Me 1982 - Lionel Richie
(Lionel Richie)

How Can You MendBroken Heart 1971 - Al Green
(Barry Gibb, Robin Gibb)

Fairy Tale of New York 1987 - Pogues with Kirsty MacColl
(Jem Finer, Shane MacGowan)

My Way 1968 - Frank Sinatra
(Paul Anka, Claude Francois, Jacques Revaux)

Billie Jean 1983 - Michael Jackson
(Michael Jackson)

Respect 1967 - Aretha Franklin
(Otis Redding)

Abracadabra 1982 - Steve Miller Band
(Steve Miller)

Wicked Game 1991 - Chris Izaak
(Chris Izaak)

Oh Carol 1959 - Neil Sedaka
(Neil Sedaka, Howard Greenfield)

Love Won't Let Me Wait 1975 - Major Harris
(Vinnie Barrett, Bobby Eli)

Let's Get It On 1973 - Marvin Gaye
(Marvin Gaye, Ed Townsend)

All Things Bright and Beautiful 1848
(Cecil Frances Alexander, William Henry Monk)

Abide With Me 1847
(Henry Francis Lyte, William Henry Monk)

Nearer My God to thee 1841
(Sarah Flower Adams, Eliza Flower)

Scotland the Brave 1870 (approx.)
(Unknown composer, Lyrics Cliff Hanley 1950)

Flower of Scotland 1967
(Roy Williamson)

The Fields of Athenry 1979
(Pete St. John)

A Soldier's Song (Amhrán na bhFiann) 1909
(Patrick Heeny, Lyrics Peadar Kearney 1910, Liam O'Rinn 1923 (Irish
Version)

Ireland's Call 1995
(Phil Coulter)

Old Land of My Fathers (Hen Wlad Fy Nhadau) 1856
(Evan James, Lyrics James James)

God Save the King/Queen 1745
(Henry Carey, John Bull)

Changes 1971 - David Bowie
(David Bowie)

My Generation 1965 - Pete Townshend
(Pete Townshend)

The Road To Hell 1989 - Chris Rea
(Chris Rea)

ABBA- FAB-U-LUSS !!
Agnetha Fältskog, Benny Andersson, Björn Ulvaeus, and Anni-Frid
Lyngstad (Stig Anderson also co-wrote some songs)

THANK YOU FOR THE MUSIC